Works by Gifford MacShane

The Donovan Family Saga

§

The Winds of Morning, Book 0.5, The Prequel
A young woman's desperate attempt to save her family
during the Great Irish Potato Famine.

§

Whispers in the Canyon, Book 1
A valiant young woman, haunted by abuse,
must learn to trust the man who killed her brother.

§

The Woodsman's Rose, Book 2
When a friendship is shattered,
can a fragile young woman with the gift of insight heal the rift?

§

Rainbow Man, Book 3
He'd follow her anywhere, regardless of danger,
but will her recklessness lead to their doom?

§

Without the Thunder, Book 4
An outcast Society belle falls in love with a Navajo man;
can they defeat the woman who's driven to destroy their happiness?

Dedication

For Jack & Janet,
a love story for the ages.

Cast of Characters

The Donovan Clan

John Patrick Donovan (b 1814), rancher & farmer, married to *Molly* (née O'Brien, b 1831)

§

Their children:
Adam (b 1853), rancher, married to *Jesse* (née Travers, b 1867)
Brian (b 1853), rancher
Conor (b 1855), ship's Captain
Daniel (b 1858), aka *The Woodsman*
Evelyn (b 1860), married to *Lowell Griffiths* (b 1861), dairyman
Frank (b 1862), farmer
Geordie (b 1862), farmer
Henry (b 1866, d 1868)
Irene (b 1869), a minor
Jake (b 1872), a minor

§

and *Rebecca Johnson*, lifelong friend of Jesse

In the Village & Surrounding Areas

Tommy Twelves Trees, Navajo blacksmith; married to ***Elena*** (deceased); their son ***Alec***, silversmith

Owen Griffiths, shopkeeper & widower; his son ***Lowell***, dairy farmer, daughter ***Annie***

Theodore Barber, doctor; his sister ***Jane***

Robert Taylor, merchant; married to ***Sarah***

William (Bill) Thatcher, banker; married to ***Nellie***; their son ***Ben***

Raymond Benson, rancher & village constable; married to ***Mary***

John Riley, widower & farmer; his son ***Tim***, daughter ***Norah***

Eli Sykes, farmer & former slave

Wang Shen, shopkeeper; his son ***Lei***, daughter ***Jenny***

Sean Flaherty, farmer, married to ***Moira*** (née Sullivan); their sons ***Michael, Rory***, daughters ***Patricia, Helen, Kathleen***

§
The Navajo

Running Wolf, Chief

Left-Handed Bear, his lieutenant

Short Feather, warrior; his mate ***Small Cloud at Night,*** basket maker; their son ***Blue Deer,*** healer

Yellow Knife, warrior & outcast from another tribe

A Short Glossary of Terms

IRISH TERMS:

This book encompasses a time when Irish people were forbidden to speak, read or write in their native language. Words were whispered and passed down secretly from generation to generation, and came to be spelled phonetically. "Mo chroi" became "Machree"; "mo chuisle" became "Macushla", etc. It is those spellings I've decided to use in this historical saga.

§

Aroon: my dear or sweetheart
Arrah: beloved (from *"grādh"*)
Bawn: fair of skin, also beautiful
Colleen: girl or young woman
Machree: my heart
Macushla: my pulse/lifeblood, also *"acushla"* *
Mavourneen: my darling/beloved (from *"muirnīn"*)

§

Note: In my books, the Donovan family uses "macushla" when this endearment is directed to the females, "acushlah" for the males. This is a little quirk that, as far as I know, occurs only in my family.

§

WELSH TERMS:

Bach: boy (son)
Caraid: my dear or sweetheart
Fy merch fach: My little girl
R'wy'n dy garu di: I love you

§

SPANISH TERMS:
Amigo: friend
Caballo: horse
Niña: girl
Niño: boy
Pequeño: small one (male)
Querida: beloved

Prologue

SPRING, 1885

It was a day of celebration. The eldest of the many Donovan siblings, Adam, had married Jesse Travers, and the community had joined them in a wedding supper at the Donovan homestead. The toast had been drunk, the gifts presented, music and dancing and food indulged in beyond all reason. But one person was feeling little joy.

Annie Griffiths' heart had been broken. Since they were kids, Annie had worshiped Adam's twin, Brian. And tonight it was obvious to all who knew him that Brian's heart had followed Adam's and now belonged entirely to Jesse.

As the first tear leaked from her eye, Brian's younger brother Daniel took her hand and led her down the slope, away from the laughter and noise of the crowd. In the orchard, where benches were arranged among the trees, he sat beside her. She attempted to smile at him.

"Annie..."

"It's hopeless. I know. I guess I've known all along."

Suppressing a sigh, she stood to go, but Daniel stepped in front of her. "Annie, there is a man who loves you."

"Daniel..."

"Yes. Daniel."

She'd listened in growing confusion as he told her of his love. Of the years he'd stood aside, knowing his words would only bring her pain. She'd listened to the voice as rough as emery on slate, listened for the first time to the Irish lilt twined around the southern drawl. And heard a music she'd never heard before.

"*Aroon*, I love you." He took her hands and kissed them with a tender passion she'd never dreamed him capable of. "Please give me a chance."

Her tears fell then, and he groaned as he pulled her into his arms, the muscles rippling under his soft buckskin shirt. One part of her marveled at the way her head fit into the hollow between his shoulder and throat; another wondered at the tenderness of the hand that cradled her head, of the strong fingers that lost themselves in her long, fine hair. A third part of her protested her fickleness—she'd always wanted Brian. What was she doing now in his brother's arms?

She stepped back and sat again on the bench, glanced up at him sideways, seeing him as if for the first time. The auburn hair worn long in the back, the flowing mustache, the eyes of so deep a blue as to be almost black. The scarf he tied tightly around his neck. His shirt, laced with rawhide thongs, fine copper-colored hairs showing between the laces. Her hand flicked toward them—she stilled it quickly as shame flooded through her body.

"Annie, I want no promise. All I ask is a chance. To show you how much I love you—to try to make you love me."

"But, Daniel, can you make love happen?"

"I can try. If you'll let me." After a moment, he added, "Will you think about it?"

"Yes," she whispered. "I will."

Chapter 1

LATE SPRING, 1886

Breakfast was never a formal event in the Donovan home, but since four of the nine siblings had moved on, it sometimes seemed quite staid. Today though, as Daniel padded down the stairs from his room, the conversation emanating from the kitchen was more animated than usual. He pushed through the swinging doors and poured his first cup of coffee, listening to his youngest brother expound on the merits of his pony.

"Dad, she's too small. She's a kid's horse!"

His father made no response as Daniel took his seat at the long table, across from his younger brothers. He murmured thanks to his mother as she set a plate of scrambled eggs before him, helped himself to ham and biscuits, then turned his attention back to Jake. The boy was sixteen, his school days over. Daniel agreed it was time to graduate from the pretty black filly Jake had raised as a pet, but he held his own counsel.

"If I'm gonna be a cowboy, I need a cow pony," Jake continued. "Fancy's too small for cutting steers. Besides, she's scared of 'em. And on top of that, my legs are just too long for her now."

John Patrick drew thoughtfully on his pipe. "And so?"

"So I need a horse I can work the cattle with. A big horse!" Jake's voice cracked into an octave above its usual range; his glance darted around, daring them all to laugh.

Daniel stifled a chuckle. In spite of the absurd vocal movement, the boy's argument was sound. A cowboy couldn't ride a filly, no matter how pretty, if his stirrups couldn't be properly lengthened.

His father's silent gaze gave the youth no encouragement, but there was a twinkle in his eye those familiar with it might have noticed. The old man was nearing his seventh decade and looked much younger. His iron-gray hair was still abundant, the fingers that grasped his pipe still strong and straight. In times of stress they might tremble a little, but no one was ever brave—or foolhardy—enough to remark upon it.

Jake fidgeted in his chair and his face began to turn red, a sure sign of temper.

"Mustangs out in the canyon," Daniel offered in a voice made gruff by a childhood accident, amusement hidden by his long mustache.

"Umm-hmm," responded John Patrick.

"Whaa...? OH!" Comprehension bloomed on Jake's face and left him speechless. His brothers had captured or foaled their own horses, and he'd have to do the same. He shot a grateful look at Daniel, turned to his father again.

"Can I go and get me one?"

"Umm-hmm." John Patrick rapped his pipe lightly against the table and, in his thick Irish brogue, added, "You'll be needing some help."

"Will you help me, Daniel?" Jake's request was almost a demand.

"Well... I've got a lot of work lined up out there."

"I can help you with it. I'll do half of what you've got to do if you help me catch a pony."

"All right, kid," Daniel said. "You be ready to leave right after chores. We'll work for Adam and Brian awhile, then go take a look at those mustangs."

THE WOODSMAN'S ROSE

The boy jumped up, knocking his chair over in the process. He skipped around in a circle, hooting his delight. Impetus drove him out the kitchen door, but he was soon back, sitting down to his half-finished bowl of oatmeal, not even reacting to the hilarity of his family.

WITH THEIR MORNING chores complete, Daniel and Jake rode west to the canyon known as Rocking Chair Ranch. It was the family home of Jesse Travers, now Adam's as well. Adam's twin, Brian lived there, too, as well as Rebecca Johnson, Jesse's good friend.

As they rode, Daniel listened in bemused silence as Jake blathered on and on about the horse he hoped to catch, never once asking what work he'd volunteered for. By the time Daniel could turn the conversation, they'd arrived at the trail's end to see a small white cabin set among the cottonwoods. Jesse jumped up from her seat on the porch swing, putting aside a bowl of half-shucked peas.

"There you are!" Her big green eyes flashed at them, and her tawny hair rippled in the breeze. "Hey, Jake, it's good to see you." Her soft voice was flavored with a deep Southern drawl.

"Came to help," the boy said. "Then me and Daniel are gonna catch a mustang."

"Oh, yeah?" Jesse tilted her head at Daniel. "How'd he rope you into that?"

"Volunteered. Dad wouldn't let him go alone."

"I should say not! Come in and have some coffee. Adam and Brian went into town, but they should be back any minute."

Inside the cabin was spotless—the old wood stove recently blacked so it shone like obsidian, the red gingham curtains and tablecloth adding cheerful notes to the space that served as both kitchen and parlor. Daniel helped Jesse as she gathered settings for the table, for she was a tiny woman, coming barely to his chest. He studied her obliquely—his sister-in-law was physically fragile, and the miscarriage she'd suffered in the fall had been compounded by a serious illness. That tragedy, coupled with a past she rarely discussed, still haunted her at times. His heart rejoiced to see the sureness of her movements and the healthy glow in her cheeks. And her face, like the weather, was sunny today.

"Sure smells good in here," Jake said.

"Rebecca made soap this morning," Jesse told him. Rebecca Johnson, Jesse's childhood Mammy, had moved back to the canyon from Prescott during Jesse's illness, and was counted as part of the family now.

"Doesn't smell like any soap I ever used!"

Jesse giggled. "It's got lilac flowers in it, and honey. She always makes it for me."

"Where is she, anyhow?"

"She went after some berries. But we made these before she left." Jesse whisked the cloth off a plate piled high with corn muffins; Jake's fingers snaked out to grab one before they even reached the table. "Help yourself! You, too, Daniel, if he's leaving you any."

Jake turned scarlet. He tried to talk but his mouth was already crammed full; he was still sputtering around the crumbs when Rebecca came in. Daniel poked him on the shoulder, so he swallowed hard and gulped some coffee. "'Scuse me. These muffins are real good."

Rebecca gave him a smile that eased his embarrassment. Tall and spare, her graying hair smoothed into a bun, she stored her empty basket on a high shelf as Jake's hand hovered over the plate once more.

"Go ahead," said Jesse, laughing. "That's what they're here for!"

"Strawberries aren't quite ripe," Rebecca said in a soft, cultured Southern voice. "Maybe next week."

"Oh, foo! I was really in the mood for some strawberry pie."

"We've still got some canned peaches, if you can make do with them." Rebecca's eyes, as deep a brown as her face, softened at Jesse's bright smile.

"Is your pie as good as your muffins?" Jake asked.

"Who's got muffins?" Brian's voice boomed through the room as he filled up the door, his wild red hair identical to Jake's.

"Better get one quick!" Daniel advised him. "Jake's about eaten 'em all."

Brian grabbed the plate of muffins and moved it to the far end of the table. "Don't you touch that," he growled, wagging a finger. "I'll break your arm right off."

Daniel made a skeptical noise in his throat—violence was no part of his gigantic brother's nature. He'd been known to catch spiders in the house and put them in the garden.

"Where's your twin?" Daniel asked.

"Puttin' up the hosses. Why'd ya bring the kid?"

"Paying his debt in advance." Daniel told him of the hunt they planned, then had to explain it once more when Adam came in.

As different from Brian as a panther is from a sequoia, Adam had the lean build of a range rider and the quiet, dangerous grace of a prowling cat. His black hair hung down over his collar and his bright blue eyes strayed often to his wife as coffee and muffins were passed around along with the conversation. The topic turned finally to the weather and the possibility of drought; after an early winter full of sleet and ice, snow had barely fallen and the spring rains had been light.

"Dad said to tell you he's planning to run more cattle in here if it doesn't rain soon," Daniel said.

"Plenty of room out by the lake," Adam answered, "and with good water, they don't need as much feed." He scraped his chair back, then stood behind Jesse and dropped a kiss on her head.

"Guess we better get t' work," Brian said. "Corral ain't gonna build itself."

AS THE SUN BEGAN TO dip behind the cabin, Daniel and Jake walked to the western end of the canyon. Two miles on, a beaver dam had created a lake where wild mustangs would come down to water every morning and evening.

After climbing a terrace beside the brook that fed the lake, they watched the horses in silence for several moments. The lake itself measured about ten acres in a natural oval bowl. Hundreds of cattle dotted the fields on each side, a few of them mixing with the horses as they drank.

"Sure is pretty," Jake said.

Daniel didn't reply. The glory of nature was something he never took for granted and here, where high white clouds scudded across a sky as blue as the water, where the deep green of the firs contrasted with the glossy leaves of tipu and the feathery fingers of ferns, where the striated canyon walls were a symphony of rust and brown—here, his soul was always at peace.

As they stood together, the difference between the brothers was almost startling. Daniel had broad shoulders and the lean body of an athlete, the powerful thighs of a runner. He wore buckskin from head to foot, a red bandanna tied tight around his neck to hide the scar from the accident that had affected his voice. His auburn hair was thick and sleek, and his mustache hid a sensitive mouth. He carried a rifle in his left hand; in his right boot a long knife lay against his leg.

As broad of shoulder as Daniel, Jake had exceptionally long arms and legs. His body seemed to consist of many angles, all at odds with one another. Where his brother stood with a silent compact grace, Jake was constantly in motion, and he moved like a fractious colt.

The bright red hair he'd inherited from his mother was ruffled by the breeze. His eyes were light blue and ginger freckles dotted his face and hands. The boy was already tall, and was shooting up so rapidly Daniel was sure his own six-foot-two-inch height would be surpassed before the summer's end. Yet their faces were alike—broad brow, strong straight nose, squared chin. Different as they were, they both looked remarkably like their father.

Jake focused on the huge white stallion that was the herd's leader, but Daniel was quick to set him straight. "That old man has been free for too many years. You might catch him, though I doubt it. Even if you did, you'd never tame him. You don't want a horse you have to fight every time you put a saddle on him.

"Besides, Jake, he's earned his freedom. See those scars on his flanks and chest? He won that herd. He fought for them and won them, and he'll hold on to them until he's too old to fight any more. Then some young stallion'll come along and beat him, and he'll slink away and die. If he doesn't die fighting.

"No, little brother, if you want him, you'll have to catch him yourself. I won't dethrone a king."

So Jake picked out a frisky young black with three white feet and a diamond-shaped blaze ending at his nose.

"A lot of horse," Daniel commented. "See that sorrel mare he sticks with?"

"Yeah." The boy answered without enthusiasm.

"She may be his dam. Alec likes to work them in pairs. If we catch them both, you can give the mare to him as payment for his help."

"Won't he be coming with us?"

"Not the way things stand right now. He's angry and it doesn't look like he'll ever get over it."

"Can't you just tell him?" the boy asked. Alec had told everyone, it seemed, that Daniel knew who had killed his mother the previous spring. "Wouldn't everything be okay then?"

"No, Jake. In the first place, I have no proof and the man who killed Elena's gone. There's nothing we could do to him. But he has kin who'd be shamed by finding out—people who are innocent and don't deserve to be hurt." Daniel sighed deep inside. Alec Twelve Trees—his friend, his brother in spirit—was so intractable, so unable to see the harm he might cause. "And in the second place, there's such a thing as honor. If I knew something that you're ashamed of, would you want me to tell Alec? Just because he's my friend and he wants to know?"

"No. I wouldn't think you were much of a man if you did that."

"Exactly. So I have to weigh my conscience against what Alec wants. I just wish he could understand."

Jake reached for his shoulder. Daniel covered the boy's hand with his in silent acceptance of the sympathy offered, then shook off his gloom and said, "We need a plan. First we'll have to find out how they get into the canyon. Then we'll figure out how to make a trap to keep them here. But before we do any scouting around out there, you'll need a new pair of boots."

"These are new." Jake displayed one of the high-heeled black boots he'd tucked his denim pants into. With the fancy stitching that was the local bootmaker's trademark, they were his most prized possession.

"They're also loud." Daniel slapped his own knee-high buckskins. "You'll get a lot closer to them in these."

"Where do we get 'em?"

"You don't *get* them. You make them."

"What! I wanna be a cowboy, not a bootmaker."

On the other side of the lake, the white stallion pricked up his ears, but Daniel only shrugged. "You wanna be a wild horse hunter and you gotta have the gear."

"Can't I just borrow a pair of yours?"

"Jake... come put your foot over here."

THE WOODSMAN'S ROSE

"Huh. Guess I'd have to cut my toes off first, like those girls in the Cinderella story."

"Don't let anyone ever tell you you're slow, kid!"

IT TOOK THREE EVENINGS to make the boots, and they spent their days working on the corral. At one point, Daniel's quick ears caught the boy voicing a complaint to Adam, whom Jake held in an admiration that was close to worship.

Leaning against his shovel, Adam focused bright blue eyes on the boy. "Before you ask for a man's advice, you have to assume he knows more than you do. So when he decides to help you out, it only makes sense to go along with what he says. If there's anyone around here who knows tracking, it's Daniel. You know what the Navajo call him?"

"The Woodsman." In sudden curiosity, Jake asked, "Did you have to make boots, too?"

"Nope." Adam's left eyebrow curled up at the middle as he grinned. "Apples was born on the ranch. Right in the corral. I just had to help his dam foal him." He slapped his brother's shoulder. "Looks like you picked the hard way. But stick it out. And listen to your brother—he knows what he's doing. It'll be worth it in the long run."

"Knowin' Daniel," Brian put in, "I think you got off real easy. Be thankful he didn' make you catch the deer first!"

Jake went back to his tasks more cheerfully. Three days later, the boots were done.

Chapter 2

THE EVENING BEFORE the mustang hunt, Daniel rode into town on his buckskin mare and knocked on the Griffiths' cottage door.

"Hello." Annie's voice was sweet and soft. Her dress of green calico hugged her tall, slender figure. Flaxen hair hung down her back in a single braid, and a few tendrils had escaped to frame her face.

He tucked one strand behind her ear, and asked, "Got a few minutes?"

When she nodded, he took her hand, drew her outside, and strolled down the wide main street of the village. White's Station was usually quiet on a weekday evening, with most of the shops closed. Down the side street Joe's Cafe was brightly lit, and tinkling notes from a piano floated out from the saloon where a few men congregated.

As they walked, Daniel told her of his plans to help Jake. "We're leaving tomorrow. I'm not quite sure how long we'll be—a week if we're really lucky, up to three if we're not." He took both her hands in his, ran a thumb over the ring she'd accepted with his proposal. "I'll miss you."

Annie cast her eyes down, but he saw the blush rising to her cheek, the curving of her lips. It was enough for him.

As he turned to lead her back home, she asked, "Is he going to work with Alec?"

"I hope so. I hope Alec understands he shouldn't hold anything against Jake—that the trouble between us has nothing to do with anyone else. But if not, I'll work with Jake. I'm not as good at taming horses as Alec, but I can get it done."

They walked hand in hand back to her home and sat together on the bench on her front porch. After a few moments, his arm stole around her and she rested her head on his shoulder. Annie had a soothing way about her, and he felt at peace with the silence between them. Together, they watched a sliver of moon rise and peek through the scattered clouds.

"I'd best be going, *aroon*. Have to get an early start tomorrow." Daniel stood and pulled her up into his arms, kissed her cheek, then swung up into his saddle.

"Daniel..." When he looked down Annie said, "I'll miss you, too."

The grin he gave her split his face in two.

SETTING OFF AT DAYLIGHT, Jake and Daniel took to the rocky trails in the canyon, searching for the mustangs' entrance.

They set up a permanent camp in a grove of pines near the lake. On the first day, the brothers observed the herd from the opposite shore. They seemed to be entering the canyon through some concealed gap in the wall, coming down the ledges where the cattle couldn't climb out.

As they sat by the campfire after dinner, Daniel explained his plan to Jake. "We'll climb up to the canyon's rim a few miles west of here and work back along the ledges to find the gap in the wall."

"Why don't we just follow them?" Jake asked.

"That might only give us one chance at them. If we follow them out in the morning, we'd be leaving our scent on their trail. If we didn't manage to catch them before evening, they'd turn around for sure as soon as they caught wind of us.

"That old king's pretty crafty," the woodsman continued, "or he'd never have lived this long. He'd either find another way in or he'd take his herd off the range completely. Either way, it wouldn't help us."

"OK. But once we find the entrance, how're we gonna catch 'em?"

"I can't tell you that until I see where they come in. If we're lucky, there'll be some kind of natural barrier we can use. Maybe this canyon will lead into another canyon we can turn into a trap. Maybe we'll have to track them all over creation."

"Or maybe," Daniel added, "we won't be able to catch this herd at all. If there's a wide open range on the other side of that rim, they can run forever."

"There won't be," Jake said. "I feel it in my bones."

"I hope your bones are right!"

They sat quietly for a while, then Jake spoke up hesitantly. "You gettin' married, Daniel?"

"Sure am. As soon as Annie's ready."

"What's she waiting for?"

Daniel's pipe had gone out and he tapped the ashes into the fire before answering. "Gran told me once that a woman's like a little bird—she'll know when she's ready to build her nest. I can't tell you more than that; Annie's not ready, and I'm just going to wait until she is."

Another silence enveloped them, and again it was Jake who broke it. "Do you miss her?"

"Sure, but it's only for a little while."

"I meant Gran," Jake murmured.

THE WOODSMAN'S ROSE

"I sure do. Especially when I need advice. Though I'll tell you something..." Daniel let out a short chuckle. "I think some of those 'old Irish proverbs' were stuff she just made up."

"Sometimes I dream about her."

"I know. I think we all do." Daniel lit his pipe and gave his brother a nudge with his foot. "You better get to bed now. Mornin' comes early these days. And remember—tomorrow night, you make the biscuits!"

AS JAKE SNORED SOFTLY, Daniel lay awake listening to the familiar sounds of the nighthawk and owl, the coyote in the distance. A small animal, probably a grasshopper mouse, was ferreting through Jake's belongings, but the food he wanted had been bound in a blanket and tied in a tree.

Bats swooshed overhead. *There must be a cave nearby, in the walls of the canyons.* This complex network of canyons and mesas was the only part of the Arizona Territory he hadn't fully explored.

He was at home with nature, felt a serenity of spirit in the remote recesses where few men ventured. The occasional crackling of the fire, the scent of the pines, the eternal brightness of the stars—all were balm to his soul. He breathed the night air deeply, content in the knowledge that he was at peace with the earth. Believing in his Navajo friends' prayer that ended "All is well."

After a while, he set his mind on the days to come. The most important thing he'd have to teach Jake was patience. A smile crept under his mustache—his brother was full of life, full of energy, and it was going to be difficult for him to even stand still, let alone accept the time it would take to catch and break these horses. *But I have learned patience, and Jake will, too. There are just some things worth waiting for.*

Like Annie.

He cast his mind back to the previous spring and the day of Adam and Jesse's wedding supper. He'd begun then to woo her gently, tenderly, unwaveringly. Until she confessed that the affection she'd felt for Brian was dwarfed by these new emotions—feelings that ran so deep, she could hardly name them.

Her face floated before him now, with her elfin smile and hair the color of a wheat field in the sun. So soft, so fine in its long braid. And her eyes...

It had taken him years to find the words to describe her eyes—green and blue and gray at once, ringed around with deep navy—the color of the wild sea. Her eyes made him believe that she was fey.

Her eyes could see into his heart, into all their hearts. And a gift, inherited from her mother, allowed her to see glimpses of the future.

He wished her good-night and the vision faded, but not before he caught a little wink. He'd be patient. Yet sometimes his patience warred with his heart. How much time would they have together? How much before Annie succumbed to the tortuous headaches she suffered more and more frequently? He watched the stars on their slow journey and offered a prayer to the ancient gods.

Let her accept me. Let us live together and be happy. Even for a little while. And all will be well.

Chapter 3

TWO DAYS LATER, THE brothers were looking down from the rim of the canyon wall as the mustangs disappeared around the bend.

"The gods must smile on you," Daniel said. "I just can't believe it!"

The trail used by the herd was some thirty feet wide below them and a quarter mile long, but at each end there were narrow gaps in the canyon rim permitting no more than three horses abreast.

"What we need to do is block off that north entrance with a fence. We can build it today and put it up tonight after they come through. Then we need another gate we can swing shut behind them when they come back from watering."

"They'll be trapped in this place." Jake eyes were alight with glee. "We can catch them all!"

"We don't need them all. And we don't have the time or the manpower we'd need to catch them all. No, we'll stick to the two we picked out. But it's sure gonna be a lot easier than I expected.

"Come on, brother, I saw a stand of young birch a ways back—they're just what we need for the fences."

They cut the trees into poles. For the north fence, they built two portable units, both high and strong, and covered them with branches to make it look like a natural barrier. They pulled the sections close to the gap—as close as Daniel thought they could get without warning the herd. Then they cut more poles for a simple post-and-rail fence for the narrower southern entrance.

That evening, the mustangs came through the northern gap without hesitation and as soon as the last few disappeared along the trail, Daniel and Jake began to drag their fences into place. They had less than an hour to situate them and lash them together with the long, tough rawhide strips Daniel produced from his pockets. Rawhide would hold up better than vine, he told his brother, and nails or barbed wire were out of the question. He was careful to explain that the barriers they built would cause no harm to the mustangs and that, if hysteria infected the herd, they'd have to set them free before any injuries occurred.

The moment the barrier was complete, the brothers retreated, climbed to the canyon wall and made their way to the southern gap, being certain to stay downwind of the herd. After drinking, the mustangs came back through and approached the branch-built wall curiously. Then the old king caught the scent of man. He snorted and turned, reared up and whistled a challenge. But Daniel and Jake were already blocking off the southern exit, sliding the rails into their makeshift fence, the posts of which leaned in against the canyon walls. The white stallion pawed the ground but didn't approach them.

The Donovan brothers made their beds on the other side of the post and rail fence. The mustangs congregated at the opposite end of the trap, and followed the white stallion in restless circles until the dawn broke.

Just after sunrise, Jake helped his brother reinforce the southern gate. They found a crevice in the canyon wall they used as additional support for the right side. On the left, they moved several boulders in to support the posts. Daniel tested it against his weight.

"All right, Jake," he commanded, "you watch me. I'm going after the mare. You sit there on the post—if any of them come near you, flap your hat at them. Don't scare them, just wave them away. Here we go."

THE WOODSMAN'S ROSE

With his lariat held low, Daniel jogged noiselessly toward the herd. They milled and turned but he ignored their activity, concentrating instead on the sorrel mare. Fear filled her eyes as she realized she was his prey. Though she was tired from the night's relentless movement, she pranced away, but he ran straight at her and when she reared, he threw the lasso high and wide. It came down over her head and one leg, and he tightened it with a deft flick of his wrist. She snorted and whistled when she realized she was caught.

The herd scrambled away. Daniel dug in his heels as she strained against the rope. He pulled himself closer to her hand over hand, until he was less than ten feet from her. Then he addressed her silently.

Little sister, you have no need to fear me. You will not be hurt. You will be changed, but you will not be hurt. Little sister, I have come to ask your help. I need your help for my friend, my brother. You will be changed but you will not be hurt.

For the better part of an hour, he stood eye to eye with her. Finally she quieted and he backed away. Reluctantly she followed his lead, though her body still shivered with fear. He led her to a tall tree at the side of the trap, tying the lasso around it, giving her little room to move.

Daniel turned to his brother and asked, "Want to try it?"

"Oh, yeah!" Jake grabbed his rope and built the noose. Like Adam, he was left-handed, and it made him seem awkward at times. But the natural skill was there.

"Concentrate on the one horse," Daniel said, "and ignore all the others. Let him know you're after him. And wait 'til he rears before you throw. Try to get the rope over a foreleg, too, so we don't have to choke him to bring him down."

Eager as he was, Jake couldn't concentrate on the single horse. His first two attempts at roping the colt had failed, and Daniel could see his frustration building, but before he could speak, Jake threw his lariat again. He was off balance and fell backward even as the rope caught the ears of a bay mare. She reared, pawing the air as he tried to scramble away. Her hoof crashed down on his left boot, pinning him there. As the mare rose up again, Daniel ran to his brother, grabbed his collar and yanked him back. Jake started to thrash and moan.

"Keep still!" Daniel's whisper was adamant as he crouched down beside him. "Be quiet. The herd's riled up. Don't do anything more to upset them."

They waited, not moving from that spot. Almost an hour later by Daniel's reckoning, the mustangs finally quieted.

"How bad you hurt?" he asked Jake.

"I'm OK. She caught the side of my leg more than the front, then kind of slid off. It hurt like hell at first, but it's way better now."

"Let's see."

Jake pulled his pant leg up and scrunched the soft buckskin boot down. A purple bruise shaped like a half moon stood out against his white skin. He poked at it gingerly.

"Ouch," Daniel commented. "Think you can walk?"

"Pretty sure."

Daniel helped Jake to his feet, watched him take a few tentative steps, and shake his leg out. He limped a bit, but it seemed no real damage had been done.

"All right, boy-o, watch and learn." Again the studied approach, the intelligent response, the perfect throw. And another hour spent in soothing and calming the colt while the herd milled restlessly.

Daniel tied the trembling pony next to his dam, watched their silent commiseration, and motioned to his brother. "Stay here and watch them while I take down the barrier."

As Daniel skirted the trap, the herd pranced away from him. The barrier wasn't as sturdy as it appeared; he dismantled it quickly. He climbed on a rock to watch the king trotting back and forth, his tail high, his mane almost sweeping the ground, his nostrils blowing out the scent of man. Finally the stallion reared, trumpeted a warning blast at Daniel, and leaped out at a gallop, whistling for his band to follow. By twos and threes they crowded out of the gap in the canyon wall, ignoring the man who sat and watched and marveled at their beauty. They ran after their king and didn't stop until they were many miles away.

"A good day's work," Daniel said as he came back to Jake and the captured horses. His brother was staring at his boots. "What's the matter?"

"I'm no damn good at this, am I?"

"You just need some experience. It's not as easy to do something as it is to watch. You think I'm good at it, but it's only because I've been doing it for eight years or so. How do you think I felt the first time I went out with Alec?"

"How?"

As he fashioned hackamores for the captives, Daniel answered, "Pretty damn stupid. There I was, with this kid who was fifteen years old—and I was a big man of twenty. I chased a roan mare all over creation, and never once came close to catching her. Then Alec made me sit down and he caught her without even raising a sweat! But I learned, Jake. The same way you will. The hardest thing is to ignore the other horses, to stop worrying about what they're doing behind you. And the next hardest thing's learning the patience it takes to gentle them. But you take these two to Alec and he'll show you how it's done. And maybe he'll take you out with him this summer.

"Now let's get these two back to the corral and stop in to see Adam and Jesse for a few minutes." Daniel grabbed his rifle and gathered the hackamores, gently urging the captives to follow in his wake. His brother walked beside him, matching the woodsman's strides with his own.

Chapter 4

THE CLEARING WHERE the cabin stood seemed deserted. Handing Jake the mustangs' leads and signaling for him to wait, Daniel stepped silently onto the porch and crossed to the open door. He saw Adam sitting in the rocking chair by the hearth with Jesse on his lap, her tawny hair disheveled, a tear lingering on her cheek. But she was asleep now, her hand caught in the bandanna at Adam's neck, her face soft and sweet in repose. As quietly as he'd entered, he backed out again.

He put his finger to his lips as Jake began to speak. Taking one of the youth's arms, Daniel guided him away from the porch.

"Jesse's sleeping," he whispered. "I'll get our horses and meet you down the lane." Jake nodded and, taking up the captives' leads, moved the mustangs down around the cottonwood grove and onto the trail that would lead them home.

Daniel took his time saddling their horses, working slowly and calmly, remembering the first time he'd seen his sister-in-law. "Little Jesse Travers" she'd been called then, and she'd had a reputation in town as a drunkard, a tramp, and a killer.

His skill as a tracker was known far and wide, and a prospector had asked Daniel if he could determine who had assaulted and robbed him. He'd tracked bootprints and then hoofprints to the canyon where Russell Travers lived with Jesse and their crippled father. Not finding his quarry, Daniel instead had spied Jesse stumbling from a grove of sycamores near the stream that ran through the canyon. He'd been surprised at the smallness, the delicacy of her—she was nineteen, but could pass as a child of ten or twelve. She staggered again and he'd thought she was drunk. Then he saw that her face had been beaten savagely, her clothes half torn off her body, her hand clutching the remnants of her blouse over her bosom. The marks of human teeth had raised a purple welt upon her neck.

The blood froze in his veins as Daniel realized the only other tracks leading to the cabin belonged to her brother. But before he could move, before he could help her, the doctor arrived to treat her father. He'd haunted the clearing for most of a month, hoping to keep her safe, but Russell Travers found another outlet for his violence, and had attacked Elena Twelve Trees in the village, in her own yard.

Daniel recognized the bootprints of Elena's attacker—the slightly turned-out left foot, the slice of leather missing from the sole—and he'd seen the purpling bite upon her neck. He blotted the tracks out, sure that Alec would do murder if he realized who had killed his mother. In spite of Alec's threats and demands, Daniel wouldn't identify the killer without more proof. He'd hoped to find evidence he could pass on to the town's constable, but only days later it was too late for justice: Adam shot and killed Travers as he robbed the town's only bank.

Over the past year, most in the village realized all of the filthy rumors about Jesse had been perpetrated by her brother to keep her away from the town. To keep the town from knowing the truth about him. But there were still those few who clung to the old gossip.

From that first time he saw Jesse, Daniel had sworn to protect her. He was one of the few who knew that the baby she lost the previous year had been her brother's. That she'd agreed to marry Adam to spare her child shame; that they hadn't lived as man and wife for more than a full year after their marriage. And he was sure Jesse was unaware of the extent of his knowledge.

Now, after an arduous ordeal, and only with Adam's help, Jesse had almost regained her trust. Had almost found a safe place to live. She was secure in the love of his large family, but the outside world could still batter her with fear.

Daniel closed his eyes for a moment, then pulled himself back to the task at hand. He needed to keep their horses calm as they met the new captives. His mare was a bit skittish, obviously scenting the newcomers on his clothes, but the black filly Fancy ignored it, and Bucky settled down when Daniel mounted her.

As he and Jake started toward home, Daniel was satisfied to see that, in spite of the tension in the sorrel mare's gait, the young stallion was in synch with Fancy, stepping out with his head held high and taking an occasional playful head-butt at his dam's side.

"Jesse's okay now, isn't she?" Jake asked.

Daniel's head whipped around—but the look of concern on his brother's broad face made him temper his remarks. "She's better, and I think that's all we can expect right now.

"Listen, Jake, let's not forget it's only a year since her father died. It would take us longer than that to get over Dad's death. And Jesse was as close to Gran as any of us, so she's got that to deal with as well."

"Gee, I didn't think about that."

"Other things have happened, too—her baby was born dead and her brother got killed."

"Bu-but..." Jake sputtered. "Why does her brother matter? He was nothing but bad."

"Maybe so, but she told me when they were kids in Texas—before her mother got sick—her brother would sometimes play hide and seek with her, and swing her from a tree in the yard."

"Hard to imagine," Jake said.

Daniel grunted. That the man who beat his sister on a regular basis and finally raped her could have been a happy child was impossible for him to believe. Yet he wouldn't discount Jesse's memories.

"Do you think she wanted the baby?"

"Why would you ask that, Jake? What possible difference would it make? You and I can't know what a woman feels. I sometimes think of having a baby with Annie and, man, the love I can feel for that child already—I can't describe it. More than I've ever felt before in my life."

Daniel's face tightened and his voice became as rough as sand on a whetstone. "A woman has that baby growing right there in her womb. That baby was forced on Jesse, but it was still there growing, then one day it just died inside of her.

"You're too young to remember Henry. He was born back in Abilene and when he died—he was only two—Mother was shattered. She cried all the time. It has to be horrible to lose a child, no matter what.

"So I don't know what Jesse felt," Daniel added. "I just know it was terribly hard for her. And it's one more thing her brother's paying for in hell."

Though it wasn't a concept Daniel held with, he knew Jake believed wholeheartedly in hell. He pulled his mare up when he realized Jake had stopped. He looked back to see the youth staring at the hands he clenched on his pummel. The woodsman was about to speak when Jake looked up with accusation in his eyes.

"You think her brother killed Elena."

Daniel turned his head away and nodded.

"Why won't you tell Alec? He deserves to know!"

Biting back an oath, Daniel answered in a voice that brooked no dissent. "He doesn't. He's too upset. He's already gone off the rails at me a couple of times, and I don't know what will happen if he knows there's nothing he can do—no revenge he can take. If he tells everyone...

"Family, Jake. That's what's most important in this world, even before friends. Even before neighbors. And Jesse is family now. We have to protect her." Seeing an argument on the boy's face, Daniel repeated, "We *have* to. Whether she knows it or not, she's depending on us to do just that."

Jake stared at him for a long minute before he nodded. His father's primary tenet could be summed up in one sentence: a man has nothing if he has no family, and he *is* nothing if he's not a good neighbor. It was a doctrine they'd all learned from the cradle.

"Family comes first," Daniel added. "What do you think would happen to Jesse if the whole town finds out? If Sarah Taylor and Jane Barber start in on her again? You know they were behind the rumors that made her out a drunk, the ones that said she was involved with Tommy since she was a kid. You've heard what they say about her living with Adam and Brian both."

One look at his brother's crimson face told Daniel his harsh words had hit home. Still the youth protested, "But that's stupid stuff."

"People believe stupid stuff every day, Jake. Every damn day. What will those two women say if they find out Russell killed Elena? They'll somehow make it Jesse's fault, and start over with the stories about her and Tommy. And who knows what else they'll make up so they can feel important. Do you think Jesse deserves that? Don't you think she's had enough hardship?"

"No. I mean, yeah." Jake scrubbed at his face. "You're right."

"Jake, I can't let you work with Alec unless you promise you won't tell him."

"Okay."

"I want your promise."

"I promise."

Daniel nodded curtly as Jake raised his eyes. "Daniel, what made him do it?"

THE WOODSMAN'S ROSE

"I don't know, Jake. I don't understand it. Tommy says some folks are born ornery—I don't know if anyone will ever understand more than that."

They began to ride again, and for a moment, Daniel wondered how he could feel so deeply for Jesse when his whole heart was given to Annie. And he regretted that his responsibility had cost him his closest friendship.

I thought it would help when I told Alec the man who did it is gone. But it hasn't made any difference at all. He's so angry—no, furious. Yet what can I do? I know Jesse isn't strong enough to bear the shame. Even after all that Adam has done for her—after all the family's done—she wouldn't be able to endure it. She's still so fragile, so delicately balanced between our love and her fears.

I cannot tell him. I couldn't bear to be the one who hurts her one more time.

Chapter 5

SUMMER CAME IN HOT and dry. Occasional storms threatened on the horizon, but the rains didn't come. Drought had hit the Arizona Territory several years before, resulting in the loss of most of the stock and produce which the Donovan ranch and farm supported. Since then they'd irrigated their fields with water from the mountain streams, which were snow-fed and never ran dry. Early in the summer they drove a thousand head of cattle into Jesse's canyon to let them water at the spring-fed lake.

Daniel had scouted out the location of their diverse herds, but he took no pleasure in the drive. Neither farmer nor cowboy, he didn't work the land he loved, yet he lived closer to it than any of his family. And unlike his brothers, who rode the range or managed the farm, he was always busiest in fall and winter. After the round-up and the harvest, in which everyone participated, Daniel would set out hunting for their winter stores. In a good year, he'd finish before Christmas. In the lean years, he hunted all winter. In the spring he made new clothes for the coming year, then helped with the planting and the tending of the orchard. And because of his agile, logical mind, he was often asked to help solve the practical problems the family faced—whether planning irrigation for new fields or installing the indoor plumbing that his father had ordered from New York.

But in the summer, when his brothers plowed and weeded and rode herd, Daniel was free to do what he wished. For the past several summers, he'd set out on the trail of the wild mustangs ranging north of the Donovan holdings. Up to the mesas he'd go with Alec Twelve Trees. For weeks they'd be gone, to return with a small string of choice horses. They'd spend many additional weeks gentling the ponies, using a method devised by Alec that resulted in work-horses that were high-spirited but not wild, tame but not broken. Daniel loved these trips to the mountains, considering them food for his soul. He was fascinated by Alec's way with horses, could watch for hours as his friend persuaded a pony to accept a saddle or bit.

But now Alec was working with Jake, and Daniel could only be thankful the rift hadn't affected his relationship with Alec's father, who ran the livery stable and was an accomplished ironsmith.

The livery stood on the north end of town, spreading across the wide dusty street and backing up to the eastern fork of the river. At the opposite end of White's Station stood the Trading Post; across from it a small chapel nestled among the sycamores. Between were several houses and smaller shops, as well as the Town Hall, the bank, a boardinghouse and the inevitable saloon.

As he approached the livery on a sunny Saturday afternoon, Daniel was amused to hear Tommy cussing.

"Ah, hell!" A Navajo with broad shoulders, narrow hips, and arms as strong as the iron he worked, Tommy had begun to use the expression in missionary school because it angered his teachers, and now the habit was ingrained. He repeated it viciously and threw down his hammer with a clang.

"Got a problem?" Daniel asked, stepping through the open doors. It was rare for the blacksmith to be out of sorts, his cheerful disposition usually shining through the angular bronze mask of his face.

"Hey, Dan'l! Boy, am I glad t' see you. I could really use your help with this." Tommy moved with a dancer's grace as he approached and shoved a piece of paper under Daniel's nose.

"What's this?"

"A leg."

"A what?" Daniel knew his friend wasn't one to talk in riddles, but the drawings bore scant resemblance to a horse's leg. Not that a horse would accept one, for that matter. "Wh—? Why don't you explain this to me."

"You know li'l Blue Deer? That sickly boy in the tribe? Well, Doc had t' cut off his leg the other day, and he's really, really down in the mouth. An' Doc said mebbe it could keep 'im from gettin' better, bein' so blue. So I thought if I made 'im a new leg..."

"Yeah, I see." Daniel pulled on the ends of his mustache and studied the drawing again, picturing Blue Deer in his mind. "He's pretty small, isn't he? If you make it out of iron, won't it be too heavy?"

"Yeah, mebbe so." The blacksmith scratched at his chin. "I jus' wanna do somethin' for the kid. He's a healer, did ya know? It's gotta be real tough on 'im, not bein' able to heal hisself. I dunno..."

"What if we made it out of wood? It'd be a lot lighter. I'm not sure how we'd attach it..."

"Doc said there should be a cup for the leg to fit in, with somethin' like India rubber to cushion it. Then there's a harness thet holds it on. Since the boy's still growin', he thought it should be easy to adjust."

"Hmm... Does he still have the knee joint?"

"Yeah. The infection didn' get up too much higher than 'is ankle."

"So he could probably use a foot, too. I could carve it easily—could you make a flat hinge for each side so it moves a little better? Can't have too much play, maybe twenty or thirty degrees. Enough to flex it just a bit."

"Sure, I see what you mean." Tommy pushed one set of his fingers up slightly with the other. "Don't want it floppin' all aroun', but jus' a li'l give so he can walk natural."

THE WOODSMAN'S ROSE

"How long should it be?" Daniel asked.

"I got everything right here. Doc measured 'is other leg. This is how long it has to be, an' this is how big the leg is, where Doc cut it."

"Maybe I'll make him boots, too. Be easier for him to hide it." Traditional Navajo moccasins were calf-high. "He'd probably feel a little better about it, too, if everyone wasn't staring at it all the time. Mind if I keep this?"

"No, Dan'l, go ahead. You think you can make somethin' that'll work?"

"I'll sure give it a try."

Tommy looked over as his son came into the livery. "Hey, Alec," he called, "come see what we're makin' for Blue Deer."

Silently, the youth approached. He wore the velveteen shirt customary to the Navajo and a heavy silver chain around his neck. His tight black embroidered pants reflected his mother's Spanish heritage and flared out over high-heeled black boots. Held with a leather headband, his hair was black and shiny as the raven's wing, and it hung long and loose. His face was dusky, his features strong. He looked at the sketch in his father's hand but said nothing.

"Whaddya think?" Tommy asked. Alec shrugged and looked from his father to the woodsman. He stared at Daniel for more than a full minute. Then, still silent, he turned on his heel and left the stable.

Tommy sighed loudly and heard Daniel's echo. The blacksmith turned to the younger man and clasped his shoulder.

"Don't be angry with 'im," Tommy pleaded. "He's so tore up—I dunno what t' do for 'im. He told me once it was my fault—that I shoulda been there with 'er. T' protect 'er." His face worked and he turned to bring a fist crashing down on the top of a stall. "*Dammit!* I wish I had been! But it was the middle o' the day... the middle o' the day in this li'l one-horse town..." His voice trailed off for a minute. "Who'd ever think, in this li'l one-horse town..."

Tommy leaned against the stall and lowered his face to his hands. The stoicism he'd learned as a boy had been eradicated by the passionate creature he'd married. He'd been taken from his family at the age of five and put in the missionary school at Flag. There he'd stayed, learning the white man's ways. Or at least appearing to. For Tommy had a facility that his teachers had never recognized—he could separate himself from the world with ease, retreat into some private place where they couldn't touch him. While he recited their prayers and read their books and learned their habits of cleanliness, he'd never given in. Only the shell had been changed.

Until Elena.

He was fourteen when she came to teach at the mission school. She was twenty-four and the daughter of a wealthy Spanish landowner. Tommy was working in the smithy, learning his trade, but after one glimpse of her flashing black eyes, he'd gone to the headmaster and confessed that he'd finally realized the advice that worthy had given him was correct—he wanted to re-enroll in classes and see if he could get a grant for college.

What Tommy had really wanted was to be near Elena. His grades were dismal, but she seemed not to care. In fact, she encouraged him to come for private tutoring sessions and basked in the obvious admiration in his eyes. Soon, what started as a whim and a game became so serious that it was reported to the headmaster. The school fired her, her father disinherited her, and on the day he turned sixteen, Tommy married her.

They left Flag amidst a furor, but neither of them cared a bit. They'd been passing through White's Station on the way to Colorado when Elena espied the white cottage on the edge of town. It had a red door, a picket fence, and a stream flowing through the back yard. It looked uninhabited. Impulsive as always, she'd stopped the stage and made the driver throw down their bags, then told Tommy to find out who owned the house. Tommy had rented it and the livery from Ray Benson, and after several years, bought the house outright.

Elena. He remembered so clearly her flashing eyes, her profile at rest as pure and clean as a cameo. But repose came seldom, for Elena was ruled by passion. She would laugh, cry, fight at the drop of a hat, and as a lover had been tender and wild by turns, and he'd worshiped her. When their son was born, Tommy felt that his life was complete.

There was an emptiness now in his life, in his heart, but he knew it was nothing compared to what drove his son. To Alec, the world had revolved around Elena. Tommy wished with all his heart that it had been he, and not his son, who had found her there dying.

The smith sighed. *I can't change the past.* Then he became aware of the strong hand that gripped his shoulder hard. Tommy looked up at his young friend—his son's friend—and saw the grim set of Daniel's face.

"No, Dan'l," he said, his voice coarse with emotion. "It won't bring 'er back. It won't help, even if Alec thinks it will." He drew a deep breath and held it or a moment. "B'sides, it ain't so hard t' figger out, is it? Only one man in these parts would've ever hurt a woman. An' if it was some stranger, you wouldn' know he was gone, would you?"

Daniel dropped his hand and averted his eyes. He didn't answer, but the smith saw that his throat was working.

"It don't matter who done it," Tommy said. "It won't bring 'er back. An' there's no sense in makin' somebody else suffer for it—somebody who's had trials enough of 'er own."

The two men stood silently for a moment, thinking of little Jesse Travers. Jesse Donovan. Who'd been Alec's staunch friend—until her brother had beaten her for being an Indian's friend. Until her brother had…

Daniel had learned that Tommy knew of Jesse's trials when he'd made a report to Raymond Benson, the town's constable. The cattleman had grimaced but shaken his head.

"I'm not the law, Daniel," he'd said in a deep Texas drawl. "The only jurisdiction I have is heah in town. An' thet's limited. I can lock 'im up overnight when 'e's drunk or when 'e shoots up the street. But I can't take 'im in an' hold 'im for a trial without hard proof. I told Tommy Twelve Trees the same thing.

"You hafta see it yerself, or she'll hafta bring in a complaint. Tommy swears she won't, 'cause it would hurt her father. I'm sorry, boy, but my hands're tied."

"Will they be tied when he kills her?" Daniel demanded.

"Not if there's proof." Benson had stared at him, seeing the hard resolve in his face. "What're you gonna do, Daniel?"

"Protect her," was the terse response.

"How?"

"Any way I can. Any way I need to." And he'd cursed long and hard beneath his breath.

"Be careful, Daniel," were the constable's parting words. Daniel had laughed without humor.

"Don't worry," he bit out. "There won't be any proof." He'd slammed the door behind him. Now, as he shook off his dark thoughts, he knew that he'd been unfair to Benson. Jesse was safe now. Even if Elena was dead.

Tommy knew the truth. Maybe someday he could tell Alec—when the pain had worn off a little bit and it wouldn't be so hard to bear.

"I'll get this started as soon as I can," Daniel said. Tommy, he knew, heard the words of sympathy that he couldn't express.

Tommy grabbed his hand and pumped it up and down. His face had taken on its usual lightness. "Thanks, Dan'l. We got a couple

THE WOODSMAN'S ROSE

weeks, mebbe a month. Doc said it won't be healed 'til then. Hey, you gonna see Jesse anytime soon?"

"Probably tomorrow." Weather permitting, the Donovan clan congregated at the homestead for dinner every Sunday.

"Well, give 'er my love, y'hear me?"

Chapter 6

DANIEL PICKED UP HIS rifle and hit the path toward home. It wasn't long before a wagon overtook him on the road.

"Want a ride?" His brother-in-law, Lowell Griffiths, pulled up beside him. A plain-featured man with light brown hair, hazel eyes, and a bone-deep optimism, Lowell was married to Daniel's sister Evelyn, and just happened to be Annie's brother.

As Daniel vaulted in, Lowell asked, "What're you smiling about?"

"Tommy's sending his love to Jesse, and I'm trying to figure out if there's a man in the Territory who's not in love with her."

"Forget it. You have to count all of us. Even me." And with a sideways look at his friend, Lowell added, "Even you."

"I wonder what it is?"

"Don't know. Maybe it's because she's not what her brother said—what everyone believed she was. Maybe we're trying to make up for that in some way. It's hard to imagine, once you know her, how anybody could've believed she was bad. Not when she's so sweet and kind." After a few minute's silence, Lowell asked, "Where you going?"

"Nowhere special."

"How'd you like to come for supper? Annie's cooking tonight." Though Annie lived in town with her father, the family often ate together at Lowell's dairy farm. At Daniel's soft, clear laugh, Lowell said, "I take it that means yes. You know, I woulda gambled on it."

"I just bet you would."

THE WOODSMAN'S ROSE

When they arrived, Daniel kissed his sister on the cheek, then stepped back to look her over. Evelyn was expecting her first child in a few months. "How are you feeling?"

"I feel fine. I just wish it weren't quite so hot." She shoved at her red hair that was curling wildly in the humidity, trying in vain to smooth it down.

"I asked Daniel to supper," Lowell told her.

His wife gave a snort of amusement. "Annie's in the kitchen—why don't you tell her Lowell's home?"

Daniel sketched a bow and drifted silently to the back of the house. At the kitchen door, he watched his fiancée for a moment as she moved from larder to stove in a spacious room that was neat as the proverbial pin. He was utterly charmed by the picture she made in her green dimity dress and crisp white apron.

She greeted him with a shy gladness. He kissed her lightly and watched a rosy blush rise to her cheeks.

"Something smells good," he told her.

"I made some bread this afternoon," Annie said, not quite disguising the pride in her voice. "And there's beef stew and pole beans. And huckleberry pie. But that's from yesterday," she added with an elfin grin. "Maybe we don't want that."

"Don't want what?" Annie's father, Owen Griffiths, stood in the doorway.

"Annie's pie. She thinks we don't want it 'cause it's a whole day old."

"Hmmph. Just gives it time to mellow." Owen pinched his daughter's cheek. He was a small, round man with a bald pate and wide, callused hands capable of fine work in leather. The rounded vowels and crisp consonants in his speech marked his Welsh beginnings. "You're a tease, girl. Always have been. Ever notice that, Daniel?"

"Nope." He watched her blush again as he took the stack of dishes from her and began to set the table.

As she helped him, Annie watched Daniel out of the corner of her eye. When his hand touched hers, she felt a sadness in him beneath the casual banter they engaged in. And when, during the meal, her father asked after things on the ranch and out in the canyon, he seemed somehow removed from their conversation.

After dessert, which resulted in the disappearance of the huckleberry pie, Owen and Annie walked the half-mile back to their cottage in the village. Daniel joined them, holding Annie's hand along the way while Owen teased them good-naturedly.

Owen retired to his workshop, leaving the young couple sitting together on the porch in the twilight. The village was quiet as they watched the sky turn from crimson to rose. He reached out to touch a stray wisp of her hair.

"What's wrong, Daniel?"

He dropped his hand and leaned his head back against the house. "Oh, Annie," he answered, his voice rougher than usual. "I don't know what to do."

"Is it Alec? What would he do if you told him?"

It didn't surprise Daniel that she'd recognized his problem. She'd always been adept at reading his emotions. "I don't know, *aroon*," he said. "I'd like to think it would bring him some peace of mind—that he could accept it. But he's so torn up, I'm afraid of what he'll do.

"He blames me for deserting him. He blames Tommy for not protecting Elena. He's not thinking straight, and he could do so much harm. So much harm."

"It's Jesse, isn't it?" she asked. "You're protecting her."

"Annie..."

She raised a finger to his lips. "Daniel, I won't tell anyone. Do you think I'd hurt her?"

THE WOODSMAN'S ROSE

"No, *aroon*. I know you couldn't." He put his arm around her shoulders and pulled her close, pressed his cheek against her hair. "Annie, I love you, but I've sworn not to tell anyone."

"I know," she whispered, "but it's in your voice when you talk about her—in your eyes when you watch her." She slipped her arms around his waist and hugged him tight.

He whispered her name and she raised her face to his. He kissed her forehead, then held her head against his shoulder with a strong, gentle hand. "*Aroon*, if you know this, tell me how to protect her. Tell me what's best."

"Your heart will tell you, Daniel."

"It tells me that to protect her, I must hurt Alec. I wish there were some other way."

"So do I, Daniel. So do I."

The sky deepened to darkness as he held her there, and she felt a gradual easing of his burden. She asked him no questions, for she knew he wouldn't answer her, yet he wouldn't have known how to refuse.

When the moon appeared, he rose to go. She walked with him to the street, where he touched her hair once more and wished her good night.

"I love you, Annie," he said. She stood on her tiptoes to kiss his cheek. He reached for her but she was gone too quickly, fleeing to the house. She turned at the door, her face on fire. He stood stock still for a moment, then his laughter, as clear and pure as a bell, pealed out behind her.

"*Aroon!*" he called. *My love.* He blew her a kiss as she ducked into the house.

Chapter 7

ANNIE'S SOFT KISS WAS, in many ways, a turning point in Daniel's life. He stood watching the door for a moment, while her smile carved itself into his heart and the warm spot her lips had left on his cheek lit a fire along his veins. He lifted a finger to his face, but didn't quite dare to touch it. Though they'd been betrothed for several months, she'd rarely spoken of love, never before offered a kiss.

His smile grew broader until it seemed to split his face, then he leaped straight up. He turned in the air and came down running, his rifle held high over his head in both hands. He wanted to shout, to laugh, to roar like a lion. Instead he ran.

Down the trail and away from the town, he sped toward home. As his feet hit the ground in virtual silence, his heart pounded with the truth that one little kiss had revealed to him. *She loves me! She really loves me! She will be mine!*

He hadn't realized that doubt until it was gone. He ran for almost two miles before slowing to a jog. At the gates to the Donovan ranch he finally stopped, bending double to catch his breath. He leaned against one of the two massive posts holding his family's brand aloft—the letter "D" encircled by the Celtic symbol of eternity. It stood high enough and wide enough to allow the passage of any covered wagon. His grandmother had designed it and a smith in Abilene had made it for the family's ranch there. When they moved to Arizona to escape the influence of what his father called "the neighbors' war", Daniel had attached the brand to two pair of

THE WOODSMAN'S ROSE

oxen, using the sides as a yoke. Their westward drive had been slowed by the pace of the oxen, but there'd been no question of leaving it behind. When they arrived, it had taken twelve men to hoist it into position.

He looked beyond it now, to a night sky alive with glittering stars. *Sometimes you can almost believe there are those beings up there—out there—who watch over us. The sisters, the bear, the king on his throne. The hunter. Do they understand us? Do they know us? Do they understand what brings us together? What makes us love?*

I don't know what makes me love her. Except that she's so beautiful. So pure and so gentle. She's like a small doe in the forest. Natural. Unspoiled. Shy. I love her. I love her.

I must be patient. Gentle. She's too beautiful to spoil. But how much I want her! Annie. My precious Annie. I will wait as long as I have to. It will be easier, now that I know you will truly be mine.

Rifle in hand, he padded toward the big white house. It stood silhouetted against the night, the lantern that hung by the door shining in perpetual welcome. It was a huge house, three stories high, constructed of sawn boards painted white. The doors and windows were trimmed in emerald green. There were those in the town who considered the Donovan home an insult, a brag of the good fortunes the family had been blessed with. But John Patrick, with his older sons, had built the house for his Molly—to try to ease the burden a pioneer's life imposed upon an Irish-born girl. To try to assuage some of the sorrow and pain she'd suffered: her parents and her younger brother, like most of her small village, had been victims of starvation, and her longing for her native land still sometimes overwhelmed her.

This house is an act of love. As much as Annie's kiss. We built this house from the ground up. The work went slowly at times, and stopped altogether when there was no money. But we didn't give up. We dreamed of it always, and finally realized the dream. This house is like my parents' marriage.

The thought stirred him profoundly. He hadn't recognized the poet, the spiritualist in his nature, believing this gift belonged to his brother Adam. But the thread of realization wouldn't be broken, and his heart told him that having Annie for his wife wouldn't be enough. It would make him happy, but he'd need to make her happy, too. Like the building of this graceful home, it would take more than love to accomplish—their marriage would require strength and patience, and commitment to the dream. They'd have to work together to build their own home. *And we'll build a home such as this world has never seen. Just Annie and me. We'll build it together. We need a piece of land. We need a plan.*

He climbed the front steps, checked the fuel level in the lantern—part of his father's dream was that the light should never be out, and no one ever turned away. He headed in to find his parents and youngest sister, along with his three younger brothers, in the small parlor behind the stairs that had been his grandmother's favorite retreat. He stowed his rifle in a corner and settled into a chair by the hearth. His parents sat together on a chaise lounge, his mother, as usual, leaning against his father's arm.

They built this home in spite of the pain and the fear and the hardship. We'll be luckier, Annie and me—we'll be able to find happiness in our own world.

But he hadn't before stopped to consider that Annie might suffer the same longings his mother did. *I wonder if she'd want to go back to Wales? I'll have to ask her. And I will do whatever she wants.*

Chapter 8

OWEN HEARD HIS DAUGHTER humming in the kitchen and looked up from his books. He stared at the wall in front of him and smiled. *If she'll just let him love her, then she'll be happy. She's been so moody lately, so changeable. Not like herself at all. I wish she'd set the date and marry him. I want her to be happy for all the time she has left.*

His happiness was overlaid with sadness as he thought of his only daughter, thought of the very short time he'd been blessed with his own wife. *She's so much like her mother, with her beautiful hair and smile. But her eyes are her own, and that little pointed chin. Makes her look like a fairy-child. And maybe she is. For Megan had the gift of reading people's emotions, and Annie shares it too.*

His wife had died giving birth. The son she had borne died, too, and Owen had found himself unable to deal with his grief. His sister had watched the children for months while he drank himself into a stupor night after night, craving the shelter of his Megan's arms, needing her love and her soft voice to whisper in his ear.

Until the day his daughter, at four years old, had taken the glass away from him and curled up in his lap.

"Mama still loves us," she said in a voice wise beyond her years. "She wants us to be happy."

He'd stared at her for a moment, seeing her mother for the first time in her tiny face. Then his baby girl had comforted him as his grief finally found an outlet. He'd wept the night through and, at the end of it, carried her to her bed and began to make plans to leave Wales. For he knew then he couldn't live there without his love, and he had a responsibility to her children—their children. Annie had made him see. So he took her and her older brother as far away as he could imagine and as far from civilization as was reasonable. They'd lived simply and quietly in White's Station.

Owen had a job first in the trading post as a clerk, and he worked in leather on the side. When cattle ranching came to the area, he found his skills in such demand that he opened the shop in this cottage and gradually saved enough money to buy the house outright. His skill as a bootmaker brought both cowboys and ladies from the entire Territory to his door.

The war had had slight effect on them here, and Owen had begun to prosper. Five years ago, he'd helped his son buy the farm on the outskirts of town. Lowell had exhibited little skill and less interest in leather, preferring to tend to his cows and to sell their milk, butter and cheese to the townspeople. He insisted his father share in his profits and so Owen, while not a rich man in the eyes of the world, had more money than he'd ever know what to do with. He wanted grandchildren, so he could spend his money on them.

He was sure Evelyn was going to be a wonderful mother. A tall, generously built young woman, freckle-faced and red-haired, she was the image of her mother. She was more outgoing than Molly, gay and lively, and Owen knew she could make his son's head whirl. Sometimes it seemed as if Lowell was putty in her hands, but Owen recognized the steel that was the backbone of his son's character and knew she depended on it. And on the strength of his love.

His thoughts returned to Annie, still humming in the kitchen. If she were to marry Daniel, Owen would be grateful as well as happy. For although he'd always enjoyed good health, he'd seen too many lives cut short in this wilderness not to worry over his daughter. Were she to marry Daniel, the Donovan clan would take her as their own if anything happened to him. She'd have a secure place in the world, as well as Daniel's love.

THE WOODSMAN'S ROSE

On the other hand, why should I worry about her when Daniel loves her so much? Wife or no wife, she'll always be taken care of.

―※―

ANNIE'S OWN THOUGHTS were an echo of her father's. She was thinking about her childhood, about the mother she scarcely remembered, about the love she'd received from her father and her brother as she grew up. She realized Evelyn was now the center of Lowell's world, and she was happy for him. Yet she wondered what marriage would be like for herself.

If he loves me, her thoughts began, but she stopped them there. *You know that he loves you. You know that he wouldn't lie, that Lowell wouldn't lie. You know that it makes your father happy to see him here. Because he loves you, and he wants you to be his wife.*

Wife. What a powerful word. It makes me tremble inside. But it makes me feel strong, too. It means we'd be partners—things wouldn't be mine or his any more, but ours instead. It means we'd be together. All the time. We'd live together, work together, sleep...

This is the root of my uncertainty. This is what I don't understand. How can I tell if I want to marry him—to marry anyone—if I don't understand what it means?

―※―

AT THE SUDDEN STILLNESS from the kitchen, Owen put down his pencil and moved to his favorite chair, noticing for the first time that the green and tan plaid fustian was wearing thin on the arms. Moments later, as he'd expected, Annie was sitting on the floor by his feet with her head on his knee. He stroked her bright hair.

"What is it, *Angharad?*"

She smiled up at him, then laid her cheek again upon his knee. How long had it been since he'd called her by her full name, the name her mother had chosen? She was silent for a while, then spoke softly. "Papa, what does it mean to be a wife?"

He continued to stroke her hair as he tried to find a way to answer. He knew what she asked, what she needed to know. *Help me, Megan,* he implored. *Help me to tell her what love is.*

"I think, *caraid*," he began, "that to every woman it is something different. There are those who marry only because they want children, and those who marry because they simply don't want to be alone. But I believe marriage should be for love. Your mother and I married for love, and I can tell you what she told me."

Annie nodded against his knee. She loved to hear about her mother, remembering only a pale, sweet face and tender hands.

"Before we married, before she accepted me, your mother told me that she expected our marriage to be a sharing. Of responsibility. Of happiness and sorrow, pain and joy. She wanted me to understand that we would stand together through everything—that never would either of us be alone.

"She also told me she expected me to be patient with her, and gentle. For you see, she was afraid, as most women are. Because men are physically stronger and can be thoughtless and cruel.

"There's always pain the first time. It cannot be helped. But a husband has the responsibility to see that his wife has as little pain as possible the first time, and as much pleasure as possible after that." Owen hesitated but forced himself on again, in honesty to her. "There are some women who never learn to enjoy intimacy, no matter how gentle a man is. And there are men who never make an effort to be gentle. But usually a man and a woman who marry for love find happiness in their bed."

He waited for her to speak, but she didn't. "Daniel is a gentle man, *caraid*," he said.

She looked up at him, her cheeks red, her eyes flashing, her voice as soft as silk. "He'd never hurt me. Never."

THE WOODSMAN'S ROSE

"The first time, *caraid*. It cannot be helped. You might talk to Evelyn about this."

She turned back to the fire. "I love you, Papa."

"*R'wy'n dy garu di*," he echoed, smoothing her golden hair, "*fy merch fach*."

AS SHE LAY IN BED THAT night, Annie could still hear the pain in Daniel's rough voice. She'd always known his voice like that—like emery on slate—though she knew at one time it had been different. He'd suffered the accident that changed his voice before the family had moved to White's Station.

The little boy had fallen into a willow tree, where a short branch had impaled him by the neck. His older brothers had been with him—Conor, they'd always say, was screaming like a banshee. While Brian held him up, Adam had used his penknife to cut the branch off the tree. They carried him home with the branch still sticking out of his neck, and it was many, many months before he'd talk again.

The voice he had now was gruff, gravelly. He thought his voice was ugly and the scar left by the accident uglier still. He wore his bandanna tight around his neck to hide the mark, and he spoke softly to hide the gruffness. She'd never seen the scar, but in his voice, Annie could hear a slow Texas drawl, overlaid with the music of his father's brogue. When he murmured in her ear, when he called her *Aroon*, she found it quite the sweetest sound she'd ever heard.

Aroon, he'd say, and his deep gruff voice would strike her heart. *Aroon*. Beloved. Sweetheart. Darling. Every other loving word she'd ever heard faded before it. *Aroon*. It fit him. It fit this place—this half-tamed wilderness tucked away in a corner of Arizona.

Aroon. An ancient word. She could almost taste it. It was made up of the song of the wind in the trees, the warning of the owl, the chant of the Navajo, the cry of the wolf for his mate. It swelled like a wave on the ocean but whispered against the shore. *Aroon.*

Arooooon...

She sighed for that word, and longed hear it again.

Chapter 9

A FEW DAYS LATER, DANIEL presented Tommy with a drawing of a functional wood and leather leg. Together they took it to the Navajo's summer encampment in the mountains. After a short conversation with the elders, they headed for a rather neglected hogan on the far side of the camp. Tommy showed the drawing to the boy and his mother, explaining that the leather cup would fit over his leg and the wide bands would stabilize it at the calf and thigh. Though Daniel understood little of their language, he could read the excitement in her face as Small Cloud at Night spoke eagerly to her son. The boy's dark eyes were glued to hers, but he gave her no response. Small for a child of twelve, he looked waxen and tired.

In his pocket, along with a handful of rawhide laces, a pencil and a scrap of paper, Daniel usually carried pemmican or dried fruit. He knelt beside Blue Deer's bed of blankets and offered him a wrinkled slice of apple.

After looking to his mother for permission, Blue Deer reached shyly for the fruit and took a firm bite, glancing once at the woodsman before averting his eyes.

"T'anks," he murmured.

Daniel pulled another slice from his pocket and puffed out his lips, then chewed so loudly and with such facial contortions Blue Deer had to laugh. "Speak English?"

The boy shook his head. "T'anks," he repeated.

"Welcome." Daniel chuckled and offered another piece of apple. Blue Deer peered around his shoulder to see if his mother was watching, then his hand darted out for the extra slice and hid it under his blanket.

"T'anks." The word was scarcely a whisper this time. Daniel winked at him.

Tommy was still talking to the boy's mother as Daniel rose and made a great show of brushing off the seat of his pants, garnering another small chuckle from Blue Deer.

"I'll see you later," the woodsman said to Tommy, throwing a salute to the sick boy and nodding to his mother. She returned a graceful wave of her hand. Turning once more to the boy on the blankets, he tossed another piece of apple to him and slipped out the door.

※

THE FOREST WAS COOL and shady, the sun creating a dappled carpet that changed with the breeze. Birds and squirrels paid no attention as the woodsman glided along on the mat of loam and pine needles. Three deer—a doe and two fawns—pricked their ears up at the slight rustling of his footsteps. But seeing only the movement of hide identical to their own, they dipped their heads to the stream again.

Daniel moved warily, leaving no trail, listening to the sounds of the forest, knowing someone was close by. When he stopped, he heard the man tracking him stop a split-second later. As he stepped out again, the footsteps that dogged him weren't quite attuned to the rhythm of his stride. The follower was taller than he. As he left the next clearing, just at the edge of the woods, the woodsman pivoted.

Like a child caught in a game of Statues, Alec Twelve Trees stopped mid-stride. In place of the flared vaquero's pants and velvet shirt he habitually wore, today he was dressed in buckskins identical to Daniel's. His hair hung loose below a leather headband decorated

THE WOODSMAN'S ROSE

with silver medallions. As the woodsman leaned on his rifle, Alec settled his feet together.

"Tell me," Alec growled.

"I can't."

"Tell me who killed my mother."

"He's gone now. There's nothing you can do."

"Tell me."

"Alec, we've been through this before. I have no proof."

"I don't care. I want to know. I need to know."

Daniel shook his head slowly. Conversation seemed useless. Still, he tried to reason with his friend. "There's family left—"

"You bastard. I'll kill you."

"No. You won't."

But Alec didn't hear—he'd turned on his heel and disappeared into the trees.

Daniel looked up to the canopy but saw only his friend's face—a face that had always been solemn and yet always calm, now twisted and tortured with pain, dark eyes smoldering with despair. He wanted nothing more than for his friend to find peace.

A deeply spiritual man, Daniel considered the outward trappings of religion nonsense. He'd found solace in nature, coming to believe that all things have a sacred meaning of their own. His beliefs had been crystallized by discussions with Alec and Tommy, and he'd accepted much of the Navajo way—he believed that a man's word was as good as his deed, that nature's bounty wasn't to be taken lightly, that waste was the greatest sin. That a man without honor is no man at all. He also found hope in the optimism of the prayer of the Navajo, which ended with, "Now all is well." He stopped for a moment, closed his eyes and tried to force the belief into his heart, but it brought him no comfort.

Letting out a long slow breath, he rubbed his face with both hands. He had no choice—he had to protect an innocent. She needed him more than his friend ever could.

He continued on his journey and, after another mile, arrived at the edge of the forest and stepped out onto his father's land. The foothills rolled gently behind him, and even more gently in front of him—down to the river and the village of White's Station.

This was his home—the Arizona Territory. From the desert in the south to the mountains surrounding Flag to the Tonto Basin, Daniel knew the Territory intimately. He loved it all, but he loved these foothills best. Here the winter could be harsh but wasn't too long, and the other seasons glided into one another much as he glided through the forest. His brothers sometimes remarked he loved his Territory even more than his family.

A smile played on Daniel's lips. It wasn't true, of course, but it made for some interesting conversations. A bit more settled in spirit, he continued on his way home.

Chapter 10

ON A QUIET SUMMER DAY, Adam and Brian went looking for Daniel and found him at home. The brothers had talked of building a separate cabin in the canyon for Brian's use, but had decided instead to add a large bedroom—one with its own fireplace, to keep Jesse from feeling the cold. The new room would be built off the main cabin opposite the two small bedrooms Jesse's father had built on when she was a child. After tearing out every inch of plaster between the logs of the existing cabin, they'd brought their plan for the new room to Daniel for approval, whose skills in carpentry were above reproach.

Daniel took one glance at it, gave a snort of disgust and handed the paper back to Brian without a word.

"What's wrong with it?" Brian demanded.

Daniel glared at them. "You know, you may be strong..." He flicked his chin toward Brian, then turned to the big man's twin. "And you may be handsome, but there ain't a lick o' sense between you."

Adam bristled and repeated his brother's question. "What's wrong with it?"

"It's a room for Jesse, right? With a fireplace to keep her warm, right?"

"So?"

"So you gonna put her in through the window?"

The twins looked at their plan then at each other, and finally at their brother, who was squatting on the ground and laughing so hard he couldn't catch his breath. Brian caught him by the scruff of the neck and hauled him to his feet.

"Are you gonna help us?" Brian's red hair was wild around his head, his cheeks almost purple. "Or am I jus' natur'ly gonna pulverize you?"

Daniel held up a hand for peace. "Tomorrow," he managed to croak. "I'll come out tomorrow and help you get started."

As good as his word, Daniel worked with them, showing them how to use wedges to support the walls while they cut a door through from the parlor. How to use the same supports to lock the new walls to the old. He cut their logs to precise measurements and helped wedge them between the logs of the outer wall. He recommended they use adobe instead of plaster to seal the walls, and raise the floor of the new room another few inches to create better insulation underfoot. He showed them how to lay the stone for the fireplace, then helped seal the roof to the main cabin. And when they'd nearly finished, he hung the shutters and the inside door for them. His brothers finally admitted his superior skill, and he laughed again.

Chapter 11

DOC BARBER STOPPED by the Donovan home at least once a week, sure of a good cup of coffee and fairly certain of a meal. Today he was accompanied by Tommy, and after dinner, they drew John Patrick and Daniel aside and told them of some disquiet in the peaceful mountain tribe of Navajo—there were several newcomers, men who'd refused to be relocated to the reservation with their own tribes, and who were fostering rebellion.

The doctor reported incidents on the outskirts of town—slaughtered cattle, stolen sheep, fences pulled over. A prospector's shack had been burned while he was in town, a squatter's wife was terrorized by half a dozen young warriors who splattered her house with the blood of chickens.

"I don't feel safe going up there without Tommy in tow," Barber said. "That Yellow Knife in particular seems like a dangerous fellow. Thought he could threaten Tommy because he lives with us white folk. Tell them how you answered him, Tommy."

Tommy snorted. "Didn' say nothin. Gave 'im what 'e deserved." The blacksmith raised a hand to one of his broad shoulders and flicked off an invisible mote. "Bastard thinks 'e can take me, I say c'mon an' try. But he ain't got the stomach for it—you wait an' see."

Nevertheless, the tribe's highest-ranking elder had asked Tommy to warn the white settlers to be prepared for more violence. "Runnin' Wolf used pidgen English, so nobody but me an' Left-Handed Bear could unnerstan'. I jus' nodded a bit, lookin' here an' there, like we was talkin' 'bout huntin' or somethin'."

"But I'm tellin' ya, it ain't no use askin' Yella Knife t' let up," Tommy continued. "He's good an' riled an' gainin' more followers every day. It's men my age mos'ly—the ones who were kidnapped by the missionary schools, before you came an' put an end t' thet."

John Patrick waved away Tommy's thanks. The practice of rounding up the Navajo children and forcing them into missionary schools had angered him immensely. There was no logic he could see for telling them their gods were invalid, force-feeding them Christianity and English, and forbidding them to speak their own language or keep their own customs. Then, for good measure, the children were dumped back on their villages at the age of sixteen, where they were considered outcasts. The girls were laughed at for trying to maintain the white man's standards of purity, while the boys were scorned for their lack of life skills. The three R's were worthless in the Navajo world, but a good hunter could save his tribe from starvation.

John Patrick had seen the same abuses suffered by the native Irish at the hands of the English, and he'd tried to stop it by argument and persuasion. Finally, he'd traded with the tribe for the land between the river and the foothills. The only way to the children now was through Donovan land, and he'd made sure both the army and the schools knew they weren't to trespass. Conflict with the schools' bounty hunters had almost become physical at one point, but the family and the village had stood together against them.

"Only made sense," John Patrick now said. "If the children will live with their families, they should be raised with their families. Still, we've not addressed the issue at hand."

"What about the old ways?" Daniel asked. "How did the tribe handle internal problems then?"

"Depends on the problem. Could be anythin' from some extra chores—woman's work, mos'ly—t' makin' restitution. Shunnin' if the problem was bad enough."

THE WOODSMAN'S ROSE

"Shunning? What's that?"

"Well, everybody in the tribe agrees t' ignore 'em. Not speak to 'em, not do anythin' with 'em—not hunt or even eat with 'em. It's us'ally jus' for a few days. But sometimes, if it was bad enough, it'd be permanent." Thoughtfully, Tommy added, "Mos' the time, the ones who got shunned jus' left on their own. They couldn' stand havin' nobody pay 'em any mind."

"What do you think?" John Patrick asked. "Would it work?"

"Wal, it'd be up to Runnin' Wolf an' the elders." Tommy screwed his face up for a minute. "I know Runnin' Wolf won't take it on hisself t' run 'em out—he'd hafta have the other elders in on it. But I tell ya they're sure mighty embarrassed by this whole thing."

"What have we to lose?" John Patrick asked. "If they refuse, all we've invested is a bit of time."

So they went together, the two Donovan men and Tommy, to sit and talk to Running Wolf and the elders. Most of their conversation was couched in an English-Spanish-Navajo patois, with subtle words that offered neither insult nor recommendation. No decisions were made, but they'd expected none. The elders would take action, or not, after a private discussion.

❦

ON A DREARY AFTERNOON that threatened rain but didn't deliver, Daniel stopped at the livery stable and found Tommy whistling as he worked at his forge.

"Hey, Dan'l. How ya doin'?" Without waiting for an answer, Tommy continued, "Me an' Doc went up t' the camp yestidday an' saw Blue Deer. He's real happy with 'is new leg. Said 'e can do all the things the other boys can. They make a li'l fun of 'im, but 'e don't really care."

"That's great. Any news about the newcomers?"

"Nothin' solid." Tommy stopped to select a rod of raw iron. "Coupl'a people objectin' to the shunnin', but I think Runnin' Wolf'll make 'em come around eventually."

"Oh, an' Small Cloud said you're t' come up an' have supper with 'em one o' these days. Feel like goin'?"

"Sure. Wednesday work for you?"

"Anythin' works for me, son, when there's food t' be had."

Chapter 12

AS SUMMER DRIFTED INTO fall, Daniel became a habitual guest at the dairy farm, arriving at least twice a week in time for dinner with the Griffith family. Evelyn was more than happy to accommodate him. A pragmatist at heart, she didn't understand the long engagement he'd undertaken. In this part of the country, courtship was normally a matter of weeks, not months, still less close to a year. She longed to tease him, but had decided to save Annie embarrassment. So she centered the conversation around her need for a longer kitchen table, expecting her brother to volunteer to make one for her. She wasn't disappointed.

"I knew you would," she told him.

Daniel gave a gruff laugh, then asked, "Did you hear about Frank and Geordie?"

Evelyn stared at him. "What now?"

There was a sly look around her brother's eyes and an undercurrent of laughter in his voice. She was always ready for the antics of the younger twins.

"They've been courting Patricia Flaherty since the spring."

"Both of them? Really?" Evelyn started to giggle.

"Really. Told her they wouldn't fight over her, and she could make up her mind between the two of them."

Annie gaped at him. "Are you serious?"

"How do you know?" Owen asked.

"Seamus told Tommy," Daniel answered. "They haven't spoken to Mother and Dad yet."

"What's your mother going to say?" Lowell asked his wife with a huge grin, causing Evelyn to go off into gales of laughter.

As they all joined her, Evelyn wondered how Seamus's daughter could have captured the hearts of both her brothers. The quiet, sensible Geordie. The garrulous, excitable Frank. Two men who looked so much alike that, in Brian's words, "the only way t' tell 'em apart's t' put 'em close t'gether an' see who twitches first." Two such different men, each enamored of a silly, flighty girl with a pretty face and a heart of gold.

"I wonder which one she'll pick," Annie said, when their gaiety had subsided.

"What if she doesn't pick either one?" Lowell asked.

"I'm sure she will."

"Which, then?" Evelyn demanded.

Annie raised an eyebrow but wouldn't answer.

SATURDAY NIGHT BROUGHT the last dance of the season to the Town Hall. Daniel wore gabardine pants, a shirt of white lawn his grandmother had made for him shortly before she died, and black leather shoes he'd borrowed from Adam. He met Annie at her father's cottage. Freed from its braid for this occasion, her flaxen hair hung long and loose, and her dress of blue moiré made her eyes seem more green than ever. Overwhelmed by her beauty, he deemed himself the luckiest of men.

She was light as a fairy in his arms as they waltzed across the floor. He shared her dances with his family and hers, then relented and let Tommy take her around the floor, while he joined Adam and Jesse on the chairs ringing the room. Jesse teased him, asking him how long he was going to make Annie wait to get married. He laughed with her, rejoicing that the girl who could scarcely look at him when they first met was now so self-assured.

THE WOODSMAN'S ROSE

When John Patrick claimed Jesse's hand for a waltz, Daniel glanced around and saw Alec Twelve Trees standing alone near the refreshment table. He seemed to be in a trance. Following his gaze, Daniel found his sister Irene at the end of it. She was dancing with Michael Flaherty, smiling vivaciously up at him, and Michael looked as if he held the world in his hands and didn't know what to do with it. Daniel couldn't blame the boy. Or Alec.

When she'd graduated to beauty, he didn't know, but the fact that Irene had was inescapable. Her thick black hair was gathered into a topknot, tendrils of it framing her face, curling on her neck. She was tall and slender, graceful as a swan, her skin white and luminous as a magnolia flower. The dress of ice blue sateen made her dark eyes shine with an ethereal light.

The band paused and Alec approached her, but as the music started, she was whisked away in Michael's arms once again. Daniel watched Alec's expression grow dark and bitter. The silversmith and Irene had long been friends, and Irene had often said he was the best friend she had. And now it seemed that friendship was less than he wanted.

When Daniel looked back again, Alec was gone, and Irene was dancing with Adam, pouting up at him, anger flashing from her deep blue eyes. He was glad his brother had intervened. Irene was, after all, just seventeen, and the old cats were ripe for some new gossip about the family. Adam had foiled their last attempt by marrying Jesse. And clearly intended to foil them again.

As the evening was ending, Daniel took Annie's hand for the last dance and a smile began to form beneath his mustache.

"What are you thinking?" she asked.

"Look at Patricia."

"Where?" Annie found the girl even as she spoke. Patricia's nut-brown hair was worn in ringlets, and her cheeks were bright red.

She was whispering into her mother's ear; both faces wet with tears that were obviously joyful.

"Oh, Daniel," Annie whispered, "do you think...?"

"It's just a matter of which one."

"Who do you think it will be?" she asked with a twinkle in her eye.

"I think we're about to find out."

Seamus Flaherty had stopped the band and was hopping around on the dais.

"If ye please, if ye please!" he cried out, "I'll have an announcement t' make. Me daughter Patricia has consented t' be the wife..."

Here it became apparent Seamus lacked some pertinent knowledge. The little man squinted at his wife, who mouthed a name, but he was more than a bit tipsy and didn't take it in. The hall began to buzz with merriment.

"Me daughter... me daughter has consented t' be..." The crowd was roaring with laughter as Seamus gave it one last shot.

"Me daughter has consented t' be... Mrs. Donovan!" he finished in triumph. "Mrs. Donovan!"

"Hurrah!" Brian shouted. "Now tell us which one!"

"It's you!" cried Adam. "You're on the hook!"

"Oh, no, not me! Aw, I'm sorry, Miss Patricia. I didn't mean no offense. But it's one o' these here boys you want, ain't it?" Brian grabbed a twin with each hand and held them by their collars. "You jus' tell me which one, an' I'll take 'im t' the preacher right now!"

"It's Frank!" Patricia went unerringly to her fiance. "You let him go! We're going to have a big church wedding. And everyone's invited!"

Geordie was released and Frank was the victim of Brian's bear hug. Then the big man planted a hearty kiss upon Patricia's cheek, as

THE WOODSMAN'S ROSE

the Donovans swarmed round. After offering congratulations, Adam and Daniel conferred with Geordie.

Daniel borrowed the band's fiddle, Geordie pulled his harmonica out, and Adam's sweet tenor rang through the hall. The crowd moved aside to give Frank room to dance with his betrothed as his brother sang:

> *Believe me if all those endearing young charms,*
> *Which I gaze on so fondly today,*
> *Were to change by tomorrow and fleet in my arms*
> *Like fairy gifts fading away,*
> *Thou wouldst still be adored as this moment thou art,*
> *Let thy loveliness fade as it will,*
> *And around the dear ruin each wish of my heart*
> *Would entwine itself verdantly still.*

What Frank whispered in her ear, no one knew, but by the end of the dance, Patricia was crying again. Her mother wrapped her arms around her and cried, too, but when his two younger daughters also started to bawl, Seamus had enough. He leaped again onto the stage. Hardly a singer of great repute, he began in a reedy baritone. Daniel took up the tune with the fiddle, Geordie's harmonica rang out once more, and Seamus sang out for all the company to hear that "None can love like an Irishman!"

The verses got more bawdy as the song went along. They belittled the prowess of the French, the Spanish, the Russian. The Swede, the Turk, the Italian. And, of course, the English.

> *The London folk themselves beguile,*
> *And think they please in capital style;*
> *Yet let them ask as they cross the street,*
> *Any young virgin they happen to meet,*
> *And I know she'll say from behind her fan,*

GIFFORD MACSHANE

That there's none can love like an Irishman!

Before the revelers departed, Molly spoke to Moira Flaherty about the wedding plans, and offered the use of her house or yard for the celebration.

"Oh, Molly, could we? Seamus planted our whole front garden with corn this year—he said he'd need the extra money for her trousseau. We were going to ask if we could use this building, but it seems so impersonal. It would be perfect to have it at the ranch.

"And you won't have to do a lick of work, I promise. I'll do everything myself, from polishing to cooking. I'd be so grateful to you!"

Molly shook her head. "Many hands make short work. We'll all pitch in. What else are families for?"

"Families... I've had none but Seamus since we left the old country. The children don't remember—no doubt they think it silly to pine."

Molly smiled to herself. If her children thought her silly, she'd never know it. Their father had taught them the importance of family—even Conor had learned the lesson and corresponded regularly from the ship he captained on the high seas, posting a letter every time he returned to his country from abroad.

As for Frank, I could not have asked for a better man. Nor could Patricia. For he is like his father in all that is important. And if he jumps around a bit too much and rarely sits in one place for long, at least he is now settled in his heart.

Moira Flaherty was thinking of her daughter. Her flighty, willful, spoiled daughter whose hands fluttered constantly with nervousness and whose unending chatter could drive her to distraction. At one time, she'd hoped to have the calm Geordie as her son-in-law, but she'd come to realize his nature was too serene for Patricia.

"I wonder what they'll need?" Molly mused.

THE WOODSMAN'S ROSE

"T'won't be furniture. Never sit still long enough to use it!"

Molly laughed. They looked at one another, thinking of an empty house, and Moira began to giggle. "I wonder if they'll need a bed?"

Molly was scandalized, but laughed just the same.

Chapter 13

THE WEDDING DATE WAS set for early October. It was unusual for a farmer's daughter to be married during harvest season, but Frank planned to take his bride to the Grand Canyon for their honeymoon, and he wanted to be home before cold weather set in.

"Geordie's got everything under control," he assured his father. "I've made arrangements for the feed we're shipping out. Adam's ready to take the extra corn and store it, and the root cellar's been cleaned out. There's enough farmhands hired, and Geordie knows just what to do."

His father tapped his pipe against his palm. He'd turned the management of the farm over to the younger twins two years ago and hadn't regretted his decision. Frank loved to keep the books, totaling the columns of figures spent and earned, estimating the harvest yield right down to the peck. He wasn't above pitching in with the planting and plowing, but it was Geordie who had the green thumb, who could persuade every kernel of corn to send up a shoot, every bean to blossom, every cabbage to grow tight and plump beneath the summer sun. So John Patrick turned to him and asked, "All right with you?"

"Sure, Dad," Geordie agreed. "We got it all figured out. It'll be fine."

"Mmmm." It was the only permission they'd needed.

Now the wedding was less than three weeks away. Both families gathered at the Donovan home on Sunday, and the conversation turned to the final stages of planning. Patricia was talking over the honeymoon plans with Jesse.

"Your trip sounds wonderful," Jesse said. "I've always wanted to see the Grand Canyon."

"But, Jesse, you live in a canyon, don't you?" School had meant nothing to Patricia, geography a concept never grasped.

Adam answered her. "I think you'll find it a bit different from our canyon, Patricia."

"Really? How?"

"Well, for one thing, it's a lot deeper. And the Colorado River runs right through it."

"Don't you have a river?"

"Just a stream," said Jesse. "But you go see it, then come back and tell us all about it."

"Oh, I will! Maybe I can draw you some pictures."

"What a nice idea! If you make some drawings, Daniel can frame them so you can hang them in your house, and you'll always have a reminder of your trip."

That Frank was proud of her talent amazed Patricia, as her father had always called it childish and useless, pressing her to more practical activities. She was thrilled to find Jesse encouraging her, too. But...

"Didn't Frank tell you? We're going to live here. Your parents said we could have the two rooms that were your grandmother's. You don't mind, do you?"

"Oh, I think that's a wonderful idea!"

"I'm sure Gran would approve," put in Adam, then smiled at Patricia's obvious sigh of relief.

DANIEL FOUND HIMSELF drawn inexorably into the planning for Frank's wedding. He was amazed at the energy his mother and sisters poured into the smallest of details, and chuckled when his advice on such things as the color of Irene's dress was accepted. But when Evelyn asked him to help stitch the hem of lace on the crinoline she and Molly were making for Patricia, he simply stared at her.

"Daniel," she begged, but he was reaching for his hat and rifle.

"I'm going for a walk." He heard her muttering behind his back about useless men and ungrateful brothers.

Some minutes later he laughed aloud, for his feet had taken the trail that led to town and he was on his way to Annie. Owen had gone to Tuba City on business and the shop was closed, so he knew he'd find her at the dairy farm. But he hadn't, after all, managed to escape the lure of the impending marriage.

"Oh, Daniel, I'm so glad you're here." Annie was flushed with excitement, her ivory skin glowing peach. The few light freckles across the bridge of her nose made a startling contrast to the streak of flour on her forehead. She wiped her hands ineffectively on her apron, then pulled him through the door and into the kitchen.

He was struck first by the mess she'd made, as even when cooking supper, she always managed to keep the room pristine. And her dress of blue gingham looked like it had been splattered with snowflakes.

"Look at the cake pans Tommy made for me," Annie said as she flitted from the counter to the table, talking all the while, gesturing with her long, slender hands, sending a small flurry of flour out to coat every surface. "And look at this picture—see how this cake is—I want to do it for Patricia. I don't know how. I need your help."

The sweetest words she has ever said. I don't care what she wants. I'd go to hell for her. And crawl all the way back if she'd just say it again.

"Daniel, I need you."

He put down his hat and rifle and stood in front of her, lifting her face with a gentle hand.

"Anything in the world, *aroon*." He caressed her cheek and tweaked a small curl that had escaped its braid. Her eyes fell as her hands came up to rest against him. He bent to kiss her.

Annie jumped back at the sound of footsteps at the kitchen door, then turned to find her brother Lowell.

"I hope I'm not interrupting," Lowell said with a wink at Daniel.

"Oh, no," Annie said swiftly. "Daniel's helping me with the cake."

"You might want to get him an apron."

The white imprint of her hand showed plainly on Daniel's shirt. She turned back to her brother, saw that he was laughing, and stamped her foot.

"You..." She sputtered and tossed her head so hard her braid flew up and slapped against her cheek. Her brother laughed louder as her hands flew to her face. She turned and fled from the room.

Daniel's arm shot out as she passed but missed her by inches. "Annie!"

"Let her go," her brother advised. "She'll get over it soon enough." He looked his friend up and down, handed him a towel and gestured at his shirt. As Daniel sheepishly wiped the flour off, Lowell imitated his father's crisp dialect, "Am I to understand your intentions are honorable, young man?"

"Yes, sir," Daniel answered, then grinned. "As if you didn't know."

"Just checking." He was, in reality, three years younger than Daniel, but the two men had been friends since childhood. If they'd ever acknowledged a discrepancy in their ages, the time had long since vanished.

"What's the story with the cake?" Daniel inquired.

The dairyman chuckled. His sister's rare outbursts of temper had always amused him.

"Annie found this picture—I don't know where." He pushed it along the table. It was a daguerreotype depicting a couple in formal wedding regalia, and in the background was a triple-tiered cake. "She got Tommy to make the cake pans in three different sizes, but she doesn't know how to put it together."

"Looks pretty easy. I'd be willing to bet the columns between the layers are dowels painted white. The layers must have some kind of platforms to support them. Looks like two sheets of wood would do. With holes cut in the cake to put the dowels through. Yeah, it's pretty simple."

"Well, don't tell her that. Let her think you're some kind of genius."

***

LATER, DANIEL SAT ALONE in the kitchen. Lowell had supplied him with a pencil and a large piece of brown paper, and he cleaned off a corner of the table to make room for it. He didn't wonder why Annie had chosen to work here, where the table was four times bigger than the one she used at home.

On the edges of the paper, he'd marked off the diameters of Tommy's cake pans, and was trying to estimate the height of the dowels by comparing the dimensions in the picture to the pile he'd made of the cake pans. He was frowning over his drawings, dissatisfied with his work, when Annie came in. She was pale and it was obvious she'd been crying. He went to her and drew her into his arms.

"I'm sorry, *aroon*. I didn't mean to hurt you."

"I know. It's not your fault. I've been so excited, I guess, and nervous... worried about the cake. I haven't been able to sleep, I just lay awake and worry. I guess I'm too tired to think straight."

"Come here then. Take a look at this and tell me what you think."

He'd sketched the framework for the tiered cake on the brown paper. She looked at it, then up at him.

"Will it work?" she asked breathlessly.

THE WOODSMAN'S ROSE

"No reason why not. I'm just not sure if the columns are the right size."

"I was going to make one today," she told him, with renewed excitement in her voice, "to try out the pans and see how long it would take to bake. Maybe we could try putting it together, too. Then, if the columns are too long, you could chop some off. Do you think we could?"

His arm was still around her shoulders, she was leaning against him, half-facing him. He bent over her and finished the kiss he'd started some hours earlier.

"Whatever you want, Annie," he said.

"Please let's try it."

"All right, *aroon*. I'll go see if Lowell's got any boards I can use. Otherwise I'll have to go into town."

He was back in moments for his hat and rifle. "Your brother's pretty worthless. Doesn't save a thing!"

She was deep in thought, studying her recipe, and looked up at him in abstraction. Another streak of flour adorned her forehead.

"Back in a while."

Her golden head bent to the recipe again.

He returned an hour later, having stopped off at the livery to use some of Tommy's tools. He couldn't find a board wide enough for the bottom layer, so he'd pieced together two half-circles for the base. He'd picked up dowels in several diameters, and carried the whole conglomeration in an old saddlebag he'd borrowed from the smith.

As he strode into the kitchen, Annie was struggling with the largest pan. She'd filled it with batter and was trying to slide it off the table onto a stool. It hung precariously on the edge. Daniel saw that her frustration had again resulted in tears.

"Hold on." He dropped the saddlebag on the floor and relieved her shaking hands of their burden. "Open the oven first." When she had, he picked the pan up, surprised she'd been able to move it at all.

"There you go," he told her, closing the oven with a flourish. Tears still gleamed in her eyes. With an arm around her shoulders, he led her into the parlor and sat next to her on the chintz-covered couch, guiding her head to his shoulder.

"What's wrong, sweetheart?"

"I guess I'm just tired."

"Do you feel all right?"

"My head aches."

"Annie..."

"No, it's not here." She touched her right temple, where the pains that could rock her into unconsciousness would occur. "It's more up here." Her fingers flicked across the streak of flour. He touched his lips to it as she settled in against his shoulder once more.

"You need some rest," he told her. "How long will this cake take?"

"At least an hour." Her eyelids began to droop.

"*Aroon*," he murmured, "do you want to lie down? I could wake you in an hour."

"Hmm?"

When she didn't raise her head, he realized she was half-asleep already. "Shhh. Never mind. Go to sleep, my love."

He roused her when he could smell the cake. He hadn't been concentrating on the time, but had lost himself in the sweetness of having her so close to him. She'd stirred once, and her head had fallen down to his breast. He'd turned in his seat and cushioned her, as he'd seen Adam do for Jesse, and heard a soft murmur as she settled into a deep sleep.

Lowell came in once and smirked at Daniel from the door, then left the house again. He trusted his friend as he'd have trusted no other—were it not for the necessity of protecting her reputation against the gossip of the old cats, he wouldn't have hesitated to leave them alone indefinitely. But since his father was out of town, the responsibility for Annie had devolved to him. *Just like when we were kids. Only then it was to see she didn't break her leg. This time the damage might not be so easily repaired.*

When he returned, Lowell found the couple in the kitchen, the cake pan emptied of its contents, and a touch of vexation in Annie's voice.

"But how long was it in?"

"*Aroon*, I don't know."

Annie was obviously trying to control her temper, which had been unusually short of late. She was pulling at her fingers, a sure sign of distress.

"What time did you put it in?" Lowell asked.

"I forgot to look."

Lowell gave her a pointed stare. "What time did you take it out?"

"About five minutes ago."

"Well, when I came in before, it was three o'clock. So that's an hour ago."

"And it was about a half-hour before that when you fell asleep," Daniel put in. "So it must have been an hour and three quarters. Maybe a little more."

"Let me write it down. It's close enough, anyway." She fumbled for a pencil, found her recipe covered in flour, and gave a little laugh. "Guess I'd better be more careful next time."

Lowell stuck a finger out toward the cake. Annie slapped it with the recipe and flour went flying up in a cloud. "Don't you dare touch that! I'll cut off your fingers!"

"I thought this was the practice cake."

"It is, but we've got to get it put together first. Then you can have all you want."

"And when will that be?"

"Soon as you get out of the kitchen," Daniel informed him. "We've got serious work to do here and you're holding us up."

GIFFORD MACSHANE

"Ex-cuuuse me," Lowell drawled. "I guess I'll just go on out to the barn, where somebody appreciates me, anyway." And he stalked out in mock indignation.

Chapter 14

IT TOOK DANIEL AND Annie another hour to put the columns in the first layer of the cake. She'd wanted four of them, as in the picture, but the woodsman convinced her the cake would be steadier if there were twice that many. The cake in the picture, he opined, had been built where it stood. Annie's cake would have to be moved, if only from the kitchen to the porch. She'd accepted his logic, but insisted the columns be set in a circle and not in the diamond pattern he suggested.

So they cut holes in the cake and placed columns of various lengths and diameters, until she was satisfied. Then he marked the base, and from those markings made a pattern out of another sheet of brown paper. He assembled the whole thing again, then placed the next smaller base on top of the columns and put the second cake pan on top of that to see the effect.

"It's going to work!" Annie clapped her hands and another cloud of flour went flying. "Now I have to make the other two layers, and you can cut the columns for them too. Oh, Daniel..."

He took her shoulders in his hands and turned her to him. "Tomorrow, *aroon*. We'll finish it tomorrow."

After a moment, she asked, "Would you like to stay for supper?"

"Ump-umm." Her face fell, but he ran his hands down her arms. "You've been working too hard, Annie. Let's go into town and eat at Joe's Café."

"What about Lowell?" Since Evelyn was working with Molly and Moira, Annie had said that she'd see her brother got supper.

"He likes Mexican food, too," Daniel reminded her. "Besides, he'll appreciate you more if he has to eat someone else's cooking once in a while."

Annie enjoyed her dinner more than she'd anticipated. The crowded cafe was bright, its walls hung with colorful weavings, its shelves filled with vibrant Mexican pottery. Over spicy tamales and beans washed down with beer, the two men teased her a bit, and Daniel repeated a story he'd told many times, of taking his eldest brothers out hunting during the previous drought years and of their inability to bring home any game whatsoever. They were all laughing as they left the restaurant, and Annie realized she'd always resented these stories on Brian's behalf, though in truth the big man hadn't seemed to mind the jests at his expense.

As she walked home with her hand in Daniel's, she was very quiet. The woodsman noted her face was serene, though. He looked ahead at Lowell, who'd again managed to give them some privacy.

"Tired, *aroon*?" he asked.

"A little."

"Annie, do you ever think of home?"

She looked up at him. "Home? You mean in town?"

"I mean Wales."

"Oh. I guess I do. Sometimes. I was so young when we left. It was after Mama died. I don't really remember it that much."

"Do you ever want to go back?"

Silence greeted his question, then she answered in a wistful voice, "Sometimes I wish I could go back in time. I wish I could remember her better. Sometimes I think if I went back, it would be easier to remember her."

"*Aroon*, I'm sorry."

After a moment, she added, "Mama died having a baby." And more quietly, "The baby died, too."

His arm tightened around her and her head drooped against his shoulder. *This must be it. She's been so reluctant to set a wedding date. She's afraid she'll die, as her mother did, in childbirth. Yet she accepts the inevitability of the pain in her head, knowing one day it may kill her. It's not logical. But I think I understand.*

When they reached the farmhouse, he sat with her on the porch, his arm still around her, her head resting again on his shoulder. The breeze played with a few stray locks of her hair as the katydids began to sing to the rising moon.

"*Aroon*, we all must die some day. It seems to me we start to die the minute we're born. For each of us, there's granted a longer or shorter time. My brother Henry died when he was two years old, yet my grandmother was eighty-nine. There's no way for us to know how long our lives will be.

"I think life shouldn't be measured by length," he continued, "but by happiness. By how much happiness we have, and how much happiness we give. Henry didn't live very long, and yet he made my mother and father very happy. And Gran, well, sometimes it seems to me she spent her whole life making us happy.

"She was really good at it, too, if you ask me, and it seems she had a pretty wonderful life. Not because it was easy—I don't think life for a widow with a baby could ever be easy. But because she found a way to be happy, and to make other people happy, too."

Annie didn't reply, but he hadn't expected anything else. He knew that her way of reflection was to turn inward, to study and consider. After a few moments, he stood to go.

"Get some rest, *aroon*. I'll be back tomorrow to finish that cake stand, all right?"

"Yes. Thank you, Daniel."

He kissed her on the lips. "I love you, Annie. You make me very happy." Her bright smile trembled. "Sleep well, sweetheart," he added as he kissed her hand. "Good night."

"Good night," she echoed. Later that night, she wept into her pillow, then dreamed of her mother. And of her mother's smiling face, beautiful and serene as a Madonna.

Chapter 15

THE DAY BEFORE THE wedding, when the Donovan ranchhouse was redolent with the scent of vanilla and a hint of mace, the parlor behind the stairs was confiscated by the cake-builders. Daniel hung a "No Trespassing" sign and posted Jake at the door as guard. Irene was kept out, for they couldn't trust her to keep the secret from Patricia. She was bursting with curiosity and begged Jake for information, but he was silent. Finally, she screamed at him and inside, Daniel was concerned—Irene's temper could be an awesome sight. But he heard Jake's voice, low and calm, "Over my dead body."

"It can be arranged, you know. But tell me one thing—is it something good?"

"You bet! You're gonna love it! Why, it's... it's phe-*nom*-enal!"

"And you're not going to tell me?"

"Nope. You'll see it tomorrow. You'll love it."

"Does Frank know?" she wheedled. Daniel heard no answer, but then she continued, "All right, but I'll remember this. I'll remember it for a long time."

"Don't I know it," Jake moaned, as Irene laughed and scampered away.

Turning to Annie, Daniel announced, "She's gone! I had a feeling Jake could handle her." He slid supports into the braces he'd attached to the base of his structure. He'd added little feet to keep it steady, painted all the pieces white, squared off the ends of the dowels, and was using his penknife to mold hollows that would hold each one top and bottom. A thin coating of Annie's icing would serve as glue for the stanchions. They were building the cake on a small sturdy table already covered with a rose-colored cloth and a length of white lace, and he was sure the cake would be secure enough to transport.

Annie, however, was fluttering around the room, flapping her apron, then smoothing it down, only to worry at it again. She wondered aloud if there'd be time for her to complete all the decorations she'd planned—she'd already made a hundred pink sugar-icing roses as ornaments. Her cheeks were flushed, her eyes too bright, as Daniel tried to soothe her.

"Annie, there's plenty of time. It's only ten o'clock, and we already know it's going to fit together. The hard part's done." She moved closer and he caught her around the waist, kissed her cheek. "Relax, *aroon*. I'll have this base put together in a few minutes. Why don't you start to make the icing?"

As soon as she began to work, Annie's demeanor calmed. Daniel watched her for a moment—her slender right arm whirled like a dervish. Whip, whip, whip! until the whites of eggs stood in stiff peaks, then beat, beat, beat as she added the sugar and powdered almonds she'd already prepared.

By the time the icing became a spreadable paste, he'd slipped the first layer of cake over the posts. Annie bit her lip as she smoothed the frosting on, then with her pastry bag began to decorate. The plain, cream-colored landscape became a miracle of confection—garlands of white with tiny pink nosegays set off with green leaves. Layer by layer they worked until, finally, she circled each of the dowels with another white garland, then propped a pink rose at its base. Daniel stepped back to admire it.

"It's beautiful. Just like the picture."

"It still needs something. It doesn't look finished." She picked up the picture again and held it up to the cake. "Look at this. I didn't make anything to put on top."

"Annie, your cake's much more beautiful than that one. No one's going to complain anything's missing. No one's even going to notice." Still she frowned. "Let's go eat and think it over. Don't worry, *aroon*, we'll come up with something."

Locking the door behind them, they helped themselves to the pot of stew Molly always kept simmering, then went along to the front parlor where Molly was arranging autumn-colored ribbons on the picture hat Patricia had borrowed from Evelyn. Jake sat cross-legged at her feet.

"Well," Molly asked, "have you finished?"

"No... yes..." Annie pulled at her fingers.

"My dear, it cannot be both yea and nay."

"Well, it's yes because I've done everything I planned to do. But it's no because I didn't plan for everything."

"I see," Molly said. "And what is it that you did not plan for?"

"In the picture, there's a kind of ornament on top. I didn't even notice it until the cake was finished. I guess I was too worried about whether or not we could put it together."

"I understand. I saw a cake once with two small birds on it. They hung from a bower of evergreens. Is it that you have in mind?"

"Yes, anything like that. But I don't have time..."

Molly patted her hand. "Daniel, in the attic there are three hat boxes of oval shape—striped, I believe black and gold. At any rate, they are the sole oval boxes you'll find. Please bring me the largest of the three."

In moments, he returned with the box.

"Ah, this is just the one we need." Tissue paper crinkled as Molly dug through the contents and removed a large, ornate hat, decorated with myriad fruits and vegetables, huge green leaves and trailing golden tulle. Daniel covered his reaction with a cough, but Jake sputtered with laughter.

"Mother, that's awful! You didn't wear that, did you?"

"Nay. In my day, hats were not so simple." She heard her son's snort of disbelief as she searched the surface of the hat and closed her hand over her prize. "Have you your knife, Daniel?"

"Do we want an apple or a cabbage?"

"It's help that you're wanting, or so I heard. Stop your foolishness and bring your knife."

"Sorry, Mother," he said with no real contrition in his voice. He cut where she indicated, then took the hat and put it back in its box on the floor. When he looked up, Annie was radiant.

"Look!" She held out two tiny birds, fashioned of feathers and nearly life-like.

"Love birds," Molly told them. "Now all that remains is to build for them a bower. You can manage that, can you not, Daniel?"

He bent to kiss her cheek. "Thanks, Mother."

"Yes," Annie joined in. "These are beautiful, and just what I need. Thank you."

So Daniel formed a bower out of wire and covered it with greens and, with the two miniature birds nestled within, he placed it on the top of the cake.

"It's perfect," Annie told him with eyes that shone.

Chapter 16

THE WEDDING OF PATRICIA Ann Flaherty and Francis Patrick Donovan took place at two o'clock on the afternoon of the hottest day of the season. It was so crowded and stuffy in the tiny chapel, both Annie and fifteen-year-old Helen Flaherty fainted. Preacher Hayes took a cue from the incidents and began to talk to the influential about building a larger church.

After Doc Barber examined his patients and declared them recovered, the throngs adjourned to the Donovan ranch, where vast quantities of food awaited them and a wooden platform had been built to accommodate the bride's wish for dancing.

Adam sang to his sister-in-law while she danced with her husband, whose expression for once was frozen in sheer happiness. Geordie claimed the second dance, kissed the bride on the cheek as he delivered her back to her groom. He retired to the punch table & didn't move from his chosen place all day, his face wearing a smile as thoughtful as his twin's was ecstatic.

As the afternoon shadows grew long, the wedding cake Annie made was presented and admired even beyond her dreams. Seven-year-old Kathleen Flaherty, who'd served as her sister's flower girl in a dress of fluffy pink organza, made a pig of herself, eating her piece, most of Patricia's, half of her father's, all of John Patrick's, and then asked for another. Moments later, she staggered up to Alec Twelve Trees, whom she considered her very best friend.

Alec wore a new black suit, a white shirt, and a bolo he'd borrowed from his father. His hair was tied back with a leather thong. Engrossed in conversation with Irene when Kathleen tugged at his pant leg, he glanced down in annoyance to see the glazed look in the child's eyes. Her skin, he noted, was pale and slightly green.

"What's the matter, darlin'? Too much excitement?" He led her to the shade of the orchard where she was promptly sick all over his new black shoes. "Ah, too much cake."

He knelt to wipe her face with a handkerchief while Irene giggled at him.

"That's what you get for wearing a suit!"

He passed the moaning child into her arms, then stood and removed his shoes and socks. He took off his jacket and tie, rolled his shirtsleeves up to his elbows and sat on the bench beside his young friend. As he touched her golden hair, she looked up at him. "Little piggy."

She gave him an embarrassed look, part smile and part frown, then hid her face against Irene's shoulder.

"It's all right, baby," Irene assured her. "Alec's not mad at you."

"Are you?" Her voice was muffled.

"No, darling, I'm not mad. But it's a silly thing to make yourself so sick, isn't it?"

Kathleen's blonde head nodded against her.

"Feel better now, sweetheart?" Alec asked.

The child nodded once more, but still refused to look at him. After a few minutes, Kathleen was snoring delicately. As he turned her face away from Irene's shoulder to ease her breathing, she moaned a little but didn't wake.

Irene was wearing a light blue gown that made her eyes bright as sapphires. Her black hair was piled on top of her head, and he wanted to touch the stray tendrils framing her face. He'd wanted to dance with her all afternoon, but each time he approached her, one of her brothers or Michael Flaherty had claimed her hand. He couldn't object to her brothers, but Flaherty's attentions had made his blood boil. This time alone with her was soothing to his jangled nerves.

"Do you want me to take her?" he murmured.

"No, let her sleep. She'll feel better when she wakes up. Isn't she beautiful?"

Again his dark hand found the golden curls. *As beautiful as you are, though so different. Oh, I wish...*

"Do you think you could find me something to lean on?" Irene whispered. In response, he reached behind her and braced his arm against the bench. She leaned into him, and a few moments later, rested her head against his shoulder. It was meaningless, he knew—neither more nor less than she'd do with her brothers. With her father. Or for that matter, with his.

He'd missed being with her. Since his argument with Daniel, it seemed his time with most of the Donovan clan had been limited. But he pushed all thought of that conflict aside. Right now, it was enough to be close to her, to breathe in the faint scent of violets. He looked over at the sleeping child.

Our children would have black hair. The thought came unbidden, startling him with its strength. He held in a sigh. Even if her family would accept him with his mixed blood, it was obvious Michael Flaherty had the upper hand.

But he's her brother-in-law now. He was wise enough to know it was hope feeding the idea and it was, in fact, more negative than positive. The two families were now intertwined—she might be spending more time with Michael than ever before. Shaking off his gloom, he closed his eyes. As the breeze blew the tendrils of her hair against his cheek, he let all thought of tomorrow drift off.

Chapter 17

AS EVENING FELL AND the guests from the outlying areas began to disperse, Annie looked around for Daniel. Her duties were done and she wanted to be close to him. She saw him leaning against a tree at the edge of the orchard and her heart sank.

His face was calm, but his eyes were narrowed and he stood stiffly against the tree. Before him stood Alec Twelve Trees, and from his gestures Annie knew what the debate was. She approached and when the woodsman saw her, he waved her away. But she continued on as she heard Alec say, "Sorry doesn't bring her back. Sorry means nothing!"

"He doesn't understand," Daniel said to Annie.

"*I* don't understand?" Alec's voice shook. "*You're* the one who doesn't understand! *You're* the one who's supposed to be my friend!"

"I am your friend, Alec. But I won't hurt someone else to prove it to you."

Alec gave him a black look and strode fiercely away. Holding Annie's hand, Daniel walked into the orchard. All day long, with the crowds and the excitement, he'd felt a hundred miles away from her. He touched the ring he'd placed on her finger at Christmas, then drew her into his arms, made an effort to dismiss Alec from his mind. He breathed deeply of the perfume of her hair, the hair that hung loose, freed from its braid for this special occasion. The peace of her flooded into his veins, and he dropped to his knees.

"Annie." Her name caught in his throat. "Annie, I love you. I need you. Won't you marry me now?"

THE WOODSMAN'S ROSE

He felt the sudden stillness of her and realized he'd been too abrupt. Her face went pale, her eyes fell. He arose again, knowing she couldn't give him the answer he wanted.

Before she could speak he said, "It's too soon, isn't it, *aroon*?" She nodded, a quick gesture of both fear and relief. He encircled her shoulders with his arm and felt her relax. His voice was warm and sincere. "I love you, Annie. I can wait." He touched her nose with one finger. "The longer I wait, the more you will love me."

EARLY THE NEXT MORNING, Daniel found her sitting on the front steps of his home. She'd stayed overnight after telling her father she was too tired for the ride to town. She'd been with them for four days now, sharing a room with Irene, working not only on the cake, but helping Molly and Moira Flaherty with the other baking. Now as he linked his hand with hers, he knew he should take her home and let her rest.

"Hello, sweetheart."

"Good morning." Her head drooped against his arm as he toyed with her braid, brought the end of it up to tickle her face. She giggled and swatted at him but he persisted in his game, until she hid her face against him.

"Stop," she pleaded.

"Say please."

"Please."

"Pretty please."

"You're teasing me."

"Hmmm." He lifted her chin with one hand, saw that her mouth was drawn up in a pout. His fingers brushed her lips and she closed her eyes, pressing closer to him. He touched her cheek, traced the line of her jaw, the shell of her ear. He heard her breath catch. When she raised her eyes, he gazed into their pale depths and whispered, "Annie, I love you." And bent to kiss her.

Several moments later, she murmured his name.

"Yes, *aroon*," he answered, but she made no response. "What is it?"

"I think I should go home."

"I don't want you to."

"I know. But I think I should."

"Do you really want to?"

"I really should."

After a brief pause he asked, "Got your stuff packed?"

"Almost. I can finish in about ten minutes."

"All right," he said, helping her to her feet. "It'll take that long to hitch up the horses."

She slipped into his arms. "I love you, Daniel," she whispered against his ear. Then she darted away, leaving him to stare after her.

AS DANIEL HITCHED UP the team, Jake sprinted into the barn.

"Where ya goin'?"

"Taking Annie home. Want to come along for the ride?"

"Oh, yeah," the lad said eagerly. "You sure you don't mind?"

"Nope. In fact, it'd be better for us to have someone else along."

"A girl's gotta be pretty careful, huh?"

"Up to the man to watch out for her," Daniel replied. "Funny the way things are—man makes a mistake and everybody just laughs behind his back. Woman makes a mistake, and she suffers for the rest of her life."

"Doesn't seem fair, does it?" Jake observed.

"Take me and Annie, for instance. If a wheel fell off this buggy and it took me 'til nightfall to get it back on, she'd get home after dark. It wouldn't be anybody's fault, and nothing wrong would have happened, but if we were alone, she'd take the blame. And the only thing for her to do would be marry me tomorrow or live the rest of her life in shame."

"Don't appear to me that marryin' her would be such a great hardship for you." At Daniel's enigmatic smile, Jake added, "Wonder if I'll ever get married."

The woodsman knew his brother had been trying to cultivate a relationship with Cynthia Callendar for a while, but didn't seem to have made much progress. "Have to be someone pretty special, wouldn't it?"

"Yeah. I guess it would."

"I've loved Annie since we were kids, and I never thought I'd have a chance with her. But Adam and Jesse have only known each other for a year and a half, and they've been married for most of it. You don't know what's going to happen, Jake. All you can do is wait and see."

Annie returned and Jake snagged her valise and stowed it under the seat, while Daniel examined the sky—the unseasonable heat of the day before had given way to cool humidity.

"Better get your coat," he told Jake. "Might get cold on the way home—it's clouding up to the west." He helped Annie into the buggy. "I've got a blanket if you need it."

"I should be plenty warm in this," she answered, gesturing at the brown wool cloak she wore. "Besides, it's going to be pretty cozy with both of you for company."

Daniel laughed at her. The only substantial width to his brother was in his shoulders, and he could span Annie's waist with his hands. Between her slenderness and Jake's lankiness, there would have been room for four on the seat. He climbed up and crowded over next to her, leaving no room at all for his brother. "Cozy enough?"

"You get back over there where you belong," she said, shoving playfully at him, "or this buggy will tip right over on its side."

He was pleased when she slid over next to him, and as soon as Jake climbed in, they were on their way. They talked of the harvest and the coming winter, Daniel predicting one colder than usual.

"Why're you saying that?" Jake asked.

"The squirrels are building their nests low in the trees, and the ant mounds are higher than usual," the woodsman said. "Add in the amount of fruit on the holly trees and acorns on the oaks... Well, you can bet your bottom dollar it'll be longer and colder than we've had in a few years. And if the leaves fall before their color change is complete—"

"Don't say that!" Annie protested. "I love the changing colors. This is the best time of the year."

To please her, they admired the aspens with their shimmery gilt, maples tending toward orange, oak leaves as deep a gold as Irish porter—all set against the green of cedars and pines. Annie tucked her hand in under his arm and allowed her head to rest briefly on his shoulder, and Daniel found the trip much too short.

White's Station was bustling along, filled to the brim with horses, wagons and buggies. Daniel helped Annie down while Jake jumped out to grab her bag and follow them into the bootmaker's. The shop was crowded with customers. Annie hung her cloak up and began to help Owen with the orders. There were a pair of cowboys who'd been customers before and knew exactly what they wanted—they'd come back for their boots in two weeks. There was a farmer looking for a pair of sturdy workboots. He wasn't picky about the fit, but had to try on several pair before Annie was satisfied. And finally, there was a man of Daniel's approximate age, holding a little girl of five or six by the hand.

"Here you are, honey," Owen said as he handed her a package. "All fixed up good as new."

She looked up at him shyly and accepted the parcel.

THE WOODSMAN'S ROSE

"How much, Mr. Griffiths?" asked her father in a brogue even stronger than John Patrick's.

"Fifteen cents if you call me Owen. Otherwise, ten bucks."

The Irishman laughed. "I'm not so rich that I can afford false pride, Owen." He counted out the change. "And it's John you'll be callin' me, is it not?"

"John or Sean?" asked Daniel.

The Irishman noticed him for the first time. "In the auld country, 'twas Sean," he admitted, glancing from the auburn head of the woodsman to Jake's flaming mop. "And 'twould not be surprisin' me t' be addressin' two more sons of Erin."

"Grandsons," Daniel explained, holding out a hand. "Name's Donovan. Daniel. And this is my brother, Jake."

"John Riley," the newcomer replied, accepting both handshakes. "And this is me daughter, Norah." She peeked around his leg.

"Hello, Norah," Daniel said. A tiny smile was his reward.

"John bought the Olson place," Owen informed them, then turned back to Riley. "The boys live out of town a ways. Donovan has a big spread to the west of town. How many of you there now?"

"Only seven left at home," Daniel answered. "Mother and Dad, Irene, the twins and us." Liking the newcomer on sight, he added, "Got two more brothers—twins as well—that live on a ranch west of us, and another brother at sea. My sister Evelyn's married to Owen's son Lowell. Oh, and my brother Frank just got married, too. That's all of us, isn't it, Jake?"

"Except Jesse. My sister-in-law," Jake put in. "Married to my oldest brother."

"A proper Irish family," Riley approved. "I've a son, also. Name of Timothy. Just the two we had. Ah, well. Norah, say good-bye now. We'll be seein' you 'round, to be sure."

The child gave them another shy smile and followed her father out.

"Hello, girl," Owen said to Annie. "Not much of a greeting to come home to, was it?"

"That's all right," she answered. "I'm glad you're so busy. Guess you didn't have time to miss me."

"When you're wrong, lass, you're certainly wrong!"

Daniel kissed her on the cheek. "Get some sleep, *aroon*. You're worn out, and I don't want you getting sick."

"Will I see you Thursday?"

"You bet."

BEFORE HE LEFT TOWN, Daniel stopped in at the livery and before he could utter a greeting, the blacksmith sang out, "Ya heard the news?"

"What news?"

"Renegades took off."

"Where did they go?"

"Don't know. Don't care." The smith gave a ringing endorsement of his opinion with his hammer. "Boy's still there, though."

"Blue Deer?"

"Yep. His father, Short Feathers, joined up with Yella Knife 'most soon as 'e got here. By the time they left, he was 'is right-hand man." Tommy drew a ladle of water from a bucket on his work bench and drank deeply, then drew another and splashed it over his head. He poured a third into the forge, sending up a thick cloud of steam.

"I'm glad of that," Daniel said when he could see the smith again. "I don't know how that boy would have survived being a nomad."

"That's what 'is mother said. She asked Alec t' talk t' the elders, 'cause she was bein' shunned, too—just 'cause she was 'is woman. Alec made 'em see it wasn't fair. This was her tribe, not his—he comes from down Piñon way. An' with the boy..." Pride in his son was apparent in Tommy's voice, in the faint smile on his face.

THE WOODSMAN'S ROSE

"That's great. I'll tell Dad—I know he'll be happy to hear it. By the way, have you seen Jake? I was supposed to meet him here."

"Just saw 'im follow Cynthia Callendar into the mercantile."

"Of course. Guess I'll have to go drag him out."

"Good luck with thet!"

Daniel threw him a salute and, as he started down the street, Tommy's laugh boomed out behind him.

THREE DAYS LATER, GEORDIE disappeared. John Patrick found his note on the kitchen table when he came down to light the stove.

Back in a few days,
G.
P. S. Don't worry, Mother.

He frowned as he read it again. He'd noticed that his son had been even more quiet than usual in the past few weeks, though Molly had said she felt sure that he wasn't in a stew. Yet the crops were ripening, and within a week it would be time to start the harvest. Hooking a thumb in his vest pocket, he showed the note to his wife.

"Did he say anything at all to you?" Molly asked.

"Asked for his wage book last week. Hope he's not done something foolish."

Apprehensive, they agreed that all they could do was wait. Geordie was, after all, well past the age of majority. But that didn't stop the conjecture when the family gathered on Sunday.

"Maybe he's gone off to sea with Conor," Adam said. John Patrick glared at him.

"Or to Dodge City to be a gambler," put in Jake.

"Or prospectin' up in the Rockies," Brian said.

"To San Francisco to buy a book for Adam," was Jesse's contribution.

"Maybe he's joined the circus," Daniel said.

"Enough!" John Patrick demanded with a clap of his hands. He'd been watching his wife's face grow more confused and anxious as each theory was revealed. "Boy said he'd be back in a few days. We've nothing to do but wait and see."

"Molly *bawn*, the boy will surely be back."

"Of course he will, Mother," said Jesse, giving her a hug. "We're just being silly. I'm sure everything's fine. Geordie will explain it all when he gets back."

Molly smiled weakly, but in spite of her family's reassurance, could find no peace of mind. No one knew where Geordie'd gone. No one knew what "a few days" meant. Not even Adam, who knew them all so well, would hazard a guess. And in this Arizona, that was so unforgivingly wild with its mountains and deserts, rattlesnakes and scorpions, and natives who might not be as friendly as the local tribe...

She lay awake at night, wishing she could stop the thoughts that plagued her and praying fervently that her son be safe.

Chapter 18

WHEN SUNDAY ROLLED around again, Molly's eyes were heavy and her hands trembling. It was only when Annie arrived with Evelyn and Lowell, wearing the secretive smile that said a surprise was sure to come, that Molly felt the tension in her neck unravel.

The family was gathered on the porch when Geordie drove up in a new buggy, his own horse tied behind it. He pulled the team up with a flourish, jumped down to help his passenger alight. She was a pretty girl of average height, average figure, with hair almost as fair as Annie's and brown eyes that matched her twill traveling suit. As Geordie took her arm and climbed the steps, Annie held her hands out in welcome. The girl gave her a half-formed smile in return.

"Mother, Dad," Geordie said, "this is Suzette Burkhardt. Suzette Burkhardt Donovan."

Molly gasped, John Patrick sputtered, and Annie stepped forward to draw the girl into her arms.

"Welcome," she said with a kiss on the cheek. "I'm Annie." *Everything will be all right. Give them a minute, just one little minute.*

Suzette looked at her in surprise, her nervousness fading as Annie's slender, gentle hand touched her cheek. Then the woodsman held out his hand, tickled her face with his mustache. "Welcome to the family. Hope Geordie told you what you've gotten into!"

Then Suzette was pressed against Molly's bosom.

"My dear, please excuse me. The surprise—but 'tis no excuse." Suzette was hugged again and, when she was released, looked up to find tears in Molly's eyes. The girl glanced at Geordie, reached out a hand to him, and they were both crushed in his mother's arms.

"My dears..." It seemed to be all Molly could say.

Finally released, Suzette gave her father-in-law a tentative smile as he approached.

"You could have told us, boy-o." John Patrick's voice was stern and Suzette's apprehension returned.

"Oh, Daddy, stop teasing!" Irene demanded as she skipped forward. She waved a hand in her father's direction. "Pay no attention to him—he's always teasing. I'm Irene."

Suzette was shocked, but the elder Donovan chuckled as he raised her hand to his lips and kissed it gallantly. "I'm afraid my daughter's right, *colleen*. And here I should be welcoming you. Please forgive an old man his rudeness." He pressed her hand between his own. She saw tears gleaming in his eyes, too. "Welcome to the family, lass. You're a lovely addition, indeed."

"Thank you," Suzette murmured, and with that simple phrase, the tension in the air vanished. Lowell, Evelyn and Jake were introduced, Geordie congratulated by all, and the couple escorted to the back parlor where a gentle interrogation was accompanied by cups of tea and Molly's scones.

"Where did you meet?" Molly asked.

"In Prescott." She answered in a mellow voice with no discernible accent. "My grandfather was a watchmaker from Switzerland who settled in Virginia. When the war came, he moved out to Illinois. My father and mother got married there, but as the war dragged on, the business wasn't doing well. My father decided to move west and try farming, and my grandfather came with us. I don't remember it. I was only two years old then, and my sister is four years younger than me."

Geordie continued the story. "I met her on the cattle drive last fall—she was working in her grandfather's shop. I don't know why I went in, but I'm glad I did. I didn't say anything to her then, since I was sort of half-promised to Patricia, but we've been writing letters for a while. I figured I could step back a little when Frankie started to moon over Patricia this summer, and I was really happy when they got engaged.

"I went to Prescott to ask her father's permission to court her. I took my wage book, Dad, so he could see I had the means to support her. I didn't say anything 'cause I thought he might want us to wait a year or two—Suzette's seventeen—but her parent are real happy for us.

"I knew I had to get home for the harvest," he added, "but I couldn't bear to think of leaving Prescott without her. So I took a chance, asked for her hand and married her before she could give it a second thought."

The smile Geordie bestowed on his new wife was beatific. They'd spent a single night together at the hotel in Prescott, emerging starry-eyed and tongue-tied in the morning to catch the stage.

"I borrowed the buggy from Tommy when we got here. We're going to take a real honeymoon after Christmas, and go back to see her folks."

When Molly offered the couple a bedroom, Geordie knew his family had accepted his new bride. But he preferred to take her down the lane to the cabin where he and Frank had been living. After supper, he drew his father aside and asked if he could buy five acres of land near the river. It was a ten-minute ride from town, and he wanted to build Suzette a home of her own.

"You'll buy nothing," John Patrick responded. "The land is a gift—a wedding gift. And don't say me 'nay.'" His eyes twinkled. "When do we begin to build?"

Geordie smiled at the sound of "we". He wouldn't have asked for help, and yet had counted on it. "I hope right after the harvest. I guess I'll have to see Daniel about the plans."

GIFFORD MACSHANE

"Aye. Else your house will have its windows, but no doors!"

WHEN THE HARVEST WAS over, it was time for the annual trail drive to Prescott. Jake was eager to hit the trail with his newly trained black stallion. He now stood taller than all of the Donovan men but Brian. He wore his black holster low on his left side, a dark blue corduroy shirt and a piebald leather vest. His denims were tucked into the tops of his high-heeled boots, and he'd rolled his deerskin boots into the blankets that would be his bed.

Jake had asked for spurs for his birthday but none of the men but Adam wore them, and none of the brothers had obliged him. Daniel had, in fact, attempted to dissuade him from ever using them, but on this subject Jake would have none of his counsel.

"I'll file the rowels down like Adam did, so they won't hurt Blaze."

Daniel had shaken his head in chagrin. Adam stopped wearing the spurs for a while after his marriage and the woodsman had hoped he'd discarded them for good. But after they went on again, Brian told him Jesse liked the silver clink they gave off—that it made her feel safer to know that Adam was near. Daniel accepted their presence, still not quite believing no harm could come to Apples.

Now as the cowboys congregated in the large front yard, Daniel stood with his mother and sisters to see them off. He'd heard his mother crying earlier in the morning, and his father's voice soothing her. Jake would be in Brian's particular care and no harm would come to him.

Molly warned them all, "I dare any one of you to step foot in this house if he is injured!"

John Patrick chucked her under the chin. "And if I or one of the others is hurt?"

THE WOODSMAN'S ROSE

She tossed her flaming hair and retorted, "If you get hurt, it's your own fool fault!" As her husband chuckled, she'd relented and hugged him close. "Bring him back to me."

"Of course, my darlin' girl. Haven't I always brought them back?"

Daniel stood next to her as Molly handed out new red bandannas to all her sons. It was part of the yearly ritual, and as Jake wrapped his around his neck, Daniel was pleased to see that he pulled it tight before tying it, rather than wearing it loose as the other men did.

The young black stallion was chomping at his bit. He'd taken readily to the saddle and the companionship of the tall youth who'd gentled him. The woodsman watched the affectionate interplay between horse and rider before Jake mounted, and hoped he'd been able to teach his brother something of the sacredness of life. Of the intelligence that existed in the animal world. Then the frisky black was trotting down the lane, his rider turning once to wave good-bye.

Chapter 19

THE BUILDING OF SUZETTE'S house had to be put off until spring, as winter arrived earlier than anyone expected and brought with it an unusual number of storms. The mountain passes filled with snow and the Navajo moved down from the mountains to their winter camp, a few miles north of the Donovan range. With a lull in the bad weather just after Thanksgiving, Daniel and Jake went out to hunt.

After a full day's effort, they'd managed to kill a pronghorn buck. They'd slung him upside-down on a branch they carried on their shoulders. As snow began to swirl around them, Daniel called a halt; digging his compass out of his pants pocket, he pointed downhill, to the southwest.

"'Bout five more miles," he said. Jake made a noise he construed as disgust. "It won't kill you. We can take ten minutes to rest."

"Wish there was something to sit on."

"Way it goes, kid. What are you doing?"

"I saw—" With that, Jake fell to one knee. The rifle he'd cocked fired as he went down.

"Jake!"

"I'm all right." The boy struggled to his feet. "I saw a snowshoe hare—but I guess I stuck my foot in a hole."

Daniel grabbed his arm and hauled him up as the mountain above them began to thunder. "Can you run? Come on! This way!" He leaped off on a course across the path of the oncoming avalanche.

"Jake! NOW!"

THE WOODSMAN'S ROSE

But his brother wasn't as agile. As Daniel sped clear, he looked back to see Jake rolling head over heels down, down, down the side of the mountain, the snow gathering him up, pulling him in, until he disappeared completely.

⁂

ANNIE HAD BEEN DISTRAUGHT all day, so when her brother said he had a delivery to take to the Donovans, she begged him to drop her off. She knew he agreed only to get away from her raw emotions. Brian answered her knock and, taking the wheel of cheese from her arms, he ushered her into the back parlor where Jesse sat close to the fire. Her eyes were too bright and splotches of fever stained her cheeks. As she took Jesse's hot hand in hers, Annie let herself relax—Jesse was here, where she'd be well taken care of. There was nothing to worry about. She felt a bit foolish, but shrugged it off.

"How are you?" she asked Jesse.

"I haven't been feeling too good." Jesse's eyes were green as emeralds against her pale skin. A racking cough overtook her and it was some moments before she could continue. "We came to see—" Again her words were cut off by the cough. Her bluetick hound, Moze, sat her feet whining.

"We come t' see Mother," Brian put in. "Irene's puttin' up some tea for us t' take home. If Mother even lets us go. Said she wants Miss Jesse t' stay a few days."

"Where is she?" Annie inquired.

"Adam drove her an' Dad t' Benson's for supper. But Rebecca's here, too. She's cookin'," Brian added happily.

"Where's Daniel?"

"Wal... him an' Jake went huntin'. They was s'posed t' be back yestid—"

"Miss Annie! Miss Annie!" Brian's arm was supporting her before Annie even realized she'd fallen off the chaise. He helped her up and sat her next to Jesse, who took her hands and rubbed them briskly.

"Get her some water, please," she asked Brian. "Annie, don't worry. Please, don't worry. It will be... all right."

Not the words but the wrenching cough brought Annie back. She put her arm around Jesse's shoulders and held her until the fit was over.

"Hush," Annie whispered. "Don't try to talk. I'm all right, really I am." The women clung to one another until Brian returned with a glass of water. Irene followed him with Jesse's tea.

"Thank you," Annie said in a tiny voice. "I'm all right now."

"Are you sure?" whispered Jesse. "Thanks, Irene."

"Drink up that tea so you'll feel better," Irene told her. "And you're supposed to be quiet. I'll find you a pencil and pad—if you want to say something, write it down!"

Jesse stuck her tongue out at her sister-in-law; Irene made a face back and rummaged through the dainty cherry desk that had been her grandmother's.

"Here," she said to Jesse, "now be still! Annie, are you sure you're okay?"

But Annie jumped to her feet and ran into the hall. "Daniel!"

"It's all right, *aroon*." The rough voice was a relief to those who couldn't see him. Brian helped Jesse to her feet as Daniel entered with Jake slung over his shoulder.

"Oh, what happened?" Irene cried. "Jake, are you all right?"

"Gosh, what a ride! I thought my gut would bust open!" As Daniel dumped him on the chaise, Jake rubbed his stomach. "Brother, you gotta do something about those bony shoulders!"

"You're all right?" Jesse was kneeling at his feet on the floor, her face ghostly pale, her hands clutching nervelessly at his knee.

"I'm fine. Really, Jesse, don't worry. It's just my ankle."

"What happened?" asked Brian.

THE WOODSMAN'S ROSE

Daniel took Annie's hand as he responded. "Not much, really. Jake fell and hurt his ankle and I had to pack him home again. That's why we're so late—he's no featherweight any more!" With that, he pulled the knife from his boot and approached his youngest brother again.

"Daniel!" Jesse's eyes were wide with horror.

"I'm going to cut his boot off," he said with a chuckle. "The ankle's swollen and I can't tell if it's broken or just sprained. Don't worry, little sister. No surgery performed today.

"Irene, could you get us some ice? And a towel to wrap it in. Annie, come on over here, please. You and Jesse can hold the top of this boot. Brian, you hold his leg still. And listen, brother," he said to Jake, "no sudden moves. Got it?"

"Oh, yeah," the lad responded. He'd seen that knife cut through fresh hide like butter. "I'm a statue, believe me."

Within seconds, the deerskin boot and the sock beneath it were removed. Jake's ankle was swollen and discolored right down to his toes. "Wow! No wonder it hurts!"

"Can you move your toes?" Annie asked him. He grimaced with the effort, then shook his head. She looked up at Daniel. "What do you think?"

"Don't know. He should be able to move them if it's only a sprain. But, boy, they sure are swollen, aren't they?"

"Mebbe I should go for Doc," Brian suggested.

Jesse shook her head vehemently. *Ask Rebecca to look at it*, she wrote.

"I'll get her." Without waiting for an answer, Annie turned and ran from the room.

"Wow," Jake repeated, as Irene brought in a towel and a basin full of snow in lieu of ice. "It's sure a beauty, ain't it?"

"Doesn't it hurt?" his sister asked.

"Some. But it feels a lot better now the boot's off." He held the boot up to his brother. "Guess I'll have to make another one now, huh?"

"Kid, from the looks of that foot, you gonna have plenty of time to sit around making boots!"

"Oh, my," Rebecca said from the doorway. Wearing a simple gray dress and white apron, she stared down at the lad's foot—where it wasn't blue, it was bright red from the cold, or black where the blood was trapped under the skin. "Looks like you did a good job. What exactly happened?"

"Well, I tripped over a root. But it didn't seem too bad then. I kept on going for a little ways until it gave out. I twisted it again, I guess, and I fell against a rock. See that cut there? That's where the rock hit it."

"Can you move your toes?"

"No, ma'am."

"Well, that's not too surprising." Rebecca knelt before him. "You say this happened yesterday?"

"Around three o'clock," Daniel put in.

"Yes, it's had a good long time to swell up. That may be why your toes won't move. Does this hurt?" She ran her finger over his sole.

"Tickles a bit."

"And how about this?" She held his foot by the heel, grasped the big toe and wiggled it up and down, then side to side.

"It doesn't feel real good, but it doesn't hurt real bad either."

"All right. And this?" She flexed his foot and he hissed in pain, his fingers clutching at the cushion of the chaise. "I'm sorry. Where did it hurt?"

He caught his breath with difficulty. "All the way up to my knee. Sort of a sharp pain, and now a pounding."

"Well, young man," Rebecca said, "it seems a good possibility you've broken a bone. I think the doctor should look at it. In the

THE WOODSMAN'S ROSE

meantime, you should keep it packed in snow so it doesn't swell any more."

He made a face as the snow was piled up around his foot and his sister draped the towel over it.

"Keep it good and cold," Rebecca advised Irene, then turned back once again to her newest patient. "I wouldn't be surprised if you wind up wearing a cast."

"No kidding?" Jake asked. "I always wondered what that would feel like."

Be careful what you wish for. Jesse passed the note to him with a sly smile.

As Brian left to fetch the doctor, Annie came back in. "Good news?" she asked.

"The best! Looks like I'm gonna be laid up for a while. And y'all be gettin' to wait on me!"

"You just hold your breath!" Irene advised him, and flounced out again.

The woodsman helped Jesse up from the floor and settled her in beside Jake, while her dog curled up again at her feet. Then he and Annie took the chaise on the other side of the fireplace.

"How are you?" he murmured.

In answer, she rested her head against his shoulder. "Fine, now that you're here."

"Why is Jesse writing things down?"

Annie started to explain, but Daniel caught his younger brother's words.

"... and when I tripped—"

"Jake," he warned.

"But it's just Jesse. She won't tell. Will you?"

Jesse's eyes were big and bright as she shook her head and crossed her heart.

"All right," Daniel said. "But no one—I repeat, no one—tells Mother a thing."

"I won't," breathed Jesse.

"I won't," echoed Annie. "What happened? I know you didn't tell us everything."

"Well, like Jake said, he tripped. What he didn't mention was that when he did, his rifle went off. Right into the side of the mountain. An avalanche started and we had to run like anything!

"Good thing we were on an open trail," Daniel continued. "The snow started piling straight down the mountain, so we ran cross-wise away from it. The tail end of it caught us, though, and Jake fell and went tumbling on down. When I first looked, all I could see was the barrel of his rifle sticking up out of the snow. I was hoping he'd been able to hang on to it—lucky for him, he had.

"Also lucky that he was sitting upright when I found him, so I could clear his face right away. But by the time I dug him out, it was too late to get home."

"So we stayed the night in this cave Daniel knew about," Jake put in. "He built a fire, but it was still pretty cold. Then this morning, he packed me on home."

"Packed you..." Jesse's eyes grew even wider with the realization of the danger they'd been in. *You could have been killed!* she wrote.

"But we weren't," Jake said, "so there's nothing to be scared about. Really, Jesse, everything turned out okay, didn't it? Worst of it is, we lost the pronghorn!"

She sank against a pillow, scribbled on the pad. *You'd better pray your mother never hears this, or she'll never let you out of the house again!*

"Aw, you won't tell her, will you?" he pleaded. "You promised!"

"Besides, it's not the worst thing that ever happened," Daniel put in. Annie moved in closer, but offered not a word of fear or reproach. "I remember this one time when me and Alec..."

THE WOODSMAN'S ROSE

JAKE'S WISH WAS GRANTED. The doctor diagnosed a broken ankle and wrapped it first in wool then in plaster of Paris up to his knee, and confined him to the house for three weeks. After examining Jesse, Barber prescribed the same confinement for her.

Brian went back to the canyon to see to the stock, and Rebecca went along to keep him company, flicking off Jesse's sly suggestion that they needed a chaperone. Jesse and Adam settled into the guest room, and Daniel made Jake a pair of crutches so he could get downstairs in the morning on his own, though he'd need help in the evening to get up to bed. Jake thanked his father and brother heartily for installing the bathroom for his grandmother, sure that his life would have been miserable without it.

For the first week Jake was a model patient, obeying the doctor's orders to the letter, drinking the comfrey root tea his mother prescribed, and reveling in the attention she lavished on him. But a love of confinement wasn't in his nature and, by the tenth day, he was surly and short-tempered.

Bundled in a thick blue robe, Jesse sat next to him on the couch. He'd grown so much over the summer that, even though he slouched, her head barely came to his shoulder. Her cough was gone, but she was still weak and easily tired from her illness.

"What did I tell you? Be careful what you wish for—didn't I say that? But noooo..." She saw a little smile beginning to form. "You had to ask for it. Well, now you've got it! And it ain't as much fun as you thought, is it?"

"No. I didn't know I'd have to drink that awful tea!"

"You should try some of the things they give me."

"I guess I shouldn't complain. But Jesse, don't you ever feel like you've just gotta get out of here?"

"Yes," she said, looking away from him. "Sometimes I just want to go home." She turned back with a deliberate brightness on her face. "Here, why don't we play checkers? That'll be good for both of us."

Jesse continued to put herself out to entertain him and at the end of the three weeks, the boyish adoration Jake had felt for her was gone, and he'd fallen deeply in love. He didn't speak of it, but the change in him was noticed by his family. He'd always been a happy-go-lucky lad, and was still bright and optimistic. But he seemed older somehow, and quieter. The gangly clumsiness of youth was gone, and he deliberated before speaking. And when he'd healed enough to leave the house, he did so eagerly and yet sadly.

Jesse pulled her cloak around her shoulders and followed him out to the porch. The day, though cold, was bright and fresh, the breeze carrying the tang of cedars down from the mountains. Jake balanced on one crutch and leaned over to kiss her cheek.

"Thanks," he said, "for everything."

"You're welcome, Jake," she answered, then gave him a passable imitation of his father's brogue, "What families are for."

He had to laugh. He hobbled down the porch steps, turned at the bottom to wave up at her, then went to the barn to visit his young stallion.

ON THE MORNING AFTER Christmas, just before Adam took her home, Jake presented Jesse with the black filly he'd outgrown. As she stood next to Fancy, Jesse's eyes sparkled with tears.

"Thank you," she said with a quaver in her voice. "She's such a beautiful little horse. I'll take good care of her. And in the spring, I'll be able to ride her."

She took Jake's hand and squeezed it while he turned crimson. He managed to bend and kiss her cheek with grace, before blurting out, "It's because she's just as pretty as you are."

THE WOODSMAN'S ROSE

It was Jesse's turn to blush, while Adam wrung his brother's hand. In what seemed to be an imitation of Daniel's voice, Adam growled, "Thanks, boy-o." He tied the filly to the buggy then helped his wife in. Jake watched in happiness as she turned and waved her thanks again as they drove off.

Chapter 20

AS WAS HIS HABIT AFTER dinner, whatever the weather, Daniel sat on the front porch smoking his pipe. For the past week, he'd gone hunting every day but had little to show for it. Trekking alone through deep snow had left him exhausted. As he looked up to the winking stars, his thoughts turned to Annie. With the insight she'd inherited from her mother, the charming, ethereal girl had a way of soothing his soul. He ached to spend even a few minutes with her. In spite of the snow, he knew he could make it to her home in the village within the hour, so he put on his snowshoes and took himself to town.

The lights were low in the bootmaker's cottage, sending a frisson up his spine. His sister Evelyn answered his knock on the door with tears on her face.

"Oh, Daniel, how did you get here so fast?"

"What? What's wrong? Tell me!"

"It's Annie. She collapsed this afternoon—the doctor's here. We haven't been able to bring her around. I sent Tommy for you—didn't you see him?"

Dazed, Daniel shook his head. He hadn't stuck to the trails, but made a beeline across his father's fields to the village. Voices rumbled above—Annie's father and the doctor.

"Give me your coat," Evelyn said with a crack in her voice. "I'll make you some coffee."

"I want to see her." He threw his jacket on the divan and, without waiting for his sister's response, climbed the narrow stairs to see the doctor standing by the window, and Annie's father sitting on the side of her bed. He looked over Owen's shoulder.

So pale, so peaceful. Please, don't let her go away now.

He brushed past Owen and knelt beside the bed, stretched his arm out around her pillow and moved his face in close to hers.

"*Aroon,*" he murmured. "*Aroon.*"

He waited without breathing and felt rather than heard her small response. No more than a quickening of her blood.

"*Aroon*, I need you." He put his lips next to her ear. "Annie, sweetheart, please come back."

Her response was barely audible. The doctor reached in to take her hand, feel for the pulse in her wrist, but Daniel didn't move.

"*Aroon,*" he whispered once more.

Daniel? Are you here?

Yes, sweetheart.

Where am I?

I don't know. Come back to me, my precious love. I need you.

Yes.

Her eyelids fluttered and fell again, then opened to recognize him.

"Daniel," she whispered. She raised a weak hand to his cheek. He turned into it, kissed the palm. In a voice full of wonder, she said, "You were always there."

"And I'm here now. I love you, *aroon*. Stay with me, please."

"Stay with me," she echoed as her eyes fell shut again. His arms closed around her as she turned toward him. "Don't go."

"No, sweetheart." He raised her up until her head nestled against his shoulder, and he stroked her hair. "Sleep now, and I'll be here when you wake up."

Her breathing became deep and regular as she lay there in his arms. He heard Theo and Owen speaking in soft tones behind him, but he concentrated all of his attention and strength on her. She murmured once against his neck and stirred once in her dreams.

Let me keep her, he begged the all-mother, *for just a little while longer. I know I will lose her one day to this thing, this pain. But not now, please not now. Give her time to learn what love is. Give us both time.*

When he looked up again, they were alone. He could hear Evelyn weeping, and Owen's soothing words drifting up the stairs. "She'll be all right now. Don't cry, *caraid.* She's all right."

Daniel gazed at the sleeping girl in his arms. How long it would last, he couldn't know, but she was all right for now. He, on the other hand, was in considerable discomfort—the knee he'd cracked in childhood was pounding in protest and there was a cramp in his lower back. He leaned away, but Annie whimpered and her hand fluttered against his chest.

"Shhh. Hush now." Without releasing her, he struggled to his feet. He lifted her carefully and moved her closer to the wall, then stretched himself out on top of her covers. She made another little sound as he drew her close again. He put his face against her hair, smelled the fragrance that reminded him of honey. He'd loved her so much—for all his life it seemed. When she was ready, they'd marry. *Let it be soon, for I do not know how much time we will have.*

※

WHEN OWEN PEEKED IN on them, he saw their heads together on his daughter's pillow, Daniel's deep auburn a marked contrast to Annie's light gold. *I should not allow this. I should dump him on the floor and beat him senseless.* Instead, he plucked a bright afghan off the quilt stand in the corner and covered them both. *I don't care. I wouldn't care if he painted himself blue and danced naked around the house. He brought her back to me. I don't know how, and neither does the doctor. We were so sure this would be the last time.*

THE WOODSMAN'S ROSE

Until the minute he walked in the door.

That very minute, the color came back to her face. She'd been so pale, her skin was almost blue. She's still pale. But not like that. God bless him. And thank you for letting him come in time. As quietly as he could, Owen left them there alone.

❦

WHEN ANNIE BEGAN TO stir against him, Daniel woke. It was pitch dark outside, but the light from the parlor stole up and around the corner of the stairs. He felt the afghan resting on his shoulders, but knew he couldn't let Annie find them sleeping together in her bed, no matter how much her father might approve. With his free arm, he pushed the coverlet aside and slipped off the bed onto his knees again.

It was only a moment before she opened her eyes. He took the hand she held out to him, then got up and sat on the bed. "Feeling better?"

She gave him a shy smile. "What time is it?"

"After nine. Are you hungry?"

She thought for a moment. "Yes, I think I am."

"Do you want to get up?" He stroked her hair. She stretched her long neck, rubbed her head against his palm like a kitten and closed her eyes again.

"I guess I should," she said.

"You don't have to, *aroon*."

"I really should."

"Let me light this lamp." Daniel reached in his pocket for his matches.

"No."

Even in the shadows he could see her blush. "Suppose I send Evelyn up to give you a hand?"

"Yes. Thank you."

He turned back at the top of the stairs, gave her a long look full of his love. She closed her eyes again, drifting off a bit, back to the first time Daniel had declared his love—the first time she realized he'd always been there when she needed him.

The previous spring, the community had gathered at the Donovan homestead to celebrate Adam and Jesse's wedding. But her heart had been broken by Brian's obvious attachment to his new sister-in-law. She'd loved Brian since they were children and never considered another, but was much too shy to ever tell anyone, much less confess it to him. But she knew the big man's heart—and it would never be hers.

The dream she'd cherished since childhood dissolved into mist. She'd been on the verge of tears when Daniel took her hand and led her down the slope, away from the crowd. And there, in a few words, he'd spoken of the love he'd cherished for years.

Later, she sat on the high seat of the buggy as her brother drove them home. Her hands laced together in her lap, still warm from Daniel's touch. She was warm all over, in spite of the damp and cooling air. Warm where his arms had held her, where his lips had touched her hair. Where her cheek had nuzzled against the soft deerskin on his shoulder. She wondered how her head could fit so perfectly into that spot—and how one small word could have made her heart turn over.

Aroon, he'd said, and the love she'd felt for his brother had been that quickly eclipsed. But how could she love him when he was so different from the one she'd always wanted?

So different, and yet so much the same. Both gentle men, strong men, men with values and morals that never bend. And yet to look at them—Brian as tall and wide as a tree with a smile for everyone and an optimism I've rarely seen shaken. Daniel quieter, more serious, slow to smile but quick to laugh at himself. His mustache had tickled her ear as he held her, muffled his voice as he whispered. *Aroon...*

THE WOODSMAN'S ROSE

"So Daniel finally spoke up, did he?" Lowell asked.

"Finally?"

"Annie, don't you know how long he's loved you?"

"How long?" she whispered.

"Ever since we were kids. Ever since the Donovans moved out here. When you were five years old, you wouldn't play with Evelyn and her dolls. You wouldn't stay in the yard with the little kids. You wanted to do what the big boys did. Me and Adam, Brian and Conor. You followed us. After a while, you followed Brian. And Daniel followed you."

"Did he?"

"Every inch of the way. Don't you remember when you cut your foot on that rock and were bleeding so much? Who made you put your foot in the air to stop the bleeding? Who tore his shirt to pieces to make a bandage, then wrapped the bandage tight with those rawhide laces he always has a pocketful of? And who carried you all the way home again?"

"Daniel." The answer came quick and soft. Again she wondered how she could have been so blind.

"Um-hmm. And who taught you to call turkeys, found the flowers in the woods for you to pick? And who, little sister, when you passed out, would make his shirt into a pillow for your head, and stay with you while the rest of us went back to our games?" Lowell turned his face away from her, still ashamed that he'd done virtually nothing to help her.

She took a long time to answer him. "What should I do?"

"Let him love you, Annie."

"But, Lowell..."

"I know, *caraid*. You've always thought about Brian and haven't considered Daniel. But he's the one who loves you. You know that now.

"Shhh," he murmured, reining in the team and putting his arm around her. "There's nothing to cry about. He loves you, Annie. He always has. What you've felt for Brian is real, but it was a childhood attraction—it won't stand up against Daniel's love.

"Daniel's always been around when you needed him. He's never even looked at anyone else. Let him love you. Give him a chance to make you love him." He tapped her nose once. "He'll make you happy, *caraid*. Just give him a chance."

Chapter 21

AFTER A HARD WINTER, with more snow than anyone but Tommy remembered, spring came early and brought with it an incessant rain. As the snow in the high mountains melted, the river rose and overflowed its banks. White's Station became a morass of mud even before its streets filled with water. Doc Barber and his sister Jane sought refuge with the Donovans, and they were only the first of those fleeing low ground. The doctor and Tommy braved the weather to visit the Navajo encampment and returned, soaked to the skin and shivering, with a load of bad news.

"Some o' them renegades are back," Tommy said in disgust, holding his hands out to the warmth of the kitchen fire. "Tribe won't turn 'em out in this weather."

"That's not the worst of it." Barber took the coffee Molly offered with a nod of thanks. "They've taken to the caves, and I'm worried about the old ones and that boy, Blue Deer. There's six or seven little ones, too. None of them are strong enough to fight off infection—influenza could wipe out the whole tribe. Not to mention cholera."

"I talked t' the elders, tried t' explain the danger." Tommy rubbed both hands over his face. "Runnin' Wolf is willin' to listen, even if some o' the others ain't. But we gotta show 'im a solid plan. They won't even talk about being broke up—they wanna stay together."

"How many would you say they number?" John Patrick asked.

"Mebbe fifty, countin' the kids."

The old man lit his pipe and puffed in silence for a few minutes.

"We've six bunkhouses with eight bunks in each." He waved a hand to cut off any protests, fully aware of the logistical problems. "Right now Flaherty has one with his family. We can double up here to make room for them.

"Geordie and Suzette have the foreman's cabin. They can share Frank and Patricia's rooms, if you and Alec take that. That leaves us with the Callendars and the ranchhands." The widow Daisy Callendar had a grown son and four younger daughters who were lodged in another of the empty bunkhouses, while the half-dozen permanent hands shared a third. John Patrick's frown deepened. They could make it work, he was sure, but he couldn't quite see his way through to it. "Jake, go get your brother Daniel."

They came downstairs moments later with Frank and Patricia, Daniel with pencil and paper in hand. Before he had a chance to sit, John Patrick had a question for him.

"Have Evelyn and Lowell any extra rooms?"

"No, sir. In addition to Owen and Carolyn, they've got the Entwerps and the new Chinese family. Oh, and the Alegrias. Benson's got the Taylors, Rileys and Thatchers, all the single ranchers and farmhands from over that way, plus his cowboys. Everybody else from town is out at Cordell's or on Miller's farm."

"What about the new man—the one who bought the Wilson place?"

Daniel shrugged, but Tommy answered, "Said 'e was goin' down t' Tuba City. Heard it wasn' so bad there."

"Well, let's hope not." John Patrick clapped his hands together. "So, how do we do this?"

It took Daniel a few moments to reply. He'd drawn boxes on the paper while he talked, and began to scribble names in each. He examined his work, then looked up at Molly. "Your room's the biggest, Mother. I think it can work if we put Daisy and Moira and all the young ones in there."

THE WOODSMAN'S ROSE

"Of course."

"You and Dad could take the guest room. Then we split the rest up by gender. Men in my room, Jake's room and the front parlor. Women in Irene's room, and in Frank and Patricia's rooms. We'll keep the back parlor open in case anyone gets sick. Plus it's the only way to the bathroom. That leaves the dining room for the hands."

"Wait a minnit," Tommy said. "Why don't ya put the hands in the foreman's cabin? Me an' Alec can bunk with the tribe. They might be more comf'table with us right there. The li'l ones won't need their own bunks—they can double up or sleep with their Mas."

Daniel could see the relief on his mother's face. She wouldn't have objected, but to have men camped out in her dining room was the last thing she'd wish for. "OK? Then we're set. Tommy, I guess we've got to go talk the tribe into moving."

※

HAVING SETTLED THE Navajo into the bunkhouses, the Donovans fell into a new routine. A breakfast of ham and biscuits was served in the kitchen in three shifts. At noon, a platter of beef sandwiches appeared and everyone helped themselves whenever they were hungry.

Dinner was served at 6 o'clock, with kids in the kitchen, adults and babies in the dining room. Supplies might have become a problem, but everyone had brought their food stocks with them, including so many canned goods that some had to be stored on the back porch.

The logistics of dinner preparation were determined by Molly, who acted as overseer and assigned teams of four women on a rotating basis. As the days went on, Irene's temper began to fray, and when old Mrs. Jonas again criticized her potato peeling, Irene threw down her paring knife and stormed from the kitchen, the swinging door crashing after her.

After a few moments in which all the women silently concentrated on their own tasks, Annie whispered to Molly, got a nod in return, and followed Irene out. The sound of sobbing led her to the small parlor behind the stairs, where Irene lay on her grandmother's velvet couch. Sitting beside her, Annie waited for the storm to pass, then asked, "Are you really this upset about some potatoes?"

"Oh, Annie, it's not just that!" Irene sat up and wiped the tears from her cheeks. "Mrs. Milligan's in my room—she thinks she might be having a baby and she threw up all over my new boots."

"I'll help you clean them up after we eat."

"Violet already did." Violet was one of Irene's school chums—a girl with a shy smile and eyes that matched her name. "But it still smells bad. Then Vi went out to the barn to tell Mr. Milligan to come in, and now there's mud all over my rug. All my things are getting ruined!"

The weeping began again. Annie put an arm around Irene's shoulders and stifled the urge to criticize.

With her temper once more under control, Annie asked, "Have you thought about what's happening to Mrs. Milligan's things?"

"What? No. Why?"

"Their ranch is downhill from the river, isn't it? It's going to be full of water and mud. They could lose all their livestock. Even if Mrs. Milligan is pregnant, she's going to have to share the clean-up with her husband." Irene tried to interrupt, but Annie went smoothly on. "Violet's going home to a farmhouse south of the river. Her mother has rheumatism, and her brother and sister are too small to help very much. So Violet and her father will have to do most of the work.

"And Mrs. Jonas lives alone in town. She's probably worried that the water's going to soak everything she owns, and she's going to have to ask for help. And you know how much she hates to ask for anything, don't you?"

THE WOODSMAN'S ROSE

"Oh." After a long silence, Irene added, "I guess I'm being a baby."

"Just a little bit." Annie smiled at her, all vestige of temper gone. "When times are hard, everyone suffers. It's something to think about."

Irene stood and smoothed down her skirts, tucked a stray tendril of hair behind her ear. "I'm going to go apologize to Mrs. Jonas."

"That's a good idea. Then we'll finish the potatoes together, OK?"

"Yeah. I wonder if she'll like your way of peeling."

Chapter 22

THE VILLAGE WAS UNDERWATER for two weeks. When the river finally receded, the streets and the ground floors of every building in town were filled with mud, and thousands of cattle were dead. The family did their share of the cleaning up and clearing out. The mud was bad enough—smelling, as Brian put it, "like socks that got worn wet for a month, then thrown in a corner t' mildew." But when it came to the disposal of steer, pig, and chicken carcasses, the stench seemed to flare up from hell. Even the camphor-soaked bandannas Molly prepared weren't enough to cover the stink of rotting meat as it burned. The men trudged home every night so nauseated, the very thought of food made them gag.

John Patrick had an answer ready for every complaint. The rich tapestry of his mother's wisdom included a proverb he found especially appropriate to the life they led in this wild land, and he repeated it often to his children. "You can live without your own, but not without your neighbor."

With the cleanup finally accomplished, Raymond Benson called a meeting of the Cattlemen's Association. He proposed a scheme of proportionality to make up for some of the losses sustained in the flood and it met with very little resistance. When a detailed agreement was hammered out, he invited all the residents of the town and outlying areas to a meeting at the Town Hall.

"Awright, folks, settle down now. Take a seat if you can find one." He waited for the room to quiet. "Awright, I asked y'all heah t'day t' see what we can do about the flood damage."

THE WOODSMAN'S ROSE

"Do?" demanded a man standing against the far wall. "What you gonna do? It's over an' done. I'm ruint an' so're the rest o' us, 'ceptin' you few with money."

"What's yore name, mister?" Benson asked.

"Sykes. I bought the Wilson place las' fall." He was a powerfully built man, with skin the color and texture of aged walnut. His dark eyes snapped at Benson.

"Well, Mr. Sykes," Benson began, in his soft Texas drawl. Sykes' face twisted into a grimace. "I'd like you—an' all y'all—t' hear me out. The Cattlemen's Association met yestidday, an' we have a proposal t' make. If it's awright with y'all, we'd like t' make a proportional distribution o' this year's calves along with their mothers."

Benson put up his hands for silence as he was barraged with questions. "Wait a minnit! Jus' gimme a minnit an' I'll explain it t' y'all.

"The ranchers who had fewer losses have agreed t' pool t'gether the calves that're born this year, along with their mothers, an' distribute 'em accordin' t' the losses each o' y'all suffered. Now, it won't make up for everythin' you lost, but it should be enough t' keep y'all goin' 'til next year."

"You're talkin' 'bout charity," Sykes declared, gripping a cloth cap between strong hands. "I won't take no charity."

"We're talking about neighbors." John Patrick's voice carried throughout the room. "All of these good people are my neighbors, and yours. We share the good times, and we can share the bad times as well."

There was a buzz of agreement in the hall, but Sykes wasn't satisfied. "What's in it for you?"

"Not a thing," John Patrick answered, "except perhaps my immortal soul." The black man shook his head. "Let me ask you this: if this building were on fire, would you join the bucket brigade?"

"Reckon so."

"Why?"

"'Cause the whole town might burn down."

"And the whole town is needed by you, as it is by all of us." John Patrick pointed his pipe, moved it to encompass the entire room. "We all need one another. Which of you would live in this wilderness alone?"

A low chorus of denials greeted his inquiry.

"But what about plow horses?" one of the farmers asked.

"I got some," Tommy answered. He'd loosed all of his horses when the river overflowed. With the help of the Navajo, he and Alec had managed to catch most of them again.

"I've an extra," added Seamus Flaherty, and three other farmers followed suit.

"Y'all get t'gether after the meetin'," Benson said. "See if you got what you need, an' if not, lemme know. Anythin' else?"

Marvin Entwerp stood up. His ranch was far south of town and he'd lost not only his cattle and horses, but most of his family's belongings as well. "First off, I wanna say thanks. An' I don't want nobody t' think I don't appreciate what you're tryin' to do here. But I lost everything, an' some calves an' cows ain't gonna be much use to me. I need cattle I can sell this year. I won't make it through another winter on what I got put away. I'm sorry, gentlemen, I hate t' be..."

"No, no," Benson said, "anybody else in the same boat?" Five or six hands went up. "Awright, jus' wait a few minnits, will ya?" Benson motioned to his committee. Daniel followed his father and Adam as they gathered in the corner with the other ranchers.

"Whaddya think?" Benson asked. John Patrick shook his head and the others looked perplexed.

"How about this?" the woodsman suggested. "We use the same calculation based on the number of new calves, but we put mature cattle in place of some of them. It actually works out better for everyone, doesn't it? We wouldn't be giving up this year's entire crop, and the others would have stock they could breed or sell this year."

"I think that's it," Adam agreed. "And if we put together a breeding program, it'll give everyone a fighting chance at some growth next spring."

"Any objections?" Benson asked, looking around at his committee. "Awright, I think that'll work. How we gonna control it?"

"Three of them, three of us," Daniel suggested. "Make the counts together. Calves have already started dropping. We can keep a running tab, and go out every two weeks or so for a recount. Deduct the ones we've already counted, and that's the new number."

John Patrick clapped his hands together. "Ray, let's get this done."

At the end of the day, both Daniel and Sykes were appointed to the counting committee. Eli marched over to John Patrick as he left. "I still don' know how I feel 'bout this, sir. I don' like t' be beholden."

"Everyone in this town is beholden, son. It's the way we all stay honest."

Chapter 23

AFTER THE FIRST ROUND of calf-counting, the committee dwindled. Ultimately four members dropped out, saying they were too busy and would trust the information Daniel was gathering. Eli Sykes, however, maintained his position.

"Not 'cause I don't trust you," he told Daniel, "but they gave me this job, an' I don't feel right 'bout letting it go."

"Then let's go out to the canyon today. Haven't been there yet, and Adam says they have at least a dozen new calves. Not that *he's* been out to count them!"

"Awright, Mr. Donovan. This Adam—he's kin o' yours?"

"Call me Daniel. And yes, he's my oldest brother. My brother Brian lives there, too."

"My name's Elijah. Eli for short."

As they rode out west of the Donovan lands, Daniel searched for a way to get some personal information from his companion without sounding too nosy. He was about to speak when Eli asked, "Where's your daddy from?"

"Ireland."

"Thought he might be. How long y'all been here?"

"About eighteen years here in Arizona," Daniel replied. "I was the first one born over here—I mean, in America. Texas, to be exact. Family moved here when I was ten." He got no response from the man at his side, so decided to elaborate. "Adam and Brian were born in Ireland—they're twins, almost five years older than me. My

THE WOODSMAN'S ROSE

brother Conor was born there, too, but he's at sea and doesn't get home much."

"Nice family. All boys, huh?"

Daniel had to laugh. "Nope. We go all the way to 'J' now." At the other's look of confusion, he explained his grandmother's method of naming the Donovan children. The first, Adam, had been named after her deceased husband. Then Molly had named Brian to honor her father, William Francis O'Brien, and John Patrick had chosen his mother's maiden name for Conor. "Gran called my three brothers her 'little alphabet'. When I was born, she suggested Daniel, or 'Donal' as it is in Gaelic. Then there's my sister Evelyn, and the younger twins, Frank and Geordie. Then Henry—he died when he was two years old, before we left Abilene. Irene and Jake were both born here in Arizona."

"Whew! That's a big family!"

"How about you?"

Several minutes elapsed before Eli spoke, his voice rumbling in his chest like a locomotive. Yet the words came out slowly as a drip of molasses. "I was born a slave." He looked over at Daniel before he continued. "Back in Mississippa, on the Big Black River. Worked a cotton plantation. We worked hard an' didn't have no days off, an' sometimes in winter the roof'd leak. But that wasn' too bad compared to what come next.

"Masta's name was Ryan, and he had jus' the one child. His wife died when the boy was five or six. Well, when the big war came the young masta, he went t' fight an' got hisself killed. Masta Ryan, he just fade away after that—let the whole plantation go straight t' hell. An' when he died, well, there wasn't nobody else left in the family, so the place got took over by the plantation down the road. An' that man—name o' Groven—he was wuss than the devil hisself. Blamed us for lettin' the place go t' rack an' ruin. Ran us twenty hours a day. An' that overseer, he'd flog you at the drop of a hat.

"My boy," he continued in a lifeless voice, "my boy was seven years old. He worked in the kitchens. One day 'e dropped a bowl o' soup. Just one bowl. An' that ol' devil Groven called out t' the overseer that this here boy don't know 'is place.

"They took my boy out t' flog 'im. But I fell right down on top of 'im an' took the beatin' for 'im. But afterwards, when they pulled me off, they was all set t' flog 'im anyway. So I just picked up a pitchfork an' I run that overseer through. Then I grabbed my boy an' lit on out."

The horses had come to a stop at the entrance to the Rocking Chair Ranch. Daniel's hands were trembling and when he found his voice, it was deeper, gruffer than usual. "You did what you had to do. I would've done the same thing."

He heard a long sigh from Sykes and glanced over to see his hands were trembling, too.

"I never told that story before. I guess the way they trust you... I been waitin' a long time t' get it off my chest."

"You did what you had to do," the woodsman repeated. "And it doesn't matter way out here. No one cares about the past—or what happened somewhere else. Where's your boy now? And your wife?"

"It was goin' on winter when the boy an' me run away. I run inta the river t' keep the dogs from followin'. I dunno how long I run—two, mebbe three days—an' I was just about t' give out when a raft come downriver. There's a white man on it, so I started t' run away, but alla sudden, he shouted out he was a Quaker. Them Quakers, y'know, they helped a lotta us escape."

"I know," Daniel said. "They're a wonderful people. They helped Ireland out when the famine hit. But that's a story for another day. You go ahead—what happened then?"

"Well, we got on 'is raft an' 'e took us to a boat further upriver. We hid down in the hold an' they covered us with bales o' cotton. It was a long, dirty ride, but the boat went up to Cincinnata. Way after dark, they pulled us out an' put us in the back of a wagon, covered us up with more cotton. An' they brought us t' Mr. Levi Coffin."

"We was sick. We was both real sick. We couldn't go on. They hid us in a root cellar, but the boy already had the grippe an' there wasn't nothin' t' be done. He died jus' a few days later.

"I was okay after a while, an' Miz Coffin give me a uniform to wear an' told me, if anybody asks, to say I was the butler an' had worked for them for 10 years. One day they told me t' get ready t' go up t' Canada. But then the war was alla sudden over. I got me a job at a warehouse—sortin' cotton if y'can believe it! I saved up my money, an' then I tried to find my wife.

"One of the first things that Groven did was sell half the women down river. I went back to the plantation an' heard she'd been sent to Baton Rouge. But she wasn't there anymore. A friend o' hers told me she went to Prescott, so I tried there, too. But no luck. I left messages there for her if she ever does get there, then I came north to see if I could find a li'l farm. I always did like t' see the crops grow—startin' from a li'l bitty seed an' growin' tall an' strong... It's just somethin'. So anyways, here I am."

"And here we are," said Daniel.

Sykes looked up to see a little white cabin with emerald green trim. He flashed a wide smile at his companion. "Ain't that pretty."

Jesse came to the door. She waved a towel gaily and Daniel waved back.

"I wasn't expecting you today," she said as they dismounted. "Come on in and have some coffee."

"Jesse, this is Eli Sykes," Daniel said. "Eli, this is my sister-in-law, Jesse Donovan."

"How do you do, Mr. Sykes." Jesse held out her hand. Sykes took it carefully, shook it gently. She was, by far, the smallest woman he'd ever seen.

"How do, Miz Donovan."

"No, please call me Jesse," she said, with a sparkle in her eye and a laugh in her voice. "Mrs. Donovan's my mother-in-law. Where'd you two come from? Come on in and sit down."

As they followed her into the cabin, Daniel explained their mission.

"Oh, I heard about that," she said. "Brian's out with the herd right now."

"Where's Adam?"

"He went to town with Rebecca. They should be back any time. So, Eli—you don't mind, do you? We don't stand on ceremony around here. Where do you live?"

"I bought the Wilson place last fall."

"Wilson...?"

"Out by the old stage line," Daniel told her. "On the way to Fort Defiance."

"Oh, my. You must've had some trouble with the flood."

"Lost alla my stock," Sykes responded, "but the house is awright. An' I saved the chickens. Put 'em up in the loft with all the hay."

"Well, wasn't that smart! Would you like more coffee? Oh, wait, that's Adam and Rebecca now!" With that, she flitted out the door, leaving Eli and Daniel chuckling behind her.

She came back in with a small parcel, followed by her husband and Rebecca, both carrying more packages. After introductions, Sykes found himself staring at Rebecca. "Don't I know you?"

"Yes, we met in Prescott. I had a dress shop there."

"I worked the mercantile there for a while," he told the others, then turned back to Rebecca with a soft smile lighting up his face. "You left kinda sudden. How long you been out here?"

"Rebecca took care of Jesse when she was little," Adam explained. "She moved here with Jesse's family. Some... things happened, and she had to leave for a while, but she came back about two years ago."

THE WOODSMAN'S ROSE

"I heard my little mite needed me again," Rebecca told him, aiming a warm smile at Jesse. "Wild horses couldn't have kept me away."

"That's awright, then," Eli said. "We thought somethin' mighta happened t' you."

"All right, men," Daniel said. "Play time's over. Let's go count some calves!"

"Stop in on the way out," Jesse invited. "We'll all have supper together."

"Yes, ma'am!" came eagerly from both men.

Chapter 24

PIPE IN HAND, JOHN Patrick gazed out at the field he called "the north pasture", though it lay east of the ranchhouse and had never been used for grazing. It was filled with dead stalks a foot or two high, many of them flattened by the rain. A few tiny buttercups had pushed their heads up through the detritus and shimmied in the breeze.

Donovan had added this parcel to his claim to prevent white people from bothering the Navajo tribe. It wasn't just the missionaries—the merchant at the Trading Post had at one time decided to offer "summer tours" of the Navajo village to newcomers and visitors to the town. When violence threatened, John Patrick had interceded and offered the chief and his council a percentage of his yearly harvest for this five-acre plot. Now anyone approaching the encampment had to trespass on Donovan land first. Few indeed were those willing to risk the old man's wrath.

John Patrick had learned a valuable lesson through that deal. The concept of land ownership was unknown to the Navajo—the elders agreed to leave the land unoccupied in return for Donovan's promise to aid them in harsh winters. They wanted beef and produce—enough to see them through to spring. The first year, he'd offered several wagonloads of food, but the tribe took only what they needed and refused to take more. Or less. On one occasion, this had placed a hardship on the family, but John Patrick had held firm. They'd live up to their bargain and tighten their own belts accordingly.

THE WOODSMAN'S ROSE

The old man considered the land's features again as the woodsman stood at his side. The wide bench on which they stood was level, but the field sloped down toward Geordie's claim and the river in front of him, and up to the foothills behind. A small brook gurgled to his left.

"You've spoken to the tribe about this?"

"Of course," Daniel replied. "Explained exactly what I want to do. As long as they have a right-of-way through to town, they're fine with it."

"I'll give you the deed, lad, though why you'd be wanting this piece of land is beyond me. You'll not be raising anything of value in that soil."

With a short laugh and a gesture at his clothing, the woodsman asked, "Do I look like a farmer all of a sudden? I'm not planning to raise anything, Dad, except a cabin. And maybe some kids."

"Hmmm. Well, the deed is yours. A wedding gift. And you'll not be telling me no." John Patrick looked into the dark blue eyes of his fourth son, and saw their edges crinkle.

"Thanks, Dad."

"And the book is yours, too," the elder Donovan asserted, filling his pipe. "Maybe those kids you're considering will be needing it."

"Dad..."

Silence followed, as John Patrick lit his pipe and took a few deep puffs. He'd offered his son a passbook earlier in the day, representing the wages he felt Daniel had earned from the age of eighteen. The woodsman had handed it back with a smile.

"I appreciate it, Dad, but I really don't need it."

"It's not a matter of need, boy-o. You've earned it."

"How? By being part of the family? By hunting in the winter and slacking off in the summer? No, Dad. I've done maybe three months' worth of real work around here every year. The rest of the time, I've lived my life the way I wanted to. I've got plenty of money in the bank from the mustangs I sold, and from hunting for the folks in town. I haven't earned that money and I really don't need it."

John Patrick understood his son's reluctance to take the money. The woodsman wouldn't take what he didn't need—not from nature, not from his family. Not from anyone. But the land he wanted was worth only a few hundred dollars and the wages, his father still felt, had been earned.

"If you don't want it now, I'll be holding it for you. Maybe your Annie will know what to do with it."

"And if she says no?"

"Then we leave it in the bank until the need is there." John Patrick clapped his hands, indicating the subject was closed. His son knew better than to argue. "What else are you needing, lad? Aside from a worthless meadow?"

Daniel laughed once more. A worthless meadow, indeed.

"Just a little help when the time comes to build. But I've got to get Annie to name the date first."

REBECCA INVITED THE family to Rocking Chair Ranch to celebrate Adam and Jesse's second anniversary. It was a warm, sunny spring day, and Daniel could tell Annie was excited—her hands were constantly twisting in her lap as they rode along in her father's buggy.

"What's up, *aroon*?"

"Jesse's pregnant."

"You're sure?"

Her only answer was to cock her head.

"Of course you're sure." He put his arm around her, gave her forehead a loud kiss. "Silly me for asking!"

The moment they arrived at the cabin, Annie jumped from the buggy and caught Jesse in a tender embrace. "Oh, I'm so happy for you!" She stepped back, caught Jesse's hand, brushed the tawny hair away from her face and, in a voice of utter certainty, said, "Don't worry, *caraid*. Everything will be fine."

Jesse was in her arms again and Adam was holding them both. Daniel joined them, wrapping his arms around their shoulders, his face full of joy.

As Brian came out of the cabin, his twin held a hand out to him. He joined them, his great arms around the waists of his brothers, the women sheltered within the circle of their embrace. There was joy here and he felt it on his cheeks. He cleared his throat with difficulty.

"Why'm I cryin'?" he demanded in a voice as gruff as Daniel's.

They laughed up at him, and Annie answered, "She's having a baby."

"Oh, Lord," said Brian. "Lord love us all." He took Jesse's hand between his two great paws. "That's the best news I ever heard." In the next moment, he had them all locked in his arms again. "Lord, love us all."

Chapter 25

AS SPRING ADVANCED, the lawn in front of the ranchhouse wore its green velvet once more. The orchard was in bloom, and the tulips on either side of the wide porch steps nodded their brilliant heads in the soft breeze. Fuchsia leaves peeked out between the flowers, and tiny purple cabbages lined the drive. Looking out across his land, John Patrick could almost see the verdure of Ireland.

On a Saturday, just a year after the passing of his mother, the old man took himself to town. The village bustled along. Farmers and ranchers shopped for tools and feed, young mothers congregated at the mercantile, their offspring jostling each other for first chance at the sourballs. Matrons and spinsters alike pawed through the fabrics beneath a huge sign promoting a sale; hunters and traders sorted their goods or gazed longingly at a fine watch or rifle. Young girls stood on the porch in giggling cliques, while boys strutted up and down on the opposite side of the street or in front of the town hall, pretending not to notice them.

A smile played on John Patrick's face as he climbed down from his buggy. He loved this village, and the liveliness meant prosperity. Not for all, perhaps, but for most. And he knew that those who had more would find a way to spread it among those who were not as blessed—his village was populated with men who knew the value of neighbors. Men who, like himself, hadn't been born here. Families whose children might have some ultimate claim to the land. And natives who lived peaceably enough with the white man and the black man, the Chinese and the Mexican.

THE WOODSMAN'S ROSE

It was an unusual town in this place, in this time. A town that took pride in itself, in its own, making work for those less fortunate than others, standing together through the bad times. In a way, an intolerant little town. For the influential among them had seen enough of war, famine, hatred and spite, and worked hard to eliminate the lingering traces of prejudice from their lives.

There were those, John Patrick would admit, without whom the village would be a better place. Robert Taylor for instance—a smarmy, manipulative man who'd inherited the Trading Post and hadn't learned the value of working with his own hands. Worse than the merchant was his wife, Sarah, a sharp-tongued, vicious gossip who didn't care if the words she spoke were true. And she'd found a kindred soul in the doctor's sister Jane. But there were many more who belonged heart and soul to the community, and it was the many who drove the town to prosperity and saw that all were treated fairly, regardless of wealth or talent.

John Patrick intended to bestow some small reward on two of its citizens. He went first to the bootmaker's cottage and found Annie there.

From his vest pocket, he drew a tiny parcel wrapped in muslin, tied with white string. Her hands fumbled with the packaging, then her eyes lit up at sight of the tiny filigree stick pin in the shape of a lily, with seed pearls to represent the pistils.

"'Twas my mother's," he said. "I want you to have this, *colleen*, in thanks for all you did for her. In remembrance. Ah, don't cry, *colleen*."

"Thank you. It's beautiful. I'll treasure it." Annie wiped her eyes with the back of her hand. He kissed her cheek and left her standing in the doorway, looking down at the gift.

He turned next to the livery and found it crowded with horses. The blacksmith wiped his hands off to give John Patrick a proper greeting.

"Busy enough?" the old man teased.

Tommy's rich laughter split the air. "I swear every pony for two hunnerd miles around needs a new shoe! But I'm not complainin'!"

"Is your boy here?"

"He jus' went home t' get me somethin' t' eat. Haven't had a bite since breakfast. So don't keep 'im too long, hey?"

John Patrick answered with a salute and made his way to the cottage next door. He arrived just as Alec came out.

"Looking for me, sir? Could you wait a moment? I've got this lunch to deliver." At the old man's nod, he hastened away to return in less than a minute asking, "How can I help you?"

In answer, Donovan held out another muslin-wrapped package. "A thank you," he said, "for going to Flag for the priest last year, and allowing the family to stay together."

"But I didn't do that for pay."

"This isn't pay, boy-o. It's a remembrance—something of Mother's I want you to have."

"It was hers? That's different then." Alec opened the box and stared at its contents. "It looks…" His voice broke and his eyes filled, for the cameo had his mother's pure profile.

John Patrick clasped the silversmith's shoulder. "Mother always told me it looked just like her. I thought you'd appreciate it."

Like Annie, Alec could only nod. Again John Patrick left him there, staring at the brooch, knowing the gift would grow more precious as the years went by.

Chapter 26

FAMILY AND NEIGHBORS gathered to celebrate John Patrick's seventieth birthday, including the newcomers, Eli Sykes and the Rileys. Only Jesse, Adam and Rebecca were absent from the festivities.

When Brian arrived, he'd reported that Jesse was suffering from severe nausea, as she had with her first pregnancy. She couldn't eat and wasn't sleeping well, and was terrified of losing this baby as she'd lost her first. The entire company, even Jane Barber, greeted the news with dismay. And for Annie, it was devastating.

She'd been restless and anxious for several days, but had been unable to fathom the cause. From the first time they met, Annie had been tuned to Jesse—even more than to her natural family—and Jesse's fear had torn at her heart. So while Daniel was busy passing out glasses of porter and elderberry wine, she told her father she was suddenly feeling tired and needed a nap, then approached Patricia. She knew the kind-hearted girl would be willing to do almost anything asked of her, and wouldn't take the time to wonder why.

"I'll come up with you," Patricia offered. "Or I could bring a cup of tea."

"Oh, no, don't bother. I just need to lie down for a little bit. You stay here and have your dinner."

"Are you sure?"

"Absolutely. I'll be fine."

Annie climbed the stairs wondering if her decision would bear fruit. John Patrick's mother, Katie, had inherited the gift of insight from her Druid ancestors. Annie's mother had shared the gift as well, and Annie thought she might be able to reach Jesse with the help of Katie's spirit—a spirit she firmly believed was still with them, and which might be most concentrated in the rooms the old lady had used for so long.

As she entered the sitting room, Annie took no notice of the velvet curtains or trellised wallpaper. She sat on the hearth before Katie's fireplace, stirred up the embers and added a few pieces of kindling, then deliberately emptied her mind of thought. She stared unseeing into the fire. The smoke wavered and curled, and Annie could almost feel the old lady holding her hand. She closed her eyes and breathed deep, concentrating all her energy on the cabin in the canyon. A strange power flowed through her. Her other hand stretched itself toward the smoke. Opening her eyes in little slits, she saw the smoke curling from the chimney of the cabin in the canyon.

Yes. The old musical voice reached into Annie's mind. What she'd expected, what she'd hoped for. Still, it made her shiver. *We are almost there. Follow the smoke, see whence it comes. Follow it into the house. Back to the fire. We are almost there. Hear his voice, find his voice.*

"Jesse, *mavourneen*, you have to talk to me." Adam's voice was gruff with emotion. Annie almost drew away, but the old lady's spirit forbade it. So she stayed with him, felt the depths of the love within him, and the terrible fear. She felt him gather up his tiny wife, move to the chair in front of the fire. She concentrated once more and heard him say, "Tell me what's wrong."

The old voice commanded, *Be with her!*

Annie's consciousness flickered to the girl. She felt warm arms surrounding her, gentle hands caressing her. The strength of him, the warmth. And the fear—the terror—the pain, guilt, fear. Annie rocked with her emotion, tried to pull away, but that faint voice

THE WOODSMAN'S ROSE

encouraged her: *She needs us. She needs you.* Her heart reached out again, though she moaned with the pain of it.

Tell him, the old voice commanded through her. *Tell him all.* And Annie heard the small voice whisper.

"Adam... Adam..." She clutched at him frantically, her little hands cold in spite of the warmth of the room.

"Yes, my love. Tell me."

"I'm afraid."

"Tell me why, *mavourneen*."

"What if... the baby... my brother..."

"What about him, my love?"

"Could the baby... be like him? He killed her..."

"Russell? Killed who, *mavourneen*?"

"H–he killed... Elena... I know h-he killed her..."

Adam's response was so strong it drew Annie back into him. *That goddamned bastard.* He struggled for breath. *Has she been living with this hell, too? How long has she known? And what else is there about that bastard I have to know? My god, don't let there be any more!*

He looked at his wife and knew the depths of his selfishness. *She's so strong in that frail shell. She puts us all to shame.*

"My sweet love," he murmured into her hair.

"I'm sorry." She was clinging to him then, seeking support for her fragile strength. Her voice wavered as she continued, "The last time he came home... before the time I shot him... he caught me in the yard... I slapped and kicked at him... he threw me down on the ground... and he said..."

She closed her eyes, swayed against him. He whispered, "Tell me, love. Tell me."

Yes. Tell him all.

"He said, 'Don't fight me, girl... or you'll die, too'. Could... the baby... be like...?"

"Never, my love, never." Her little hands clutched at him again. "Oh, Jesse, I swear. On your mother's grave, I swear."

Annie felt the certitude flowing from him as he repeated it over and over again. And finally, she felt the acceptance flowing into his woman.

"I... I was going to tell the... next day. But Alec was my friend... I knew he'd kill him... in cold blood. And then... be hanged. I... couldn't..."

"And then... he was dead... you told me... he was dead... and I didn't... have to tell..." Her voice cracked, her small reserve of strength used up.

"Hush, love. You couldn't have told—who would you tell? There was no proof. Even Daniel said there was no proof. It's all right, my love. If you want Alec to know, I'll tell him. But, Jesse, are you sure you want to?"

"I... I..."

"What else, Jesse?" His tone was like velvet over steel. He supported her with one arm, stroked her cheek with his other hand. "What else?"

She reached for him blindly, sobbing so terribly the words came out in a jumble.

"I... didn't want... *his* baby... murderer... shame... your name."

Annie pulled back, but it was too late—too late. The knowledge was like a brand, burning into her soul. The first baby—that poor stillborn baby—*not Adam's but her brother's!*

"No, no..." Annie rocked and held her head with both hands, trying to expunge the knowledge she'd gained. The old voice spoke again.

Forgive me, macushla. Believe that it was necessary. Believe that we have helped her. She will be well now.

THE WOODSMAN'S ROSE

Forgiveness came at once, but it didn't ease the pain. She rocked and moaned. She tried to stand but flopped down again, whimpering.

Call him. Call him and he will come.

She opened her mouth, but no words would come. *Daniel.* She reached for him. *I need you. Daniel.* But there was no answer and her tears began to flow.

Within seconds he was at her side. She reached for him again and this time felt the strong warmth of his arms, the deep rough voice of comfort in her ear. Real he was, and close and loving. She held him tight and trembled violently.

"*Aroon*, what is it?"

But she couldn't speak.

"Annie," he whispered. *Precious Annie.* "Come with me, sweetheart."

He picked her up and carried her to his room. He laid her on the bed and turned to close the door. When he came back to her, her arms were reaching for him again, tears streaming down her face. He gathered her in, held her as if she were an infant, and made soft noises of comfort against her hair.

She began to sob and he turned her head against his chest to stifle the sounds, for he realized that he'd compromised her. He should have taken her to the guest room, gone for his mother or sister. Almost in a panic, he tried to soothe her.

"Hush, *aroon*," he begged. He slipped off the bed, knelt beside it, her arms still around his neck, his still holding her tight. "Sweetheart, don't cry. Oh, Annie, please."

His words finally penetrated and she drew a deep shaky breath, held it until she'd brought herself under control. But she did not, could not let him go.

"*Aroon...*" He stroked her hair, kissed her forehead. "My precious girl, tell me what's wrong."

Her tears started again, but she managed to speak. "Jesse..." Her voice juddered and broke as her body trembled. "How... could he hurt her? How could he... hurt her so much?"

He groaned in denial, in helplessness. "I don't know, *aroon*. I don't know." But his heart demanded, *How could this happen? When I've tried so hard to keep it from her?*

The old lady's voice answered him. *It was necessary. Believe that it was. I am sorry, acushlah. We have done what we must.*

But as he bent again over the girl he loved, he found it hard to accept. *How many more people will he hurt? When will this ever end?*

Chapter 27

WHEN ANNIE SLEPT, DANIEL covered her with a quilt. He looked down at her as she rested on his pillow, then cursed himself for a fool. If anyone should find her here...

Softly he closed the door behind him, quietly he descended the stairs. Silently he slipped into the parlor where the guests were gathered. His heart stopped when he saw Jane Barber. He'd forgotten about her—one of the worst gossip-mongers in the village. His need to protect Annie escalated to desperation, but he looked in vain for Evelyn.

Luckily, Jane sat half-turned away from him. He made a small urgent motion to Jake, hoping Alec had taught him some of the hand-signals they'd used while gentling ponies. *Come quickly,* it said, *come quietly.* The youth was sitting on the floor beside the hearth but got up and joined his brother at the door. He'd attracted no attention, and Daniel felt his panic dissolve.

"Where's Evelyn?" he asked in a low voice.

"In the kitchen. They're making coffee."

"Go get her for me? Tell her to meet me in the hall. Do it as quietly as you can, okay?"

The lad disappeared through the kitchen door as Daniel slipped out into the entryway again. He found himself pacing, stopped and ordered his thoughts under control. When Evelyn came out, he was leaning against the newel post.

"Jake said you wanted me?"

"Need you is more like it. I did something stupid and I need your help."

"What is it?"

"Annie was in Gra... in Frank and Patricia's room. I don't know why, but she was crying when I went up." He lied blatantly but felt no guilt. "Evelyn, I put her in my room. She's asleep."

"Daniel..." His sister gaped at him.

"I said it was stupid. But she was so upset, I didn't think."

"We can't let anyone find out. Owen wouldn't mind—he trusts you. But there are so many other people here. And Jane... it would be terrible."

"Help me, please. I can't let her suffer just because I'm stupid."

"All right. You get back in there—no, go outside then back in by the kitchen door. Make yourself conspicuous. I'll go upstairs. I'll think of something."

"Thank you, *mavourneen*. I knew we could count on you."

As Evelyn flew up the stairs, Daniel sauntered around to the kitchen to help his mother and Carolyn with heavy trays of cups. No one, it seemed, had noticed his absence from the gathering. As he passed coffee around, he heard everyone planning the Fourth of July festival. The town would be fifty years old, and they all wanted a special celebration.

They were talking about the horse races as Evelyn approached Owen and put a hand on his arm. "Papa, Annie's upstairs and she's not feeling well."

"It's not headache, is it?"

"Oh, no, just a bit of indigestion."

The tension left Owen's face. "Indigestion" was the word his Annie used to describe any discomfort that wasn't headache. "I'm going to bring her some peppermint tea. But it might be better if she were to sleep afterwards. She could stay here tonight."

"Are you sure it's no trouble?"

THE WOODSMAN'S ROSE

"None at all, Owen," Molly answered. "You must know that by now."

"The guest room's already made up," Evelyn added. Daniel had some trouble hiding his laugh. Again the statement was true, and Owen need not know it was he and not Annie who'd spend the night there.

"Should I go up and see her?" Owen asked.

Evelyn patted his arm again. "Maybe later." She was gratified when he sank back into his chair. She made a wicked face at Daniel as she left the room, was rewarded by a grateful smile.

Molly saw it, though, and stared hard at him. He got up to follow as she motioned him into the kitchen. "What goes on?"

Evelyn explained the situation while her brother stood silent. Molly looked him up and down. "Haven't you the slightest bit of intelligence at all?"

"No, ma'am."

"It wouldn't be so bad were Jane not here. And yet it seems that she has changed somewhat—she seems not quite so bitter as before. Still, we cannot allow anyone discover this. Oh, Daniel, I once did think you had a brain."

"Once he did," Evelyn put in, "but that was before he fell in love."

"Aye." Molly eyed him once more. "And that was quite some time ago, I fear. Now get yourself back in there, and for pity's sake, do no more thinking tonight!"

He kissed her cheek and obeyed. He joined in the plans for the festival, offering half a dozen wooden toys for the craft table competition. Jane Barber volunteered to help the ladies make rag dolls for prizes, and the surprised silence was broken by Carolyn who, as always, offered to host the lemonade stand.

DANIEL ESCORTED EVELYN, Owen, and Carolyn out as the party broke up; Evelyn had convinced them Annie was sleeping soundly. Lowell had their buggy ready and, as good-nights were exchanged, Evelyn gave her brother a broad wink. He sent her a salute of thanks as they drove away.

He walked down the lane and leaned against the corral fence, his chin supported by his arms. The sky was glittering with stars, and he tried to drink in the serenity of the night. Then, directly behind him, he heard the soft footsteps of his Navajo friend.

First Jesse, then Annie. Now Alec. I don't know what I ever did to deserve this day.

"Daniel." The voice that was so rich and deep, that soothed nervous mustangs and comforted frightened children, just now made the woodsman's hackles rise. "Who killed my mother?"

"I can't tell you. I have no proof."

"You told my father."

"I've told no one."

"My father knows."

The woodsman shrugged.

"You told him," Alec averred.

"No."

"Then how does he know?"

Something within him snapped, and Daniel's voice was no more than a growl. "I don't know, Alec. Maybe he figured it out for himself. Maybe if you weren't so damn stupid, you could figure it out, too!"

Horrified by the insult he'd thrown, Daniel reached out and grabbed at the air, as if he could snatch the words back. Then he realized that Alec had paid no attention to the slur but was deep in thought, staring hard at the ground before stalking away. Daniel sank to his knees beside the fence post, rested his head against it and groaned aloud. *What have I done?*

Chapter 28

THE MORNING SUN STREAMED through the window and touched Annie's face. She was warm under a soft quilted cover, but it wasn't hers. The pillow beneath her head had a familiar scent but it, too, belonged to someone else. Her awakening mind thought, *The Navajo build their hogans to face the east. The rising sun must waken them each day.*

But it wasn't a hogan in which she'd slept, though a bearskin rug lay on the floor and the walls were hung with pelts. The room was clad in wood and the ceiling had rough-hewn beams. A peaceful, calming place.

There was that which she didn't want to remember, so she concentrated on the scent of the room. Leather. Tobacco. The dying embers of the fire. And one thing more. She turned into the pillow and breathed deeply. Felt the warmth, the security it promised. Her heart responded. *He will take care of me.*

A soft knock on the door. He came in with an armful of wood, leaving the door open behind him. She watched him stir the fire into flame and place the logs upon it. *Daniel.*

He padded over to her, touched her hair, bent to kiss her cheek. Then he was gone again, the door closing behind his silent steps. *He will take care of me.*

When she woke again, Annie knew she'd been changed. The first thing she realized was that there was a block before a certain part of her mind. She didn't question it. Sitting up, she realized she was still in her clothes, though her shoes had been removed. She hunted around, found them under the edge of the bed and put them on, then turned her attention to the room.

It's neater than my room. Every single thing has its place. Wandering around, she touched the deer pelts that hung on the wall. Softer than she'd imagined. Some had been decorated with beads and silver medallions—Alec's work. More were rolled lengthwise and stood together in a corner, each tied with a single rawhide thong. *He always has a dozen of these laces in his pockets.*

She studied the map above the fireplace. *The Territory. He claims it as his home.* She moved to the desk, brushed her fingers over its polished mahogany surface, found the plans for indoor plumbing, the sketch for the framework of her cake. The design for the canyon gates he'd made so Tommy could insert the large iron brands the smith had created for Adam and Jesse, and that had given the canyon the name of Rocking Chair Ranch.

He saves everything. Her attention was caught by the shelves above the desk—dozens of books, wooden trains and toys, tools and metal parts of every description. And in the corner, sitting alone, a fat, bedraggled teddy bear with a single eye.

She picked it up, stroked its worn body, carried it to the bed and held it close against her. *Poor little one. Has he been ignoring you? After you have brought him such comfort in the past? Oh, Daniel, I remember the children we were. Life was so very simple then. Why has it changed?*

As if she'd conjured him out of the air, he was again at the door. He left it open but came to sit beside her on the bed. His gentle smile was half-hidden in his mustache as he reached out and touched the head of the bear in her arms. She leaned toward him and he drew her into his arms. She rested her head against his beating heart.

The old voice, cracked and melodious, fluttered into her mind. *I am here.*

Yes.

THE WOODSMAN'S ROSE

He will protect you.
Yes.
Our work is done. She will be well. Do you understand?
Yes.
The pain is over. The guilt is gone. The sorrow will remain for some time. None shall harm her. And none shall harm you, ever. He will protect you. He will be with you for as long as you live. There is nothing to fear. Do you believe?
Yes.
And slowly, the curtain rose. She cringed with the first touch of horror, and trembled there in his arms, but the old voice came again.
It is over. None shall harm her. He will be with you always. Have no fear.
She felt the sorrow well up from her heart and overflow, as the horror that had been so real faded like an early morning fog. As he rocked her in his arms, she became calm once again. But the sadness remained.
He whispered into her hair, "My precious girl. I love you."

※

WHEN HER FATHER ARRIVED, Annie was sitting with Molly and John Patrick in the back parlor. The fire burned cheerfully, for the day was gray, windy, and unseasonably cold. Irene had let him in and offered tea, which he gladly accepted.
"Feeling better today?" Owen asked his daughter, although the answer was obvious. Her eyes were shining, her smile bright. She reached for his hand as he sat next to her. There was a peacefulness about her that had been missing for some weeks, and it seemed to Owen she'd regained her usual serenity. He hadn't realized how much he depended on her composure until it was gone.
At Molly's invitation, they stayed to lunch. Daniel, Jake and Irene joined them at the table, along with the younger twins and

their wives. When they were ready to leave, Daniel walked out with them to the buggy. He had two burlap bags: one held a heated brick he placed at Annie's feet. The other he laid in her lap. He said not a word, but took her hand and kissed it before tucking the carriage robe in around her, then stood watching as they drove away.

Owen looked over at his daughter, saw the movement of her hands under the robe, struggling with the bag. "Got a present? Is it alive? If it is, I hope it doesn't eat too much. I'm a poor man, you know."

She sighed in mock sympathy. "Poor Papa."

"Nobody gives me presents."

"You don't need them. You have me!"

He laughed at that, then still feeling the urge to tease, Owen began to hum. But again she surprised him, as she joined in the song.

I've no sheep on the mountains nor boat on the lake,
Nor coin in my coffer to keep me awake;
Nor corn on my garner, nor fruit on my tree,
Yet the Maid of Llanwellyn smiles sweetly on me.

They sang until the cold wind took her breath away. Then he wrapped the robe more closely about her and pulled her in against him. She snuggled up as if she were a child and whispered, "I love you, Papa."

He put his hand on her hood and turned her face away from the wind. "*R'wy'n dy garu di, caraid.*"

When he stopped the buggy at their cottage, Owen jumped down and trotted around to help his daughter out. She was tangled in the robe, though, and they had some trouble extricating her. They were laughing at their clumsiness when, behind them, the town erupted.

Chapter 29

OWEN AND ANNIE TURNED to see Tommy Twelve Trees striding down the middle of the wide street, marching his son before him. Alec's hair was flying about his face like a wet black mop. His velveteen shirt was wet down to his breast, his arm twisted up behind his back as his father held on grimly. Though the silversmith was tall, slender, with the strength of a whip-cord, his struggles were ineffectual. Tommy had the advantage of three inches in height and forty pounds of muscle and, were it not for his fierce expression and the painful grimacing of his son, the scene would have been comical.

They could see Tommy's lips moving but his words were lost in the wind. At the doors to the livery, Tommy shoved his son inside. Alec went sprawling against a stall, then fell in a heap in the straw.

The street behind them filled with the curious, and Carolyn ran up to grab Owen by the arm. "Oh, Owen, you won't believe what he's done! He's been drinking all day."

"*Tommy?*"

"No, Alec. He's been in the saloon since last night—he broke in! He was there when they opened the bar at noon. Oh, Owen…"

"Carolyn, tell me what happened."

"He's told everyone Russell Travers killed his mother."

"Oh, dear God, no!" Annie cried. "Who was there—tell me quickly! Who was there?"

"Only Sam at first. He opened up and found him there. But then some of Benson's cowboys came in. One of them told Taylor, and now Sarah's spreading it all over town."

Annie turned back to the livery. *How did he find out? Only Daniel knew. Who could have told him?*

Rushing to the stables, Annie heard Tommy shouting, "Don't you know what you done? Don't you realize, don't you see the harm you done?"

Alec must have answered, for Tommy shouted again. "Dan'l? What's Dan'l got to do with it? He can beat th' hell outa you for all I care! Dan'l can take care of hisself!"

As Alec staggered to his feet, Annie saw his lips move, but still she didn't hear. Though the crowd had pressed closer, none dared come too near the raging smith.

"How can you say you don't know what you done? Don't you know she's been sick? Whaddya think this is gonna do—make 'er well again?"

With every question he roared, Tommy pushed his son backward until the youth was staggering into the corner of the stall. Then with a fierce grip that split the back of the velveteen shirt, he pulled Alec close, thrust his face into his son's and snarled, "I'll tell you what you done to her. I'll *show* you what you done!"

He let go and Alec slumped to the floor. As the youth struggled to his feet, using the stall as a crutch, Tommy reached for a buggy whip and advanced upon him with deadly intent.

Annie gasped and struck her mouth with her fist. Before another instant passed, she stood between the smith and his son.

"Annie!" Owen cried.

She put up a hand to keep her father from coming closer. *Stand still, stay there!* The smith was looking over her head, fixated on the stall behind her.

"Get outa my way." His voice was fierce.

"No."

"I'll kill 'im."

"No, Tommy."

THE WOODSMAN'S ROSE

"Get outa my way!"

"No."

"He deserves it."

She didn't argue, but reached out for the whip. He looked down at her. Her head came barely to his shoulder; she was slender and delicately built.

"Annie. Get outa the way."

"Give it to me, Tommy." She knew he would not, could not hurt her. He rocked on the balls of his feet as she repeated, "Give it to me."

He was a big man, a man of immense physical strength and the confidence that comes with it. Yet the whip fell from his hand and his head drooped.

Annie motioned again to her father, who clenched the blacksmith's arm and led him away.

SILENT AND BROODING, Tommy let Owen lead him home. But when his door opened, the first thing he saw was his worn chair by the fireplace. It was there that he'd held Jesse, soothed her battered spirit after his wife had soothed her bruises. He'd promised her protection there, and realized his love for her. He fell to his knees.

"My son." He buried his face in his hands. "My own son..."

As Owen stepped closer, Tommy stretched himself out facedown on the floor and reached for the chair. His words were little more than a moan.

"Oh, Jesse, Jesse... please. I'm sorry."

Chapter 30

OWEN STOOD ABSOLUTELY still. In his friend's voice, he'd heard more than the anguish of a neighbor or friend. Of a father. In his friend's voice, he'd heard the torment of a lover. And he didn't want to hear more.

As he looked down at the blacksmith, he knew it would be impossible to move him. He knew that, if he spoke, Tommy was beyond coherent response. Owen didn't consider himself a coward—if Annie hadn't been so quick, he'd have tried to protect Alec himself. He knew Tommy could have shaken him off like a fly, that he'd have to protect Alec with his own body. And he knew he would have done it.

Still, he wanted no more knowledge of the smith's love for Jesse. The rumors he'd heard, he'd discounted. He wouldn't speculate, wouldn't wonder. And he'd certainly never admit to anyone that he knew Tommy loved her.

We all love her, he consoled himself as he closed the cottage door and started back to the stable. *We are all upset by her illness. If some of us feel it a little more deeply, it is only natural. John Patrick is upset. His hands were shaking even today. Daniel is affected, though he has looked at no woman but my Annie.*

And no one needs to know if one of us is more upset than he is expected to be.

In the street, constable Ray Benson had been sending the crowds about their own business; at the livery, Owen found that Annie and Carolyn had covered Alec with blankets. The youth was blubbering in drunken, disconnected phrases, punctuated by pitiful moans. His daughter was white and shaking, and Owen hurried to her side.

He was less than an inch taller than she was, barrel-chested and solid of body and limb, though age had given him a tendency toward stoutness. Annie held onto him tightly, her head on his shoulder. Carolyn closed the doors so the dispersing crowds had nothing to see.

As Annie composed herself and stepped away from him, Owen saw the narrowing of her eyes that told him she was in pain. She froze for a moment, took a deep breath and held it. After another moment, she gave him a strained smile.

"You need some rest," he said.

"I can't leave him alone."

"I'll stay with him. You go on home. Carolyn will go with you. I'll send word when he comes to. Oh, and Carolyn, do you think you could bring me back some coffee? And maybe a blanket or two?"

"Of course. I'll be about ten minutes." She bustled off, coaxing Annie along with her. Once in the cottage, she took Annie's cloak and, noticing the girl's movements were slow and jerky, climbed with her to the loft and helped her into bed. Annie's eyes were closed before Carolyn had finished covering her.

"Do you want your laudanum?" she asked.

"No, thank you. I'll be all right."

"You rest now, dear. We'll let you know when he comes around."

"It's very important." Annie's voice was fading.

"I know, dear. Rest now. I promise to come get you as soon as you can talk to him."

"Thank you."

Carolyn descended to the kitchen and began to make coffee and a sandwich to take to the barn. She knew where to find everything she needed in this cottage, for she and Owen had been keeping company for some years. They'd arrived in White's Station almost at the same time, and a few years later, Carolyn's husband had run off with a dance-hall girl from Prescott, leaving her destitute but not despondent—she'd recognized his faithlessness early in their marriage.

Were it not for the Donovans and Owen, she'd have been hard-pressed to keep body and soul together. The inheritance she'd had from her mother was gone—gambled away. It was John Patrick who suggested that she turn her large home into a boardinghouse, and Owen who'd taught her to manage her money. She'd taken on a Mexican couple as chambermaid and cook; at first giving them only room and board. But as things got better, she paid them as well. Now María helped her embroider linen sheets and napkins, and her husband José had recently opened Joe's Café with their son Antonio.

She sliced ham and slathered the bread with Annie's home-made mustard, waiting for the coffee to boil so she could pour it into a Mason jar. As she worked, Carolyn ruminated on the citizens of White's Station. *We are a community of immigrants. For we've come from Wales and Ireland, Texas and Pennsylvania. From Sweden, Mexico, Kentucky, China and Louisiana. Only some of the children were born here and have a first-hand claim to the land. Only our few children. And Tommy.*

The community had accepted him and his wife as they accepted all decent, hard-working men and their families. There was too much danger in this wilderness for logical men to draw invisible boundaries between them. There were those who'd tried—newcomers who hadn't lasted long. For the real power in the community was vested in those men like Donovan, Benson, Griffiths and Twelve Trees—men who had the intelligence to realize that neighbors must live together. Or die together.

Russell Travers was an anomaly in this town. His drunkenness and thievery were tolerated because of his father's crippled condition. He wouldn't listen to Ray Benson's advice, and one of the Donovan boys—I

THE WOODSMAN'S ROSE

don't remember which, perhaps Brian?—beat him almost senseless for crippling a horse. But Russell never learned and he finally went too far, and he paid for his wildness with his life.

It's too bad that all of his evil deeds didn't die with him.

Chapter 31

WHEN CAROLYN KNOCKED on the door of the livery, Owen removed the bar to let her in. He took the blankets from her and she set the coffee and sandwich on Tommy's workbench.

"How is she?" he asked.

"She should be asleep by now. She said she'd be fine, didn't want her medicine."

Owen let out a long breath as the youth on the floor snorted and mumbled, deep in a drunken stupor.

"Poor thing," Carolyn said.

Owen put an arm around her shoulders and kissed her cheek. When she blushed, he thought her quite the prettiest woman he knew.

"Stop that!" she protested, but she didn't move away.

"How did he get so wet?"

Carolyn let out one small giggle. "I shouldn't laugh. But they were a sight. Ray Benson came to get Tommy when Alec started breaking things up in the saloon. Tommy got there in time to hear... Anyway, Tommy grabbed him and hauled him out to the street and dunked his head in the horse-trough. For a minute, I didn't think he'd let him up again. And then... but you saw the rest." She was serious again. "I wonder what will happen between them now?"

Owen had no answer as he escorted her to the stable doors. He'd been careful to let her stay for only a few minutes; the sodden youth in the stall wouldn't pass muster as a chaperon. But he did kiss her cheek again as she left, and when she'd gone back to his daughter, he

THE WOODSMAN'S ROSE

settled himself into the one chair available, glad for the warmth of the blankets and coffee, wondering how long his vigil might be.

He woke with a start, feeling another presence. The gray light of day had faded; it was just bright enough in the stable to let him see Tommy leaning over the stall and looking down at his son. *I must not have barred the door when Carolyn left. I wonder how long he's been here.*

The chair creaked as he got up to stand next to the smith. Tommy's bronze face was haggard and lined with pain.

"Don't worry, Owen. I won't hurt 'im now."

The bootmaker put a hand on his friend's arm and they stood quietly for a minute.

"How did he find out?" Owen asked.

Tommy shrugged. "Dan'l knew, but I don't think he woulda told 'im." After another moment's silence, the smith continued, "It's the only logical answer. Only one man 'round here woulda ever hurt a woman. An' Dan'l told us 'e was gone, didn't he? So we knew it wasn't some stranger. An' nobody left town 'round that time, so it musta been someone who died.

"Who died after Elena was killed? Jim Callendar fell offa thet ladder an' hung on for a coupla days. But 'e was a li'l, timid guy, an' Elena—she'd'a chewed 'im up an' spit 'im out. Then ol' man Travers died, but 'e hadn't been outa that cabin in three years 'r more. So who's left? Jus' Russell. You'd think everybody woulda figgered it out long ago." Tommy let out a long breath. "Not that it woulda hurt 'er less then, than it will now. I jus' hope..."

"So do I, Tommy."

Once more, silence descended between them. Then Owen realized the blacksmith was speaking to him again.

"You wanna go get some supper?"

"I told Annie I'd stay with him 'til he comes to."

"Won't be for quite a while, if he's anythin' like 'is ol' man." Tommy turned around to lean against the stall. "I got good an' drunk once m'self, when the school fired Elena. I figgered she'd be goin' back home t' her papa an' there'd never be another chance for me. Didn't come 'round for close t' two days. An' when I did—boy, I wisht I hadn't.

"Was she mad—madder'n a hornet that got swatted! Lambasted me up one side an' down t'other. Said I shoulda known better. Said I oughta learn what love really means. Didn't lose much time teachin' me, either, if you get my drift!" The smith became serious again. "She'd know what t' tell 'im, Owen. But 'e don't listen t' me. That's the hell of it. I don't unnerstan' him, an' he don' unnerstan' me. We jus' sit an' jaw at each other, an' neither one o' us gets anywhere.

"We're jus' so differnt. We look differnt, we act differnt. We even talk differnt. Sometimes I think 'e swallowed a book as a kid, way 'e talks."

The bootmaker essayed a small joke. "You walk the same, though. Nobody ever hears either one of you coming."

"Guess thet's somethin'."

"But I know what you mean. I went through it with Lowell. Came a time when he thought he knew everything. Wouldn't listen to a word. But he got over it, and Alec will, too.

"We're old men to them, Tommy. Old and foolish. But I remember when I thought my father was a fool, too. Surprised me how quick he learned everything after that."

"Las' time I saw my father, I was five years ol'. I remember thinkin' he knew everythin'. He was a healer—what you folk call the medicine man. An' what 'e couldn't cure couldn't be cured. There was always folks comin' round t' see him, bringin' him presents. He was the biggest man I knew, any way you wanna measure it. That's what I wanna be for 'im. But somehow it always comes out wrong."

THE WOODSMAN'S ROSE

Owen didn't know how to respond. After a moment Tommy spoke again.

"Cold in here, ain't it? Lemme light a fire in the forge. There's more coal over there in the bin for later." After the fire was roaring, he added, "I'm goin' down t' Joe's. Want me t' bring you somethin'?"

"Sounds good. Make it those hot tamales, and about a pound of cornbread." Owen held out money but the smith ignored it.

"Nope, it's on me. Can't let you folks take care of everythin'!"

Chapter 32

EARLY THE NEXT MORNING, Annie returned to the livery with no trace of the headache. She looked down at her father, a smile playing on her lips. Owen was sleeping in the chair, his chin resting against his chest, the top of his bald head looking out at the world like an expressionless face. She shook his arm gently.

"Papa," she murmured. "Papa, I brought you some coffee."

"Uh... hmmm?"

"I brought you some coffee."

"Hmm. Good girl." He stood, stretched and groaned, held out a hand for the cup. The fire in the forge had died down to embers and it was cold again. But the north wind seemed to have blown itself out and the day was calm and still. Owen replenished the fire. "By the way, Tommy came in last night after dark. He wasn't mad any more—just hurt, I think. And confused."

"Oh, I'm glad. I hope we can help them sort this out."

In his half-sleeping state, Alec heard the voices discussing his father, but his mind couldn't grasp the content of their speech. He moaned and rolled over onto his back. He lay motionless, his breathing irregular and punctuated with little sounds of pain. His tongue was thick, his lips cracked and dry, and his head pounded to the rhythm of their words. *Why do I feel so lousy? Where the hell am I?*

He forced his eyes open. Peering out through slits, he realized that he was in the livery stable, lying on the floor in the hay. *What's happened? Where's my father?*

THE WOODSMAN'S ROSE

Like a clap of thunder, memories exploded in his brain. Daniel's insult was overlaid with his father's threats, in turn drowned out by the realization of what he'd done. He'd betrayed his friend, shamed his father. And caused such anguish for a girl who'd been his only close companion as a boy. He writhed in agony.

I am worthless. He heard his father's muttered words again. *How could you do this? Your mother would be ashamed of you.* Then his mother's voice. *A man does not take actions which will cause his friends to be hurt.*

I am worthless. Groaning with pain, he raised himself up enough to reach the long knife in his boot. *I do not deserve to live.*

His hands were weak and shaking and the knife was taken from him. He moaned again. "Let me die."

"No." The voice was sweet and low, and stirred an older memory.

"I deserve to die."

"No. You have only made a mistake." He lay back helplessly in the hay, closing his eyes as a gentle hand touched his cheek.

"Mama," he whispered brokenly. "Mama." And the dam he'd created, that had held the tears for so long, crumbled into bits and he lay sobbing on the cold, hard floor.

Through the hand that caressed his hair, Annie heard the torment in his heart.

No one understands.

I understand. My mother has also gone.

Were you there? Did you see it?

Yes. And I could do nothing.

Nothing! So much pain. And I could do nothing.

Yes. I know.

It was my fault.

No.

I should have been there.

You could not know.

I should have known.
No. It is not for such as you and I to see.
I want her. I want her back!
I know, caraid. We all want her back. She was so lovely. So loving.
It isn't fair!
No, caraid. It is not fair. Yet there is nothing we can do to change it. We must accept it. For her sake. She would not want us to suffer so.
She loved me.
She loves you still. Caraid, love does not end. Love lives forever. Long after this world is gone, she will love you. Love you as she has loved no other.
I have shamed her.
She forgives you.
No.
Yes. Her love knows no bounds.
I have shamed my father.
He will forgive you.
He doesn't understand.
You must explain. You must listen. You must try to understand.
He doesn't grieve.
He does, caraid.
No. He laughs, he talks. He acts the clown.
It is his way, as yours is silence. Listen with your heart and hear his grief.
He grieves?
He does. As you do.
I have hurt my friends.
They will understand. They will forgive you if you ask.
She will hate me.
She will not. This I know for certain.
How do you know?
It was told to me. By one who sees.

THE WOODSMAN'S ROSE

I must make amends. I must apologize.
All will be forgiven.
Do you forgive me?
Yes, caraid, I forgive you.

OWEN WATCHED HIS DAUGHTER stroke the hair of the sobbing youth. In something less than a minute, Alec's wild grief had abated, though his breath still came in shuddering gasps and his body shook as with ague. When less than another minute had passed, he reached up for Annie and was folded into her arms. Not a single word had been spoken between them. Yet as Owen watched the dark head resting on his daughter's shoulder, he knew she'd found a way to comfort him.

He closed the stable doors and slid the bar into place. He laid a blanket over them and went back to his chair.

She was fey. He'd always known it. And now she had realized the fullness of her gift.

Chapter 33

IT WASN'T LONG BEFORE Alec slept again. He didn't thrash or moan and the twitching of his body had stilled. As Annie slid her arm from under his head, Owen rose and helped her to her feet, brushed the remnants of hay from her clothes.

"I'm sorry, Papa, but could you stay with him for a while longer? I need to talk to Tommy." With an elfin grin, she added, "I promise to make you two breakfasts when we get home."

There was no answer to her knock on the red door, but Annie let herself in. The smith was sitting in his chair by the fire, deep in thought or dreams; Annie took off her cloak and sat on the edge of the hassock at his knee. For several moments he was silent, then he looked over and took her hand in his.

"I'm sorry, Annie. You know I'd never hurt you."

"I know, Tommy. I wasn't afraid."

He reached out to remove a straw from her hair. He studied it for a minute then asked, "How is he?"

"He's sleeping now. I think he'll be all right. But, Tommy, he needs you."

The smith laughed without humor, flicking the straw into the fireplace. "No, Annie. I'm the last thing he needs."

"That's not true, Tommy. He thinks you don't understand him, that you blame him. He thinks it's his fault Elena died."

With narrowed eyes, the smith regarded her, then turned his attention back to the fire. "He told me once it was my fault."

THE WOODSMAN'S ROSE

"He doesn't believe that. Maybe he was trying to shift the blame from himself. Tommy, he needs you."

"He hates me."

"No, he doesn't. He needs you. He's so full of pain. He needs to talk to you about it."

The smith pushed his face up close to hers, his black eyes brilliant with unshed tears. "What about me, Annie? What about my pain? She was my wife—my life! Does he need t' talk about that, too?"

"Yes. He needs to know he's not alone in his grief. And so do you." She pressed her palm against his face. "Tommy, he's like a ship that's lost at sea. He can't find a star to steer by. You're the only one who can help him."

He sat back, silent again, staring into the flames. Slowly his eyes closed and he leaned his head against the chair.

"Tommy." She waited for him to look at her. "He wanted to die. I took his knife away."

As his face worked, he squeezed her hand so hard it hurt. "I guess you saved us both from ourselves, girl. Thank you, Annie. More'n I can say."

He stood, pulled her to her feet and hugged her tightly. "You're sure he wants me?" He looked down upon her in wonderment, his voice gruff with emotion. "You better be right, girl, or I'll have you over my knee!"

"You'll have to catch me first!"

He turned at the door, serious once again. "Thank you."

"Any time," Annie replied.

※

THE SMITH SENT OWEN home to his breakfasts. Then, as he'd done the night before, he leaned against the stall, watching his son sleep. Always had the boy been a mystery to him. His somber mien, his sensitivity, his brooding and questioning nature were foreign to the big-hearted, open-handed blacksmith. Nor did he inherit these tendencies from Elena, whose elemental nature seemed to change from one day to the next.

Elena. With her flashing eyes, her profile at rest as pure and clean as the cameo. But repose came seldom, for Elena was ruled by passion. She would laugh, cry, fight at the drop of a hat, and as a lover had been tender and wild by turns. The only constant thing about Elena was that she was always changing. He had worshiped her.

Since she'd been killed, there was an emptiness in Tommy's life, in his heart. But he knew it was nothing compared to what drove his son. Tommy wished again that it had been he, and not his son, who had found her there in the yard, beaten and ravished. Dying.

He hung his head for a moment. *She was the glue that made us a family. Without her, we are just a man and a boy struggling with our problems. And with each other.*

Owen's words filled Tommy's mind. But he'd never thought his father a fool. He'd never had a chance to really know him, for the man they called Twelve Trees was killed when his son was ten years old and caught in the grip of the missionary school. They told him his father had been mistaken for an Apache warrior and killed in retaliation for a raid on a southern settlement.

He'd never believed it.

My father was a quiet man. A man who thought tradition and ritual were important. A man who took life seriously. Maybe my son inherits this from him. Maybe I can talk to him as my father talked to me. Maybe I can find a way to teach him as my father taught me.

He turned away, deep in thought, and began to putter around his shop. The instinct of years took over as he stoked the fire in the forge and reached for his tools. Soon the rhythmic hammering of metal on metal began.

The sound disrupted Alec's dreams, the vision of his mother fading. The rhythm of the hammer didn't break as he struggled to his

THE WOODSMAN'S ROSE

feet. He made an effort to brush some of the straw from his clothing and ran his fingers through his damp, matted hair. He saw his knife in the hay, bent to pick it up, slipped it into the sheath inside his boot. His father was still at the forge, oblivious to his movements.

I could kill him now, and he would have no chance to defend himself. How many times have I wished him dead instead of her? On silent feet, he moved to the wall and grabbed a buggy whip.

Chapter 34

TOMMY LOOKED UP FROM his work as Alec approached and offered him the whip. The smith put down his hammer and the horseshoe he was working on, wiped his hands on his shirt. He took the whip, gave it a good look, then threw it into a corner.

"I deserve it," Alec admitted.

"Mebbe. But I'm not in the mood."

Alec stared hard at his father, his eyes narrowing.

"You did wrong, boy," Tommy said. "You hurt Jesse. An' I hafta tell ya, I jus' don't unnerstand why."

"Because I am a fool. All I could think was that, somehow, if I knew who did it, it would make it easier. But it didn't. It didn't make any difference at all.

"And I just couldn't..." Alec went on. "I'd waited so long to find out, and it didn't make any difference at all. I just wanted to forget. I thought—I don't know what I thought any more. I didn't mean to hurt her. I just wanted to forget."

"Did you?" The question was spoken softly, but cut to the bone.

"*NO!*" Alec swayed on his feet. "No. How could I ever forget?"

"Do you still want to?"

"No." It was hardly more than a whisper. "I just want it not to hurt so much."

A long arm reached out to him. A strong hand fastened itself behind his head. He was pulled in against the broad chest, held by arms that seemed made of steel. He clutched the sleeves, pressed

THE WOODSMAN'S ROSE

himself tight as if to draw on the strength of his father's body, and gave way to sobs once more.

"I want her back!" he cried. And heard the deep, sonorous voice whisper brokenly.

"So do I, boy. So do I."

LATE IN THE AFTERNOON, when the stable was warm with fire and steam, Annie returned. At his workbench Alec sat engrossed, engraving a silver medallion. Approximately the size of a silver dollar, but an irregular shape, he'd carved the upper portion with tiny leaves, and was now working on the lower half, carving in the trunks. He was still wearing the torn velveteen shirt.

She stood behind his shoulder as he worked silently. She'd never been at ease with him, although they were close in age. They'd been in school together for several years and Annie had grown up in the cottage next door, yet they'd never become close, for her shyness was as pronounced as his reticence. He put his tools down finally and picked the piece up, showing her that the reverse side was identical.

"It's beautiful," she murmured.

He took her hand, opened it, and placed the medallion in her palm. "For you. With my thanks."

"Thank you!" She held it up to let the light sparkle through. "I've always admired your work. I've always wanted one of these."

From his forge, Tommy watched them and was satisfied. *Maybe he'll learn. Maybe it won't be so bad after all. He's started to make amends. I only hope Daniel can forgive him.*

He said he'd go tomorrow. I guess he has to work up the courage. It ain't easy to tell your best friend you're a fool. And who would know better than me? I once accused John Patrick of prejudice, just because he forgot to invite me and Elena to some little shindig when he first moved here. *Wasn't he the only man who ever came to these parts and talked to the tribe before he moved onto the land?*

I guess we're all fools from time to time. I guess that's why we need our friends so bad—keeps us humble. His hammer rang with every thought. *I hope Daniel can forgive him.*

THAT AFTERNOON, BRIAN rode into town to pick up supplies and returned to the canyon with the news that Jesse's secret was a secret no more.

Adam's eyes narrowed to slits and his jaw grew hard. He paced endlessly up and down in the barn, trying to find a reason, any reason, not to tell her. *How can I face her with this?* But she was sure to hear it sometime and he cursed himself as a coward. *How can I let anyone else?*

With that final thought, he crushed out his cigarette and strode to the house, stalking past his brother and Rebecca at the kitchen table, knowing he'd lose his courage if he hesitated at all. At the bedroom door he faltered, his hand on the knob, the knot in his heart choking him. But she called out to him.

He went in slowly, like a condemned man to execution, and saw the faint tinge of rose in her cheeks. She was still so sick, her small strength used up combatting the nausea she suffered. He took her hands and brushed his lips over them.

"What's wrong?" she asked.

He could scarcely reply. "Jesse, there's something I've got to tell you. It's bad news, love. Brian heard it in town." He stroked her bright hair, fighting for words as her troubled frown questioned him.

"Jesse," he managed to say, "it's about your brother. And... and Elena. Alec told... everyone in town..."

He couldn't go on. His wife nodded silently and closed her eyes against the day. She didn't respond and she didn't cry. But it was

THE WOODSMAN'S ROSE

a long hour before her trembling stopped, and another before she slept.

Chapter 35

AS HE LEANED AGAINST the porch railing of his parents' house, Daniel pulled at the ends of his mustache and regarded the youth who stood before him. Alec had confessed his guilt, explained but not pleaded, and declared himself willing to make whatever amends were necessary. He'd promised nothing, but apologized for the the distress he'd brought to his friend. To his brother.

He has acted like a man. A man and not a boy. He understands he was wrong. He's so proud—it's his pride that makes him admit he was wrong.

The woodsman spoke slowly, deliberately. "I was trying to protect you, Alec. To protect you and Jesse."

Alec's dusky face became splotchy, but his eyes didn't waver. "I understand that now."

"What you did to me wasn't so bad—it was just a lack of faith. Maybe I would have felt the same if I'd been in your shoes. Maybe from your point of view, I was wrong. Maybe it would have been better for you to know right away.

"But I had to do what I thought was most important. It was a hard choice. You were in pain, I know. But Jesse wasn't strong enough, and I had to protect her."

"Yes. You did what I failed to do. She was my friend, too. Almost as long as you have been. And I have failed her."

"What you've done to her, Alec, is infinitely worse than what you've done to me. And if it weren't for that, there would be nothing between us to forgive."

THE WOODSMAN'S ROSE

The tension in the silversmith's face relaxed. "I don't know if she will speak to me. And no matter what I say, it won't take away what I've done. I can't change that. But if she will see me, I will apologize."

Daniel gave him a word of caution. "Adam may not let you in." Adam's temper wasn't a thing to be taken lightly. Still, his brother was a fair man, and Brian would be there to make sure no actual murder was committed. It might be a very good thing for Alec to face him—it might bring home to him just how important Jesse was to them.

"I'll go see her tomorrow."

"Why not today?"

Alec held out his hands. "Today I have only words."

"You can't buy it, Alec," Daniel responded, looking his friend in the eye. "And if you could, she wouldn't sell it to you."

"I only meant to show her how much I have valued her friendship in the past."

It was the woodsman's turn to consider, but before he could speak, Alec added, "Perhaps if she can forgive me, I will bring her something to show my thanks."

After some hesitation, he offered Daniel his hand, which was accepted immediately.

"I'll go now," the silversmith said.

He leaped onto a wiry pinto mustang and set off for the canyon. Not infrequently, the urge to turn back possessed him. He stopped for a moment to touch the gates his father had made—the pair of brands with the initials *A* and *J* entwined to form the stylized rocking chair that had given the canyon ranch its name. His shoulders were just a bit squarer, his spine a bit straighter as he rode down the trail to the cabin.

He pulled his horse up and slipped from the saddle, knocked lightly on the door. The man he faced was as tall as he was, broader of shoulder, lean and hard of body. His left hand clenched, seeming to waver over the gun he didn't wear. His voice was little more than a hiss as he demanded, "What do you want?"

"To see Jesse."

"Haven't you done her enough harm?" Adam's eyes blazed blue fire.

"I have come to apologize."

"I should horsewhip you."

The silversmith stood his ground. "I'd like to see her first. Then you may do with me what you wish."

"And if she doesn't want to see you?"

"Then I will go, and I will come back when she will see me."

Without another word Adam turned on his heel, shutting the door in Alec's face. After several long minutes, he opened it again and stood aside, motioned for Alec to come in. As he passed, Adam gripped his arm and held it hard, pulled him in face to face. "If you hurt her again, I will horsewhip you!"

Though scarcely audible, Alec knew it wasn't an empty threat. He approached the door to Jesse's room and his first look at her, lying on a bed close to the fireplace, tore at his heart. He took the hand she stretched out to him, sank to his knees beside her. *So small, so delicate. How could I have hurt one who is so helpless?* He bent over until his forehead rested on her hand. He could find no words to say.

"Alec." Her voice was small and breathless, and he looked up. "I'm glad to see you."

"Jesse." He choked on her name. "Jesse, I'm sorry." He struggled with his breath, brought himself under control again. "I have come to apologize. Jesse, I know I've hurt you. I can't explain why, except that I am a fool. I don't ask you to forgive me. I don't deserve it. But please believe I am sorry. And that I will never be so thoughtless again." Again he had to stop and breathe. "You were my friend for many years. Please believe that I did not mean to hurt you."

THE WOODSMAN'S ROSE

"Alec, I'm still your friend. I know you wouldn't do anything to hurt me."

"But, Jesse, I told... everyone. About Mama. About..."

"About Russell. Alec, did you do that to hurt me?"

"No!" He calmed himself with an effort. "No. On my mother's spirit I swear to you. I did it because..."

"Because you were angry." She completed his sentence again. Silently he nodded, swaying on his knees. "I'm glad you told. Now everyone knows. And I don't have to worry any more about someone finding out."

"Jesse... " He couldn't quite believe what he'd heard. He bent down over her hand once more, kissed it fervently. He stood beside her bed for a moment, watching as her eyes fell closed. Then he turned quietly and left her.

He stood before her husband in silence. Adam gestured toward the door.

"Get out of here." But there was no threat. Alec took one last look at the peaceful sleeping girl and left them.

Adam went back to his wife at once. He touched the fragile hand lying on the quilt and found it cold. He tucked it in and spread another afghan over the bed, but was still not satisfied. Slowly, gently, he wrapped the covers around her and lifted her in his arms. He carried her to the old rocking chair in the parlor and sat with her on his lap. She murmured once, then curled in against him. Between his warmth and that of the fire, she'd be safe.

He bent his dark head over her bright one and rocked her back to sleep. *Dear God, don't let there be any more. Let this be the end. Let us deal with this pain and help her recover. Let all of us who know defend her against her fears. Make her well. Make her happy. Keep her warm. Protect her.*

GIFFORD MACSHANE

BRIAN WATCHED FROM the doorway and gave his twin a look full of hope. The big man had had a long, secret talk with Daniel. He knew the woodsman blamed himself for telling Alec, though he'd only given his friend the same clue he'd given everyone else long ago. Brian guessed that there was much more Daniel hadn't told, but he'd asked for no details, knowing he'd receive none. What his brother knew about Jesse would go to his grave with him. The only person he might confide in was Annie. *And Annie can no more hurt anyone than she can fly. I trust them both.*

Daniel's mighty lucky to have her.

Chapter 36

IT HAD BECOME A TRADITION for the Griffiths to gather at the dairy farm on the one day Owen closed his shop, and Daniel had fallen into the habit of spending Sundays with them. Annie had a cold and was content to curl up on the sofa by the fire with her head on his shoulder. As Evelyn brought her a tisane and peppermint drops, Daniel teased her. "Spoiled rotten, aren't you?"

Her elfin grin answered him.

"You leave her alone," Evelyn demanded. "She deserves a little spoiling now and again."

"Thank you," Annie said.

"It's the least I can do." Evelyn gave her a wink. "After all, you'll be taking him off our hands soon. Might as well be spoiled now, before the misery begins!"

Daniel laughed at his sister's retreating back, then bent to kiss Annie's forehead.

"Soon?" he asked, playing with the ring on her finger.

"Daniel..."

"All right, *aroon*. I just thought I'd ask."

"I love you, Daniel," she whispered.

"I know, my love. And I can wait as long as I have to. But Annie..." He looked deeply into her pale eyes. "I want you."

She murmured, "I know," and hid her face against him.

When she'd spoken to her father about marriage, Annie had been satisfied with his answer, but as time went on, she found there was a gap between what her father had said and what she needed to know. She loved Daniel. She loved his kisses, his embrace, the way his fingers played in her hair. The way his deep gruff voice sounded in her ear. The way he pulled her close against him, making no secret of his desire. She loved him, and the fluttering in her heart, in her belly, told her she wanted him, too. But she needed to know what he'd do to her and she was too shy to ask him.

She'd spoken to Evelyn, who rhapsodized about her husband for a full fifteen minutes. Annie was glad that her sister-in-law was so content in her marriage, but the response had included nothing in the way of fact and she was as unsure as ever. She spoke to her father again, who told her not to worry and repeated that Daniel would be gentle. *But how will he be gentle? How will he touch me? How will he know if he hurts me?* As he took his leave of her that evening, Annie found herself clinging to him. She wanted so much from him, and realized for the first time that she was afraid.

She was trembling when their kiss ended and she whispered his name.

"I love you, Annie," he murmured, the rough voice low and soft. He took her face between his hands. "I love you, *aroon*. And I'll wait." She sank against his chest, felt his fingers playing in her hair again. "I won't rush you, sweetheart. I know it's a big step. I want you to be sure." He brushed his lips against hers once more. "Good night, *aroon*. Take care of yourself."

"Good night," she whispered. "Thank you."

He kissed her one more time. "Thank you, sweetheart. For loving me."

ANNIE'S COLD WASN'T serious and within days she was feeling fine. But the rain still came, fine and soft, and confinement to the cottage was making her jumpy. Owen was busy filling orders, but there were few customers in the shop for her to wait on.

THE WOODSMAN'S ROSE

She woke one morning with the urge to bake. In contrast to the big, airy kitchen at her brother's dairy farm, her own kitchen was set in a tiny alcove between the back door and the stairs to the loft. Its single window faced north and it would have been dreary but for the cheerful yellow curtains, and the shining copper pans hung from the ceiling.

The floor space was largely taken up by a table and two chairs, so Annie had to plan each step carefully. She made the dough for two loaves of bread and put them on the windowsill to rise, then decided to make some pies. When the first one came out of the oven, she put the second in and kneaded the bread again. As she placed the bread back on the windowsill, she caught a glimpse of Tommy returning to the house next door. She called out to him and was answered with a broad smile. On impulse, she grabbed her cloak and the warm pie and ran out into the misty rain. Tommy was holding the door open for her when she got there.

"Whaddya doin' out in the rain?" he demanded.

"Bringing you a pie!"

He took it from her, sniffed at the aroma of apples, cinnamon and nutmeg, let out a long sigh as he headed for the kitchen. "You know where t' hang your coat," he said over his shoulder. "I'm gettin' me a knife!"

She hung her cloak on a peg in the hall and followed him through to the kitchen. He'd already put two plates on the table. As she entered, he asked, "Coffee or milk?"

"Milk," she decided. "Gotta keep my brother in business!"

He laughed with her and handed her a fork, then brought two large glasses of milk to the table. He sat down and cut a quarter of the pie, put it on a plate and offered it to her.

"No, thanks," she said. "I'll have about a third of that."

"Don't like your own cookin', hey?" the smith teased, as he cut her a piece that was just slightly smaller. Without waiting for her answer, he dug in.

"Oh, Annie," he sighed, "you are some wonderful cook!" He finished his piece quickly and eyed the remaining slices. "Think I might have another," he said in an undertone.

"The cook would be flattered."

He helped himself to another quarter. When he finished it, he patted his stomach while he eyed the remaining piece. "Guess I really should save some for Alec."

"Guess you really should," she echoed with a twinkle in her eye. "But you could finish this piece."

"Annie, you're a wonderful girl. I dunno why Dan'l ain't married you yet!"

Her blush was just fading when he finished the pie. He studied her face closely.

"I say somethin' wrong?"

"No. It's just..."

"You wanna talk about it?"

"No," she said. "Yes. I don't know."

A moment later he was standing at her side, helping her to her feet. "He done somethin' t' hurt you?"

"Oh, no. It's nothing like that. It's just... I just..."

"You jus' don't know what you're gettin' inta. Is that it?"

She nodded, looked up at him quickly before she turned her face away once more, but not before he saw the fire on her cheek.

"Let's go inside an' set down," he suggested. She followed without protest. He leaned back in an armchair and patted the hassock at his knee.

She sat, giving him a shy smile. Tommy was more to her than a friend, more than a favorite uncle. His wife, Elena, had taken the

THE WOODSMAN'S ROSE

place of the mother she'd barely known, and Annie regarded Tommy as a second father.

"Annie, if you're scared, it's only natural. Girl," he said, reaching for her hand, "don't be ashamed. Don't ever be ashamed o' your feelin's. You're entitled t' be scared. Jus' like you're entitled t' be in love with 'im."

The brightness of her cheeks faded to rose; she blinked back the tears that threatened. Tommy settled into his chair and gazed into the fireplace.

"Women," he said, "are a lot differnt from men. A man does a lotta things by instinct, sorta by the seat o' his pants. But a woman likes t' plan things out, likes t' know what's happenin' every step o' the way. A woman likes t' know what she's gonna get at the end o' the recipe. A man don't always care, long as it's somethin' he can eat.

"But, Annie, life's not always gonna run accordin' t' plan. An' love—well, love's hardly ever what you plan it t' be. Man has an advantage then, 'cause he can be satisfied with what happens, long as 'e knows 'e's loved. But a woman wants certain things, an' sometimes, if they don't happen jus' so, she's afraid it ain't really love after all.

"Now, you could ask me what's goin' t' happen b'tween you an' Dan'l. You could ask me how Dan'l's gonna love you, but there's jus' no way for me t' know. Every man's differnt. Every man's got his own way o' talkin', o' walkin', o' makin' love. An' there's no one who can tell you what that's goin' t' be. In fact, 'til he does it for the first time, a man don't rightly know hisself.

"The most important thing for you t' remember is you don't hafta let him do anythin' you don't want 'im to. A man has no right t' hurt a woman. Not her body, an' not her feelin's. If he does anythin' you don't like, you jus' tell him t' stop.

"An', Annie, he will stop if you ask him to. I know he will." He leaned toward her again. "You unnerstant me?"

"Yes. Tommy..."

"Ump-umm. You have any trouble with thet boy, you jus' lemme know an' I'll beat the livin' hell outa him!"

"You won't have to," she said softly. "He'd never hurt me."

"I know it, an' you know it. You do. Now all you hafta do is let yourself trust 'im."

Chapter 37

THE WEATHER CLEARED on Friday and a warm breeze dried the puddles and left the world sparkling. Early Sunday morning, Annie packed a picnic lunch and waited impatiently at the farmhouse for Daniel.

She didn't care where they went. "Just someplace pretty," she said. He took the basket and her hand, and they cut across the farm and fields, heading toward the foothills. They walked in silence, but her hand closed tightly on his from time to time and she was supremely content.

They climbed a little hill and at the top of it, he brought them to a stop.

"Oh!" she gasped. Two steps into the field brimming with wildflowers, she sank to her knees. "Ohhh," she sighed, looking out across the open meadow. It stretched before her for several acres, a whole valley full of flowers, white and gold and purple and red and pink. Her arms reached out as if she could embrace it all.

"Ohhh. How beautiful!" she breathed. "Oh, Daniel, thank you! I... oh, how I needed this!" She stretched herself out, buried her face in the flowers and sighed again.

When she rolled over, his face was right there. She reached for him, locked her arms around his neck and gazed into his dark blue eyes. And there in the warm soft sun of spring, in this field of flowers nodding gently in the breeze, she felt her fears disperse.

She met his kiss with lips that hungered for him. He pulled her close against him and cradled her head in his hands. She reached for his shoulders, then ran her fingers down his back. He pressed her closer and she sighed, then sought his lips again.

"*Aroon.*" His voice was deeper, rougher than she'd ever heard it. "I want to see you."

In a moment, she lay naked among the flowers, and the sun and his warm hands were touching her where she'd never been touched before. She knew she'd helped him with the buttons, the laces, yet she felt no shame.

His lips followed his hands now and her breath caught in her throat. She felt herself straining toward him, reaching for his hair, losing her fingers in its softness. He raised his head, looked down at her, and slowly pulled himself away.

"*Aroon,*" he whispered, his voice ragged with passion. "Annie, stop me. Before it's too late."

She gazed up at him through hooded lids and saw the sunlight glinting on the copper-colored hairs showing between the laces of his shirt. She'd wanted for so long to touch them, to see if they were as warm and soft as they appeared. She lifted her hand, tangled her fingers in the laces, brushed them over his chest.

As he moaned, his head tilted back. She could read his desire in the corded muscles of his neck, the labored heaving of his chest. She slipped her other hand up inside his shirt and watched in awe as he surrendered to his need of her. With one smooth motion, he stripped the shirt off and threw it aside, bent to take her face in both his hands. His mouth claimed hers and she felt the longing deep within him. The copper-colored hairs brushed against her and she wrapped her arms around him. She heard his soft moan as he slid her body in beneath his. Her blood took fire from his. He whispered brokenly into her ear.

Love you... want you... need you... want you... Then with a knowledge as ancient as her bloodlines, she shifted under him,

THE WOODSMAN'S ROSE

listened as his words descended into moans, and knew she echoed every one.

Chapter 38

ANNIE WOKE IN THE SHADE of the pines, her head pillowed by his shirt. Her dress had been buttoned, but her feet were still bare. She heard the stream babbling close by. *There are some who'd say I should be ashamed. But I love him and I know now I can be happy being his wife.*

Her lips twitched as she thought of the pain she'd been prepared for and realized that, for others, it might have seemed arduous. But she'd known pain that could bring her to her knees, so swiftly and violently would it strike. Pain that was unremitting for hours or days, that could make her moan through her unconsciousness. It was that pain she'd anticipated. And hadn't found.

She was half asleep again when she felt his hand in her hair. She looked up at him, his deep blue eyes, his mustache, his wide shoulders, and the soft covering of copper-colored hair she loved. She reached for him, found herself cradled in his arms like a baby. With his face in her hair, he whispered her name.

"*Aroon*, forgive me."

"*Arrah*," she answered, "I love you."

He thought his heart would burst. He couldn't catch his breath. It was his word, his language, not hers. *Arrah*. Beloved. He pulled her close, held her tightly, felt the joy that stung his eyelids. And breathed again into her ear, "I love you, Annie. I love you so much. Marry me, *aroon*. I need you."

He sought her lips, a long and tender kiss, then she answered, "Yes."

THE WOODSMAN'S ROSE

"Tell me when." It was a demand, a plea. He brushed her hair back. "Tell me, *aroon*. Please."

"Beltaine." An ancient day, a rite of spring and of fertility. A day when all the world wore green. A day for lovers. A day just ten little days away.

"I love you. Oh, Annie, you are the most beautiful thing in this whole world." *She'll be mine forever. I will never let her go.*

When he looked down at her again, the little smile was still there. She bit her lower lip and reached up for his scarf, tugged at the knot. He groaned in protest, but he couldn't stop her. He'd seen her, all of her, and wouldn't deny her the same right.

He looked away, out across the field, and when the scarf slipped off, he closed his eyes.

"*Aroon*," he whispered. A delicate touch on the depressed scar, and he groaned again. A single finger stroked it, round and round. "Annie, don't."

Arrah, does it hurt you?

Yes.

Tell me.

It's so ugly.

No, my love. It is beautiful.

No. No, how can it be?

You were afraid.

Yes.

So very much afraid.

Yes.

And yet so brave. Such a brave little boy.

Aroon, no.

Yes. My brave little boy. So silent, so stoic. So brave. It is the badge of your courage. It is beautiful.

Aroon.

Her lips touched it softly and his heart surrendered to her. "I love you, Annie. I am yours forever."

"No," she whispered, pulling his lips close to hers. "We are one forever." The warmth, the sweetness, the purity of her settled in him. And slowly, gently, tenderly, he gave her all the love he had.

Chapter 39

THEY SPENT THE REST of the day there in the field, laughing and playing like children. At some point they ate, but he couldn't have said when or what. Afterward, she jumped up and ran from him. He chased her, marveling at her supple grace, encouraged by the teasing look she threw back over her shoulder. When he caught her, he tumbled her over and over again in the flowers, and her hair came free and tangled round him, a silken web against his face, arms, chest.

She looked down at him, saw the fire in his eyes. She came to him again then, her body warm and willing. He swore his love to her forever, pledged his life in defense of hers, and vowed upon his soul that anyone who touched her would die by his hand. Startled by the vehemence of his words, she looked deep into his eyes, found the memory that still haunted him, the rage that still smoldered. And accepted his pledge. She'd impose no limits, no restrictions, but trust in him, in the beauty of his nature and his deep love of all that lived.

He wove a chain of flowers for her neck, a garland for her hair. They spoke of a quiet ceremony, just her family and his, a few of their friends. They talked of his grandmother, who hadn't lived to see them wed. They cried together for the old lady who'd loved them so much, known them so well. Their grief was mingled with gratitude, for she'd sharpened the girl's gift, and brought the man to an understanding of her love.

He held her quietly for a while then, but the shadows were extending and they were far from home. He helped her up and drew her into his arms, kissed her tenderly. As she packed the basket up again, he shrugged into his shirt.

The red bandanna lay unnoticed in the grass as he took her hand and led her back the way they'd come. As darkness descended, they began to run. Some hundred feet from the house, she stopped abruptly, almost pulling him over.

"What?" he demanded in a whisper. "What is it?"

"My shoes," she whispered with a giggle. "Where are my shoes?"

"Oh, no," he groaned. "*Aroon...*"

There was no time to go back, and she couldn't get home after dark. She couldn't go alone, or without them.

"Look in the basket," he hissed.

It was a desperate suggestion, but with another small laugh she grabbed them and waved them around. She sat to slip them on but didn't lace them, then held out her hand. He tugged her upright and they ran again, reaching the farmhouse porch just as the first stars shimmered into the sky.

Annie started to giggle. He stared at her for a moment, then joined in. When Evelyn came to the door they were clinging to each other, almost hysterical, and she regarded them as if they were insane.

"What's so funny?" she demanded.

Annie controlled herself long enough to answer. "Nothing," she said demurely, and Daniel laughed again. She fell against his arm while Evelyn shook her head.

"Well, if you two can control yourselves long enough to wash up, dinner's almost ready."

***

A FEW MOMENTS LATER, Owen came out of the barn. Daniel's head was bent low over Annie's, and he saw the radiance of his daughter's face, the deference in the woodsman's touch.

THE WOODSMAN'S ROSE

I should beat him with a whip. But she is so very happy. Ah, Megan. My Megan, do you remember the day...? He sighed deeply.

Daniel straightened up then, stood almost at attention. Taking Annie's hand in his, he turned them both to face her father.

"Papa."

"Owen."

They'd both spoken at once. Owen raised an eyebrow. "Hmm?"

Daniel knew it was his place to speak. "Sir, she... Annie... I mean, we..."

"Spit it out, son."

"She's picked a date. May Day," he said in a voice full of wonder. "We're getting married. May first."

Trying hard to keep a straight face, Owen glared at Daniel for a long moment. It was only when he saw the younger man's confusion that he blurted out, "It's about time!" His round face broke into smiles and he held his arms open to his only daughter.

"Papa!" She ran to him, hugged him tight, then pounded on his chest with a fist. "You old tease!"

He laughed at her and kissed her forehead, then extended his hand to the woodsman. "Congratulations." He pumped Daniel's hand hard. "It's about damn time."

The woodsman reached out to touch the golden head that rested on Owen's shoulder.

"It was worth the wait," he said. She turned to him, her smile bright and soft, and was folded into his arms again.

"She's a beautiful girl, isn't she?" Owen asked. "You treat her right, boy, or you'll answer to me."

"Yes, sir."

"You don't have to worry, Papa. He'd never hurt me."

She's still so sure. Maybe I'm wrong. But he looked again and saw the worship in Daniel's eyes. *No, I know what they've done. How can I be angry with her—with them? When she is so happy? What a wonderful thing love is.*

Later that night, Owen sat in the cottage with his daughter's head upon his knee. She looked up once, then turned back to the fire.

"Papa..."

But he didn't want to hear her confession. "Are you happy, *Angharad*?"

"Oh, yes." Low and reverent the answer came, almost a prayer.

"That's all that matters." Her cheek rubbed against his knee, as he thought of a sun-drenched cove on the coast of Wales. *Ah, Megan. My little witch. She is so much like you. For you needed to know also, and you took my hand and led me there and shamelessly seduced me. You took my soul right out of my body and kissed it. And now she has done the same to him.* He stroked the golden hair and loved his daughter more than he ever had. *She'll be safe now, and I need worry no more. He'll take care of her.*

Chapter 40

BEFORE HE LEFT HER, Daniel raised Annie's hands to his lips. Evelyn had demanded the details of the wedding, but they'd had none to give her. "I'd like to make the plans, *aroon*. Will you trust me?"

"Of course."

"Is there any special thing you want?"

"No. Just something quiet—simple." She crinkled up her nose. "Not a thousand people."

"Not like Frank and Patricia?"

"No. It... it just wouldn't feel right."

"I love you, Annie. I want to do this for you."

Her kiss gave him all the permission he needed. He left her reluctantly, knowing he wouldn't be alone with her again until they married. His desire was as strong as ever, but the edge had been taken from his need. He didn't regret the day, but he'd wait until she was rightfully his to touch her again.

His heart was full as he walked home and he found he was singing aloud—the same song over and over and over—until he reached the gates of his family's ranch. Then he stood and watched a silver crescent peek from behind the trees and he sang it once again,

> *The farmer rides proudly to market and fair,*
> *And the clerk at the ale house still claims the great chair,*
> *But of all the proud fellows, the proudest I'll be*
> *While the Maid of Llanwellyn smiles sweetly on me.*

He checked the fuel level in the lamp and went into the house. His steps made no sound as he entered the back parlor. Molly was reading to Jake. John Patrick was smoking and staring into the fire with Irene sitting at his feet, and Brian was dozing in the armchair. Daniel stood before his mother, took the book from her hands. He pulled her up and held her close, unprepared for the strength of his own emotion.

"What is it, my son?"

"May Day." His voice was barely more than a gurgle. "She'll marry me. May first."

Their words hadn't been heard by the others in the room. John Patrick exchanged a glance with Jake, who shrugged helplessly. Brian was still sleeping and Irene seemed not to know of the woodsman's presence until her father nudged her away. John Patrick left his pipe behind, went to them and drew them both into his embrace, saw that Molly's face shone with happiness.

It's all right, then. I was afraid for a moment that he'd lost her. His voice was louder than he intended, and gruff. "I take it you'll be married."

Daniel's head bobbed up and down erratically.

"The first of May," said Molly. She hugged her son again, then turned to her husband. "The first of May."

"*Yippee!*" cried Jake.

Brian started up. "What? What?"

"Daniel's getting married!" Irene sang out. "Oh, let's go tell the boys!" She ran upstairs, shouting for Frank and Patricia, while Jake took off for Geordie and Suzette's cabin. Soon the room was filled with laughter as they congratulated and teased their quiet brother, pounding him on the back.

John Patrick broached a keg of porter and handed glasses around. He offered his mother's Homeric blessing:

THE WOODSMAN'S ROSE

There is no fairer thing,
Than when the lord and lady with one soul
One home possess.

They raised their glasses to him and drank, remembering the lilting, ancient voice that had first spoken the words. They could all feel her presence, knew that she shared their joy. They fell again into each other's arms, laughing and crying, happy and sad, demanding the details he couldn't yet give them, and offering their help and anything else he wanted.

WHEN THE OTHERS HAD all gone up to bed, the woodsman sat with Irene curled up against his shoulder like a kitten.

"Daniel," she asked, "do you think I'll ever get married?"

He chuckled inwardly—it seemed no time at all since Jake had asked him the same question. "Of course, *mavourneen*. You'll have your pick of men. You're the prettiest girl in the Territory. Aside from Annie, of course."

"Of course." She rolled her eyes and Daniel poked her in the side. Laughing, she said, "I wonder who it will be."

"Well, I know of at least two possible candidates."

"Who? Tell me who!"

"Nope. It's up to them. But Irene, don't rush into anything. Be very sure you love the man you accept. 'Cause you'll be stuck with him for a good long time."

"I know," she sighed. "I think I want a man like Adam. Or like you."

"Thank you, darlin'. That's the nicest thing anyone's ever said to me. Now I think it's time for you to be in bed."

She turned back to him at the door. "I'm happy for you, Daniel. I think Annie's a very lucky girl."

IN THE MORNING DANIEL took himself to the Rocking Chair Ranch, hoping he'd find Jesse in good health. Hoping Brian had honored his wish to be the one to break the news. He was thankful to find her with rosy cheeks as she greeted him with a hug.

"The boys aren't home," she told him. "Adam went out to the lake to see if there are any new calves and Brian went to town for supplies. Come and see Fancy—you won't believe how fat she got over the winter!"

He let her pull him into the barn where he admired not only the filly, but her pet calf Li'l Feller. As they walked out into the sunshine again, a huge tawny cat presented his mistress with a dead mouse.

"Thanks, Boy-o," she crooned at him. She dangled the creature by its tail in front of Daniel's face. "See what kind of presents you get when somebody loves you?"

He laughed as he tossed the creature into a clump of weeds beside the barn. The cat gave him a look of pure disgust, turned his back and began washing his tail.

Jesse giggled. "Got quite a way with animals, haven't you? But let's go have some tea. Then maybe Adam will be home. I want to hear all the news. How's Evelyn feeling? And what about Annie?"

"Evelyn's fine, but the doctor's got her resting most of the day. Lowell says she's getting kind of restless, but she's feeling good."

"Oh, I'm glad."

"You're looking fine, too. How do you feel?"

"Great! Mother made me a new tisane when the other one didn't work. It's taken most of the sickness away. You want another cup of tea? We could take it out to the porch—it's too nice a day to spend indoors."

"Sure."

Jesse settled herself on the swing. "Daniel, you haven't said one single word about Annie since you got here. Is something wrong?"

THE WOODSMAN'S ROSE

"No, *mavourneen*, I was just waiting until Adam got back to tell you the news."

"Tell me. Oh, Daniel, are you getting married? Tell me now."

"First of May."

He barely had time to put his cup down before she jumped into his arms, hugging him, laughing and crying, kissing his cheeks, then hugging him again.

"Oh, I'm so happy for you! Oh, I know you'll be so happy!"

"Thank you, *mavourneen*. I'd like to ask you for a favor."

"Anything," she promised rashly. "Anything at all."

"Annie's left all the plans to me. We'll be married at the house. I think she'd like you and Evelyn to stand up with her."

"Oh, Daniel..." Her face was radiant through her tears. "Oh, thank you. I'd be so proud." He caught her up in his arms again as she began to cry in earnest.

He turned his head at the sound of a horse, saw his brother's appaloosa approaching. Adam dismounted, a frown creasing his brow. "Not bad news, is it?"

The woodsman shook his head.

"Oh, Adam," Jesse said, reaching for his hand. "Daniel's getting married! On May first. Next week!" Shyly she added, "He just asked me to stand up with Annie."

Adam wrapped a long arm around Jesse's shoulders and leaned back against the porch rail, and regarded Daniel seriously.

"About damn time!" he said. "You're a lucky man. Why she'd want you, I sure don't know, but then I've never understood women."

Daniel gripped his brother's hand and drawled, "Don't guess I ever will. But I'll tell you somethin', brother." Adam raised a single eyebrow in question. "I'm sure not complainin'."

Chapter 41

ANNIE HAD A LENGTH of Japanese silk in the palest of jade greens. It had been a christening gift.

"My mother's cousin's husband," she told Evelyn, "was a merchant in Oriental goods. They lived in London and sent this to me when I was born. I never met them, but I saved this because it always seemed like such a special gift."

"It's beautiful," Evelyn agreed, feeling the delicate texture. "And it'll be perfect with your eyes and your hair."

She knew Annie was disappointed not to be able to wear her mother's wedding dress, which Owen had saved for her. But her mother had been a tiny woman, no taller than Jesse, and there wasn't enough material in the dress to make it long enough.

"It'll be perfect," Evelyn repeated. "Besides, you should wear green on the first of May." She began to sing, "*Green is the color of my true love's dress...*"

"Isn't it robe? *My true love's robe?*"

"The important thing is, it's green and you wear it!" Evelyn held the fabric up and measured it against her arm. "There's about three yards here, and it's not too wide. It'll have to be a fairly simple pattern. I don't think I have anything we can use. Why don't we go up to the house and look at some of Gran's old books? I remember there was a dress in one of them—oh, it was so pretty." Her hands began to move in excitement. "It had a high waist, and a long, slim skirt, and something I don't know—braid or something, all here and here."

THE WOODSMAN'S ROSE

"It was Egyptian, I think, or maybe Greek. Simple, but oh, so elegant." She regarded her sister-in-law. "Just like you."

Annie cocked an eyebrow. "So now I'm simple, am I?"

"No, no, I just meant you like things that aren't all fancy and full of doo-dads." Evelyn flushed with embarrassment, then caught the gleam in Annie's eye. "All right, so the truth is out. Who but a simpleton would marry my brother anyway?"

"Who would marry mine?"

"Guess it makes us both pretty simple, doesn't it? But come on, what do you say? Let's go look at those books and see what we can find."

At the ranch, they spent the afternoon with Jake in the back parlor. The boy had taken a fall off his horse earlier in the week and reinjured the ankle he'd broken the past winter. He threw himself into the dress hunt with the alacrity of the extremely bored. Eventually Evelyn found the pattern she remembered.

"It's beautiful," Annie said, "but it's got no sleeves or anything. I'd be embarrassed."

"Okay," Evelyn said, "let's see what else there is."

They were on the verge of resignation when Jake called for Annie. He'd picked up a book after they'd discarded it and was flipping pages when a picture caught his eye. He held the book up for her to see. "Look at this here. It looks pretty elegant to me."

A slender woman stood alone on the page, with flowers in the black hair piled on her head, held in place by a wooden comb. Her skin was flawless, her eyes as dark as her hair.

Annie caught her breath as she gazed. "Isn't she beautiful?"

"It says she's from Siam," Jake said. "Isn't that somewhere near Japan?"

"I think so. Somewhere in the Orient, anyway. Evelyn, come look at this."

"Oh, that's pretty," Evelyn said. "I think it's in two pieces. A dress with a long skirt—it would be almost like the Greek dress we saw. But the jacket would cover your shoulders. The sleeves are long but the bodice is short." She looked at Annie with a dressmaker's eye. "We might have enough. Or we might have to make a shorter sleeve. One that just covers your elbows." She pored over the picture again. "I don't see how it closes. The jacket must have a placket with the buttons hidden inside.

"I've got some muslin at home—let's see if we can make one out of that. If we run into trouble, I bet Rebecca will help us out."

Annie leaned over to kiss Jake on the cheek, then laughed as his cheeks flooded with color. "Thank you, brother-to-be. I think you may have found my wedding dress for me."

※

TWO DAYS BEFORE THE wedding, Evelyn delivered the dress to Annie. It had turned out perfectly. By foregoing the triple folds of a placket in favor of white frog closures, Evelyn was able to fashion sleeves that came nearly to the wrist. And there were enough scraps of fabric left for Owen to make matching slippers. Annie tried on the dress and slippers, and wept with delight.

"Oh, my baby girl," sighed Owen, "you are so beautiful."

"Oh, Papa, thank you. I'm just so happy." She flew up the stairs again to remove the dress.

Evelyn spoke carefully. "Have you decided what to do, Papa? You know you're welcome to come to the farm."

"I know, girl, and it's not that I don't appreciate it. But you've got your own lives, Evelyn, and soon you'll have your little one to worry about. I don't want to be in the way."

"Don't be silly. You'd never be in the way."

"Don't be too sure now," he cautioned. "Before we came to this country, after Megan died, my sister lived with us—me and the kids.

THE WOODSMAN'S ROSE

She was a wonderful woman—been dead these past five years. But she was a wonderful woman. And I remember wishing she'd just go home.

"I loved her, but I wanted her to just go home and leave us alone." He lit his pipe and pulled on it. "I don't ever want anyone feeling that way about me. So I think for now, we'll leave things the way they are.

"You might see me a bit more often at the dinner hour," he added with a chuckle. "Be too far to walk to Annie's."

"Do you know where they're going to live? Daniel won't tell me a thing."

"I'm sworn to secrecy. Can't even tell Annie!"

"She doesn't know?"

"Says she doesn't care, either. As long as he's happy."

"Oh, my Lord! Maybe she is a simpleton. Imagine trusting a man with something like that!"

Owen began to laugh, then got up to answer the knock on the door. "Well, speak of the devil!"

"Annie home?" Daniel asked.

"Upstairs. Should be down in a minute. You've missed supper, boy."

"That's all right. I can only stay a minute, anyway."

As he entered the parlor, Evelyn jumped up and grabbed his arm. "Tell me," she pleaded in a whisper. "Please tell me where you're going to live." As he shook his head, she pouted. "You told Owen."

"Owen knows how to keep his mouth shut."

"Oh, please. I won't tell her. But if you tell me, I'll tell you what her dress looks like."

"See what I mean? Evelyn, I love you, but you've never kept a secret in your life."

She stomped her foot, pleaded and begged, and finally she sulked. But he remained adamant. In two days, all the world would know.

She sighed. "That means you won't tell me?"

"In two more days, you'll know everything."

"All right. I guess if nobody else knows, either..."

He gave her a noncommittal smile. He didn't tell her John Patrick and the younger twins had helped him build a platform for the tent he'd erected on a wide shelf of the leeward knoll overlooking the meadow. Didn't tell her Molly had helped him with small decorative touches, and Brian had helped him build a small rope corral for his few horses. Or that, in a moment of uncertainty, he'd told Jesse every single detail of his plan. *Least said,* he told himself, *soonest mended.*

He turned at the sound of Annie's footstep on the stairs. As she held out her hand, he could see she'd been crying. "*Aroon,* do you feel all right?"

"Yes, I'm fine."

"Been crying?"

"Just a little. You know they say the bride is supposed to have the jitters."

"No second thoughts?"

"Silly!"

"Come out to the porch for a minute."

Annie stepped out into the soft night. Daniel wrapped his arms around her and she leaned back against his chest.

"I just stopped by to tell you I love you," he said. She lifted a beaming face to him and he bent to kiss her, whispered her name. She turned toward him, pressed her head into the hollow of his shoulder and lifted her arms up around his neck.

"I love you, Daniel." Her voice had the soft sound of a laughing brook. "I miss you so much."

"Two more days, *aroon*. Two more days and we'll be together." When he pulled himself away from her lips again, he said, "We'll get

THE WOODSMAN'S ROSE

married at the house. The preacher should be there at two o'clock. All right?"

Her smile was radiant.

"Mother said you can come any time. The guest room's ready for you. Owen can use my room—I'll bunk with Jake."

He thought of the pelts and books he'd transferred to their temporary home, wondered if she'd bring the teddy bear. Owen had given him a key to their cottage and his brothers were ready to move her bed to the tent as soon as she arrived at the ranch. Maybe he'd tell Brian to bring the bear as well.

He lost himself in her eyes, stood and gazed into them until Lowell arrived to take Evelyn home. Stepping off the porch, Daniel took her hand in his, slipped the ring off her finger. He'd made it for her—three strands of copper, silver and gold, entwined in the Celtic symbol of eternity. He kissed the place where it had rested, then looked up into her stricken face.

"*Aroon*. No, sweetheart. Oh, Annie." He tried to pull her close again but she pushed at him, staring at his hands. "I'm sorry, *aroon*. I thought you'd know." He held the ring out to her. "I need to have it back, sweetheart, so I can give it to you. At the wedding. Sweetheart, how could you think...?"

But she was grabbing frantically for the ring. He passed it back to her and she thrust it onto her finger, turning it round and round as she stared down at it.

"Oh, Annie, do you think I could ever let you go? It's yours, sweetheart. I'd never take it from you. I'm sorry... I thought you'd realize... I'm sorry. I love you, *aroon*. I'd never take it back."

She gave him a strained smile, then leaned against his chest again.

"I guess it... I guess I'm kind of silly," she whispered. "But when you took it away, I felt so alone."

"It's all right, sweetheart. I should have told you. I didn't think." He put his hand under her chin, raised her face to his once more and kissed her. "You keep it. I'll find another one for us to use. I love you, Annie. I'll never leave you."

"I know. I don't know why..."

"It doesn't matter. You keep it safe." He kissed the ring and said, "I love you, Annie."

"I love you, Daniel."

"Good night, *aroon*."

He turned at the gate and saw her gazing down at the ring, turning it round and round on her finger. Her hair caught the sparkle from the stars, her face was like a white flower in the moonlight. When she looked up at him, the love in her eyes warmed him through.

Chapter 42

AT DAWN ON HIS WEDDING day, Daniel walked to the meadow. He spent several minutes looking out over the valley full of flowers, then climbed the knoll to where the brook sang merrily—where he'd carried Annie after she fell asleep in his arms. There were two steps up to the platform on which the tent stood—he took them in one stride.

Annie's bed was inside, his bear resting on her pillow. His pelts hung on the walls, his map sat atop the dresser. Their clothes mingled on pegs fastened to the wooden framework he'd constructed to support the walls. Until he could build their cabin, this would be home.

He gathered an armful of flowers for the vases his mother had given him. Then he stepped out once more. The day was beautiful, soft. A passing shower had dampened the field in the hours before dawn, so the flowers stood bold and proud, curtsying in the breeze. He picked enough of them to weave a garland for her hair, starting with a crown of daisies, then tucking in blue flax and penstemon, pink storksbill and evening primrose, adding tiny green leaves to fill the empty spaces. Annie needed a bouquet, too—Jesse had told him that. And Jesse had slipped her own wedding ring from her finger when he brought his newest problem to her.

He got to the ranchhouse just in time to greet her. Jesse rode her black filly Fancy, wore the black riding outfit he remembered. Adam had a carpet bag on the back of his saddle; Jesse took it and the garland of flowers, and ran up the stairs to Annie.

"Big day finally got here," Adam said. "It's about damn time!"

"Tell Annie that!" Daniel turned to Brian. "It's your turn next, isn't it?"

"Oh, no, not me! I'm the irresponsible kind."

"Who'd want you anyway?" Adam gave him a punch on the shoulder.

Brian poked a finger at him. "Why, I'll have you know—"

But his words and gesture were broken by Adam's soft benediction. "My dear God. Isn't she beautiful?"

They looked up to see Jesse beckoning to them from the front door. She wore her own wedding dress—a sprigged muslin Evelyn had made, creamy white with tiny red roses and emerald green leaves scattered over it. Her hair was pulled up into a topknot, wisps of it playing against her temples and neck.

As Adam took the steps in twos and threes, his silver spurs jingling like coins in a pocket, and bent over the hand she held out to him, Daniel murmured, "She certainly is."

Brian nodded silently as Adam returned to them.

"Annie sent you this." He handed Daniel Annie's ring. "Said if you lose it, she'll have your head on a silver platter. Said she'd have Alec make it special, just for you."

The woodsman laughed as he exchanged the ring for Jesse's, then slipped it into the embroidered pocket of his shirt. "You know, brother, we really have had the luck of the Irish!"

ANNIE WORE THE DRESS of jade green silk, her father's delicate slippers, and she looked to Daniel like a fairy-child. Her blonde hair hung long and loose. The garland and his grandmother's stick pin were her only jewels. She floated down the stairs with Evelyn and Jesse, to find him at the door with the bouquet. He took her hand and kissed it, then led her to the preacher.

THE WOODSMAN'S ROSE

Two large rooms in the Donovan home were used only for special occasions. One was the formal parlor, and it was there that they were married, before a fireplace of Connemara marble. Jesse and Evelyn stood at Annie's side, while the family gathered behind them. Daniel had asked Lowell and Alec to stand with him, and the only other guests he'd invited were Tommy and Carolyn. Softly he and Annie exchanged their vows, gently did he slip the braided ring onto her finger.

After the ceremony, family and friends drank a toast and presented their gifts. There were linens and china, blankets and canisters. Mugs and knives and a crystal vase. Annie couldn't keep track of it all, so Evelyn bent to whisper, "Don't worry, dear, I'm writing it down for you."

But two gifts Annie could never mistake. From Jesse, an embroidered wall hanging with Katie's Homeric blessing. When she unwrapped it, Annie's eyes overflowed with emotion. Then from Alec came a gift in two boxes—one for each of them. Two halves of a single medallion surrounded by a braided circle—gold, silver, copper—each with one initial engraved. Annie's on a delicate chain, the initial "D"; Daniel's on a heavier link, the initial "A". The two pieces fit together as one. Neither of them could say a word. With perfect timing, John Patrick raised another toast, and the room resounded with laughter and cheers.

They adjourned to the dining room for the wedding supper. Molly and Irene had decorated the room in emerald green and white. White tablecloth, green napkins. White flowers in green vases. Huge green and white bows tied to the chairs the bride and groom were to occupy. The room was the epitome of May Day.

After dinner was eaten, the preacher and his wife departed, and the guests gathered again in the parlor. Daniel picked up his violin and played *The Maid of Llanwellyn*. Annie beamed at him, and remembered her first reaction to the song.

It was their first dance, their first date. She'd answered his knock on the cottage door and stared at him until the color rose to his cheeks.

"Evenin'," he'd said in his deep gravel voice.

"Daniel," she answered breathlessly.

"What do you think?" He turned around slowly, his shoulders shrugging as he came to face her again. She didn't know how to reply. Gone was the woodsman she knew. Gone was the buckskin suit with its rawhide laces, the knee-high boots with their long fringe. But the man who stood before her made her heart beat fast and hard.

He wore serge trousers and soft black leather shoes that made his feet look small. His white shirt had full sleeves that had her remembering the pirates she'd read about as a child. The shirt had a slit at his throat; the ends of a black bolo he'd borrowed from Tommy fell on either side of it. His mustache had been trimmed and shaped, and even the hair that usually hung down over his collar had been clipped. *What will it be like to dance with him? He's never been to a dance that I know of—not since we were kids.* His soft, self-deprecating laugh helped her pull herself together.

"Do you hate it?" he asked.

"No, no." She was still breathless, her heart beating fast. "But you look so different. Like an old Spanish pirate. Or an Irish one, if there ever was such a thing!"

"I'm sure there were. And maybe there still are—who knows what Conor's been up to lately?"

As they strolled to the Town Hall with Evelyn and Lowell, he told her how his grandmother sent for him just an hour before they were to leave the house. He'd been trying to decide between his buckskin shirt and a maroon corduroy one—the former he felt would be too casual, the latter too warm—when Katie had presented him with the white shirt. He showed Annie the embroidered pocket; it was a derivation of the Donovan brand, the Celtic symbol of

THE WOODSMAN'S ROSE

eternity surrounding a pair of embroidered "D"s. It had been years since she'd made a shirt for any of them but Adam, and he knew it had taken her many weeks to make his.

"For once, I didn't have anything to say."

Knowing him as a man who spoke only when necessary, Annie giggled. As they arrived at the hall, he stopped and stood before her, placing his hands on her shoulders.

"*Aroon*," he said, "you are beautiful tonight. More than ever before."

His hands were warm on her shoulders and she quivered as she looked back up at him, unaware of the throngs around them. He raised her hand to his lips as she felt the heat rise to her face, then he tucked her fingers under his arm and took her inside.

They danced their first dance together and Annie felt light as a fairy in his arms. So graceful was he, so strong, that she seemed to be carried across the floor, her feet hardly touching down. He'd shared her dances with his brothers, her father and his, and with Tommy, who teased her as he waltzed with her and made her blush. At the end of that dance, the musicians took a break and Daniel led her over to her father, then offered to get them refreshments.

"Having a good time?" Owen had asked her.

"Oh, yes. I can't remember when I've had so much fun!"

"Daniel's all gussied up. Sarah Taylor asked me who he was."

"Did she want to dance with him?"

"You're a tease, girl. I hope Daniel knows what he's getting into."

She sought him out, saw him speaking to the fiddler and taking his instrument. With breathless anticipation, she waited for the jig or reel to begin. Instead, the song was slow and lilting. Annie recognized the ancient Welsh air and turned to her father, her eyes snapping, her jaw set. Owen quickly turned her face away from the band.

"Don't be foolish, child," he said.

"He has no right!"

Her father put his arms around her and danced her into the crowd. "What has he done?" At her stony silence, he continued, "He's learned a song from your country. Is that so bad?"

"But, Papa... it's a love song."

"Because he loves you. Is it such a crime?"

"Everyone will know." Her face was on fire. She hid it against his shoulder.

"Who will know? Who will know but you and me? And Lowell? Perhaps Evelyn? No one will know, *caraid*. And he has meant no harm. You do him wrong to think so."

"Papa," she protested again, but he went on as if she hadn't spoken.

"His song is a gift, Annie. Take it as such. And take his love, too. He'll make you happy, *caraid*." Moments later, he was singing in her ear:

> *Rich Owen will tell you, with eyes full of scorn,*
> *Threadbare is my coat, and my hosen are torn,*
> *Scoff on, my rich Owen, but faint is thy glee,*
> *When the Maid of Llanwellyn smiles sweetly on me.*

And now as the song ended once more, with her heart full of joy, Annie could think of no greater gift she'd ever received.

WITH THE CELEBRATION over, Daniel took Annie's hand in his, led her from the ranch house and across the fields. At the sight of the tent, she stopped for a moment, her heart beating so rapidly she could scarcely breathe. He pulled gently on her hand, leading her through the sunset field, then opened the flaps and lifted her in his arms. She touched his face.

THE WOODSMAN'S ROSE

"*Aroon,*" he whispered, "I love you."

"Daniel." It was all she could say. Inside, he lay her on her own bed and knelt beside it. She looked around in wonder. "How did you know?"

He knelt there with a tender smile on his face, until she reached for him. Then he, who considered himself the least sensitive, the least gifted of his family, made love to his young bride with such tenderness of tone and touch that she wept in his arms.

He cradled her head against his breast. "*Aroon,* have I hurt you?"

"Oh, no." Soft, sweet denial.

"Then what, sweetheart?"

"Oh, Daniel... there's too much happiness inside me. There's just not enough room for all of it. I don't know how else to let it go."

"I love you, Annie," he whispered. He held her close and watched her fall asleep, her slender hand pressed against his heart, her golden hair mingling with the copper on his chest.

Thank you, mother. Thank you for this day. Let me keep her for a little while. For now all is well. Now all is well.

Chapter 43

THE DOOR TO THE TENT faced south; a flap in the side wall created a window. The rising sun glanced through to warm her face, and Annie wakened to find a happiness she'd never imagined would be hers.

Daniel lay behind her, next to the wall, and her body nestled in against his. She felt his breath upon her shoulder. One of his arms was under her head, the other wrapped around her waist. The security she felt as she'd fallen asleep was now multiplied a hundredfold and it washed over her in wave after wave, like the tide upon the shore. A single tear trickled from her eye, but she didn't move to wipe it away.

After a few moments, she began to take in the details of the room. It was ten feet square, the bed sitting in a corner. On the opposite wall, under the small triangular window, low shelves stood. His books and hers, his toys and the music box that had been her mother's. Their shoes lined up together in the corner. She smiled at the neatness, at the mingling of their things.

In the far corner, more pegs held her pots and pans, a metal rack her utensils. Dishes and cups, spices and foodstuffs, jams, dried berries, canned vegetables, jars of rice and flour. And a contraption she recognized as a small forge Tommy had discarded years ago—it seemed to be a brazier that would serve as both stove and furnace. Against the front wall of the tent stood a table and two chairs.

He's thought of everything. He's brought his rug, the pelts for the walls. And all these beautiful flowers. Four, no five vases full of them.

THE WOODSMAN'S ROSE

It's so beautiful, so warm and cozy. So perfect. I could live here for the rest of my life. With him.

She felt the pattern of his breathing change and lay quietly. But the very stillness of her wakened him.

"*Aroon,*" he murmured against her ear.

"Daniel, I love you." She turned for his kiss. "This room is so perfect."

"You really like it?"

"It's perfect."

"I have a plan for a cabin—I thought we'd build it here on the hill. This level shelf is just wide enough for it. And maybe a little garden for vegetables. Want to see?"

"Yes. Right now."

He slipped over her and out of the bed. She hadn't noticed his desk at the foot of it. He brought a scrolled paper back to her, flipped it open, and began eagerly to explain the design to her. A large room, divided into kitchen and parlor. The fieldstone fireplace went from floor to ceiling and had bookshelves built in on each side. Two separate bedrooms on the east side, with a loft above that looked down on the big room, a narrow stairway leading up between them. Water would be piped to the cabin from the stream. He'd build the house of squared peeled logs, and thought he could make a sealant from the resin of the pines to use in place of mortar. The cabin would be the light yellow of natural pine and he'd trim it in white. There were windows in every room.

She touched the drawing, the large front bedroom they'd share. There was a window in the side wall. "A window to the east, so the morning sun comes in."

"I love the feeling of the new day, when everything starts over. It seems to me every day's a new chance—no matter what happened in the past, a new day is a new beginning. Even when the sun doesn't shine, it's the east that brightens first." Softly, he added, "It gives me hope."

Her hand reached for his and she found herself in his arms again. He held her close for a few moments, then stroked her hair and said, "Better get up, *aroon*. No telling when we might have company."

Laughing, she agreed. Evelyn wasn't the only one curious about their new home, and they both knew the extent of her impatience.

But they were left alone for a week. They spent the days much as they'd spent their first day there—laughing and playing like children, making love in the flowers or under the pines. Or talking of the future. He wore neither shirt nor bandanna, and she left her shoes in the corner.

Annie couldn't get her fill of the view from the hill—the vale of flowers filled her heart with joy. She asked Daniel to add a wide front porch to his plan so they could just sit and look at the end of the day. He sketched in the garden on the east side of the cabin and an orchard on the west. A small corral for horses behind it. An outhouse, and perhaps a chicken coop. At that, they both agreed nothing could be done to make the plan more perfect.

ON SUNDAY, THEY WALKED to the Donovan ranch. It was less than four miles over the fields to the ranchhouse, and just over six in the opposite direction to the dairy farm. They walked hand in hand, sharing a smile now and again. As they entered the yard, they waved at Adam and Jesse, who were sitting on the porch. Jesse tripped lightly down the steps as Annie broke into a run. Laughing, Daniel sprinted behind her.

Evelyn and Lowell arrived in a buggy, just as Brian and Jake came out of the barn. Adam helped his sister to alight—she was round and awkward in the advancing stages of her pregnancy. He'd scarcely let

THE WOODSMAN'S ROSE

her go when Annie and Jesse fell on her with glad cries. Adam looked over their heads to his brother-in-law, shared a rueful smile.

"Women," said Lowell, but there was fondness in his tone.

"Looks like a family reunion," declared John Patrick from the porch. Descending the steps, he took his turn hugging the young women. "Your mother says lunch is waiting. Brian, you'd best stay out here—I don't know that she was expectin' all this company."

The big man laughed and followed them inside. They all knew Molly's meal would be generously served. The memory of starvation had never been eradicated, and her family wouldn't go hungry as long as she lived. Yet there was no waste, ever. She prepared carefully, managed left-overs frugally, and wasn't averse to packing up a basket and sending it home with the preacher when he came to call.

At the end of the meal, Daniel regarded his brother. "Brian, I think you've been outdone. I think Jake finally managed to eat more than you."

Jake grinned as Brian's brow furrowed.

"It's 'cause I ate breakfas' so late," the big man complained. "Put me offa my feed."

The ensuing hilarity was broken by Irene's question. "Annie, where are you living? Daniel wouldn't tell us anything!"

The whole family clamored for details, so Annie described the field and the tent which was now her home.

"A tent!" Evelyn turned a look of accusation on her brother. "Daniel, you're making her live in a tent?"

"He's not making me," Annie retorted. "I love it! It's the most beautiful room you've ever seen."

"Come and see it," Daniel said.

"Me, too?" asked Irene.

"Can we come?" echoed Frank.

"Sure. Everybody's welcome."

So they helped Molly with the dishes, then set out across the open fields. Lowell insisted that Evelyn go in the buggy, but the others decided to walk. The day was warm and breezy, the air fresh and clear. Only Brian grumbled.

"Shoulda brought my hoss. This walkin' jus' ain't no good for my legs."

As they laughed at him, Jake stuck out a buckskin boot. He'd run upstairs to change into them before setting out. "Oughta make you a pair of these. Makes walkin' a whole lot easier!"

"Catch me makin' boots!" Brian scoffed. "I been a cowboy for thirty-four years, never had t' make my own boots yet!"

"You've had sore feet for thirty-four years, too!" laughed Adam. "Better take the kid's advice!"

But Brian's laments continued until they stood on the crest of the hill overlooking Annie's valley.

"Now, ain't that purty," he said, breaking the few moments' silence, realizing he hadn't taken the time to really look at the scene when he was helping Daniel with his plans. "Miss Annie, you jus' fit right int' this place. Jus' like the Lord made it especial for you."

"Thank you, Brian," she said shyly, her cheeks coloring. "But you don't have to call me 'miss' anymore! I'm your sister now."

"You'll never convince him," Jesse said, smiling fondly at her husband's twin. She was still "Miss Jesse" to him, in spite of the fact they shared a home.

"Well," he boomed out, "let's see this here tent you call home!"

She took them proudly, then showed them the plans for the cabin and, in the end, even Evelyn was satisfied. She sat on the edge of the bed, taking it all in once more.

"It's perfect, Annie. It's just like you. He thought of everything, didn't he? I should have known."

They joined the others outside. Patricia and Suzette were sitting at the edge of the meadow with their husbands. Irene was lost in

THE WOODSMAN'S ROSE

daydreams, staring out at the acres of flowers. The men had looked at Daniel's sketch and agreed the plan needed no improvements, while Molly and Jesse whispered about roses for the front porch. John Patrick put their thoughts into words.

"A little bit of heaven, right here in Arizona." And he asked no more why his son had laughed about this worthless piece of land.

Chapter 44

DANIEL ASKED FOR HELP cutting the logs he needed for the cabin and snaking them down through the hills to the homestead, promising in return to help build Geordie and Suzette's new home. So each day John Patrick and one of his younger sons would arrive. The woodsman chose his trees carefully, for not only should they be tall and straight, but he wouldn't leave an obvious gap in the forest.

At the end of the last day of cutting and hauling, Annie was making dinner while Jake introduced his frisky black to Daniel's buckskin mare. The woodsman sat with his father on the steps to the tent.

"Did I tell you I found a small stand of wafer ash near the lake in the canyon?" Daniel asked.

"Ah, good. Hops seem not to be thriving this year—the merchant in Flag sends excuses in lieu of goods. I'd come to the conclusion we'd have no porter for this winter. And your mother was complaining just yesterday that her stock of stomach remedies is low."

"So I'll pick her some leaves next time I go up there, and I'll look for the seed pods come fall."

"A good plan," his father said, then waved his pipe to encompass the meadow at their feet. "It keeps growing prettier, does it not?"

Daniel answered in a sly voice, "A worthless piece of land."

"Aye, as some would say Tara is these days." For the ancient home of the Irish High Kings had fallen to ruin long ago. John Patrick had taken Molly to see her ancestral home before they departed for

America, and the sadness he found in the memory crept into his voice. "A view of heaven that was. The green for miles around, the sky blue as a robin's egg. But this... This comes as close as anything I've seen.

"The flowers are a difference, yet the feeling is the same. You should be naming this place, lad, the way the old ones named their homes."

"When I look out at it, I think of the stories Gran used to tell of the little people. There was a word she used—I've tried to remember it—it meant the hill they lived on."

"*Sidhean.* That's a fairy hill."

"Then we could call this place *Sidhean Annie*, and it would mean *Annie's fairy-hill*, wouldn't it?"

The old man reached out to ruffle his son's long hair. "Aye. And you'll be building her a little fairy-cabin to go along with it." He stood and stretched, tapped out his pipe and ground the ashes beneath his foot. "*Sidhean Annie.* Your Gran would approve."

With that blessing, the cabin began to take form. Daniel squared off his logs, saving the long slices of bark for the roof. He tapped the resin from a dozen trees, experimented with mineral spirits, turpentine, and various heavy oils until he found a combination that would spread smooth and dry hard between the logs. He had help he hadn't counted on, for his father sent one of his brothers a few days a week and Alec came often, intrigued by the building process. Annie was eager to help; he taught her to use a plane to smooth the rough spots, and she'd help him spread the sealant, or sometimes hold a support while he built the walls higher.

Her illness created a disharmony in her body—her energy came in spurts. In no time, Daniel realized her strength followed the same pattern as the waxing and waning moon. Ten days of normal activity would be followed by three or four days during which she was tense, nervous, and high-strung. Then ten days of quietude as the moon faded, followed by a period of listlessness and fatigue, amounting at times to total exhaustion.

He began to plan their days around the rhythm of her cycle. For ten days they'd work side by side, then he'd distract her—taking her visiting or shopping, or exploring in the foothills behind the house. He taught her to ride a horse, to read the signs of weather and mark a trail. They worked on their plans on her days of lassitude, or he'd regale her with folklore. One of her favorite stories concerned the willow trees near the stream that flowed behind the house: a willow once heard a cat mewling in distress, so she reached down into the water to save the cat's kittens from drowning. In remembrance of the tree's good deed, wherever the kittens' feet touched her branches, catkins would grow. Annie couldn't hear this story too many times.

If Alec came to visit on her quiet days, he'd sit with her beneath the trees and talk to her about his mother. Or sometimes Daniel would spread a blanket in the field so she could lie down. He'd tell her stories of Ireland or of the Navajo traditions, while he wove chains of flowers for her to wear. Or he'd lie beside her in the sun and empty his mind of every thought except her love, leaving her to sleep peacefully in his arms. He'd hold her, cosset her when she was ill. He made no demands whatsoever on her strength.

She didn't realize the extent of his care, yet Annie knew that a stress she'd never fully recognized was removed from her life. She no longer felt the need to live as she'd seen other women do, to fill each day with chores and domestic accomplishments.

At the end of July, the rains began. The roof of their new home wasn't quite finished and Annie was restless with confinement to the tent. Early one morning, she started to work in the corner kitchen. Her hands were trembling with nervousness—she dropped the skillet and then the coffeepot. When Daniel bent to pick it up, she snapped at him.

THE WOODSMAN'S ROSE

He looked up at her from his crouch, saw her fist jam itself hard against her mouth and her eyes fill with tears. He pulled himself up and gathered her into his arms.

"It's all right, *aroon*. Don't cry."

"I'm sorry," she sobbed out. "I'm sorry."

"It's all right. Sweetheart, don't cry."

With an effort she controlled her tears, then whispered again, "I'm sorry."

He hugged her close. "Don't worry about it."

"I didn't mean it."

"I know, sweetheart." He kissed her forehead. "Come sit down a minute."

She followed him to the bed and sat beside him, her head drooping on his shoulder.

"What's the matter, Annie?" he asked. The face she raised to him was streaked with tears. "Tell me what's wrong."

"I just... feel... so..." Her hands were restless again, trying to explain what she didn't have a word for.

"Confined?"

"Yes..." The fluttering hands were still once more. "Sometimes it's like I can't even breathe." She said it softly, as if afraid he'd laugh.

"I know what you mean. Alec and I got stuck in a cave in the mountains one time during a blizzard. We were in there for four days and by the end, we both felt the walls closing in. We knew it couldn't be true, but it sure did feel that way."

She took a deep, shaky breath and held it for a moment before she let it out. "Yes. Like I'm a bird in a cage that's too small."

She looked up quickly—she hadn't meant any criticism of him or of her temporary home.

"It's all right, *aroon*. I know what you mean." He held her close for a moment, felt her relaxing against him. "I'll bet there's someone else who's feeling the same way right about now."

"Who?"

"Evelyn." In her last month of pregnancy, Evelyn had been house-bound even before the rains. "By now she's probably chomping at the bit. What say we go see if we can cheer her up?"

Annie's arms crept up around his neck. "I love you, Daniel. You always make me feel better."

He bent to kiss her, felt her warm response. It was quite some time later in the day when they set out in the buggy for the dairy farm.

As he'd surmised, Evelyn was beside herself with boredom. She had difficulty getting to her feet and the doctor had cautioned her about overexertion, so she was spending most of her days on the couch. She begged her brother to let Annie stay for a few days.

"*Aroon?*" Daniel asked. The eagerness with which she accepted the offer made him chuckle. "I'll go get some things for you. Or am I invited to stay, too?"

Evelyn had the grace to blush. "Of course you are, you big dope! Do you think I'd dare to separate you two?"

He bent to kiss her cheek. "I really wouldn't advise it." He touched his wife's hair. "I'll only be a little while. Don't spoil her too much!"

He left them giggling as Lowell walked him out.

"Thank God you're here," Lowell said fervently. "She's been going crazy! And I'm about at my wit's end. She wants these things to eat—oh, God, all kinds of things—braised potatoes one day and celery soup the next, then something else the next day. I've been begging Carolyn for help—but how many times in a week can she drop everything?"

"Celery soup?" Daniel's face screwed up in disgust. "What did that taste like?"

"Beats me. I just make the stuff—I don't have to eat it." Then he repeated, "Thank God. At least Annie knows how to cook—maybe

THE WOODSMAN'S ROSE

she can show me how to make some of this stuff. Trouble is, you never know what she's going to ask for next!"

For a week Annie indulged her sister-in-law's culinary whims while Daniel helped Lowell with repairs to the house and barn. At the end of that time, the rains began to let up. When the morning dawned with a warm mist rising from the ground, he told Annie he wanted to finish the cabin roof. "Do you want to stay here a few more days? I could come back tonight."

"Would you mind? I think just a day or two. I think this baby's getting a little impatient!"

"Think so? You think I should tell Lowell to let Doc Barber know?"

"And maybe tell your mother, if you don't mind going all the way out there."

He had to laugh. Sometimes her perceptions took him by surprise. Having lived in the village all her life, she considered the Donovan ranch the outskirts of civilization. To him, it was still part of the town. He wondered how she'd react if he told her he'd once run almost the entire distance. "I think I can make it that far. I love you, *aroon*."

Her kiss said more than words could have.

"I'll see you later."

"Be careful," she called as he left her.

⚜

WHEN THE DAY WAS DONE, Daniel was satisfied that the roof would need only one more day of work. He walked through the fields toward the dairy, grateful for the feel of the damp grass beneath his feet. *Annie's right. Even in the big farmhouse, you can feel like the cage is too small.*

A scream splintered the peace of the evening. He broke into a run, then realized Annie's premonition had come to pass. He heard one more scream as he drew near, but silence greeted him at the door. He sprinted into the house, taking the steps by threes and fours until he reached the landing on the second floor. Molly came from the bedroom and took Lowell by the hand, but Daniel couldn't hear their voices.

By the time he reached him, Lowell slumped against the wall, his face as white as the best Irish linen. The woodsman put a hand on his shoulder and he looked up.

"A s-son," the dairyman stuttered. "M-my son."

Daniel put a rough hand in his hair, then hugged him tightly. "Congratulations." His gruff voice was full of joy. "They're both all right?"

At the sound of a tiny mewling cry, Lowell seemed to come back to life. "I have a son!" he said, loud and prideful. "We have a son!" He fell into his friend's arms once again, pounding him on the back, then demanded, "Where in blazes were you when I needed you?"

Chapter 45

ADAM GRIFFITHS WAS healthy and strong, and squalled in the Donovan family cradle. The family had gathered for dinner at the dairy farm on the evening of the last dance of summer. His women were decked out in their finest, his sons in their Sunday best, and John Patrick was happy as he looked out over the table at their shining faces.

Evelyn sat on his right. She was fully recovered from childbirth and radiant with the joy of motherhood. Lowell doted on her and his new son, and Rebecca had been staying with them for a few weeks to let the household settle into a routine. He watched now as Rebecca reached up to touch the watch pinned to her dress. He'd found it amongst Katie's jewelry and given it to her in gratitude for her care of his mother, her help to all the family. He caught her eye now and smiled. She nodded in acknowledgment, in thanks, but the slight shake of his head told her that she wasn't in his debt. Her calm, serious face lightened for a moment and she nodded again.

Next to her sat his younger twins with their brides across from them, Patricia engaging in vivid conversation while Suzette listened intently. Next to Patricia was Irene, her whole body alive with excitement as they talked about the evening's dance. Her eyes were a blue as deep as the ocean, flecked with green. Her complexion was perfect and her black hair, lately worn in a braid like Annie's, was piled on her head in a topknot. *She is a beauty. She has the very face of Ireland. We could have named her Rosaleen.*

Owen sat next to Jake. He was a man of average height, which made him quite a dwarf in the present company. Only Annie and Jesse (and of course little Adam) were shorter than he. *But he's quite the big enough man. A few inches wouldn't change him. I'm glad his children are happy with mine. Lord knows that mine couldn't be happier.*

Carolyn Hodges had joined them, too. News had come from Flag that her erstwhile husband had died, shot for cheating at cards, and speculation was rife within the Donovan clan as to whether—or really when—she and Owen would marry.

The old man's attention shifted to the argument his older sons were having at the far end of the table. The last thing to be done before the winter was to create another entrance to the Rocking Chair Ranch. With Jesse's baby due in January, they couldn't take the chance of her being snowed in. He and Adam and Daniel had agreed there was no way to keep the narrow, quarter-mile-long entrance to the canyon free of drifting snow, but the woodsman had found a smaller outlet where the brook babbled through to join the river. The canyon wall was only seven feet wide there and the existing tunnel was high enough for a man to crawl through. If they could build a small bridge and make the opening high and wide enough for a buggy to pass, the problem would be solved.

"You can't just chip away at it," Daniel was saying. "In the first place, you've got to control the amount of falling rock so the whole wall doesn't cave in on you. And in the second place, if you let too much debris fall into the brook, you'll create a dam. We've got to build some kind of boardwalk first, while the hole's still small, to keep the brook free of falling rock. And then we've got to find a way to control what falls."

"How are we going to do that?" Adam asked in exasperation. They'd come to the same point in their discussion before.

"I don't know how. I just know it's got to be done."

THE WOODSMAN'S ROSE

"Riley said he worked on the Central Pacific," Owen put in. All eyes turned toward him, speculation and confusion rife.

"That he did," responded John Patrick, "but what can it mean to us?"

"They tunneled through the mountains, didn't they?" Owen asked. "With dynamite? I wonder..."

"Right," said Daniel. "That could work, 'cause what we've got is a little tunnel to start with. If he knows how to blast it, to support the walls at the same time, that's all we need to know. And if he doesn't know how to do it himself, maybe he can tell us who to get. I'll talk to him tonight if he's there. He usually brings his kids, doesn't he?"

"They're such beautiful children," Jesse said. "It's a pity they have no mother."

"I'll talk to him," repeated Daniel. "If he's not there tonight, I'll go into town tomorrow. We need to do some stocking up anyway, don't we?"

He addressed his last remark to Annie. She wore her dress of jade silk and when she'd put it on, he'd fallen in love with her all over again. He'd spent most of the meal involved in his own thoughts, trying to find a way to refuse to let her dance with anyone else. Between her father and his, his brothers and hers, not to mention Alec and Tommy and anyone else who asked, he'd be lucky to have every second dance with her. He caught her hand under the table and held on tight. He'd let the evening bring what it might, then take her home and show her exactly how much he loved her.

And maybe Jesse will dance tonight, though it's on the verge of propriety. His sister-in-law wasn't one to stand on tradition when there was fun in the air. They'd be careful of her, all of them, but if she wanted to dance, they'd indulge her. It was no hardship to make her happy.

And dance she did that evening, but only the waltzes. Daniel knew she didn't care a whit what the old ladies whispered behind their fans, but she sat for long spells, waited on by Donovans, Griffiths, and Twelve Trees. After the first with her husband, she had only one dance with each of her brothers-in-law, and one with Alec. She danced, finally, with Eli Sykes, then put his hand in Rebecca's with a sly little grin. Later, Adam led her to the dance floor for the last waltz.

"Look," Annie whispered to Daniel, as they glided around the room. "Look at Jesse."

Daniel stole a glance at her: her cheeks were rosy and her eyes sparkled with delight. She met his glance and sent him a smile before Adam's steps turned her away.

"She's almost as beautiful as you are. And he's almost as lucky as me." Daniel saw that same look steal across Annie's face and thought, *We have been blessed, my brother and I. I wonder what we ever did to deserve them.*

"I love you so much," he whispered. He pressed his lips against her forehead and her small sigh made him content. *Tonight,* he thought, *tonight I will show her exactly how much I love her.*

Chapter 46

JOHN RILEY HAD BEEN a blaster in a coal mine in Ohio before coming West to work on the railroad. He agreed to examine the canyon's potential new entrance. He told Daniel he'd left his work upon the death of his wife, for he couldn't leave his children alone all day. "Aye, here I am with the most dangerous job in the wide world, and Grace it is that dies. Of appendix-itis, while the doctor's off to Sacramento for some damn convention or other."

"I'm sorry," said the woodsman.

"Aye. What's done is done and can't be undone. I just wish me wee Norah could get over it." Riley made a conscious effort to pull himself together. "But let's go and see this tunnel you're talkin' about. Be nice t' hear the boom-boom of dynamite again."

At the canyon, they showed him the tunnel the brook had made. He shook his head. "Nay. Ye've no way t' keep the whole wall crumblin' down on ye. 'Twill never do."

The Donovan men exchanged glances.

"What is meant to be will be," John Patrick muttered as he started toward the entrance to the Rocking Chair Ranch.

"Yon lassie wants her babe at home?"

John Patrick's voice held a note of desolation. "Aye. She's lost one already."

They'd just come through the gates and entered the narrow trail to the cabin when Riley pulled his horse up. "Y'know, there's a way to widen this trail here. Most o' that wall is shale, it breaks up easy.

It's the reason ye canno' blast o'er the brook—it breaks up that easy ye canno' control the fall.

"But here..." He pointed with his pipe. "Here ye've no brook to worry ye. And the blast shouldn'a carry far enough to disturb it. But we can reinforce it, just in case. Have ye got a place to take the gravel?"

"We'll find one," answered Daniel. "You're telling me we can blast this entrance wider?"

"Be a helluva lotta work, but it can be done."

"What does it take?"

Dynamite, men and wagons. And a place to take the gravel—tons of it. It wasn't a day's work or a week's, but a month's work—easily. Riley would be glad to help if arrangements were made to look after his children. His son Tim was in school, he said, but Norah rarely left the house. Mrs. Hodges had agreed to watch her today but Norah was panic-stricken when he left, fearing that he, like her mother, wouldn't come back.

John Patrick shook his grizzled head. "Poor mite. 'Tis always hardest on the little ones." After a few moments' thought, he asked, "Does she like animals? Cows and such?"

"Aye, loves all the critters. Cows an' ducks an' geese. An' kittens—loves kittens best."

Donovan's eyes sparkled. "There's a new litter of kittens at the dairy farm. My daughter Evelyn would be glad to have your little girl in her home. Evelyn has love to spare, and an understanding of a child's mind beyond my ken. Tim could perhaps do some little chores for Lowell and maybe learn about cows to keep himself occupied."

The younger man sat thoughtfully on his horse for a few moments, then stuck out a hand to John Patrick. "Aye, seems 'twould benefit all around. Suppose we start on Monday. I'll need time t' get me gear together. Do ye think," he added, "that the little ones could go for a visit t' the farm first? Before they'll have t' stay, that is?"

"Good idea. Bring them Saturday. We'll have a picnic lunch and let them explore the place. You know where it is?"

"Aye. An' maybe I'll learn a thing or two about farmin' meself!"

The arrangements were made. Norah was as happy at the farm as she was anywhere, and Tim spent the hours after school trailing behind Lowell and giving him more help than the dairyman would have thought possible. Knowing Daniel didn't want her to be alone in the cabin, Annie divided her time between the farm and the canyon. She and Jesse became even closer, and it was Annie who became little Norah's confidante, who soothed her pain and assuaged her grief, and played with her and the infant Adam for hours on end.

Norah's shyness with Evelyn soon resolved itself into love, for the tall red-haired woman had a gentle touch and a tender voice, and taught her lullabies and let her help with the baby's bath. The children were happier than they'd been since their mother's death, and John's absence for part of each day helped Norah to conquer her greatest fear.

One morning the little girl came from the barn with a kitten under her arm. "Where's Annie?"

"Annie has a headache today," Evelyn answered.

Norah was quiet for several minutes, watching Evelyn dry dishes. Unheeded, the kitten scampered away.

"Will she die?"

Evelyn pulled out a chair. She held her arms out, and Norah crept into her lap.

"Annie gets headaches sometimes," Evelyn explained in a gentle voice. "Sometimes they make her very sick. But, Norah, people can get sick and not die." She stroked the girl's fair hair. She'd already sent Lowell to Daniel—the headache wasn't too serious and Annie was still conscious, though in great pain. Evelyn was sure she spoke the truth to the little girl in her arms. "Norah, some day Annie may get sick and die. But not today. Some day," she said, "some day, everyone is going to die."

"But I don't want her to. I don't like it when people die."

"No, my love, I don't like it, either. But there are some things you and I can't change, aren't there? Like the sun coming up in the morning, and the wind that blows and messes up our hair. We like the sun and we don't always like the wind. But the sun doesn't always come out, and sometimes the wind feels nice. But there they are, and we can't change them.

"Annie will be all right, and she'll be here in a few days to play with you. In the meantime, why don't you say a prayer that her headache doesn't hurt too much?"

Norah closed her eyes and her lips moved silently as she prayed for her friend. When she'd finished, Evelyn hugged her tight. "You're a very good girl. I'm sure Annie feels better now." A small smile appeared on Norah's face. "Why don't you go find your kitten? I think he went into the parlor and maybe he's climbing the draperies!"

She skipped off happily, eagerly, and Evelyn said her own prayer for Annie's recovery. *It isn't fair. But then I guess it's one of the things I just can't change. If I had one wish in all the world...*

Chapter 47

DANIEL'S THOUGHTS WERE an echo of his sister's. He'd been awaken before sunrise by the whimpering sounds his wife made in her sleep. He could see the erratic pulsing of the vein in her temple. He slipped from the bed, went out to light the brazier, and before she opened her eyes, he was ready with her medicine and a hot cloth for her head.

"Da...el." Her first word was little more than a moan. Her eyes were half-open, the pupils like black points in the sea.

"Yes, *aroon*, I'm right here."

"...hurts..."

"I know, sweetheart." He lifted her head off the pillow. "Drink this now. It'll make you feel better."

She drank it slowly, her hands shaking as she helped him to hold the cup. "Oh, it's horrible," she whispered and forced a smile.

"I know." He brushed the hair from her face, knowing she was trying to mitigate his worry. "Here..." He draped the cloth over her eyes. "This should help, too."

"Mmmm." She brought one hand up to press it close over her right eye and temple. Her other hand reached for him. "Don't go."

"I'm right here."

"Daniel." The medicine made her voice weak. "Tell Norah I'm sorry."

"I will, sweetheart. Don't worry about anything. Norah will understand. You just go back to sleep now. I'll be right here."

"Dan...iel."

"Shhh. Go to sleep, *aroon*. Sleep now and don't worry."

She surrendered at last to the pull of the laudanum. He sat there with her until he was sure she was deeply asleep, then heated the cloth again. She whimpered once more as it touched her face, and curled over on her side. She'd sleep for four hours or more and maybe when she woke, it wouldn't be as bad. *If I had one wish in all the world,* he thought with a sigh. *Gran always said if wishes were horses, beggars would ride.* He thought of the old lady and whispered, "Help her, Gran. Help her. Let it not hurt so much."

Jake came a little later, for his father was concerned: Daniel had been joining them every day to help with the work in the canyon. Lowell came shortly after and to each he gave the same answer,

"She's all right. She's in a lot of pain, but it's not serious. She'll be all right."

He was sitting at her side late in the afternoon when she opened her eyes again. Her breathing hadn't been regular for several minutes—telling him the pain wasn't completely gone. But her hands were stronger as she reached for him and her smile wasn't forced. He held her close and kissed the top of her head.

"Better?" he asked.

She nodded against his shoulder but said nothing. She wouldn't use her voice, as it would waver and break for some time after she woke, a side-effect of the medicine. She snuggled closer and he stretched out on the bed and cradled her head against his chest.

He felt the little catches in her breath, the momentary spasms that told him the pain was still there. He waited for a while as it sometimes faded after she woke up. When he knew it hadn't diminished, he poured about one-third of an envelope of laudanum in a glass of water and offered it to her.

"But it's better," she protested.

"Liar," he said with a laugh in his voice. Though the drug induced a sense of being out of control, of drifting, she'd told him she minded

THE WOODSMAN'S ROSE

it less when he was with her than she ever had before. Again she made a face at the bitter taste. "Wonder if it'd taste any better if I put some honey in it? I'll have to ask Doc if that's okay."

"We're supposed to go honey-hunting," she said, her voice trailing off weakly.

"End of the month. We'll have to find a big hive, too. Mother said she's out of mead. Maybe we'll have to find two." He stroked her hair, watched as her eyes closed again. She'd sleep for an hour or so and he'd have a light supper ready when she woke again, in case she wanted to eat. And tomorrow, he felt sure, she'd be better.

She was hungry when she woke—a good sign. She wanted to get up and sit at the table but he made her a tray instead. She ate the soup, the bread, and asked for more. Then, as he cleaned up the kitchen, she sat and watched, smiling every time he looked over at her.

Just after sunset, he came back to her. He'd hung his clothes on the pegs in the corner and she smiled again at his neatness. At his strong, solid body. She slipped over toward the wall as he got into bed, then moved in close to him and brushed her fingers against his chest. He pressed his hand over hers, stilling the motion, and he gazed down into her eyes. "*Aroon*, you need your rest."

"I need you."

He hesitated. Never had she denied him, and he didn't want to hurt her by refusing her now. But he was afraid her strength wasn't as great as she thought it might be. He lifted her fingers to his lips, then placed his hand against her heart to feel the beating. It was strong and regular. His hand then rested against her temple, felt that the fluttering in the vein had stopped, the erratic pulsing was calm.

"Annie," he whispered against her ear. "I..."

Arrah, are you afraid?

Yes, *aroon*. Of hurting you. Of harming you.

Do you love me?

More than life.
Do you need me?
Yes, *aroon*. More than I need the sun.
Do you want me?
Oh, my love, more than anything in this world.
You are so good.

She turned her cheek against his shoulder and nestled in against him. *He'll protect me. I must trust him, trust in him and I will be safe.* She heard the long breath he let out, then closed her eyes and let him hold her until she slept again.

IT WAS LATE THE NEXT morning when she woke. She got up carefully, knowing she might be dizzy and weak. She washed her face, put on a dress and brushed her hair. Then, barefoot, she stepped out into the sunshine and found her husband sitting on the edge of the porch.

He held a hand up to her. She took it and descended the few steps, came to sit between his knees. He put his pipe down and began to braid her hair.

"Mawnin'," he drawled when he'd finished. She turned her face up for his kiss. "Feeling better today?"

"Much better." With a touch of shyness, she added, "Thank you."

"*Aroon*," he chastised, and quoted one of Katie's bits of wisdom, "'*I want not thanks nor money, but your love.*'"

She made a happy sound, leaned back in his arms. "You know you have that."

"I know. And I wouldn't give it up for all the thanks or money in the world."

"Daniel?" The few minutes' silence was broken by her question.

"Mmmm?"

"I've been thinking about the money your father gave us. It seems a shame for it to just be laying there in the bank, not doing any good."

"But I can't seem to convince him we don't need it." A bit of frustration leaked into Daniel's words.

"Why don't we do something with it, then? If he says it's ours, we could do what we wanted, couldn't we?"

"We don't need it, *aroon*."

"I know. But that doesn't mean no one does."

"Oh? What do you have in mind?"

"I thought we could tell Mr. Thatcher to let Doc Barber draw on it. For when he needs medicine someone can't pay for. Like Mrs. Callendar's little ones or the Navajo up in the hills. There's really a lot of folks around who don't have extra money—why shouldn't they have the medicine they need? Or why should the doctor always have to pay for it himself?"

"*Aroon*, you are the most thoughtful girl in the world. It's a great idea. It'll help out the people who need help the most. Do you want to go tell Dad?"

"After lunch," she replied. He laughed—she'd had nothing to eat since the day before, and only one meal then.

"I love you." He pulled her to her feet and into his arms. He shook his head and laughed again. "Let's get you fed! I can't wait to see Dad's face when he hears this!"

After they presented her idea to John Patrick, Daniel left them talking together and joined his mother in the kitchen. Over a cup of tea, he told her everything he'd learned about Annie's condition and asked for her help.

"You and Gran gave Jesse so many things to help her when she was sick. Is there anything you can do for Annie? Even if you could make her a little stronger, it would mean so much to her. I know you can't cure it—but can't we make her life easier?"

And a little longer. Molly heard the unspoken plea and considered her reply carefully. "There are many things in your grandmother's books that will help with all kinds of illnesses. But, my son, I am not sure we know exactly what Annie's illness is. Let me first talk to the doctor and see what he can tell us. Then I will consult the books to see what may help.

"I make no promise, my lad, but I will do everything I can. For her, and for you."

"Thank you, Mother. I'm sure you'll find something."

"Aye, we should. If only to lessen the pain."

"If you could do that..." He'd give her the world, the stars, the moon.

"If I can do that, 'twill be thanks enough in itself."

Chapter 48

THE FOLLOWING DAY, as Molly talked to the doctor, Daniel, Annie and John Patrick met with the village's banker. William Thatcher was a man in his mid-fifties with a full head of graying hair and a voice that was steeped in magnolia tea. He carried himself with authority and radiated unflappable competence, giving assurance to those he dealt with. When John Patrick explained what they wanted, he pulled a three-page form from his drawer and began to ask questions in a precise tone.

"Do you want a revocable instrument?"

"What's it mean?" asked the elder Donovan.

"Do you want the right to withdraw the money once it's deposited?"

"No." Daniel's tone left no doubt that his was the final word on the subject.

"Do you want to establish a foundation?"

"What's it mean?" John Patrick repeated.

"Do you want to be able to add money to the fund from time to time? And do you want other people to be able to contribute to the fund?"

"Why not?" was Daniel's opinion. "That means it can go on indefinitely, right?"

"As long as funds are available," the banker intoned.

"It sounds right to me," said Annie.

"All right," said the banker. "Do you want to limit the amount that can be paid to any one individual?"

"No." It was unanimous.

"Do you want to pay for medicine or for medical expenses?"

"What's the difference?" A frown cut deep lines into John Patrick's brow.

"Well, if the deed of trust states it pays for medicine, then that's the only covered expense. But if, for instance, you have a child that needs to go to Flag for treatments with a specialist, the fund wouldn't cover that. You'd have to specify that it would cover all medical treatment. If you want the cost of the trip to be covered, too, you'd specify *all medical treatment and related expenses*."

"Say that, then," said Daniel. "Whatever a sick person needs."

"Do you want to limit the beneficiaries of the fund?"

"Bill." John Patrick's tone was desperate. "Just say what you mean."

"Well, you could set this up for children only, or Indians, or those of Irish descent—"

"Or exasperatin' bankers," put in John Patrick. He rose heavily to his feet. "Thatcher, you know what we want. Tell the doctor about it and work out the details between you, then bring the papers for us to sign." He saw the hurt look on his friend's face and added in a more moderate tone, "Bill, we trust you. And we trust Theo. Set it up between you and we'll sign it. If you bring it out on Sunday, I'll make sure Molly sets an extra place at the table. And one for Nellie, too."

The banker stood and offered his hand. John Patrick took it and shook it, then turned to go.

"There is one more thing," Thatcher said.

With an irritated noise, Donovan asked, "And what might that thing be?"

"The foundation needs a name."

"A name? What's it need a name for?"

"It's a legal entity," the banker explained. "It needs a legal name. You could call it the Donovan Fund, the Annie Donovan Foundation, or anything like that. But it needs a name of its own."

John Patrick sighed and Daniel hid his chuckle with a cough. "Just bring the papers Sunday, Bill. We'll have a name for you then."

But by Sunday when the banker and his wife arrived for dinner with the family, they were no closer to a name for the fund than they'd been in his office. Thatcher was annoyed.

"We can't execute these documents without a title for the account."

"So what's the problem?" asked Adam. *"A rose by any other name..."*

"It's the other name that's the problem," Daniel explained. "Dad doesn't want to call it the Donovan Fund, because it was Annie's idea. Annie doesn't want to call it the Annie Donovan Fund because... well, just because. So we're stuck without a name."

"Why not call it *Garryannie*?" Adam inquired. John Patrick clapped his hands together, Daniel's eyes sparkled, as Adam had once again earned his reputation as the poet of the family.

"That's pretty," said Jesse, "but what does it mean?"

"It means *Annie's Garden*." Adam turned to Annie. "You've planted a little money—seed money, you might say. Now we just sit back and watch the good things grow."

"THE GARRYANNIE FOUNDATION TRUST FUND," the banker intoned. "It certainly has a ring to it. Someone spell it for me." He filled it in on the papers before Annie could object. "And now that it has a name, I'd like to be the first to make a contribution." He took a cheque from his pocket, already made out for one hundred dollars, and assigned it to the foundation with a flourish.

In the weeks that followed, several more citizens of White's Station did the same. Tommy and Alec contributed in Elena's memory, came to tell Annie about it with tears in their eyes. The doctor's sister began to put in a few dollars a month out of her "egg money". The Griffiths contributed as a family and the younger Donovan twins took the money they'd earned with the excess produce and gave it to the banker. Jake contributed a mustang to the auction Carolyn Hodges organized to benefit the fund.

Adam had spent his accumulated wages on the repairs that had been needed in the canyon, but Brian had a few hundred dollars left after their cattle purchases. He contributed it in the name of Rocking Chair Ranch, and Jesse cried when he told her what he'd done.

"After all," the big man said, "we're partners, ain't we?"

Chapter 49

THE BLASTING WAS FINISHED and the resulting gravel had been cleared from the trail. Most of it had been used to create a low wall on the north side of the Donovan holdings, while the remainder bordered the flower beds in front of the ranch house and cabin. The entrance to the canyon was now only twenty feet long and graduated from twelve feet wide at Tommy's gates to almost forty feet wide at the far end. It might yet fill with snow but removal would take only hours, not days.

Annie came visiting a few weeks later and found Jesse sad and listless. On this date, two years before, she'd delivered her stillborn child. From time to time during the day her eyes filled with tears, but she managed to fight them off. Annie spoke of the good things the past year had brought them, especially little Adam Griffiths, and she gave Jesse assurance her own baby would be as healthy. But she saw that, today, Jesse had to struggle to believe her.

It was mid-afternoon when John Patrick came in, for he too remembered the day. Adam and Annie made some excuse to take themselves outside, leaving him alone with her.

When Jesse offered him tea, John Patrick insisted on making it himself, for he'd seen her trying to hide the trembling of her hands. When she spilled hers, he took the cup gently from her, then sat close beside her. Her body trembled with a force that shook the couch as he put an arm around her and drew her head down to his shoulder without saying a word.

She began to weep, and he held her silently until she quieted. Then he took one of her hands and spread it on her swollen belly. His own hand, wide and gnarled and tender, pressed lightly on top of it. The baby gave a lusty kick and she laughed.

"He's so strong!" she said in wonder. He watched her face as she began to understand.

"Thank you," she whispered, then rested her head on his shoulder once more. He held her and considered how much he loved her. More than if she'd been his natural child.

There was no physical attraction—the only woman he'd ever desired was Molly, and the very thought of infidelity would make him shudder. *Nonetheless, I would crawl into a pit of snakes for her. For she has seen and survived more tragedy in twenty short years than most men face in a lifetime. And has come through it with her spirit intact. Even stronger. And it is not so much what a man endures, as it is the spirit in which he endures it. She is a miracle of spirit.*

Then in the half-world just before sleep, she lifted her face to him, her eyes barely open. "Daddy?"

One little word, yet it filled his heart. He guided her head to his shoulder and answered, "Yes, little girl. Your Daddy's right here."

⁂

THANKSGIVING WAS THE last time the doctor would let Jesse travel. He'd initially forbidden her to leave the cabin at all, but she'd begged and cajoled and given all manner of promises, and he'd relented. Daniel once more converted the largest of the Donovan buggies to an invalid coach, creating a wind-proof, weather-tight carriage using deer hides. Then the brothers came to pick her up.

Arriving at the ranch, Jesse was handed down to John Patrick and taken to the small parlor behind the stairs that had been Katie Donovan's retreat. Adam came in after her—he hadn't been in this room since his grandmother's death. He expected a renewal of pain and grief, but found instead a quiet sort of sorrow and peace. He sat in Katie's accustomed seat and Jesse sat beside him, her bright head on his shoulder. The few tears they shed were for the empty places in their lives, and offered up in gratitude to the woman who'd brought them so close together.

Owen and Carolyn came to dinner, and Daniel had invited Eli Sykes. They were also expecting the doctor and his sister Jane. When Molly heard this, she said to her husband, "Why don't you ask John Riley and his little ones to come as well?"

Molly set her table up so Riley's children would sit on each side of him, and Jane Barber would sit next to his daughter.

Jane had continued to change over the past months. Her brother was reading every word he could find on the new science of psychology. Barring emergencies, he'd set aside an hour after supper to listen to her, and had weaned her from the influence of Sarah Taylor. When he had emergencies to tend to, she went with him, and he'd found she had a real talent for nursing, especially when the patient was a child. Jane loved children and a good part of her bitterness had sprung from the fact that they were afraid of her.

It wasn't long before Jane lost her heart to little Adam Griffiths.

"Would you like to hold him?" asked Evelyn.

"Oh, may I?" They settled her in a chair and placed the baby in her arms. He looked up at her and gurgled. "Oh, you are so beautiful," she cooed at him and her face was radiant.

Her brother and John Riley were both watching her. One thought of the happy little girl he'd lost and somehow found again. The other thought of the Madonna. And Molly Donovan smiled a tiny, secret smile.

At dinner, Jane went to great pains to entertain Norah, for the noise generated by some twenty adults was overwhelming for the girl. Jane coaxed her to eat and talked to her beneath the din.

Dinner at the Donovan home was always followed by music. After each guest had cleared their plate from the table, Molly declared a moratorium on the clean-up and they adjoined to the formal parlor. With its blue chintz furnishings and marble fireplace set off by dark floral carpets and cream draperies, the long room had a warm, cheerful quality. The adults sat around the edges of the room; the younger people arranged themselves on the floor.

Norah was standing by Jane's chair when the singing began. When she was offered a place on Jane's lap, the little girl accepted shyly. And Molly saw Riley watching Jane again.

John Patrick caught the gleam in her eye and reached out for her hand as he began to sing,

> *Oh, Molly bawn, why leave me pinin'*
> *All lonesome waitin' here for you?*
> *While the stars above are brightly shinin'*
> *Because they've nothing else to do.*
>
> *The wicked watchdog he is snarlin'*
> *He takes me for a thief, you see,*
> *For he knows I'd steal you, Molly darlin'...*

They all took a turn starting a song, and Jesse convinced Eli to sing as well. In a deep, rumbling bass, he began,

> *I am a poor, wayfarin' stranger*
> *Come wand'rin' through this world of woe,*
> *But there's no trials, heartache or danger*
> *In that bright world to which I go.*

After the first verse, Geordie picked up the tune on his harmonica. Rebecca hummed along and when the song was finished, the crowd was silent for several moments.

THE WOODSMAN'S ROSE

"You have to teach us that," Jesse told him. "It's really beautiful."

"I learned it from my Mam," Eli said, clearly flustered. "It's someone else's turn now."

Daniel began to play again. All the family looked to Adam, who sat with his eyes half-closed and his hand in Jesse's. Slowly he stood and walked to the fireplace. He threw his cigarette into it and stared at the flames until the music came around to the verse once again. He didn't face the company, and there was a throb in his voice as he began to sing his grandmother's favorite song.

Oft in the stilly night, ere slumber's chain has bound me,
Fond mem'ries bring the light of other days around me.

After a short pause, pregnant with emotion, John Riley joined his son Tim in "The Dingle Puck Goat." Tim was just three years older than his sister, but with the help of his father and Brian, he managed to complete all eight verses of the ditty. The entire company cheered for him. John then began "Norah O'Neale" for his daughter, and the Donovans joined in for the chorus.

Norah sighed happily, her father watching all the while. *I've no use for doctors, and yon lass is the doctor's sister. Still, this one seems to know his business, and I've not heard complaint of his absence. Ach, what are ye thinking? She's but an old maid. Not even pretty, though she does smile quite nice. And Norah likes her. What are ye thinking?* He shook his head but continued to watch as his daughter fell asleep on Jane's shoulder.

When the conversation came around to the Christmas party, Annie found an excuse to take Tim from the room. The woodsman asked for Jane's help with the wooden puppets he'd make for the children. Jane blushed and Riley smiled at her.

"You did a wonderful job last year," said Daniel in his gruff voice. "I thought I'd make a few more this year, maybe even some for the girls."

"Oh, that would be wonderful! I really enjoyed painting them. Maybe some of them could have little skirts and I could paint braids down their backs."

"Or some with pig-tails. And, Daniel," Jesse added wistfully, "I want one, too."

They all laughed but the woodsman promised her a puppet. And Carolyn, as always, offered to make the punch. She was sitting with Owen and he was holding her hand. They'd been quite open about their courtship. He wanted to get married right away but she'd demurred, stating they should wait a decent interval.

"He's been gone for nine years, Carolyn! How much longer does it have to be?"

But she'd stood firm. She'd always wanted a June wedding. He'd given in, gracelessly at first, then in fondness. She was a good woman and she loved him, and it was worth waiting for.

Carolyn had no illusions about Owen's feelings for her. She knew he was lonely since Annie moved out. She also knew he was fond of her, though much of his heart had been left in Wales. He wanted comfort, companionship, and loving attention, and would give her all the love he had left in return. And she wanted him—a good man, a faithful man. A man who was gentle and understanding and true to his own beliefs. She didn't want Megan's place—she wouldn't have believed him if he'd offered it to her. She wanted all the things he wanted, and she wanted to make him happy.

At the end of the evening, as Riley took his daughter from Jane's arms, Annie turned to her husband and whispered gleefully, "I bet there are two June weddings!"

Chapter 50

AFTER THE GUESTS HAD gone and his family had taken themselves upstairs, John Patrick sat in his mother's back parlor, a well-worn journal in his hand. He began with his personal prayer of thanks and proceeded to make notes, as he always did, of the accomplishments of the year just past.

He was pleased with the way his younger twins had handled the farm. The projections Frank offered in June were accurate to within bushels of the harvest, and he'd given them permission to put two more fields under cultivation, and to sell any produce that wasn't needed by the family or the Navajo.

And both the boys now married. Two more different girls I cannot imagine, and still they've become fast friends. Patricia is as she's always been, a flibbertigibbet. Yet she has a kind heart. Frank is happy, and Geordie moons over his own bride. Suzette may be only seventeen years old, but there is a grace and maturity about her that belies her age. She is shy, there's no mistaking it, but she is neither silly nor gauche. My sons have done well.

With his pencil, he made more notes: he'd rarely seen a busier year. The ranges, both his own and that in the canyon, were well-stocked with cattle. After the new room for Jesse was completed, he'd helped paint the cabin inside and out, made another green flowerbox for the new room's window and installed Franklin stoves in the other two bedrooms. He was of the opinion the cabin would be hotter than hell in the winter ahead but had, as usual, kept his views to himself. And the finished product was beautiful—a small white house with green trim and silvery cedar-shake roof. It reminded him of home.

Geordie's house had been built—the ranchhouse in miniature, with two stories instead of three, and a single porch across the front. There were details still to be attended to, but they'd accomplish them as soon as the fabrics and wallpapers Suzette had ordered arrived. The orchard and gardens would wait for spring, but the all-important outhouse was complete.

And the cabin now standing on *Sidhean Annie*, finished and furnished. Water flowed in two pipes to the kitchen—one hot and one cold, for Daniel had added a covered porch outside the kitchen door, taken the brazier and built it into a well of stone, and hung an iron cauldron on a frame above it. A series of pipes kept the cauldron full. Annie had only to step out and light the coals; in twenty minutes she would have warm water, in an hour it was boiling. She could pump it directly into her kitchen sink, or into a large canvas tub. She'd have the luxury of a hot bath without the chore of heating a dozen kettles of water, all because Daniel had discovered that hot compresses brought some measure of relief for the pain in her head.

And they'd built a smokehouse, an outhouse, a post-and-rail corral, and a fence for the garden she'd plant in the coming spring. The pine bark Daniel had saved was too rough for shakes, so it became kindling, and this cabin, too, had a cedar-shake roof. They'd grafted fruit trees from the Donovan orchard to transplant, and Jesse had donated cuttings of her mother's favorite roses for the square columns of the porch.

The roses blended perfectly into the scene, for they were almost the same light yellow as the cabin. They glowed with peach undertones, and John Patrick felt they were a perfect symbol of their Annie, with her light golden hair and peachy complexion. He'd mentioned his feelings to his son.

THE WOODSMAN'S ROSE

"There's something called the wood rose, isn't there?" Daniel had inquired. "That might fit her—she's always seemed to me like a little sprite in the forest."

"But the wood rose, now, 'tis brown and crinkled. Not like our Annie at all. I'd say," he'd added with a twinkling eye, "she is more like the Woodsman's rose."

He could see he'd pleased his son, and Tommy had told him the name had been accepted by the tribe in the mountains. How it had traveled that far, he wasn't sure, but Daniel had long been known and respected among the Navajo, and his father felt there must have been some good deed done and never mentioned. On the other hand, Tommy had a way of taking the puns and proverbs John Patrick spoke and broadcasting them far and wide. And without much concern for the interest of his audience.

He wrote those two words on the page now, and let his thoughts wander to his younger daughter. Irene was as deep as her eyes. *Not serious and shy like Suzette, nor a flighty hen like Patricia, she is nevertheless a vexatious little minx, sure of her own beauty and her power to persuade. She's had us all 'round her tiny finger since the day she was born. And she'll have her pick of the men in this Territory.* There were already three of them looking wistfully at her: Michael Flaherty, not quite as empty-headed as his sister; Alec Twelve Trees, somber and silent in love as in grief; and Ben Thatcher, the banker's son, who'd come home briefly after graduating college, before his parents sent him on the Grand Tour. Ben had asked her to wait for him, but she'd turned her eyes down and answered demurely, "We'll see."

Vexatious minx, to give the boy hope. For it will be a man who wins her. A man like her brothers, solid and true and strong enough to be gentle. It's a shame Owen hasn't another son, for certainly Evelyn and Lowell have made a happy union.

As for Jake, it seemed that at seventeen, his youngest was a man. His voice had settled to a deeper register. He was taller now than all of them, and had spent the better part of the summer in the mountains with Alec. They'd brought back a dozen mustangs, including a blue roan that had caught John Patrick's eye. He found his son an astute trader—they'd haggled the price down to the penny and he'd been happy with the value of the mare for the money. Then Jake had laughed, handed him the reins, and ruffled his hair.

"Do you think I'd *sell* you a horse?" he demanded. "Did you sell me my bed? No, Dad, take her. You've paid more than enough for her."

He'd protested but Jake stood firm. The summer sun had browned his skin and burned the childishness from him forever. *And yet there is still an innocence there, a simplicity. Like Daniel, he's in love with life. As well as with our little girl.*

He gave thanks again to his Lord, for Jesse was well—the lassitude she'd suffered in the spring had evaporated over the summer, and there was no doubt now she was stronger and healthier than she'd ever been. *And why not? Since she was thirteen years old she had the care of an invalid and her brother's brutality to contend with. And then her baby's death, the illness following, her husband's withdrawal into grief, and my own mother's death—all had sapped her strength. But she is pampered now, waited on by Adam and Brian and Rebecca. Her fears have been calmed, the scars of abuse almost healed. And she has a family to depend upon—to love her and protect her. And to bless her for bringing Adam back to us.*

He almost wept with gratitude. He hadn't known what to do when Adam withdrew from them. He hadn't been able to find a way to comfort him. But Jesse had somehow brought him back. He knew his son didn't believe that he deserved her love, but faith had returned, and he accepted it now on the basis of his grandmother's words: Love is a gift.

THE WOODSMAN'S ROSE

Ah, macushlah. Her son's heart was still sore from the loss he'd suffered. *How much we miss you. How much you are still a part of our lives.*

He owed gratitude there as well to Rebecca. *She has filled a place in our lives we never knew was empty. She gives so much, wants nothing in return but our little girl's happiness. But each time there is need, this loving woman steps in to lend her hands.*

And the family at the Rocking Chair Ranch would not have been complete without Brian. No home and family for his son, except that which he shared now. It might have been sad but for the obvious happiness the big man had gained. *Like me, my sons have been late to find their hearts' mates. Even my younger twins are twenty-five. It seems the past two years have given them something they lacked before—a vision of the future. And it is all since our little girl came to us. And the most deeply affected has been Daniel.*

The woodsman has changed. No longer totally independent, no longer remote and restrained. Jesse's advent into our lives has given him an opportunity for happiness he never thought to have. He's loved his Annie since childhood—even through the years when it seemed she would marry his brother. He could never understand why Brian didn't return her love, yet Brian would not have been the right man for her. None of us had seen it, until Jesse came. She loved Adam, but she needed Brian, too—needed him to be the brother she didn't have to fear. Needed his strength, his kindly wisdom to help her through her trials. She does not know that Brian loves her as a man, not as a brother. And we will not tell her. But his dedication to her happiness has made Daniel's dream a reality.

There is a bond between my son and Annie that defies description. It is as if they are one person in two bodies. The strengths of one are physical, logical. Of the other, insightful and giving. They have both changed these past months—they have grown more like one another. My son will never have insight, yet he has come to understand our small sorrows and joys. His wife will never have physical strength, yet he has taught her that it is enough to do all that she can. He is so solid, so earthy—she is a fairy-child. And their love has given us a double blessing. For he is more ours now, and less his own. And she has taken us into her heart.

And finally, his thoughts turned to his Molly. What would his life have been like without her? He grimaced at the thought. *An empty landscape,* he answered himself, *with nary tree nor bird nor cottage to redeem it.*

She was fifty-one years old, but it seemed to him she was still the girl of seventeen he'd met and married in an instant. She'd given him a look full of promise before she retired, then turned as Brian spoke to her. Longing now for the privacy of their bed, John Patrick tucked the journal into his vest pocket, dropped the pencil into the desk drawer, and stirred the embers in the fireplace before wending his way up the stairs.

Chapter 51

ANNIE BEGAN TO SPEND more time with Jesse, who was convinced now her baby would be healthy. Annie's presence made the days of confinement easier. Jesse wondered aloud if she'd ever get to the Christmas party. Eyes twinkling, Annie promised, "I'll bring you a piece of cake!"

Daniel was hunting with Jake and Alec most days, and was happy to leave Annie in the canyon. Jesse pestered her for news, and Annie revealed that Norah Riley had started to go to school, and Jane Barber was "stepping out" for the first time in her life.

"With John Riley?" Jesse asked. Annie nodded sagely then giggled. She bit her lower lip.

"Tell me. Tell me what you know!"

"I think," said Annie, "I think they'll get married."

"Oh, how wonderful! Everyone should be married—don't you think so?"

ADAM WENT TO TOWN ONE day with Jesse's Christmas list and returned to find the doctor had visited in his absence. Rebecca met him at the door with the news. She was wringing her hands, a gesture completely at odds with her normally stoic character, as she told him the doctor had ordered Jesse to bed.

"What else?"

"Jane came with him, and after the doctor was finished, she asked to see Jesse alone. I don't know what she said, but our little mite's been crying."

Adam went in and sat beside his wife. She was asleep, lying on her side with her hair falling over her face. He brushed the tawny curls back to find her cheeks wet with tears. *I'll kill her! If she's said anything to hurt her, I'll kill her with my own bare hands.*

"Jesse... *Mavourneen*, wake up."

"Adam," she murmured, and one little hand came out from under the quilt. He took it in his and touched her hair again.

"How are you?"

"All right. Just tired. Doc said to rest as much as I can."

"Are you warm enough?"

"Shore am," she replied in a drawl more pronounced than usual. "Y'all did a wonderful job with this room—I'm snug as a bug!"

He glanced around at the white-washed pine walls, the cheerful blue striped curtains, the white quilt Moira Flaherty had made for them. Then his left eyebrow curled up from the middle as a frown furrowed his brow. "Rebecca said Jane came in to see you?"

She closed her eyes and nodded. A tear spilled from the corner of her eye and he wiped it away.

"Tell me, *mavourneen*. What did she say?" When she didn't answer, he repeated, "Tell me."

"She said she was sorry. For all the mean things she said. She said she was wrong, she was jealous. And she was sorry."

"All right, love. Don't cry." He wiped her tears with a corner of the quilt. "Please, *mavourneen*, don't cry."

She reached for his hand again and took a deep, shaky breath.

"It's just... it makes up for so much. She didn't have to do it. She never said anything to me, so I wouldn't have known. Don't you see?"

THE WOODSMAN'S ROSE

"Yes, love, I do," he answered. "And I'm glad she did. But, *mavourneen*, don't cry. Please."

"Come here, love. I want to hold you." He lifted her in his arms and took her out to the old rocking chair. She snuggled up close to him and he covered her with an afghan and held her tightly. But she was quiet. Too quiet. *I will kill that woman. I'll kill her right now. Because I know she's done something—said something that hurt.*

"Jesse, what else did Jane say?" He felt the little start she gave. "Tell me, *mavourneen*."

Tell him, a lilting old voice said. *Tell him all. He will understand.*

"She..." She caught her bottom lip between her teeth, trembling violently. Her breath came in little gasps. "She said... that Sarah Taylor told her... that..."

Tell him, it crooned. *Tell him and let him heal it. He will understand.*

"That Tommy... that Tommy and me... we... we..."

"Hush, my love," he whispered. "Hush. That wicked old bitch doesn't have enough to do. That's why she makes up stories. No one would believe that, Jesse. No one at all."

But her trembling didn't subside and a sobbing noise escaped her.

Tell him.

"Russell... believed it... that's why he... he said if I... was good enough... for... an Indian..." She clutched at him frantically. "Adam... Adam..."

He held her even closer, whispered in her ear. Any words of comfort he could find while in his heart, he cursed her brother to hell for all eternity. Cursed the wicked woman who'd manufactured that lie, who'd put them through this horror.

God damn that Taylor woman! Keep me away from her. Keep me away from her or I will beat her to death. I want her to hurt, to bleed, to be terrified. I want her to feel what she has done to this innocent girl. My little girl. Oh, dear God, how could you let this happen?

He felt Annie's hand trembling on his shoulder and looked up into her tear-streaked face.

She needs you, said the pale eyes. He controlled his rage, and pressed his lips again to his wife's forehead. He murmured into her hair.

"Adam?" It was a plea. "You don't..."

"No, my love." He lifted her face to his. "How could I believe anything so silly? Jesse." Deep and tender, yet with the hard edge of steel. "Jesse, *mavourneen*, I know I am the only one."

Annie sank to her knees and blessed him. For his words had struck Jesse's heart, removed the fear she'd lived with for so long, that he'd someday hear the rumor and believe it. Annie heard the groan that went up from Adam's soul.

Let it be over! Let this be all. I do not know how much more I can stand.

As she reached for him, Annie caught Jesse's hand also, and the girl looked up at her. Her tears had stopped falling and there was a serenity in her smile that went beyond the surface. Went all the way down into the depths of the spirit on which she lived. There was no more. No more fear. No more secrets. No more. Annie took her hand and closed it around Adam's, then wrapped her own over it.

It is over.

Relief flooded his being as he freed his hand to stroke his wife's bright hair. He looked down at Annie. *Thank you,* his heart said, and her soft smile acknowledged it. He turned to the woman in his arms, wiped the traces of tears from her face with his thumb.

"Did Doc say why he wanted you to stay in bed?" he asked.

"He said not to worry. There's nothing wrong. But the baby's getting so big and I'm so little—he doesn't want it to come too soon. We have to defy gravity and keep this little one in here a few more

THE WOODSMAN'S ROSE

weeks." She held his hand against her. "But I think he's got a mind of his own."

"He? Does 'he' have a name?"

"I think we should name him after your brothers."

"Brian?"

"Mmmm." She cocked her head at him. "I thought after all of them."

"But, Jesse, how many names can he have?"

"Oh, we'll pick out one for everyday. You know, when we call him and such."

"You don't really mean you're going to name him 'Brian Daniel Frank Geordie Jake'? Be serious, love."

"You forgot Conor," she told him, "and Henry."

"Jesse..." He knew she was teasing him and was thankful for it, for the calmness he felt in her. So he sighed in mock exasperation. "All right, love. If that's really what you want."

She was still giggling at him when Daniel came for Annie.

"What's the joke?" the woodsman asked.

"No joke," his brother responded. "Just a name for the baby. Jesse's sure it's a boy."

"Great! So what's his name?"

"I thought we'd name him after his uncles," Jesse replied.

The woodsman was quiet for a moment. "I think that's a fine idea."

"Daniel!" Adam found himself laughing. "Okay, I'm outnumbered. Poor kid's gonna have seven names. But what if it's a girl?"

Suddenly serious, Jesse replied, "Katherine." For his grandmother.

He took her hand, raised it to his lips and kissed it with utmost tenderness. "Thank you," he whispered in a voice thick with emotion.

"You wonderful girl. I love you so much." He hugged her close and Daniel patted her bright hair.

"We'll see you tomorrow," he said. But Annie shook her head.

"Tomorrow's Sunday," she said in a strained voice. "We're going to Evelyn's."

"Monday, then," he told Jesse.

"Say hello to little Adam for us." She grabbed for Annie's hand and pulled her down to kiss her cheek. "Thank you so much."

Annie smiled but didn't respond.

Chapter 52

ANNIE REMAINED SILENT as Daniel helped her into the buggy and they drove off. After a few moments, he asked, "You all right, *aroon?*"

"I want to go to town."

"It's kind of late. Sure it can't wait 'til Monday?"

"I want to go now." Her voice was small but fierce.

"Tell me what's wrong. What happened?"

They were several miles away before she answered him and when she did, he had to piece together her narrative, for it was broken by sobs and a struggle for words. When it was over, he was holding her tightly against his side. "Oh, for— What on earth ever possessed that woman? She'll be lucky if Adam doesn't kill her."

"I'm going to tell her. I'm going to tell her what she's done."

"You can't do that, *aroon.*"

"I can!" Her pale eyes flashed at him. "I can and I will!"

"No, Annie—"

But she'd realized they were on the trail to *Sidhean Annie.* "Take me to town," she demanded. "I want to go now."

"Annie—"

"If you don't take me, I'll walk myself." Her chin was quivering. "Stop this buggy here and I'll walk myself."

"Let's go home and talk about it."

She pushed away from him. "I don't want to talk to you. I want to talk to Sarah. If you're afraid to come with me, I'll go by myself."

"*Aroon—*"

"Will you take me?"

"No, Annie, I won't. I—"

"Then don't speak to me! I'll go by myself."

She sat on the outer edge of the buggy seat in stony silence, turned as far away from him as she could. He saw that her jaw was set but her fist was pressed against her mouth to control its trembling. For once she didn't look at the meadow, didn't admire the few flowers still braving the cold.

My sweet girl. There's been nothing in her life to prepare her for something like this. But she'd never forgive herself. She'd never forgive me for letting her go.

"*Aroon...*"

"Will you take me?"

"Annie, we need to talk about this."

"I don't want to talk about it! Don't you understand? Don't you know what she's done? He hurt her because he believed it! He killed Elena because he believed it! She's a wicked, spiteful bitch and she's responsible! *Don't you understand?*"

As he pulled the horses up at the cabin he turned to her, but she jumped from the carriage and ran across the meadow toward town.

He sprinted after her, gaining slowly, close to being winded when he caught her by the arm. They went tumbling, but she was on her feet in a flash. She turned to scream at him but he lifted her, slung her over his shoulder. She was still screaming, kicking her feet and pounding her fists against his back. She pulled his hair and he grunted in pain, but continued his march to the cabin. She flailed at him but the blows had no strength. He was more worried about the harm she might do herself than any she'd do to him.

He kicked the door open with his foot. Annie was startled into silence—violence was no part of his nature. He took her in and dumped her on the bed, then slapped the bedroom door shut. He leaned up against it for a moment, breathing deeply.

THE WOODSMAN'S ROSE

She sat on the bed, her face buried in her hands. On silent feet he approached, then touched her hair.

"*Aroon*..."

She pulled away from him, back to the wall, shaking her head and sobbing.

"Annie. Look at me." Never had he used that tone—a command that wouldn't be brooked. She was frightened again, but still she shook her head. "Look at me."

He knelt beside the bed, one hand almost touching her. She looked and sobbed, looked again, and turned her eyes away.

"Annie, look at me," he repeated. "You've got to listen to me for one minute. For just one minute. Then if you still want to go to town, I'll go with you. Will you listen?"

"Yes." It was barely even a whisper, but it was enough. His hand found her knee and this time she didn't draw away.

"I know you're upset, Annie. I am, too. But I don't think you should do this."

"Why?"

"Because it would hurt her."

"What do you care about her? Why should you care about Sarah?"

"Do you think I give a damn about Sarah Taylor?" he bit out. "Do you think I wouldn't like to see her flogged? Do you think I could care less if Adam kills her? That I don't want to kill her myself?"

Annie's fists were pressed hard against her mouth, her eyes huge gulfs of fear. He realized he'd been shouting, grabbed a lungful of air and let it out slowly. He got up and sat beside her. She stared at him for a moment, then reached out tentatively.

"I'm sorry, *aroon*," he murmured as he drew her into his arms, "I didn't mean to yell at you. But I don't care about Sarah. They could take her out and hang her and it wouldn't bother me at all. But don't you see who'd really be hurt? Don't you see what would happen if this started all over again?

"We have to think of Jesse. Of how much it would hurt her. Annie, you don't want to do this."

Her eyes grew wide as wagon wheels. "Oh, no," she sobbed. "No, no." She wrapped her arms around him. "Daniel, I'd never hurt her. Never." Her face was hidden on his chest as she sobbed again, "I'm sorry."

"All right, *aroon*." He held her close, his hand gentle in her hair. *Poor little girl. Such a heavy burden for such a little girl.* "Sweetheart, don't cry. It's over and no harm's done."

"I hit you." Her voice betrayed her shame.

"I'm a big boy, sweetheart. You didn't hurt me."

"I'm sorry." A tiny voice now, like a frightened child.

"It's all right," he soothed her. "Don't cry, my love. Everything's all right."

"Forgive me?"

"Of course, *aroon*. Here..." He lowered her to the pillows. "Lie down with me. That's better. Now stop your tears."

But it was several minutes before she stopped crying and several more before she spoke.

"Daniel?"

"Yes, *aroon*."

"I love you."

He kissed her forehead. "I love you, too, Annie."

"I'm sorry."

"I know, sweetheart. It's all right." With a tender hand, he lifted her face to his. "Got a kiss for me?"

She did, and it left him breathless. He nuzzled into her hair and heard her whisper his name again.

"Mmmm?"

THE WOODSMAN'S ROSE

"Don't you think something should happen to her? For being so wicked?"

"Yes, I do," he answered, "and tomorrow I'll go tell Dad about it. He'll find a way to handle it without hurting Jesse. As Gran would say: *"Coimhéad fearg fhear na foighde."*

"What does it mean?"

"Beware the anger of a patient man."

Annie nodded against his shoulder. "Daniel?"

"Mmmm?"

"Thank you."

"You're welcome, *aroon*," he answered, and again his rough voice was sweet as honey in her ear. "Got another one of those kisses?"

Chapter 53

JOHN PATRICK WITHDREW his custom from Taylor's mercantile. He marched in on Monday morning and canceled his outstanding orders for both winter feed and spring seed. He left the merchant stuttering behind him and paid no heed whatsoever to the pleas raining down upon his back.

He'd thought it through carefully: there'd be enough time to wire Prescott if necessary to arrange for winter feed. First, however, he'd try the new shop. It had been established only a few months before, but Evelyn had told them she was pleased with the yard goods. The quality was better, she'd said, and the choice wider. And Jake had found new pants there when the mercantile had none long enough for him.

John Patrick led his mare down a side street and came upon an unpretentious sign:

Hardware, Feed and Dry Goods
Wang Shen, Prop.

He had Molly's Christmas list in his pocket and found every item save one. He approached the small man who stood behind the counter. "Have you something called a camisole?"

The proprietor turned to the shelves behind him. He had a long, thin braid that reached past his waist. Pulling a box from the shelves, he asked, "What size, sir?"

"Don't know." The list in his hand simply said *white camisole for Irene*. "Got a white one?"

THE WOODSMAN'S ROSE

"Oh, yes, sir. All white." The proprietor held up a flimsy piece of silk which looked like no more than two handkerchiefs sewn together. The old man let out a sound that was close to "Hrrmmph." Eyeing the silken trinket in perplexity, he muttered, "Needs to fit Irene. How would I know?"

"Irene, sir? Irene very pretty girl. Very tall, very slender. Very beautiful. This one fit Irene." He took what to her father seemed an even flimsier garment from the box. The older man touched it tentatively.

"You're sure this is a camisole?" Where on earth did his Molly ever hear of such things?

The proprietor nodded.

"All right, wrap it up. All this other stuff, too. Can you deliver it?"

"Yes, sir. To Donovan Ranch, sir?"

John Patrick nodded, impressed. "Can you get me some winter feed?" He watched the merchant consult a chart of what seemed to be hieroglyphics.

"How much?"

"Four wagonloads to start."

"Yes, sir. Tuesday week, two wagonload. Thursday week, two wagonload. Deliver to Donovan Ranch?"

"No, to Rocking Chair Ranch—out in the canyon. You know where?" Again the man nodded and Donovan asked, "Shall I pay for them now?"

"Not necessary. Pay on deliver. Or in town next time."

"All right. How much for everything?" The merchant named his price and John Patrick was satisfied. "By the way, do those camisole things come in different sizes? Bigger, I mean?"

"Yes, sir. All size—fit woman big and small."

"Well, why don't you wrap up another one? For Molly," he added cagily. Wang Shen shook his head. "You know Evelyn?"

"Oh, yes, sir. Evelyn with beautiful hair like flame. And lovely baby boy."

"Molly's like Evelyn." Her husband's hands were expressive. "Only just a little more."

Wang Shen's eyes twinkled. "Yes, sir. Deliver, too?"

"No, I think not. She may open it if she sees it. I'll come back for it later."

"Very good, sir."

He heard the merchant humming as he walked from the store. He left his horse there and strolled down the wide main street to the livery, where he expected to find Alec. But Tommy was there alone.

"He should be back t'morrow," the blacksmith offered. "He went with Dan'l up t' the hills for some elk. Got a hankerin' for it m'self. Anythin' I can tell 'im for you?"

"You saw the shamrock he made for Jesse last year?"

"Sure. You lookin' for somethin' like it?"

"For Molly. But I thought more of a brooch than a necklace, and maybe a little larger. Think he can fit it in?"

"I'll ask 'im. I don't like to speak for 'im, but he told me yestidday he was almost caught up. Course I don't know what might've happened since then."

"Be grateful if you'd mention it. Tell him to send word if he's too busy. I'll have to think of something else in that case."

"Sure. Got a price in mind?"

"Lad's never cheated me yet."

Tommy laughed. "More'n you can say for some folk roun' here. By the way, you been down t' the Chinaman's shop?"

"Just came back. You've been there?"

"Sure. Do all my buyin' there now."

John Patrick tapped his pipe out over the forge, then refilled and lit it. "Any special reason?"

THE WOODSMAN'S ROSE

"Calls me *sir*," the smith answered, nudging his friend with an elbow. "Nice t' do business with someone who likes you, y'know?"

"Aye. Just did some shopping there myself. Took Molly's Christmas list. Ever heard of a thing called a camisole?"

"Can't say I have. What is it?"

"Come 'round on Christmas and ask Irene to show it to you." Her father knew he was making mischief, for Tommy would bring his son as he always did on Christmas. It would be interesting to see Irene's reaction to the smith's request.

"Where's Christmas this year? Out in the canyon?"

"Can't leave our little girl out of the fun."

"She'd never let you hear the end of it!"

They laughed for a minute at the thought of Jesse being left out of anything, then John Patrick took himself to Owen's shop. He'd ordered new hats for Adam and Brian, leather gloves for the younger twins, and boots for Jake—two sizes bigger than his last ones. He contrived to bring the conversation around to the new shop and was satisfied to hear Owen was placing all his new business with Wang Shen. The invitation to Rocking Chair Ranch was offered, but the bootmaker had decided to spend a quiet day with Carolyn after seeing his children in the morning.

John Patrick returned to the shop for Molly's gift and his mare. As he rode out of town, he decided to pay a call on Jesse, just to see how she was doing.

He found Annie and Rebecca with her. A short time later, Adam and Brian came in with a fir tree. Rebecca popped some corn and, with the berries she'd dried in the summer, the three women sat with needles and thread and hot cider, making garlands.

He sat and smoked by the hearth, listening to their conversation while Adam dipped pine cones in white paint. John Patrick took a fine brush and tipped them in red, and passed them to Rebecca and

Annie, who tied lengths of yarn to them and hung them from the tree and the mantle.

He sent Adam out for evergreen branches and wove a wreath for the front door. Rebecca added a grand bow she fashioned from a length of red gingham. Brian produced sheets of colored paper he'd squirreled away in childhood and cut chains of dolls, birds and stars, while Jesse crocheted some two dozen small white snowflakes to add the finishing touch to the tree.

As he left, John Patrick called Adam outside and filled him in on the details of the family's Christmas plans. As he rode home, the old man was happy. Their little girl was well. Her baby would be healthy, and he would see that justice was done.

Chapter 54

THE FIRST SNOW FELL on Christmas Eve, cloaking the earth in thick white velvet—enough to bring a peaceful hush to the canyon but not enough to make traveling treacherous. It clung to the bare branches of the cottonwoods and sycamore, gave the conifers cat-whiskered limbs. The sun shone pale upon them, making subtle patterns that reflected in the windows of the cabin.

Daniel and Annie were first to arrive on Christmas morning and found Jesse lying on the couch in the quilted pink robe Evelyn had given her the year before. While Daniel drank coffee in the kitchen with his brothers, Annie went to sit beside her.

Adam saw Jesse take Annie's hand and press it against her stomach. The baby evidently gave a good kick and Annie's face lit up. He'd known his brother's wife since the family had first moved to Arizona; still she was an enigma to him, with her child-like innocence and her seer's eyes. He was glad she was now so close to Jesse, for her assurances had brought much comfort to his wife. They both believed she was fey.

His mind wandered back to the times he and his three oldest brothers had played with Lowell. Always had Annie tagged along. First she followed her brother, then gradually she became Brian's shadow. Just as Daniel became hers.

She'd been afraid of nothing, and they'd had to curtail their adventures whenever she was too small to follow where they led, but Daniel would most often help her over the rough spots. Yet for all her tomboy ways, Annie was an utterly feminine being—her long, fine hair the color of sun-bleached wheat, her body lithe and graceful even through the awkward years. But it was her eyes that had enchanted Adam, and he'd wondered at times if her ancestry included oracles or priestesses.

One incident was vivid in his memory: she'd been brought to her knees and rocked in silent agony as the pains shot through her head. She'd fallen face-down, unconscious, and they'd thought she was dead. Daniel had opened her dress enough to feel for the pulse at her throat. When he found it, they all breathed again. His brother had carried her into the shade, laid her on a soft mat of pine needles and cushioned her head with his shirt. They'd waited hours, it seemed, until she opened her eyes. With great relief, the other boys went back to their play, leaving her in Daniel's care.

Amazing that none of us ever realized how much he loved her.

BY NOONTIME THE CABIN was filled to overflowing with Donovans. Every one of them had brought their gifts, and there they sat in piles under the tree—big packages and small, wrapped in white or brown or bits of colored paper—some even wrapped in wish-book pages—and all tied up with bright yarn or ribbon in red, green, and blue.

Jesse still sat on the couch, still in her quilted robe. Irene had tied a green ribbon in her hair, Annie sat as before on the stool at her side, and Jake stood at her feet looking down in silent worship. Adam stood behind the couch and stroked her shoulder, and she responded with a radiant look.

Molly and Evelyn had brought an ample lunch—sliced meats and bread, butter beans baked in molasses and cinnamon, hot cabbage with apples and honey. But they had to eat in groups of six, for no one had thought to bring extra plates. There was much laughter, and threats from those who were waiting against those who were eating. Brian took a plate with the first wave and somehow held on to it through the second and third.

"Hey," he said, "I live here, I'm entitled!" But they booed and jeered and slapped him resoundingly on the back. Rebecca's rum punch was passed around and the younger twins returned to the bowl again and again, until their father snuck outside and came back with two huge snowballs to rub in their faces. At that, all the men and most of the women ran out into the snow.

From the window Jesse could see the flying missiles, and also hear each grunt of surprise or pain as one found its target. She dozed off for a while with little Adam at her side, while Molly and Rebecca cleaned up. When Adam came in, he knelt beside her and kissed her forehead. Behind him came the wave of antagonists, all in various states of dishabille. Frank had evidently taken the brunt of the offense—he was covered in white from head to foot and the brothers were teasing him.

"You shoulda stood still," laughed Brian, "then we none of us coulda hit you!"

"Yeah," came Daniel's granite sally, "you shoulda stood like a mountain sheep—you'd've been safe then!" With that, the tide of teasing was turned and Brian became its next victim.

After the noise diminished somewhat, John Patrick clapped his hands together and demanded, "Who gets the first gift?"

"*JESSE!*" They all shouted at once.

"Good choice. Adam, you've something for her?"

From under the corner of the tree, Adam took a tiny white box and handed it to her. He'd put a red ribbon on it and her hands shook as she untied it. When she opened the box, she gasped.

"Let's see!" they demanded. "What is it?"

She held up a delicate pin that matched the gates to the Rocking Chair Ranch. "It's beautiful," she said breathlessly. "It's beautiful." She turned her face up for his kiss.

"Now you know how this works," John Patrick said. "The one who got the last gift gives a gift, but not to the person who just gave the gift. Understand?"

They understood. It had been tradition ever since they could remember, and the younger twins had explained it to their wives. So the gifts went round and round and round until there were only three left under the tree. Annie had received the last gift—a long coat of shearling wool which Daniel had made for her. She was still wearing it when, with her husband's help, she took up an awkward, heavy package and brought it to Jesse.

"But you already gave me one," Jesse protested. She'd gotten a coat just like Annie's, except it was a deep tawny color to match her hair while Annie's was an ivory hue. And in the pocket of the coat she'd found a little jointed puppet.

"This one's for baby," Daniel said. Jesse's eyes got big and bright as she struggled with the wrappings. Annie helped her uncover a cradle—a hand-made oak cradle with deep sides and a hood to protect the baby from the sun. On the head and foot were carved replicas of Katie's design—the letter "D" with the Celtic symbol of eternity surrounding it.

"You made it." Tears streamed down Jesse's cheeks. "You made it for me."

"We all did," Daniel told her. "I designed it. Dad and Geordie made the body, Brian and Jake made the rockers. Frank did the carving. Patricia and Suzette made the mattress, and Mother and the girls made the little quilt. Annie made the pillow."

Jesse was speechless but the rapt look on her face was thanks enough for all of them.

"Thanks, y'all." Adam imitated his twin's drawl. They nodded at him but continued to watch Jesse as she caressed the wood, the quilt, the pillow.

"Well, missy," John Patrick broke in. "Have you anything left to give?"

"Oh, yes! That little one there." Irene brought it to her and she handed it to her husband. "It's for you," Jesse whispered. "Merry Christmas."

He took the gift and her hand, kissed her fingers. He opened it, stared at it, then at her.

"Oh, Jesse," he murmured. He took the ring from the box and handed it to her, and she slipped it onto his finger. He caught her hands and held them as the family crowded around to see the heavy signet ring whose design was identical to the one carved on the cradle. His grandmother's design. The Donovan brand worked in silver. His heart was full, his lips were trembling. He bent to kiss her face.

"Thank you, my love," he whispered into her hair.

After surreptitiously wiping his eye, John Patrick cleared his throat. "There's still one left here. Whose is it?"

"It's mine," Adam answered in a voice not quite steady. They passed it to him and he took it to Jake. "Here you go, boy-o."

Jake whooped as he unwrapped a pair of Mexican silver spurs. "Wow! These are great! Thanks!"

Adam had to reach up to ruffle his hair. "You've earned them," he said. And there was something in his words that made Jake proud.

As the day advanced, friends and neighbors dropped in—Tommy and Alec, Eli Sykes, the doctor and his sister Jane, Ray and Mary Benson. The Rileys and Flahertys, William Thatcher and his wife Nellie, even Owen and Carolyn. Before they left, the assembled guests built a snowman in the yard for Jesse, with buttons for eyes and a carrot for the nose. They used twigs for the smile and the eyebrows, one of which turned one up at the middle. Sticking a cigarette butt in its mouth, they hung an old gunbelt from its left side. Annie ran in and grabbed Adam's new black hat to complete it. When he carried her to the door to see it, Jesse laughed until she cried. She waved in response to their goodbyes, and called out, "Thank you—all of you! For everything!"

And they shouted back, *"Merry Christmas!"*

⁂

ANNIE SNUGGLED UP AGAINST Daniel in their buggy, half to ward off the cold and half for the pleasure of being next to him. She'd felt so close to him since their quarrel, so sure he had done the right thing. She was grateful, but even more, she was impressed by his wisdom.

"Guess what?" she whispered.

"Mmmm?"

"It's a boy."

He looked deep into her sea-green eyes and smiled. "Good. That'll make her happy." They rode along silently for a while then he bent to kiss her.

"I love you, *aroon*. Merry Christmas."

Chapter 55

THE HOUR WAS EARLY, before daybreak, when Annie rolled over and nudged her husband awake.

"What is it, *aroon*?" His hand went instinctively to her temple.

"No, not me. Daniel, we've got to go."

"Right now?"

"Yes."

While she dressed and stuffed a carpet bag full of towels and sheets, he threw on his clothes and lit the brazier, put two bricks on top of the coals, and hitched the horses to the buggy while a fine, wet snow fell. Then he went back inside to start a pot of coffee.

"We don't have time," Annie said as she tied her cloak.

"We'll have time. The bricks have to heat up—it'll take fifteen or twenty minutes. And you need to be dressed more warmly." She began to protest but he put his hands on her shoulders. "*Aroon*, I don't want you sick. It won't help Jesse if you are." He stroked her cheek with one finger. "And you know you have to stay warm."

It was the doctor's advice and it, along with Molly's medicines, had reduced the number of severe headaches she suffered. She stood on her toes to kiss him and went to the bedroom to find more layers of clothing.

She's better. And she's beginning to believe it. It had been a gradual change—Molly had warned them it would be. For his mother had gone to the doctor with the information she'd gathered, Barber had given his opinion readily.

"I know what the specialists have said, but I've also known Annie for a long time. I always thought she had two conditions, and not just one. But when I tried to ask her questions about her cycle, she'd just freeze up. She was so embarrassed, it was painful to watch her.

"What you've told me confirms my feelings. The headaches she gets in her temple and her eye—the ones she wakes up with in the night—these are tied to her cycle. They're called megrim, and they're caused by the fluctuation of hormones and chemicals in the body. At least that's what the scientists say. She gets them once or twice a month, according to what you've told me, and always at the same phase of the moon. Well, Molly, I don't have to tell you how those phases tie in to a woman's body." Molly nodded and the doctor wondered why he'd never asked her to talk to the girl before.

"The weakness she experiences," he went on, "could be related to the megrim, or it could be from an unusual loss of blood. You'll have to ask her and see if she'll answer you. If her flow is very heavy, we can try to build up her blood before it—about a week before, we could start giving her some extra red meat. Or they say some of the root plants are rich in minerals, 'cause I know Annie doesn't like meat too much to start with. Anyway, that's the condition we can deal with. It may sound cruel, but thousands of women experience this kind of pain every day and live through it. It's frightening, it's agonizing, but it's not fatal. We can't make it go away, but it'll gradually disappear after she's forty or so."

The doctor paused in his explanations and took a long, deep breath. Molly knew somehow that the worst was still to be revealed.

"The other condition," Barber finally said, "is the one that makes her faint. I think it's caused by pressure on her brain. I think there's a growth that presses on her brain from time to time."

"A growth?" Her voice was low with fear.

"A tumor. She told Lowell she could sometimes feel it growing. I think it's at the base of her skull, where there are a series of tiny

THE WOODSMAN'S ROSE

arteries that bring blood to the brain. When it presses on them, it inhibits the flow of blood and makes her lose consciousness. And sometimes it causes her great pain. In a matter of hours or just minutes, the pressure shifts away from these vessels and she comes back to us again.

"Molly, someday it will kill her. But I don't know when. It could be tomorrow—it could be when she's seventy. There's no way to tell and, as far as I know, there's nothing we can do. But if you find something in Katie's books, I'll be more than happy to let you know if I think it will help. Although," Theo added, "maybe we don't have to know it will help. Maybe we just need to know it can't hurt her.

"As for the megrim," he said after a short pause, "we can try to build her blood up, and maybe regulate her hormones. And keep her warm—it seems strange, but she shouldn't let her hands and feet get cold. On a day when there's high wind and a glaringly bright sky, she should stay indoors in a darkened room. They say it helps even though, again, they don't know why." He pushed himself to his feet and took the hand she offered him. "I'm sorry, Molly. I wish I could have given you better news."

"'Tis better than I expected. At least we may be able to help with the pain."

"Anything you find, you let me know. If it can't harm her, we'll give it a trial, see if it helps. Who knows? Maybe there's something that got lost along the way. Maybe we'll find the cure for all the ailments in the world."

After a private discussion with Annie, Molly returned to the doctor with some of Katie's medicinal digests, and he agreed the treatments she recommended could do no harm. If the old ones were right, they might even help.

"I've seen things in the mountains with the Navajo," Theo said, "that I know shouldn't have worked. And yet they did. Sometimes it's a chant or a dance over somebody who should already be dead. But the next day, they get up and go about their business.

"I think a lot of illness is in our perceptions—in our minds. Maybe if we give Annie some hope, then her mind will accept it and make her feel a little bit better."

Molly wasn't sure the doctor's words were realistic, but in her knot garden she found feverfew, which was said to relieve pressure on the brain; licorice root, which she knew would control the hormones; and red clover, which she'd read would reduce the rate of growth of a tumor. Then she diced some beets, hung them over the stove in bleached muslin bags to dry, and pounded them into a powder. The old books recommended it for those with weak or pale blood. The first three ingredients she mixed into a tisane. The fourth, she poured into a glass jar and took to Annie with the recommendation that it be added to her soups, stews, and any other dishes she might want to try it in. From time to time, Daniel grew tired of the taste of beets, but had only to look at his wife's cheeks, glowing now with health, to subdue his complaint.

She came out of the bedroom in her new sheepskin coat, wearing so many layers of clothing beneath it she was almost shapeless. She had a pair of leather gloves Owen had made for her in one hand, and a furry hat in the other. She put them on the table and accepted a mug of hot milky coffee. Daniel poured the rest into a glass jar and wrapped it in a small towel—it would keep her hands warm for a while, then they'd drink it. He'd collected a sheepskin and bearskin rug.

"Ready?" he asked. She nodded and drew on her gloves and he handed her the jar of coffee, then draped the cloak around her with the opening in the back—if her face got too cold, he'd draw the hood up over it.

"My hat," she reminded him.

THE WOODSMAN'S ROSE

He pulled it down over her ears and tied it under her chin, then kissed her quickly.

"Let's go," she said, "it's awfully warm in here!"

He laughed, but put his own coat on and gathered up the skins. He spread the sheepskin on the seat and lifted her up onto it, then took the hot bricks wrapped in burlap and placed them beneath her feet. Finally he climbed in beside her and tucked the bearskin in around her.

"I can't move," Annie complained.

"Are you warm?" he asked, and she gave him a pout. He moved in close to her, sharing the heat of his body, and clicked the reins over the horses' backs.

As they drove, the stars began to fade in the west. The sun came up behind them. It was the time of day he liked best. And today would be a good day—another little baby would come into the world. Annie had told him everything would be fine; she only wanted to go in case Jesse needed her reassurance.

They didn't use the trail which led to the Donovan ranch but skirted instead to the south, making the trip shorter by several miles. As they rode along, Annie told him of a conversation she'd overheard between Jesse and Adam a few days earlier.

He already knew that, since Christmas, both Adam and Brian had found excuses not to leave the clearing where the cabin stood. They popped in frequently during the day. Jesse had laughed, for Rebecca never left her side and Annie was usually there, too. But the day had come when Adam wouldn't leave her for more than a minute.

"When's this baby supposed to be born?" he demanded a few days ago.

"In January," Jesse responded.

"Isn't it January now?"

She laughed merrily. "Yes, dear, and it will be for at least twelve more days."

The woodsman had to laugh at his brother, too. But he wondered at the same time how he'd feel in Adam's place.

Chapter 56

WHEN DANIEL AND ANNIE arrived, both Adam and Rebecca were in the bedroom, holding Jesse's hands while she moaned in pain. Annie took Adam's place and he went out to fall weakly on the couch.

"How's it going?" Daniel asked.

"Rebecca says she's doing fine. Everything as it should be. But it sure is good to see you."

"Annie wanted to come. Doctor on the way?"

"Brian went for him about two o'clock this morning. He should be back by now." The anxiety Adam had managed to keep hidden from his wife found its way into his voice.

"I heard there was an outbreak of fever up at the Navajo camp."

For a moment, Adam stared at him. "Oh, God! If he went up there, Brian'll never get him back in time."

"I could go get Mother."

"Would you?" Adam leaped to his feet and herded Daniel toward the door. "Take Apples, he's the fastest. Here's your hat. My saddle's on his stall."

"Can I take my coat, too?"

"Take anything you want—just go! Now!"

With the woodsman gone, Adam began to pace up and down in front of the hearth, smoking incessantly and listening to his wife's moans. On occasion, Annie or Rebecca would come out for fresh towels or water and tell him Jesse was doing fine. He struggled to believe them, and her first scream hit him like the blow of an ax. He stood still then, just outside the bedroom door, ready to run to her if she called for him. Or if she were afraid. He was standing there when his mother arrived.

The sun had passed its zenith; he couldn't believe so much time had passed. Molly took his hand and guided him to the rocking chair.

"Sit here, *acushlah*," she said as if he were a child. She brushed his black hair back. "You need your hair trimmed, my lad." He gave her a half-hearted smile as she squeezed his hand. "There is no need to be afraid. She will be fine. The baby will be fine, I feel it. Do you remember your Gran said the sorrowful times are over?"

"Almost," he replied, "almost over."

"Yes, for she knew that she would soon leave us, and that we should have sorrow for that. She said you would find great happiness. Have you?"

"Yes." It was like a prayer, reverent and low.

"Then believe in it. Believe in your grandmother's vision."

Adam's eyes popped open as Jesse screamed. "Go to her," he begged. "Help her."

"Yes, *acushlah*, and soon we shall have another little Donovan."

Daniel came in moments later and Adam held out a hand to him. "Thanks. For bringing her. And for bringing Annie."

"How is she?"

"They're still telling me she's fine. But, brother, it sure don't sound like fine to me."

As if to punctuate his sentence, Jesse screamed again, her voice starting as a low rumble, then traveling up the scale to a note that would make a prima donna envious. He heard his mother soothing her, saw Annie run out to the kitchen with the black bag, heard Rebecca's voice in encouragement. He closed his eyes, unable to bear the sounds any longer, and an old, melodious voice whispered in his ear. *All will be well.*

THE WOODSMAN'S ROSE

Molly had sent Annie out to prepare a tisane for Jesse. She'd listened to the beating of the baby's heart, felt the strength of the last contraction, and determined that Jesse's small body was ready to deliver her baby. The tea, when it came, was comprised of white willow bark, which would dull the mother's pain without making her lethargic, and trillium, or Indian shamrock, to strengthen her womb and her contractions. Jesse drank it without protest. Within minutes, whether by nature's design, or God's or the medicine's, Molly was holding the baby's head.

"All right, *mavourneen*, one more time for the shoulders, then it will be easier. There's a good girl."

Annie and Rebecca stood on either side of the bed, Jesse clenching their hands hard. Her moan escalated to a scream but she continued to follow Molly's direction, as the perfect little baby fought his way into the world.

Molly bound the cord in two places and cut it swiftly; she cleaned the infant, clearing his tiny nose and mouth. Then she picked him up and jiggled him, slapping him gently on the seat to make him breathe. He let out a lusty yell, and Jesse opened her eyes wide, reaching for him. Molly swaddled him and laid him on his mother's breast. She touched the tawny head and said, "You've done a wonderful job, *mavourneen*. He's beautiful." But Jesse didn't look up.

Molly washed her hands and left the room. Her eldest son stood outside the bedroom door. Brian had made it home, too, and was just taking off his hat and coat. Daniel sat by the fireplace and they all beamed when she said,

"Another little Donovan baby. My son..." She took Adam's hand and squeezed it as her voice dropped a notch. "You have a son."

"Thank you." He hugged her hard. "Is she all right? Can I see her? Can I see him?"

"She's fine. They're both fine. Give us just a few minutes to straighten up."

He nodded speechlessly and turned to his brothers, found himself enveloped in Brian's bear hug. Scarcely able to breath, he hugged his twin back. Then Daniel was pounding on his shoulder so hard it staggered him. He couldn't say a word as they congratulated him—his wife was fine, and his baby was alive. The sudden absence of a fear he hadn't recognized made him dizzy. Then his mother beckoned to him from the doorway.

He went in slowly, quietly, as Annie and Rebecca came out. Approaching the bed with reverence, he saw his infant son at his mother's breast. He went down on his knees, put his head on her pillow, stroked her hair, then touched his son's perfect little cheek.

Annie was peeking around the door, and motioned for the others to come close. They heard him say, "Oh, Jesse, *mavourneen*, I love you so much."

"*Acushlah*," he said to the baby, "you are the most beautiful thing I have ever seen. Except for your mother." Raising his head, he asked, "Does he have a name?"

"Kevin."

"Kevin." He'd been sure she'd choose Brian. "But Jesse, you said..."

"I said *after*," she said with a sly look. "*After all your brothers*. And K comes after J, doesn't it?"

Chapter 57

DOC BARBER STOPPED at *Sidhean Annie* one afternoon and brought news from the Navajo camp. Short Feathers, the father of Blue Deer, was displeased that Daniel had made his son an artificial leg. The boy had been ecstatic when Daniel and the doctor had first presented it; the leather cuff fit over his thigh and a series of criss-crossed leather bands buckled around his leg and waist. Tommy had crafted a jointed foot, and between the boy's long pants and his new knee-high moccasins, the wooden leg was never seen. Blue Deer walked with a slight sideways limp, and treated the prosthesis with devotion.

But Short Feathers had forbidden the boy to wear it, and his son was again being tormented by his peers, while the old ones were once more ignoring his gifts. Theo told them the boy was heartbroken and had taken to sitting silently in his hogan, which displeased his father even further.

Leaving Annie at the dairy farm one morning, Daniel asked Tommy to accompany him to the Navajo camp. They visited with the elder Running Wolf, whom Daniel had counted among his friends for years. Though he was no chief, his people had followed him without question, but now Running Wolf was losing his influence over the tribe.

When the old chief had died, his son had ascended to power in his place. But the young warrior hadn't lived long, dying the following spring of the measles. He had no heirs. Though his people wanted Running Wolf as their chief, he wouldn't accept the position, stating he wasn't wise enough to lead them. Since then, the men would meet occasionally for the ostensible purpose of choosing a new leader, but it was never finalized. The tribe was happy following Running Wolf, who respected their traditions and made no decisions without consulting them. The older people were secure in his care; the children were safe from the missionary schools and were continuing to learn the traditions of their people.

It was the youth who were unhappy, those who'd been segregated from their tribe at the missionary schools. They'd found no place in the white man's world, found that their place in their own world had been irretrievably denied them, and the reappearance of Yellow Knife was turning some of them against the wisdom of their elders.

The woodsman listened carefully to Running Wolf's words. They spoke a patois of English, Navajo and Spanish, each man understanding more of the other's language than he could speak, with Tommy interpreting where needed.

Yellow Knife had come back with six more warriors. The tribe hadn't turned them away, for the way of the Navajo was to welcome all. Here the elder gestured at Daniel. The same, he said haltingly, as the way of the Donovan. The woodsman accepted the compliment with a nod.

But the young people had been restless and the hatred Yellow Knife bore for the white man had infected them. Running Wolf could no longer control them. Their parents had lost contact with the children through the long years of missionary school, and the bonds of mutual respect hadn't been forged. Criticism was met with rage and accusations of cowardice. The harmony of life had been disrupted, and Running Wolf tried to express his regret. But the elder's parting words were not lost on him.

"Go no more alone. Go careful. No more alone."

The message sent a chill down the woodsman's spine. He offered the older man his hand, then turned and picked up his rifle as a

THE WOODSMAN'S ROSE

warrior came into the camp. Younger and slightly taller than the woodsman, his face was set in a sneer. His bare chest was broad and muscular, his arms corded with veins. His hips were narrow, his legs as heavily muscled as his arms. His skin had an unmistakable tint of yellow, indicating a white ancestor somewhere in his past. Daniel wondered if it accounted, at least in part, for his hatred of whites.

The warrior came close, stood in front of Tommy, and spat out some words Daniel didn't understand. But Tommy waved a dismissive hand at Yellow Knife, flicking him off as he would a fly. Having forty pounds of muscle on the interloper, and no lack of confidence in his own skill as a fighter, Tommy was obviously not in any awe of Yellow Knife.

But he'd still be a formidable opponent, Daniel thought, then wondered at it; they had no quarrel, yet it was plain the Navajo was antagonistic to him as well as to Tommy.

Rifle in hand, Daniel nodded once again to Running Wolf, then turned and slipped into the forest. He looked back once to see perplexity on the face of the young warrior and smiled to himself. It had been a long time before the tribe had accepted his accomplishments as a hunter and tracker. White men, they were sure, were no more at home in the woods than mule deer would be in the town. Evidently Yellow Knife shared this prejudice. *Someday it might stand me in good stead.*

Again he wondered at the thought, turning it over and over in his mind. A nagging suspicion couldn't be eradicated. *I'm getting like Annie—I'm trying to read the future. But she's the one with the gift, not me. And it will only frighten her if she senses this fear in me.* So he beat his uneasiness down, but slipped cautiously through the woods until he was on Donovan land again.

Chapter 58

SPRING ARRIVED EARLY and as quietly as the two babies would let it; Kevin had a touch of colic and Adam was teething. Molly gave Jesse a tisane of catnip and licorice root which soothed her baby's stomach, while Evelyn dipped her finger in the best Irish whiskey and rubbed it on her son's gums. The mothers were together as often as they could arrange it, meeting at least once a week at the Donovan ranch. Rebecca, Molly, Irene and the sisters-in-law doted on the children and spoiled their mothers. John Patrick and his sons were proud as peacocks, and discussed each gurgle, burp and hiccough as if it were the greatest of accomplishments.

Kevin looked just like his father—soft black hair and bright blue eyes, wide brow narrowing to a pointed chin. The first time he curled one eyebrow up from the middle, they laughed for hours.

His cousin, Adam's namesake, presented them with something of a quandary. He had a shock of bright red hair but his light blue eyes had turned to hazel. His face was round, his nose turned up a bit at the end. Any exposure to the sunlight caused freckles to form on the bridge of it. The discussions as to which of his parents he resembled became quite lively at times, until Annie put an end to them.

"Don't you see? He looks just like Papa!"

Jesse upheld her opinion and, when Evelyn stood behind her father-in-law and draped her bright hair over his head, they had to admit that, if Owen had been blessed with a mass of unruly red

THE WOODSMAN'S ROSE

curls instead of a bald pate, there would have been no question whatsoever.

Jesse rarely got to town—Adam felt it was too long a trip for her and Kevin to make. Come summer, she'd change his mind and he'd learn, as his father had, that babies were hearty. Meanwhile she appreciated his solicitude and respected his anxiety, and came to the ranch to catch up on the news.

There was no doubt White's Station was changing. John Riley had transformed the squatter's shack he'd purchased into a charming cottage complete with blue shutters and a tiny lilac bush. Daniel and John Patrick had helped him irrigate and transform the patch of barely arable land into a respectable farm. It stood on the south end of town, only a short walk from the Barber's, and Riley and his children passed many a pleasant evening with the doctor and his sister. Miss Jane now smiled almost continuously, and the attempts Sarah Taylor made to involve her in gossip were futile.

The merchant's wife wasn't an astute woman, but finally even she had to admit there was no longer enough merchandise leaving her husband's store to support them. The traders were stopping at Wang Shen's first, for he had an unerring eye for quality and offered fair prices for their goods. The trappers went to him for the same reasons—Wang Shen would pick through their pelts carefully, turning away only those which were of particularly low quality, offering the same scale of prices to all comers.

The Navajo traded with Wang Shen, for he let the tribe run an account against the blankets, baskets, furs and silver articles they promised to deliver. They quickly learned he wouldn't accept second-rate goods in trade and respected him the more for it. The poorer families traded with him because he didn't harass them about their balances and would accept payment in kind—eggs, jams, jellies, fresh vegetables, hand-made quilts and coverlets, even knitted gloves and mufflers. Again his scale of payment was applied equally to everyone. If he made a change in price, he'd post it on a slate board by his cash register, and in advance whenever possible.

News got around that Wang Shen was creating work for the poorer families by accepting their hand-crafted and home-made goods. Most of the community was closely-knit, neighborly, its members more than willing to lend a hand to those in need. There was no shame attached to poverty, no sting of charity to remind them, for their help was solicited whenever the village needed anything talent or effort could supply. The town hall was a shining example—every family was expected to contribute to the upkeep of the building, whether by painting, cleaning, or repairing. No one was asked to do what he couldn't do, contribute what he didn't have. And no offer of help was ever turned down.

Wang Shen was a round peg in a round hole and the citizens of White's Station wanted him to stay. So they patronized his store and in return were treated fairly and with dignity. Until even Sarah Taylor realized something had changed.

Robert Taylor dated his store's decline not from the arrival of Wang Shen, but from the closing of the Donovan accounts. He'd been paid in full within a week of his last conversation with John Patrick and the money kept him going through the winter. He'd fed himself on the hope that Donovan would forget whatever had aggravated him and return to the mercantile for his spring purchases, but he watched with a sinking heart as Brian, Frank and Geordie drove away from town with loaded wagons. Finally he forced himself to admit that, whatever the reason was, the effect hadn't been temporary.

And my stupid wife had to go and tell everyone she knew that the Donovans weren't buying here. He didn't remember that Owen, Tommy, and others had patronized the new shop before John Patrick made his move, and he was sure his store had been ruined by a single man's preferences. In fact, the influence the Donovans exerted, though subtle, was nonetheless real; many of those who wouldn't ordinarily have committed themselves to any kind of change were swayed by the absence of the family in the mercantile.

Rumors abounded. The Donovan accounts were said to have been closed because the merchant had cheated them, because the winter feed hadn't been delivered on time, because Molly had found weevils in the flour. In fact, every ill deed Taylor had ever done, was accused or even suspected of, was expounded as the reason for the Donovans' defection. The elder Donovan had given strict orders to his family that nothing be said, whether in denial or verification of the rumors. He told them only that Jesse had been hurt by the merchant's wife. They accepted it without question.

Wang Shen was both happy and anxious over his new status as the town's primary supplier. He'd hoped to attract enough custom to run his shop as a general store for a year or two, then specialize. For he was a lover of machinery. Any machine, big or little, any part, any tool—he knew them all intimately. A farmer could come to him and ask for the *"thingamabob that makes the whatsis go round"* and in a matter of minutes, have the right part in his hand. For the right price.

It was his son who handled the ordering of the foodstuffs and dry goods—a young man of eighteen who understood fabric and clothing and household supplies as his father understood hardware. But Wang Lei had been granted a college scholarship to an Eastern university and would be leaving the family business in September.

Owen had grown friendly with the new proprietor and listened to his complaints. When Taylor put the "For Sale" on the Trading Post, Owen took himself down the side street for a serious conversation with Wang Shen.

Griffiths was a born shopkeeper, enjoying the busy-ness of his own small business. Many times he'd considered branching out, but lacked the space in his cottage and the vision to see that the town could support two stores. Wang Shen's success had fired his imagination.

Owen had worked in the Trading Post under its founder, Cyrus White, and he knew the required routines. He could hire a clerk to wait on the customers while he filled his orders for leather goods. The room at the rear of the store, which had been filled with farm implements, could be cleaned out and become his new workshop. And, best of all, the second floor was a spacious three-bedroom apartment. The smallest room would become his office. The disposition of the other rooms he'd leave to Carolyn.

They planned to be married on the tenth of June and he worried about the change it would make in her life. She never mentioned it, but he considered the cottage too small for her—she'd been living in a twelve-room house for years. He was afraid she'd find the space too confining, though she hadn't had more than two rooms for her private use since she'd established the boardinghouse so many years ago.

Owen approached Wang Shen first and worked out a scheme of merchandising. Then he told Carolyn of his plan and found she was equally excited by the possibilities it presented. Carolyn made only one adjustment—the clerk would be replaced with a stock boy and she would wait on the customers herself. Finally, Owen went to Thatcher at the bank and asked him to make an anonymous offer for the property.

"He knows me, Bill, and will probably up the ante if he realizes I'm the buyer. I don't want to scalp him, but I want to pay a fair price. You know how much I have, you know how much the property's worth. Make me a deal within my means and tell him I'll pay cash. If he accepts it, then get ready to draw up a partnership agreement between me and Wang Shen to cover both stores."

The banker agreed and within a week the deal was consummated. Taylor would move out in the middle of May.

Chapter 59

THE FOLLOWING SUNDAY, the Griffiths gathered at the farmhouse as usual. For several months, Carolyn had been joining them as a member of the family. As Owen spilled his well-kept secret to his children, Daniel noticed the little woman was beaming with excitement. She talked to Annie about new curtains, a new, informal look for the store, and ways to use merchandise as decoration—the Navajo blankets and the trapper's pelts could be hung from the walls, much as Daniel had done in their home. The baskets could hang from the ceiling, and they would buy some outright as displays for small articles. They'd add a table and chairs to encourage wishbook browsing, and a children's corner, where the little ones could play while their parents shopped. There would be a free sourball for any "patron" under fifteen years of age.

"I've always wanted to measure and cut and find things for someone else," she said, telling them of the time she'd helped Jake to pick out a wedding present for Adam and Jesse, then adding, "I've never felt more useful and admired in my life!"

"What about the boardinghouse?" Annie asked. "The town needs that, too."

"Well, I went to see Daisy Callendar yesterday and she's going to run it. In fact, she's going to buy it from me. She hasn't really been able to run the farm since Jim died, so she'll sell that. And her four girls will be all the staff she needs. They're old enough to make the beds and do the dusting, and she won't need to serve meals.

"We don't need the money right away," Carolyn continued, "so Bill Thatcher's putting together a... what did he call it?"

"Long-term lease-purchase agreement," Owen answered.

"Yes, that. She can lease it for five years for a monthly payment that's based on the money she makes—just like Tommy's been leasing the livery from Ray Benson. If she stays for five years, half of the house is hers. If she stays for the whole ten years, she'll own it outright. And," she added, "Young Jim will be our stock boy."

"That's such a great idea." Daniel measured every syllable. "Daisy's had such a hard time of it this past year, and heaven knows that piece of land they've got takes a lot of work to farm." He got up from the table and went to take Carolyn's hand. "You," he said, his admiration plain, "are a wonderful woman." He bent to kiss her cheek.

She blushed becomingly and the woodsman suddenly understood why his father-in-law was so attracted to her.

"It was Owen's idea, too," she said.

"You can give her my kiss," the bootmaker joked.

Daniel did so, kissing her other cheek gallantly. He looked over at his sister. "Pretty lucky, aren't we?"

"Oh, yeah," Evelyn said. She took Lowell's hand and squeezed it as her brother returned to his seat by Annie.

"Oh, yeah," the woodsman echoed.

DANIEL AND ANNIE STAYED at the farm until almost midnight, talking about the new enterprise. As he walked with her over the fields, he could see she was a bit tired, but the hour was unusually late for her. *She's doing so well. She's so happy. I must remember to get a gift for Mother, to thank her for everything.*

They strolled across their meadow, arms about each other's waists. Annie had taken off her shoes and carried them in one hand.

THE WOODSMAN'S ROSE

Her other hand was under his shirt. The night was warm, soft, lovely, the scent of the flowers sweet and strong. The moon peeked between the strings of clouds and told him the new day had begun. He walked more and more slowly, until he was hardly moving at all. She began to caress his side and he pulled her in against him.

"It was today," he murmured into her hair. She looked up, her pale eyes shining like diamonds. He took the ribbon from her braid and unraveled it. She closed her eyes, lost in the gentleness of his touch, the magic of the memory.

"*Aroon*, do you remember?"

A little sound, something like a sigh and something like a laugh. "Yes."

"You were so beautiful then. You are so much more beautiful now. Annie," his voice was low and sweet, "I want to see you."

She remembered the words. Remembered the sunlight and the warmth of his hands. Remembered the kisses he'd rained down upon her, and her whole body yearned for him. He felt the response, lifted her from her feet and sank to his knees, lay down with her among the flowers, kissed her forehead, her eyes, her lips. Her long white throat. Again her fingers worked with his—the buttons, the laces were undone. Again the deep intake of breath as he looked at her, the catch in her voice as she whispered his name.

The pale moon watched silently. It turned her creamy skin to gold, her bright hair to spun silver, her little noises into prayer. Then shifted suddenly in its orbit, rocked by the love that they shared.

⁕

SHE SLEPT IN HIS ARMS, as she'd done before. When the first rosy streaks appeared in the sky, he carried her to the cabin and took her to their bed. Her eyes flickered open, closed then opened again, and her arms wrapped around his neck. She nuzzled into the hollow of his shoulder.

There was a fluttering deep in her belly and she turned her attention inward. Her body, so sensitive to every nuance, every fluctuation in temperature, every beating pulse of blood, had discovered a change in itself. A duplication of senses, a shifting of spirit.

"Daniel. Oh, Daniel..." She looked up at him.

"Yes, *aroon*?"

"Daniel." Her voice was filled with awe. "A baby. Oh..."

Burying his hand in her hair, he drew her head to his shoulder. Could it be true? She'd wanted a baby for so long. He'd felt the magic of the night, felt something happen in her that had never happened before. But he hadn't dreamed of this.

"*Aroon...*" He looked deeply into her eyes once more, found absolute certainty there. "Oh, Annie..."

He was overjoyed and terrified at once. Her baby—their baby. The miracle of it! But was she strong enough? Would her spirit, her joy carry them through?

"Oh, Annie, I love you." He slipped down and kissed her smooth white belly, rested his head against her, as her fingers played in his hair. Her happiness was there in that touch. He'd told her once that happiness was the meaning, the goal of life. He'd hide his fear. He couldn't be so selfish as to deny her joy now.

He kissed her again and offered a prayer. *Dear mother, make her happy. Give me what you can, what you will. But please let her be happy.*

Chapter 60

ALEC TWELVE TREES WAS more than usually silent and his father was worried. Ever since Annie had stepped between them, then found a way to bring them together, their relationship had improved immeasurably. They could talk without shouting, disagree without anger. Tommy was proud of Alec for the way he'd stood up to his mistake, apologized, and made amends. He knew his son still mourned for his mother in the night, for he could sometimes hear a sorrowful chant echoing through their cottage. Yet when he asked, Alec told him there was nothing wrong. Tommy didn't believe it, but he'd learned not to push his sensitive son.

The silversmith entered the stable one morning; Tommy dunked a horseshoe into the vat of water, then laid it aside.

"Pad." It was an abbreviation of "padre" which Alec had invented as a boy and had recently begun to use again. Tommy heard the hesitation in his tones but decided to ignore it.

"What's up?" he inquired. When his son didn't answer, he asked more seriously, "Something on your mind?"

"I want to talk to you."

"Sure. What's up?"

"I've been thinking of buying Owen's place."

"Oh, yeah? How come?"

"I thought it would be a good idea to set up a real shop. Not that I don't have enough room here..." Alec's hand flicked toward his workspace. "I just feel it's time for me to be... more professional."

"Hmmm," answered the blacksmith, imitating his friend Donovan. He'd realized recently that it was a good way to stall for time. Trying to read between his son's words was no mean feat, for Tommy wasn't given much to deep thought. What was his son really feeling? Loneliness in the house where his mother had lived? The need to strike out on his own as all young men did eventually? Stifled by his father? Or maybe, just maybe, getting a home ready for his future wife? Tommy knew how his son felt about Irene Donovan, though he'd made no attempt at courting her. Was he trying to impress Irene, show her he was older and more mature—more able to support her than the other young men who admired her? Tommy couldn't dismiss the idea, though he didn't know how much of a chance Alec might have. Yet he couldn't help but smile at the thought of the vivacious beauty as his daughter.

"Seems like it might be the right thing t' do. Need any help?"

Alec's breath of relief wasn't lost on the smith. "Not just yet. But later, I want to turn the big room back into a parlor, and the bedroom into my shop. I thought I'd ask you and Daniel to help with the plans."

"Sure thing. You get Dan'l t' draw somethin' up an' the three of us'll put it t'gether. You talk t' Owen yet?"

"I wanted to talk to you first."

Tommy's heart thudded in his chest, but he just chuckled. "You make sure he don't take all your money, son. You need enough left t' have a sign painted!"

But the sign, when it was time to hang it, was carved by Frank Donovan. He copied the symbol of Twelve Trees and added a single word, **SILVERSMITH**. Tommy hung it proudly while his son looked on.

It was the third new sign to go up in White's Station in the month of May. For Owen had found the mercantile's original sign in the back room and asked Annie to repaint it. His store now boasted

THE WOODSMAN'S ROSE

it was the **WHITE'S STATION TRADING POST**. Wang Shen had hung a new sign, too: **HARDWARE AND FEED**. His partnership with Owen had resulted in the transfer of the dry goods business to the Trading Post, and the bootmaker had, in turn, turned over all of the farm implements and tools to the Chinese proprietor. Wang Lei was working with Owen on stock and suppliers until he went off to school, and Wang Shen would handle most of the bookkeeping for both stores, a task Owen had always hated; all Owen had to do was track the individual credits and debits.

They'd agreed that both shops would run a single account for each customer or family—purchases at one store could be offset by payments at the other, or acceptance of goods at either. Shen would continue to deal with the traders and the trappers, while Owen would take in the Navajos' goods and display them in his store. Both stores were supplied with common foodstuffs—rice and flour, beans and salt—but the seeds were at the hardware store, along with the hoes and plows. Ready-made clothes as well as fabrics were found at the mercantile along with most of the food, household supplies, lamps and bric-a-brac. John Patrick declared the scheme to be "eminently practical."

BEFORE ROBERT TAYLOR departed, he took himself out to the Donovan ranch. He was sure he'd been cheated—that John Patrick had closed his accounts in order to let his friend get a better deal on the trading post. He was ready to accuse and to demand his rights when he rapped on the green door.

It was opened by Irene. Taylor had been infatuated with her for years and the look of scorn she gave him deflated him completely. When he asked for her father, she told him to wait and shut the door between them. He cringed at the snub—the Donovan home was always open to any who came to call.

By the time John Patrick came out to the porch, Taylor was crushing his hat in his hands. He followed Donovan down the steps and only stopped when the older man did, right beside the buggy. John Patrick had not said a word.

The merchant gathered up his scant courage. "Why did you ruin me?" he asked in a strained, pitiful voice. "What did I do?"

The older man looked out over his land, toward the canyons in the west. "Your wife, Taylor, has a tongue that is sharper than a serpent's tooth. She has been the cause of two deaths in this town." He stared at the merchant, his lip curling, his brogue becoming thick. "You are not welcome here. I had never thought to say that to any man. But in my country, a man is responsible for his wife, for his family. I hold you responsible for the harm she has done." He took Taylor's arm in his weathered hand, helped him ungently into the buggy. In a voice of quiet rage, he continued, "She will slander me and mine no more. And if you have the brains of a moon-calf, you will shut her mouth. Before someone beats her to death."

The old man's anger finally penetrated Taylor's weak mind. He turned his buggy around, setting the horses at a gallop down the lane. But when he got to the gate, he pulled up to stare at the Donovan brand overhead. His eyes filled with tears. He'd been proud of his place in White's Station, enjoyed the prestige of being heir to the town's founder, reveled in the power of owning the only mercantile north of Prescott. Now it was gone—all gone. And he'd never see Irene Donovan again.

By the time he got home, Taylor had worked himself into a state of hysteria. He flew up the stairs to his apartment and ran through the rooms shouting for his wife. He found her dusting in the spare bedroom, grabbed her by the arms and pushed her onto the bed. "What did you say to him? What did you say to Donovan?"

"Nothing. What, when? Nothing." She stood, one hand reaching for his arm, but he shoved her away.

"What did you say about him? about his family?"

"Nothing." She cowered against the wall, her face white and screwed up in thought. "What do you mean 'his family'?"

"Family! You know, his mother, his wife, sons, daughters. The Griffiths. The Travers girl. The grandchildren. They're all his family!" He saw the light of revelation on her face. *"What did you say?"*

"Oh, it was nothing, really,"—she waved a careless hand—"just that thing about the Indian."

"What thing?"

"You know, about the Travers girl and the Indian."

Taylor groaned and clutched his head in both hands, swayed on his feet. Two deaths, the old man said. And her brother had killed the smith's wife. But what about the other—who else had died? The brother. But Adam Donovan had killed him—that couldn't be her fault. There must be someone else. The old man. Old Man Travers. Could it kill a sick old man to hear something like that about his daughter?

"You made it up?" He grabbed her, shook her. "Was it a lie? *Was it?*"

She shrugged. "Well, you know how he'd go out there visiting when the brother was in jail. It could have been true. It certainly seemed that way to me."

He slapped her hard across the mouth, and then again. She fell on the bed, blood running from her lip, a scarlet stream against her pallid face.

"It seemed that way? It could have been?" He hit her again, then collapsed in a heap on the floor. "You've ruined my life! You've ruined me!" He buried his head in his hands, sobbing wildly.

When he was able to look up again, she was still staring at him. He remembered John Patrick's words, "before somebody beats her to death". He was sorely tempted. But he got to his feet, turned his back on her, swayed against the doorway, then pulled the door shut behind him, fumbled through his pockets for the keys, and locked her in.

Staggering like a drunk to the stage office, he purchased a single ticket to San Antonio, another to California. He marched unsteadily into the bank and withdrew all his money in cash over Thatcher's protests, who begged him to take a draft. Back at home, he packed a carpetbag with clean clothes, grabbed his best hat and slapped it on his head. Leaving two hundred dollars, the key to the spare room and the ticket to San Antonio on a table in the hall, he took a long look around, his head bowed and shaking.

She's the devil's own spawn. My mother warned me. Turning one final time, he left the best portion of his life behind.

Chapter 61

FOUR HOURS AFTER THE west-bound stage departed, Jane Barber heard Sarah calling from the back window of the apartment above the Trading Post. Jane went home to wait for her brother, then sent him to see what the trouble was. The doctor returned in high spirits.

"Well, my girl, be glad you got out of it when you did, for she's paying the piper now. Taylor's off to California. Left her high and dry. No," he amended, "not quite dry. Left her a ticket to San Antonio and two hundred dollars and all their personal belongings except some of his own clothes. And she says she doesn't know why." Theo shook his gray head. "I guess you've got to believe it. She's never understood anything in all her born days. Why should she start now?"

Jane didn't answer, but regarded her brother with a heart that acknowledged his part in her transformation. How easily she could have been in Sarah's place—the laughingstock of the town, left to go home to a family she'd alienated long ago. Instead she had security, affection, and the love of a good man and his children. She put down her embroidery and went to her brother. She bent to kiss the top of his head. "Thank you, Theo."

"You're welcome, Janie. I'm glad I could help."

SARAH'S STORY SPREAD like wildfire through the Territory. There was much laughter at the deserted wife's expense at the next Donovan family gathering, but Jesse didn't join in.

"It's so sad," she murmured to Adam. "She must be so unhappy."

Sitting on the floor near her feet, Daniel heard her remark and changed the subject abruptly, telling everyone of a beehive he'd found in the foothills, promising them fresh honey in the fall. Adam gave him a grateful look and took his wife's hand. Annie reached out a toe, nudging Daniel to invite Jesse along on the hive-hunt.

"When will you go?" Jesse was smiling slightly at her brother-in-law.

"Late September, early October," he replied. But she shook her head. "Why not?"

"Oh," she said airily, "the doctor will probably want me home in bed again."

A puzzled silence fell, then John Patrick sputtered and Molly beamed, while Irene burst into joyful crowing.

"When? Tell me when!" Evelyn demanded.

"About Christmas," Jesse said.

"That's why the doctor laughed!" Evelyn slapped her husband's arm affectionately. "He told me Christmas, too, and then he laughed. Right out loud!" Another joyful chorus went up.

"What?" demanded Jake, and Brian echoed, "What?"

"Babies!" Irene cried. "There's two babies on the way!"

"Who's having a baby?" Patricia demanded. Suzette repeated the news to her and they both began to squeal.

"Three," said Annie so softly only Jesse heard her.

"Three?" she cried out. "Oh, Annie—you, too? When, oh, when?"

"January," she answered, and her voice was even more shy than before. "Right around Kevin's birthday."

THE WOODSMAN'S ROSE

Adam stuck his hand out at Daniel, who grabbed it and held it hard. Then the whole room exploded, the men pounding each other on the back, the women sharing tearful embraces. The babies complained of all the noise and suddenly everything quieted.

Into the hush, Evelyn said, "You know, it might actually be four babies." They looked at her in confusion and she blushed bright pink. "The doctor said mine might be twins."

Mouths fell open and eyes grew wide. The silence was broken by Annie's delighted crow. "That would be wonderful! Daniel, then we'd get 'O'!"

Chapter 62

SEVERAL WEEKS LATER, the doctor stopped in at the yellow cabin on the knoll to check on Annie; he brought with him news from the Navajo camp. Thanks to the Garryannie Foundation and the banker's liberal interpretation of "medical treatment" to include preventive measures such as sound nutrition, all the children of the tribe were healthy for the first time in years. There was no fever, no influenza, no chicken pox to contend with. Theo was more grateful than he could manage to say.

He reassured Annie her pregnancy was progressing normally, but later he drew Daniel aside and cautioned him. "Watch her carefully, and let me know if anything unusual happens—even if it doesn't seem serious. I don't know how it might affect her fainting spells. I have a friend in St. Louis—we went to medical school together, and we still keep in touch. He's a surgeon and he does a lot of work with different brain conditions, and he likely knows more about Annie's ailments than I do. With your permission, I'll write to him and get his opinion."

"Sure, Doc. You don't think she's in any danger, do you?"

"No, I don't. Everything seems fine. I'd just like to know if there's anything special we need to do for her. She's a fine girl, Annie is. And I want to make sure we do everything she needs us to do."

"All right." Daniel brushed a hand over his mustache. "So things are good up at the camp?"

Here Barber demurred. The interlopers had recruited some followers and the elders had cautioned the doctor once more: do not go about alone. "I'm not going back up there without Tommy or Alec along."

"You think it's that bad?"

"Bad enough for me not to take any chances," he answered as he climbed into his buggy. "Tommy said he saw that Yellow Knife in town the other day, and not for the first time. He was skulking around—maybe looking for something. Or somebody. So it wouldn't hurt you to be closer to civilization, either."

Daniel didn't respond, and Theo drove away wondering if his advice had fallen on deaf ears.

ANNIE INSISTED ON HELPING with the preparations for her father's wedding. Carolyn had come to Molly and asked if she could be married in the formal parlor—the small, intimate ceremony Daniel had arranged seemed to her the perfect wedding. She told Molly she felt it would be a most appropriate setting for a second marriage.

"Besides," she'd said, "we're old folks, Owen and me. We don't need all the fuss the young people want."

Molly had protested: Carolyn was only three years older than she was, and Owen two years older than that. She'd agree to their use of the Donovan home only if Carolyn would refrain from referring to her as "old folks".

A few days before the wedding, Daniel arrived at the ranch house as Molly, Irene and Annie were completing the preparation of the dining room. They'd chosen the colors of royal blue and gold—the blue to complement Carolyn's gown of sky blue and the gold to signify Owen's heritage, for he was descended from the royal line of Theodor or Tudor, which included Owain Glyn Dwr, the most celebrated Prince and ruler of Wales. Against the backdrop of cream-colored wallpaper with trailing ecru vines separated by rows of deep red, the room appeared fit for a prince and his consort.

"Nice," the woodsman said with a look around the room. It was high praise from him and they accepted it as such. He saw his wife's cheeks were bright with excitement and held out a hand to her. She ran to him, hugged him tightly around the neck.

"Only two more days—we've got so much to do!"

"Got your cake ready?"

"Yes." Annie had planned only two tiers for this small gathering, and Daniel had already caught the scent of almonds and mace. "I'll ice it tomorrow if you'll put it together for me."

"Sure. You ready to go now?"

"Why don't you stay to supper?" Molly asked. "'Twill be ready in a few minutes."

"Okay with you?" Daniel asked his wife.

"Sure. If I don't have to make it, it always tastes better!"

So they ate Molly's stew and strawberry tarts, and later Daniel found an opportunity to speak privately to John Patrick about the interlopers. The old man agreed to take a warning to town in the morning. It might be difficult, he remarked, to get the people of White's Station to take it seriously. Though the Apaches still fought and raided to the south and west, it had been a long time since there was trouble in this corner of the Territory.

"Why don't you stay with us awhile?" John Patrick asked his son. "Just 'til this thing blows over."

"I'll talk to Annie in the morning." At his father's frown, Daniel added, "We'd have to go back and pick up some clothes anyway."

As he walked home with his wife, Daniel deliberately cleared his mind of the possible trouble to come. The days were at their longest and the first rosy blush of sunset had turned Annie's skin to peach, like the roses climbing on their porch. *The woodsman's rose. How lucky the woodsman is.*

THE WOODSMAN'S ROSE

"What are you thinking about?" Annie asked.

He smiled at her. He'd been thinking she was beautiful, and would have been a princess in her own country had the Anglos not disrupted their history. Much as he would have been a prince in his. The thought had given him pleasure and he'd wondered if Alec could make her a little silver crown for her birthday. He pulled her into his arms, kissed her tenderly, and began to tell her how much he loved her.

WHEN ANNIE AND DANIEL didn't arrive in the morning, Molly's first concern was for Annie. Her daughter-in-law had been much healthier lately, and the disability she suffered from headaches had been somewhat lessened. *Still, it is possible that she is ill. We know we have not cured her—only made the pain less.*

She called for her youngest son and sent him to *Sidhean Annie*. The cake needed to be iced and if Annie couldn't do it, she'd have to try it herself. She was sure her attempts wouldn't compare to Annie's, yet they needed a cake for the bridal couple. Jake could put the frame together for her. But only if Annie was too sick to come.

Jake stopped to pull on his buckskin boots then headed out over the fields on foot. The day was beautiful, soft and warm as many June days begin, and he was whistling an Irish ditty as he crossed the boundary of his father's land to *Sidhean Annie*.

He stopped for a moment to admire the field full of flowers—it seemed to get prettier every time he saw it. Hoping his sister-in-law wasn't too sick, he started off again but stopped in his tracks at a low moaning—a sound he identified as human pain.

He wondered if Annie could somehow have come out of the cabin into the field. Wouldn't Daniel have taken her back in? He stood perfectly still until the sound came again, then located it to his left. After three strides he broke into a run, for his brother lay face-down in the meadow with the hilt of a knife protruding from his back.

"Oh, my God." Jake knelt beside the woodsman. "All this blood!" It had soaked the woodsman's shirt and still trickled from the wound.

And where was Annie?

Chapter 63

JAKE SHOUTED FOR ANNIE and looked around wildly, then realized he was close to panic. He took a long, deep breath and forced himself to calmness. He felt for the pulse in Daniel's neck. It was regular, though not strong. His hand hovered over the knife, but he remembered the advice he'd had from Alec when a cactus thorn was caught in his leg: *Don't take it out unless you're sure of what it is, how it went in, and unless you're ready to stop the bleeding.*

He couldn't remove the knife. He needed his mother, his brothers, his father. He couldn't move Daniel, for his brother was a big, solid man. Besides, it might make the bleeding worse. He needed help.

And he needed to know if Annie was safe.

It was four miles back to the ranch but only sixty yards to the cabin. He sprinted to the door, found it locked and kicked at it. It flew open and a quick search told him Annie was gone. *She could have gone into town for help,* he told himself. But he didn't really believe it. Annie should have been right there, or on her way to his mother. He would have seen her. No, she was gone, and whoever had stabbed his brother had taken her.

I need help. I need Mother and I need Alec. If I go for Alec, Daniel may die from loss of blood. If I go for Mother, we may lose Annie's trail. But it's two miles farther to town than back home. If I take his horse, I'll be at the house in ten minutes and it may save his life. This happened a long time ago—if the trail's still there, another hour or so won't make any difference.

His decision made in the time it takes lightning to strike, Jake grabbed a bridle and forced his hands to stop trembling as he placed it gently into the buckskin mare's mouth. Then, not taking time to saddle, he leaped on her back and urged her across the open fields.

He found Geordie out inspecting his crops, and shouted, "Daniel's hurt! He needs help. Get out to the cabin!" His brother took off at a run toward *Sidhean Annie*.

As soon as he could see the ranchhouse, Jake started shouting again.

"Mother! Dad! Frank! *Mother!*" They spilled onto the porch as he pulled the horse up. She was winded and trembling.

"What is it?" his father demanded. "What's wrong?"

"Daniel's hurt. I sent Geordie." He slipped off the mare's lathered back as his mother disappeared into the house after her medical kit and Frank ran to the barn for horses. "Dad, he's been knifed. In the back. Looks like he's been bleeding all night." Jake struggled for calmness, for breath. His father's horse was saddled and ready to go. Slamming the corral gate after Daniel's horse, he grabbed the reins to the roan mare. "I'm going to town for the doctor and Alec."

"Why Alec?"

"Annie's gone." The words hung in the stilly air until the old man groaned.

"Dear Lord." He pulled a trembling through his gray hair as Jake swung up into the saddle. "Oh, dear Lord. You'll have to tell Owen." He slapped the mare on the flank. "*GO!* And get back as quick as you can!"

Jake needed no further urging. An excellent horseman on a superb horse, he made a direct run for the town, galloped in at the north end, and pulled the horse up before the silversmith's cottage.

Tommy came running from the stable as Jake pounded on Alec's door.

THE WOODSMAN'S ROSE

"What's wrong?" he demanded, grabbing the youth by the arm as Alec opened the door.

"What's wrong?" the silversmith echoed.

"Daniel's hurt. Annie's gone. We need you," he added to Alec.

"Where?"

"*Sidhean Annie*." Jake was gone again, running down the street to the doctor's house.

"I'll saddle the horses," Tommy told his son. "You pack some food and water."

By the time Alec had packed and put on a buckskin suit and boots, his father had four horses ready and the stable door closed behind them. Jake was once again running up the wide street. The citizens of the town were gathering behind him.

"Where's Doc?" the youth demanded.

Tommy stared at him for a moment. "Oh, no, no, no! He went out t' see the new farmer—what's 'is name? The one who bought the Wilson ranch—out there by the stage line. Look, I... I'll get Jane—she's jus' over at the Callendar's checkin' up on the li'l girl. I'll bring 'er out in the buggy." Tommy had taken two steps before Jake called him back.

"Tell her we need... whatever she has to stop bleeding." Then he added so no one but the smith could hear. "Daniel's got a knife in his back.

"And Tommy, please... tell Owen. I don't know what to say." With that, he jumped onto one of the fresh horses and sped away with Alec at his side.

Tommy stood for a moment, trying to collect his thoughts. It would break the bootmaker's heart if anything happened to his daughter. And Carolyn—the wedding. He tied the extra horses to a rail and padded down the street to the Trading Post.

As he entered, he found the "Closed" sign in its usual spot and placed it in the window. The only customer was a trapper and as he left, Tommy locked the door.

"What are you doing?" the new merchant asked with a little laugh. "It's too early for lunch. Besides, Carolyn will be here any minute."

The blacksmith didn't respond as he led Owen to the chair behind the counter. "Sit down, Owen." He put a firm hand on the bootmaker's shoulder. Owen sat.

"Tommy?" He looked up in confusion, then clutched at Tommy's wrist. "Tell me."

"Dan'l's hurt," the smith replied, his deep voice shaking. He tried to go on, but the words wouldn't come.

Owen's hands were groping at his friend's arms. "Annie… What about Annie?"

"She's gone, Owen. Alec's gone t' look for her."

"Gone? Tommy, where'd she go?"

"We don' know yet," the smith replied, his face set in a mask of hope. "Alec's gone t' find 'er."

"Find her? Oh, dear God, what's happened to her?"

"We don' know. Maybe Dan'l can tell us."

"But he's hurt? How bad is it?"

"I don' know. But Jake came for the doctor."

"Tommy." Owen's voice was rigid, demanding. "I want to know what's going on. I want to go out there. I need to be there."

"Horses are saddled," replied the smith, surprised and pleased by the strength in his friend's voice. "You wanna tell Carolyn first?"

"Of course." Owen got shakily to his feet.

They met Carolyn in the street and broke the news to her. She agreed to stay in town and send word if any news came back. She'd go to Wang Shen and get one of his clerks to help her in the Trading Post, and she'd try to keep the rumors in check.

THE WOODSMAN'S ROSE

"Carolyn..."

"Don't be silly, man. You go out there and stay there until she's home again. How could we get married without her?"

Speechlessly Owen hugged her tight, then planted a kiss on her cheek.

"She'll be all right," Carolyn said. "Everything will be all right."

"I love you. Pray for her."

"And for you. Now get going. And don't come back until she's home again."

The two men hurried down the street toward the horses. Tommy gave Owen a leg up onto one of them.

"Aren't you coming?"

"I gotta go get Jane. You go ahead an' tell everyone we'll be there soon's we can."

Chapter 64

OWEN STOPPED AT THE dairy farm long enough to tell Evelyn and Lowell as much as he knew, then rode for *Sidhean Annie*. He forced himself not to think at all, clinging desperately to Carolyn's words, "Everything will be all right."

By the time he arrived at the knoll, Molly had stopped the seepage of blood around the knife. John Patrick and the twins had managed to get a blanket under Daniel by rolling him first to one side then the other, and the four of them had carried him into the house and laid him on the couch. Then John Patrick sent Frank to the canyon to notify the family there.

Within half an hour, Tommy and Jane arrived. She'd been unsuccessful in persuading Tommy to wait for her brother and she was trembling. As she stepped onto the porch, the smith put his hands on her shoulders and turned her around to face him.

"Listen t' me, girl." Tommy spoke calmly but there was force behind his voice. "You gotta do this. There's nobody else. Jus' you. We need you t' help Dan'l, so he can tell us where Annie is. You unnerstand?"

Jane gulped but nodded, and entered the cabin with her shoulders straight.

She examined Daniel's wound and found it not nearly as bad as she'd expected. It was high on his back, about four inches long but narrow and straight. The knife seemed to have glanced off the shoulder blade. It hadn't hit the lung—if it had, the woodsman would be long dead. But when she removed the knife, copious

THE WOODSMAN'S ROSE

bleeding started. She applied pressure bandages, but that didn't control it. "We need some ice."

"I'll get it," said Geordie and took off on his father's horse. The quietest of the family, he was also the most level-headed. By the time his parents and twin had arrived, he'd lit the brazier so they'd have hot water to clean the wound, gathered all the towels he could find, found the medicine kit the doctor had given Daniel and Annie, and had taken it, a blanket and a single towel to his brother. He'd taken Daniel's knife and cut his shirt open. With the towel he'd begun to staunch the flow of blood, giving this task over to his mother when she got there.

Before Jane's arrival, Molly had added the herb shepherd's purse to a bowl of boiling water and let it steep. The herb was both styptic and astringent and Jane used it to clean the wound. But the bleeding, while lessened, wouldn't stop. Molly poured what was left of the solution into the cold water they were using for compresses and prayed it would have some additional effect.

Jane was worried. The cave the Donovans used as an ice house was a few miles past the ranchhouse and it would take Geordie most of an hour to return.

Tommy looked over her shoulder at the clean, gaping wound. "I once saw my father sew a man's leg t'gether t' stop the bleedin.'"

Jane glanced up, surprise quickly turning to enlightenment. "They sew people up after surgery, too, don't they? What do you remember, Tommy?"

The smith screwed his face up in concentration. "It took two of 'em. One man held the edges close t'gether while my father sewed. He used a long needle made o' bone—boiled it first t' clean it. An' boiled the laces—thin rawhide laces. He sewed it loose, but the laces dried an' pulled it tight. He used a lotta stitches close t'gether. An' I think 'e tied each one off as 'e went along. The bleedin' stopped li'l by li'l, as the stitches tightened."

"Can you help me?"

"Sure. Anythin' you need."

Jane asked Molly to find a long needle and cotton thread—white, she said. She wasn't sure what dyes were made of and the bleach that made the color of white thread consistent seemed harmless enough. She told Tommy to wash his hands then showed the smith how to use the compresses while she did the same. She had Molly boil the needle and thread, explaining their plans to her. Molly's face blanched, but she offered her help.

So as Tommy held the gaping edges of the wound together and Jane used the needle and thread, Molly wiped away the blood that accumulated. When the job was done, the wound was still seeping, but not dangerously. Molly made a poultice of the shepherd's purse and applied it to her son's back, then covered it with a towel she filled with the ice Geordie brought. She sat at Daniel's side, one hand on the towel, the other in his hair, and prayed for him and for his lovely wife.

Like Owen, she dared not think of what might have happened to Annie, except to realize she must have been taken away. She would never have left her husband's side voluntarily. She was pregnant, she was ill, she needed treatments against the pain she suffered. But most of all, she was a creature of innocence, of joy, and Molly's prayers grew desperate with the fear she fought against.

Chapter 65

ALEC RETURNED TO THE cabin having found no tracks in the meadow, no sign of anything except the spot where his friend had fallen. But the knife was of Navajo make and the tribe's summer camp was less than an hour away by horseback. He was going to go see what he could find there. The men agreed if Daniel came to and could tell them anything, Jake would follow with the information. In the meantime, they could do nothing but sit tight and wait.

They did very little sitting. John Patrick paced in front of the cabin, pulling on an empty pipe. Jake and Geordie made the rounds of the meadow, corral and house, each finding comfort in the other's silence. Owen crossed from one end of the porch to the other, stood and stared out over the meadow, then turned and began again. Tommy leaned against the door frame, muttering to himself, wondering what his son would find at the camp. Jane sat by her patient's side, willing her brother to arrive.

It was a long while before she came out on the porch and addressed John Patrick.

"The bleeding has stopped and his pulse is getting stronger. I think he should be coming around in a few hours." She watched the old man carefully to make sure he'd taken it in. "I'll send Theo out as soon as he comes home. In the meantime, Molly knows what to do."

John Patrick held out his hand. Jane found herself near tears as she shook it. "I'll be back before nightfall if Theo doesn't get home."

"Thank you, Jane. We'll most probably take him to the house."

"You're welcome." She tried to smile, flicked her other hand toward Tommy. "But you actually need to thank your tall friend over there."

John Patrick went to the blacksmith, put a fond hand on his shoulder but said nothing, then went inside and stood behind his wife, gazing down at his son. He knelt beside them and bowed his head, felt Molly's hand in his hair. Like Alec, he believed the Navajo warriors were responsible for this. *Let us find her. Let no harm come to her. Protect her from her illness and from harm.* He rested his head against his wife's breast, put his weathered hand over hers there on his son's back. Molly's arm stole round his shoulders. *Let no harm come to her,* he begged once more.

IN A FEW HOURS, DANIEL began to moan and move about in pain. When his eyelids first flickered open, he saw his father's face. He tried to reach out, but the pain in his shoulder made him groan. It was only by the greatest of efforts that he was able to fight the blackness off again. His voice came out in a deep croak.

"Annie."

"Drink this," he heard his mother say. Molly had prepared a tisane of white willow bark, which would dull the pain but not the senses. He turned his head toward her, but the angle was too great and the tisane spilled on the blanket beneath him. His father took his good arm and stretched it over his head, helped him to roll slightly. He moaned in agony, but the pull of darkness wasn't quite so strong, and after a moment he raised his head for the cup again. They put a pillow under his head, and his ragged breathing become more regular. When his eyes opened again, his voice was stronger, too.

"Annie..."

"She's not here, lad," his father said. "Tell us what happened."

THE WOODSMAN'S ROSE

"Where is she? Is she hurt? What happened?" The questions were broken by the struggle for breath, the fight for consciousness. Why couldn't he remember?

He had to work to concentrate on his father's voice. "We found you here, lad. Jake did, this morning. Someone put a knife in your back. Do you know who it was?"

"Knife," he echoed. There was a memory trying to surface... something... a knife. The warrior. Sudden pain. Then Annie's voice. His precious Annie. Screaming as she'd once screamed at him. *No! No! Let me go! No! Daniel! DANIEL!*

He groaned again, his anguish this time not for himself. He'd seen Yellow Knife carry her away, slung over his shoulder like a sack of grain. Seen her small fists pounding on his back, her feet kicking at the air. Seen the sneer as the warrior looked back, then the earth came up to strike his cheek.

"*Annnn-ieee.*"

It was a mortal cry. John Patrick took his son's free hand and squeezed it hard. Owen pounded in, followed by the blacksmith and by Alec, who silently shook his head. Jake and Geordie gathered behind him.

"Tell us what happened, lad. Tell us." The sternness in his father's voice penetrated Daniel's anguish and he stumbled over his words.

"Walking," he said. "Sunset. Coming home. Stopped to... kiss her." Agony in his voice but his father grunted and he concentrated again. "Yellow Knife... from nowhere. Should... have known... should have known..."

"All right, lad. You rest now." But the woodsman grabbed his father by the arm, ignoring the stabbing pain.

"He... took her. She's... frightened. Got to... find... her. Got to... should have... known." He tried to sit up but the effort was too much. The blackness threatened again. He gasped at the fire burning in his shoulder, then turned his face into the pillow, weeping silently.

The men moved away as Molly brought him another tisane. Not willow bark this time, but lobelia to soothe him, chamomile to fight off depression, beet root to help restore his blood. And one drop of poppy juice, to induce a restful sleep. Five or six hours, she guessed, for he was a man of solid muscle and heavier than he appeared. When he woke, he'd be more coherent. Stronger. Able to help them plan. And that would be the best medicine of all.

The men gathered on the porch and after a few moments of silence, Alec spoke.

"They weren't there. They took everything, but left in a hurry. Not more than twelve hours ago, I'd say."

"Any sign of Annie?" Tommy asked.

"No sign of anything. Couldn't find a single track outside of the camp. But that means they have something to hide."

"Do you think they might have..."

"No, Owen. They wouldn't be gone if they'd killed her. All they'd have to do is hide her body and wait for us to show up, then deny everything. I'm sure Yellow Knife thought Daniel was dead. He'd never have left him alive to be a witness against him. So that's in our favor. We know who did it, but he doesn't know we know. And Running Wolf won't let him hurt her, Owen, once he finds out who she is."

"He an' Dan'l been friends a long time," Tommy put in. "He'll figger out who she is. He won't let anybody hurt 'er."

John Patrick put his arm around Owen's shoulders. "Believe in it. If something bad were going to happen, Annie would have known. She would have told us."

Owen let out a deep sigh. He believed fervently in her gift, believed she would have hidden nothing from her husband. And above all, believed that Daniel would have done anything in his power to protect her, even if it meant leaving his beloved Territory. He closed his eyes for a moment and concentrated on faith.

THE WOODSMAN'S ROSE

Molly came from the cabin and put a sympathetic hand on Owen's arm as she addressed her husband.

"He's sleeping now, Pat," she said. "If we're going to move him, this is the time." It was for more than the convenience of the big house—it would give them something to do, something else to think about.

John Patrick turned to Owen. "Come with me to get the wagon."

The bootmaker grabbed at the chance for activity. As they rode out across the meadow, Molly returned to Daniel's side. Alec spoke to Tommy, Jake and Geordie. "I'm going back up to see if I can pick up their trail. If not, I'll start circling the mountain and see if I can find where they left it. Maybe they just went higher up. There's water up there and plenty of game this time of year. And it won't be too cold at night."

"I'm coming with you," stated Jake.

"No. You'll have to follow with Daniel. I'll mark the trail behind me—you can follow straight north from their camp unless you see another sign. Don't worry about your own trail unless you see a blue feather hanging from a juniper. Then hide yourselves and wait for me to come back.

"If you see the tribe but don't see me, the call is for nighthawk, screech owl, and nighthawk again. If you see us both and want me to know you're there, it's nighthawk, screech owl, then mourning dove. Got it?"

"Yeah," Jake replied. Alec picked up his rifle and left them without another word.

"Good luck," Tommy whispered behind his son. "An' be careful."

Chapter 66

RETURNING TO *Sidhean Annie* with a wagon full of loose hay, Owen and John Patrick helped Tommy and Jake pick Daniel up, using the blanket to carry him. Geordie and Jake climbed in to sit behind their brother and cushion his back so he wouldn't roll over, and Owen sat in front of him for the same reason. The woodsman hadn't moved at all and groaned only once, so deep was the spell of the poppies. John Patrick and Molly settled themselves on the seat of the wagon. Tommy gathered the reins of the horses, guiding them slowly and carefully through the fields.

The family had congregated at the ranch—Adam and Jesse, Rebecca and Brian, Evelyn and Lowell. Anticipating a stay of at least several days, Brian had already sent two of his father's hands out to the canyon to take care of the stock there. Frank met them at the barn and helped with the horses while Adam, Geordie, Brian and Tommy carried Daniel to the couch in the back parlor.

Kneeling by his side, Jesse brushed the hair from his face. His breathing was regular and deep. She kissed his forehead and detected no fever. Irene rushed in and started to cry.

"Daniel!" she sobbed. "Oh, no, Daniel!" She tried to put her arms around him but Jesse held her back. Adam drew her up to her feet, into the far corner of the room, and into his arms. She sobbed against his shoulder.

"Hush, *mavourneen*," Adam soothed her. "Don't cry, little one." They were the same words with which Daniel had once comforted her, and she sobbed more wildly than before.

THE WOODSMAN'S ROSE

"Irene." Her brother's voice was low but stern in her ear. "Pull yourself together now. You're not helping him. He's asleep, but he may hear you. So stop your crying. He needs his rest, and he needs his strength. He needs us to be strong for him."

Her shoulders quaked as she wept silently. Adam held her closer and murmured words of comfort. "Good girl. Hold on tight and don't cry. He wouldn't want you to cry."

"But I'm scared," she whispered.

"I know, love. We're all scared. But we can't let him see it. He's got to be strong and we've got to help him. He needs us, Irene. He needs you. So stop your crying. Do it for him."

She looked up at him, fighting her fear, her grief. The tears had almost stopped. He drew her head down to his shoulder again.

"That's my good girl. Just hold on until it's gone."

Finally, she stopped shivering and stepped away from him, wiping her eyes with the back of her hand. He took off his bandanna and offered it to her. She smiled weakly in thanks.

"What about Annie?" she asked in a voice that still quavered.

"Tommy says she'll be all right, even though the Navajo have taken her. He says the elder, Running Wolf, would never let them hurt her." He prayed the blacksmith was right, that their exquisite little seer would be protected from harm.

"But what if she gets sick?"

He had no answer for her. "We'll have to pray that she doesn't." Her head was on his shoulder again and she whispered his name.

"Yes, little one?"

"I love you."

He chuckled. "I love you, too, *mavourneen*." He raised her face, pinched her cheek. "Better? Good! Then let's go see what we can do to help."

Chapter 67

ANNIE SAT CLOSE TO the fire, trying to warm her hands and feet. She was cold—not as cold as she'd been the night before, but she was frightened.

She'd been with the tribe for five days now, and things had been easier once the elder discovered who she was. Even before, he'd protected her from the warrior who claimed her. Her lips twitched at the thought of the things she'd done to the warrior.

Though it was close to dawn, she was still kicking and screaming when he carried her into camp. She knew his back was sore from the pounding it had taken from her fists, his arms weary with the effort of hanging on to her. And she hoped he had a headache from the voice that had screamed constantly in his ear.

When he flung her down to the ground, so hard it jarred her teeth, she'd leaped up and turned her back on him. When he touched her braid, she turned and saw the hope in his eyes. She stood as straight as she could and gave him a look of such withering contempt, the light died immediately. If he were looking for a maiden to swoon at his feet, he'd be sorely disappointed.

She knew where her strength came from, for Katie's soothing voice rang in her ear. *None shall harm you, ever. He will be with you for as long as you live.* She fed her soul on the hope it promised. He'd come for her. She'd know in her heart if he were dead. He lived, and he'd come.

But the warrior reached for her, taking her arms in his big hands. She'd resisted but he was too strong. When his mouth came close to

THE WOODSMAN'S ROSE

hers she turned her head and his slavering kiss fell on her jaw. She reared back and spit in his face.

He was so startled that he let her go. She stumbled but managed to remain standing. There was rage in his eyes as he pulled her back into his arms. She fought him desperately and felt his rough mouth on her throat. She screamed and flailed at him. Abruptly, he went still.

She fell as he stepped back this time, for her legs wouldn't support her. She looked up to see the speartip resting against his neck, followed the shaft of it to the old man who was holding it, and gave him a smile of pure gratitude. The spear was lowered as the elder bit out an order. Words of anger were followed by words of rage, of accusation. Then the old man pulled himself up pridefully and spoke with authority. The warrior stared hard at him, then strode away muttering, maybe cursing, beneath his breath.

Another man helped Annie up. She stood, straight and determined, before the elder.

"Who you?" Running Wolf demanded.

"Annie Donovan."

He pointed at her hair. "No Donovan. Donovan red, black. No gold." He shook a finger at her. "No Donovan. Who you?"

"Annie Donovan. My husband is Daniel Donovan."

"Hus-band?"

"My man." She showed him her ring. "Husband. Daniel Donovan."

"You Donovan woman?"

"Yes." There was pride in her voice, in her eyes. "Daniel Donovan is my man."

"Dan-el? Red?" He made a gesture, signifying the wild red hair of Jake or Brian.

"No." Annie made a smooth movement over her own head. How to say auburn? "Hair like copper. Smooth, shiny like copper." What else distinguished her man? She growled out, "Daniel Donovan."

The elder made the sign of a mustache.

"Yes." She imitated his sign.

"Woodsman."

"Yes!"

"You Rose?"

"Annie." She tapped her chest and repeated, "Annie Donovan."

But he recognized her now, by the description he'd been given months ago. Delicate, and fairer than the red rose. Hair bright as buttercups, skin pale as the new moon.

"You Rose," he told her. "Woodsman dead?"

She shook her head firmly. "Hurt. Not dead."

"Come for you?"

"Yes."

The elder frowned and spoke again. She shook her head and he repeated it. She shook her head again and shrugged.

He started barking orders and the crowd around them dissipated. Women and children began to pack their belongings, the women packing up food and pots, wrapping their babies against the dew. Young men ran for horses, gathered them together in a group as the older men conferred in rapid undertones with their chief. For Running Wolf had claimed the title at last, knowing it was the only power that would protect his friend's woman.

In less than an hour, the tribe was ready to move. A half-dozen horses were packed with their belongings; the women carried baskets of foodstuffs. Annie was given a small bundle to carry and made to walk with the women. After the tribe left the campground, the young men sent the rest of their ponies scrambling through it, effectively erasing all traces of their flight. The horses would come back, or

THE WOODSMAN'S ROSE

would be captured again. Or the men would go to the mesas after new ones. It was now more important to protect their families.

⁂

IT HAD BEEN SUNSET, two days ago, when they finally stopped climbing. They'd come around a rim of rock to a small glade in the forest and begun to unpack. A few yards away in the pines, a brook babbled. They were fairly high and the air was cool. Exhausted and aching from exertion, Annie shivered in her light calico dress.

The pack was taken from her. She was given food and one blanket, a place to sleep with the young women and older children. She curled up as close to the fire as she could safely get, knowing she must keep warm but hesitant to ask for what wasn't given to her. Concentrating on Katie's words, she fell asleep wondering how long it would be before he came.

She measured her days by the sunrises. She was never alone, for the elder had set guards around her; they watched her so subtly she was unaware of their scrutiny. They followed her every step—four of them, together or separately. Annie would have died of shame if she'd known how closely she was watched.

The attentions of the warrior hadn't diminished, but he no longer grabbed at her. He brought gifts of food and jewelry which she refused. He'd take her arm but drop it when she pulled away. He'd sneak up behind her to touch her hair. Once, when she went to the stream to wash her face, he met her on the way back and stood in front of her on the path, making a gesture she interpreted as conciliation. She stared at him until he stepped aside, but felt his lips brush against her cheek as she passed. Deliberately, roughly, she wiped his touch away.

Yellow Knife didn't understand her. After seeing her for the first time in the Trading Post, he'd become obsessed, haunting the alleys between the buildings to catch a glimpse of her in her father's shop.

After she married, he'd lost track of her for several weeks and had hung around the outskirts of town at all hours, his passion driving him nearly insane. It was only by chance that he'd seen her riding home in the buggy with Daniel after an evening at the dairy farm.

Jealousy was not an emotion he recognized, yet it ate at his insides like lye.

Now, he had taken her. She needed a man, for her man was dead. Had he not proven how brave and bold he could be? Did he not bring her gifts? In his world, a woman wanted the best man, the one who was strongest, wisest, or most handsome. He considered himself the best the tribe could offer.

The other young women fawned over him, longed for his touch, his caress, his attentions. Yet she, whom he felt the most desirable, didn't want him at all.

The looks of scorn she gave him made him feel like a cowering child. Foremost in his memory was a teacher at the missionary school—a sour-faced blonde woman who'd regarded her charges as pagans and savages. He'd tried in vain to please her, but she'd hated him and his classmates. The contempt she'd shown him was reflected in Annie's eyes. The chief's threats had kept him from hurting her the first day. Her courage and scorn had kept him from hurting her since.

The elders were angry. Each day Running Wolf called him, ordered him to take the woman back, and each day he'd refused. Five days, five refusals. The chief had determined if a sixth refusal came, the danger must be removed. Yet Yellow Knife was the strongest, the most fearless, and there were none his equal with a knife. He'd have to be executed.

It wasn't this tribe's preference to kill in cold blood, yet the woman must be returned or they faced annihilation. Already her four guards had volunteered to kill him—they'd eliminate the barrier and take her back.

THE WOODSMAN'S ROSE

The woodsman would be fair, the chief knew. If he still lived. If they could get to him before other white men found her with them.

He looked at the golden head shining in the campfire's light, saw her shiver as she rubbed her temple, and signaled to one of his people to bring her an extra blanket.

Annie smiled at the woman, found the effort monumental, and bowed her head into her hands. What she'd feared most was coming to pass. She'd been five days without her tisane and was weak and dizzy. The pain in her temple had begun. She was cold, she was frightened, and the old voice came no more.

She knew the Navajo were superstitious—if she became ill, would they take it as an omen and desert her? Would she be left to the questionable mercy of Yellow Knife? Could she live through the shame he'd inflict on her? Live long enough for Daniel to find her—to take her home again? What about her baby? She turned her wavering attention inward, found that delicate pulse telling her that her baby was well. She concentrated on that, deliberately ignoring the pain in her head. She wove a spell of hope around the tiny heartbeat and did not hear the sudden silence descend over the camp.

Chapter 68

IT WAS ONLY A FEW HOURS after they took him home that the woodsman regained consciousness. He reached for the woman who knelt beside him, looked deeply into the big green eyes set like jewels in a heart-shaped face, and found there hope and faith.

"Jesse," he whispered.

She ran a hand over his hair. "How do you feel?"

"I've been better." He didn't dare to look at her as he asked. "Did they go for her?"

"Alec went." He sensed her hesitation and opened his eyes again. He stared at her, willing her to go on. "They left their camp in the middle of the night. He went to find them. He said he'd leave a trail for you to follow."

"If they left, they've taken her with them. She's still alive."

"That's what Alec said, too. And he said the elder would protect her."

"Running Wolf. If he can, he will. If he knows who she is. Jesse, help me up."

"No, Daniel. Not yet. You're too weak. If you get up now, it'll do more harm than good."

He couldn't face the thought of doing nothing while his wife was missing. "Help me. Please."

"Yes, *acushlah*, as you have helped me so many times." Her smile was warm, generous, and he felt it reflected on his own face. "Can you eat? It will make you stronger."

THE WOODSMAN'S ROSE

"Yes." He would do anything she said to gain his strength back, anything that would take him one step nearer to his beloved wife. With an effort at levity, he said, "Bring everything you have. I'll eat it all."

"She'll be all right, Daniel." Jesse touched his cheek. "She told me once that Gran said she would never come to harm. Believe in it." He nodded as she stood and left the room.

Moments later his father and Adam came in. His brother took his free hand and held it, sympathy and strength flowing from every pore in his body. Daniel drank it in, then whispered, "Thanks."

Adam gave his place to John Patrick and sat on the floor. The old man looked at his son's pale face and fought back misery.

"Feelin' better?"

"Some. Any word from Alec?"

"Not yet." They didn't expect any word, and Daniel knew it. The longer Alec stayed on the trail, the better it would be. He felt another hand upon his cheek, saw Irene out of the corner of his eye.

"Hello, little one. Come sit where I can see you."

She came around and took his hand from her father's. He smiled at her, seeing the difficulty with which she held in her tears. He squeezed her fingers until she squeezed back.

"It's all right," he told her. Her tears began to fall. Adam stood and reached for her, but Daniel didn't let her go. He used his good hand to pull her head down until it rested against his neck. His father and brother retreated, and he held her as closely as he could.

"It's all right, *mavourneen*. I know you're scared. I'm scared, too." She looked up at him, a question on her face. "There's no shame in being scared, Irene. Everyone's scared sometimes. You just can't let it take over everything.

"Bravery isn't about not being afraid," he told her. "It's about not letting your fear take over. Nobody who hasn't been afraid has ever been brave."

"Really? Are you really scared?"

"More than I've ever been."

"Daniel..." Her chin still quivered, but she didn't cry. "Do you think we could maybe try to be brave together?"

"It's a deal," he whispered. "We'll be partners—partners in bravery, okay?"

"Okay!" She chewed for a moment on her bottom lip. "Can I do anything for you?"

He accepted her help, and his parents' and brothers' and sisters'-in-law. Tommy's and Owen's, Lowell's and Evelyn's. He ate everything they would give him, drank everything they told him to drink, and rested when they commanded it. On the next day he sat up, his pain somewhat relieved by the willow bark. By the end of the day he was standing on his own. And walking unaided by the next morning, flexing his arm after the doctor removed the stitches, finding enough mobility to feed himself. In the evening, he told them he was going after Alec.

Silence greeted his announcement. As they all stared at him, Jesse asked, "Are you sure?"

"Yes, *mavourneen*. I've got to go."

"You can't go alone."

"I'm ready," Jake stated. Molly gasped. "It's all right, Mother. Nothing will happen to us. We'll just follow Alec's trail. We'll find the camp and we'll find Annie, and we'll bring her home."

"It's all right," he said again, very gently. Molly closed her eyes and nodded.

"Thank you." Daniel spoke to both his mother and his youngest brother. Jake was the one he needed. Not the biggest or the strongest, or the most experienced. But he could hunt, track, hide himself in the forest, glide through the glades and parks, and understand the hand signals Alec had created. And since Alec had entrusted him

THE WOODSMAN'S ROSE

with the call they would need to make contact, Daniel knew that Alec wanted the youth along, too.

"We'll leave before daybreak," Daniel said.

"Best get to sleep then." Jake winked at him. "Mornin' comes early these days."

Chapter 69

AFTER TWO DAYS ON THE trail, Jake was worried. They'd ridden their horses only as far as the original camp, having made one stop first at *Sidhean Annie*. Daniel had packed Annie's medicine and given Jake precise instructions on the dosage she might need. Just in case. Then Daniel had looked longingly at the meadow as the sun rose over it, closed his eyes and whispered a prayer, "Let all be well."

"Amen," Jake answered. The woodsman's grip tightened on his arm, then they were on their way again.

There were no real trails north of the campsite, so they left their horses there and began to climb. North was always their direction, and every fifty rods or so they found Alec's sign, directing them always onward, upward. The trek was exhausting, for Daniel wouldn't waver from his chosen course. They crashed through bramble, crawled through brush, climbed through zones of broken shale and twisted pines. Always up, always north, and always finding Alec's sign that led them further on.

They stopped at noon to drink at a brook and eat some of the food Molly had provided. She'd stayed up all night preparing a pack for them. Jerky and biscuits, pemmican, cornmeal, apples, bandages, salve and blankets. She'd boiled down the willow bark and lobelia into a tincture, so that two drops in a cup of water would equal a cup of tisane. In the morning, as she helped Jake strap the heavy pack on his back, her hands had trembled with fear for them. But she was clear-eyed and her voice was firm as she explained the importance of clean dressings for his brother's wound and the need for Daniel to eat well. At the last moment she added a small paper sack filled with beet root powder, and told Jake to see that his brother drank at least a spoonful in water with each meal.

My mother, Jake decided, *is the bravest person I know.* When he offered the beet juice to his brother as they sat in the shade next to the stream, the woodsman laughed aloud.

"Can't get away from that stuff for nothin'!" he complained gruffly, but reached out with his left hand to ruffle his brother's hair. "Thanks, kid. Guess it's a good thing you're here."

But when they camped that night, having stopped over three miles north of the cabin, Jake discovered that Daniel's wound was bleeding under its thick bandage.

"Clean it off and wrap it up. We're going on in the morning."

"But, Daniel..."

The woodsman grabbed his arm and held it so tight it hurt. "I'm going after her, Jake. Come along if you want, or go back home. But don't try to stop me."

"All right. I'm going with you. But lie down and let me do this right." He covered the wound liberally with salve, added several layers of padding, then wrapped it with linen strips. In the morning, the bleeding seemed to have stopped. But as the day went on and the climb became more arduous, flecks of blood appeared on the back of his brother's buckskin shirt. As they stopped to camp just after dark, Daniel drew the shirt off over his head and Jake saw a rivulet of blood running from under the bandage and down his brother's back.

They were camped again by a stream and Jake filled a tin cup with water, then dug in the pack for the willow bark. He put two drops into the cup and handed it to his brother.

"Drink it," he commanded. With a slow smile, the woodsman obeyed. "I've got to..."

Daniel held up a hand for silence. They heard the raucous call of a nighthawk, followed by the shrill cry of an owl. And then it came, unsuited to time and place, the lonely little trill of a mourning dove.

Chapter 70

RUNNING WOLF WAS WATCHING the Rose, unable to decide if it were sorrow or pain affecting her, when he heard the call of the dove. He signaled abruptly and a hush fell over the camp.

The forest greeted it with silence. His lieutenants waited for him to speak, but he listened until it came again. The nighthawk, the screech owl. And even more foreign than before in the utter quiet, the dove.

Someone has found us. Friend or foe?

He didn't wait long for an answer. A tall, slender young man stepped into the clearing. His hair was dark as the raven's wing. Soft and glossy, it was held by a silver-studded headband and fell past his shoulders. His face was dusky, not bronze, his eyes black and his expression stern. He faced the elder silently.

"Twelve Trees," the chief acknowledged, a shade of deference in his voice. This was his friend. Was the woodsman's friend. Was known and respected in the tribe. And hadn't long ago been a boy and not a man to be reckoned with.

The chief stole a look at the golden head, still bowed in pain or sorrow. But the somber quiet of the man before him drew his attention again.

"Twelve Trees, why have you come?"

"You have no need to ask," Alec replied in his father's tongue.

The elder made a quick movement of his head, signifying his acceptance of the words. "You have come for her?"

"You have no need to ask."

"She has not been harmed. She is well."

"She is not well. She has pain." His hand flickered over his forehead, then he placed it on his breast. "Her heart is heavy. She does not belong to you."

"She belongs to me!" The voice came from his right, but Alec didn't acknowledge it. He continued to stare at the chief, anger gleaming in his eyes.

"She does not belong to you," he told Running Wolf again. "Or to any of your tribe."

Yellow Knife pounded on his chest as he stepped between the chief and Alec. "She belongs to me! I have killed her man. She will stay with me."

"You have killed no one. You are but a weakling. I would talk with a man!"

The warrior's voice was brash as he struck his chest once more. "I have killed her man. I have killed the one they call woodsman!"

The man's voice had finally penetrated Annie's pain. She looked up. Alec's back was to her and yet she recognized him. Hope flared instantly, knocking out the desperate tension of her body, leaving her weak and faint. She didn't understand his words.

"You have killed no one." Alec's voice dripped with contempt. "The woodsman lives."

"You lie! The woodsman is dead. For I have killed him."

"The woodsman lives." A fourth voice. As a body, they turned to it.

Daniel stepped into the clearing, stripped to the waist, the campfire light glinting in the copper hair on his head, his face, his chest; gleaming off the silver chain he wore, the half-round medallion that hung below his throat.

"The woodsman lives," he repeated in English. And heard his wife scream.

THE WOODSMAN'S ROSE

She'd leapt to her feet and stood frozen when she first saw him. Her lips opened but no sound issued forth. When he spoke the second time, she screamed his name and would have run to him but for the arms that surrounded her, the hand that closed over her mouth. She struggled frantically.

"Take it easy, Annie," Jake murmured. "Just take it easy."

She fell back against him, clutching at his arms.

"Quiet now," he said as he removed his hand from her mouth.

"He's hurt." Her voice was ragged, sobbing, but low, as she watched the trickle of blood that ran down Daniel's back. "Jake..."

"He's all right."

Annie trembled violently. Jake was supporting her and without him to lean on, she would have collapsed. He realized for the first time that she was more delicate, more fragile even than Jesse, and he was more afraid for her than for his brother. He sank down until she was sitting again on her blanket. She pressed back against him.

"I'm afraid," she whimpered.

"Shhh. He knows what he's doing. And Alec's right there. It'll be all right."

Alec would know what to do. They'd found him less than a rod from where they'd stopped, around the corner of the ridge that had hidden the encampment from them. He and Daniel had worked out their strategy in low tones, then the woodsman turned to Jake.

Daniel's eyes had been dark as sapphires, his voice so rough it had been almost unintelligible as he'd commanded, "Go to her. Hold her there. Don't let her go and don't leave her. No matter what. Do you understand? No matter what!"

The woodsman pulled off his bandanna, tore the bandage from his shoulder, and tested the weight of the knife he drew from his boot. He'd made the knife himself with Tommy's guidance, and he remembered Tommy telling him, *"It should fit into your hand as naturally as a woman's breast."* At the time he'd had only a vague idea of what the smith meant, but now he'd use this knife, that fit his hand so closely, to save his woman.

As he slipped it back into its sheath, he jerked his head toward the campfire. His brother stole away into the trees. He'd waited until he could see Jake behind her—she was just looking up and his heart stuttered at the sight of her lovely, innocent face. Then he turned his attention to Alec and the warrior, before the need to comfort her could outweigh the need to save her.

Now he stood before Yellow Knife as the warrior took his measure. He wasn't as tall, as blatantly muscled, but he could move as quickly as a cat and knew that the Navajo wouldn't anticipate his expertise with a knife. Nor realize the advantage he had in weight.

The blood that trickled from his shoulder didn't bother him. Every ounce of his blood would be given before he'd surrender.

If I must die, so be it. But this bastard will die first.

The sneer on the warrior's face deepened, for one of his followers stood in the crowd and signaled that the woodsman was wounded. *It would be more honorable to fight the half-breed, young as he is, for at least there is glory in fighting one who is whole.*

Annie shuddered as the crowd drew back from the two men, while the outer fringes pressed closer. The confrontation was silent. Tension tasted like an old, dirty penny, and she swallowed hard.

"Jake..." Desperately, she tried to break free but he held her firmly.

"Stay here, Annie. You can't do anything that would help."

She moaned—she couldn't help herself. Then she made an intense effort to relax. Until the long knife appeared in the warrior's hand. It slashed out at the woodsman, who leaped back. Jake closed his hand once more over her mouth.

"Quiet. Let him concentrate."

She grabbed at his arm, her body so taut he thought it would break.

THE WOODSMAN'S ROSE

"Don't make a sound," he whispered. "Don't distract him. He doesn't need to think about us now." She nodded and he let his hand relax, but kept it there on her cheek.

The two men were circling less than seven feet apart, their arms dropping lower and lower as they began to crouch. Daniel's hand was almost at his boot when the warrior feinted again. His knife made contact this time, slashing across the woodsman's chest. Tiny droplets of blood appeared on his breasts. But by some magic—some sleight of hand—another knife gleamed wickedly in the firelight, stabbed out at the warrior and caught his face. Deflected off his jaw, it left a ragged cut from ear to forehead.

The hot spurt of his own blood enraged Yellow Knife. This was a white man, soft and weak. Already wounded. It was luck that allowed him to strike that blow. But he'd die for that. Die so his woman saw that he was dead. Then she'd want him, for he was the stronger.

He closed in on the woodsman, but Daniel anticipated his move. He grabbed the wrist that held the blade as Yellow Knife grabbed his. They grunted and strained in a macabre dance until the warrior slipped his foot behind the woodsman's ankle and they went tumbling to the ground. Daniel groaned as he fell on the injured shoulder but didn't weaken his grip for an instant. The Navajo crashed on top of him. There was utter silence from the ring of spectators and Daniel took advantage of it. The hoarse cry he gave startled them all, including Yellow Knife.

"Bastard!"

The minute break in the warrior's concentration was all he needed. With his left arm he shoved the man over, came out on top. "Coward!" he spat out. But the moment's advantage was gone. The trick wouldn't work twice.

The two men were evenly matched in strength, in experience, and it dawned on Yellow Knife that victory was not going to be as easy as he expected. The man hadn't died the first time he was wounded, and had already drawn blood. So he must die. Now.

The watchers scurried back as the opponents rolled across the campground, the advantage first to one, then the other. Annie had both fists crammed against her mouth, but managed somehow to remain silent as she watched. Her fear was so strong that Jake could feel it, and he held on tight and whispered to her when he could. The prayers he sent up were disconnected, incoherent, even desperate. But he watched his brother in awe, in pride, for the fight had lasted much longer already than he ever thought it could.

Although he felt no pain, Daniel's right arm was weakening. He could use the knife with either hand—Tommy had taught him well. But he couldn't shift the blade unless his left hand were free. And it wouldn't be free until he could get rid of the warrior's weapon.

As Yellow Knife tumbled him over again, Daniel used the impetus of the roll to overbalance him. With his foot, he pushed hard against the warrior's stomach, kicked himself free. Yellow Knife landed on his back with a grunt, was on his feet again in an instant. But the force of his landing had knocked the knife from his hand.

Both men scrabbled toward the dagger as the crowd jumped back again. Daniel switched his knife to his left hand and grabbed for the other with his right. But Yellow Knife was faster. He snagged the hilt and stabbed up at his opponent's throat. But his grip wasn't tight and the blow glanced off the silver medallion. The knife flew away to land in the fire.

There was one knife now. One knife and two warriors. Annie tried to close her eyes, tried to turn to Jake and hide her face against him, but she couldn't move. She watched as they rolled again, saw her man come out on top. She cried his name out silently and saw the sudden stiffness in his spine.

Daniel knew he couldn't hold out much longer. The loss of blood had drained him. He heard his wife's strangled cry deep in his heart,

THE WOODSMAN'S ROSE

and it was all he needed to revive his flagging strength. He looked down at the warrior beneath him—saw the smirk as Yellow Knife pushed his hands back, pushed the knife back. And suddenly the face beneath him changed. A bold face, weak-chinned, vicious, and pale. A flashing memory of tawny hair, a battered face, torn clothing. A great purpling welt, and then its twin.

And Tommy's words again, *as naturally as a woman's breast.*

His woman. His precious love. Who fit into his own hands as if she'd been made by him. His hands descended together over the man who thought to claim her. Who thought to touch her. The muscles in his arms corded and veined, the strength in his hands greater than ever before. And the rage in his heart burned cleanly as his blade touched the warrior's breast.

Yellow Knife didn't comprehend. Yet he knew he was beaten. There was some strength in his opponent that he hadn't considered. If he must die, the warrior's death was the most honorable. If he couldn't have the woman, at least he'd have respect in death.

But the woodsman read the look of pride and gathered his scant energy, spit down into the Navajo's face. Saw the darkening there of fear and dishonor and, raising himself as high as he could, he plunged the blade straight down into the warrior's heart. The jerk of his body, the spurt of blood, the grunt of surprise were cut off almost before they'd begun.

The warrior lay limp, eyes rolling back, face clouded with disgrace. As the woodsman fell sideways onto his injured shoulder and the black pit yawned before him, he heard his woman scream again.

Chapter 71

SHE SCREAMED AGAIN and he fought the darkness off, made it to his knees before he fell face-down. He began to crawl, but a firm hand held him back.

"No, my friend," said Alec. "We'll bring her to you." He signaled to Jake, who took the trembling, sobbing woman up into his arms and carried her to her husband's side. Alec spread a blanket for her and Jake set her down. Daniel's arm wrapped around her and she pressed her face hard against him, shuddering, sobbing, terrified.

"*Aroon*," he whispered. "Hush, my love."

"Dan... iel..." Her hands plucked at him nervelessly.

"Shhh... it's all over now." Again and again he repeated it, until her sobs began to subside. But still her body vibrated with the remnants of her fear. "Hush, sweetheart. It's all over."

"You're hurt." Her voice shaking, too, and very small.

"I'm all right, sweetheart. Don't worry." He wished the last of his strength into her. "Hush, *aroon*."

She whispered his name again and he pulled her so close there wasn't a hairs-breadth of space between them. He murmured sweet words, comforting words in her ear and felt the easing of terror, the acceptance of safety.

Alec covered them with another blanket. Annie wrapped her arms around him beneath its sheltering warmth. Deep and long was the sigh he heard as her quaking finally abated.

"*Aroon*," he whispered. "Oh, Annie, I'm so sorry."

THE WOODSMAN'S ROSE

She raised her face to his. She was pale and her lips still trembled. Her cheek was stained with his blood. There was blood in her hair too, but her eyes gleamed in the firelight.

"I knew you'd come." Sweet words of faith that erased his guilt. "I knew you would."

He brushed the blood from her cheek with the back of his hand. "Did he hurt you?"

"No." Her eyes told him that she didn't lie.

"Did he touch you?"

"No. The elder protected me."

Deeply he breathed, then asked one more question, the one that frightened him the most. "*Aroon*... the baby?"

Her eyes turned inward and her small, joyful smile was answer enough. He pressed his lips against hers. "I love you. I love you. *Aroon*. Oh, Annie. My precious love."

His brother brought a cup of willow bark and lobelia for him, a cup of her medicine for Annie. They drank and before she slept, she raised her face to his.

"*Arrah*," she whispered. "You killed him."

"Yes, *aroon*." He looked into her pale eyes, then pulled her head in against his breast once more. "He would have come back."

She shuddered once, then closed her eyes and nestled against his heart.

※

JAKE HAD SLIPPED A drop of poppy juice into Daniel's cup and waited nearby while Alec dealt with the elders. When he'd finished extracting their promises to return to the lower camp and banish the followers of Yellow Knife, promised in return that no vengeance would be taken for the deed of the dead man, and accepted their gifts of conciliation, it was well past midnight. When the tribe retreated, he insisted they take the body with them. Then he returned to the two who slept as one beneath the blanket and signaled for Jake. There was work to be done before they awoke.

Alec removed the blanket carefully, for the blood from Daniel's wound had dried into it. As he pushed it aside, he saw that the woodsman had managed, before he slept, to unbutton Annie's dress and slip his hand inside against her breast. Alec's eyes met Jake's—as intimate a gesture as it was, it didn't embarrass them. Rather, it touched them deeply, and as Jake moved her aside and adjusted her dress, Alec thought, *It's as if he wanted to hold her heart right there in his hand.* Annie whimpered, her hand stretching out, searching for Daniel, and when it found him, she breathed deeply and slept again.

Alec looked away into the campfire, dreaming for a moment of another girl. Would he ever earn the right to touch her? Hold her? Would he ever be the one she loved?

With a slow shake of his head, he pulled himself back to the business at hand. While Jake washed the blood from Annie's face and hair, Alec rolled Daniel over onto his back and examined the wounds on his chest. They were shallow, almost superficial, but full of dirt. With a clean cloth, he scrubbed at them until they began to bleed again. He let the blood flow for a minute to help wash out the dirt, then used Molly's salve to contain it. Then he turned his friend over onto another blanket and peered at his back. The gash was bleeding still from the highest point, where the knife had gone in deepest. The edges of the wound were red and inflamed, and one corner was full of pus.

He drew his own knife from the sheath in his boot and held it to the fire, motioned for Jake to hold his brother still while he applied the hot blade to the wound. Flesh hissed and burned and the woodsman groaned in spite of the poppies. Annie whimpered again. Alec repeated the process on the lower edge of the gash.

When it was over, Jake's hands were white and trembling, so he gave the youth a slight smile and said, "That's it. Cover it with the salve, then bandage it good and tight. And don't worry, he'll be all right." With a sudden grin, Alec added, "You'll live through it, too."

Afterwards he stood guard while Jake slept, and roused him before sunrise. He'd prepared a light pack and saddled a pony; he gave Jake a rifle and directions to the Donovan ranch—an easier way down than they had coming up. He should be at the ranch by sunset and should send two wagons and at least three men up to them in the morning. Jake set the mustang to a brisk trot, eager to be bringing the good news home again.

The patients slept until almost noon and woke to the smell of coffee. Annie had snuggled in against him sometime during the night, and Daniel held her close and silent. When she raised her face, he kissed her tenderly. She smiled up into his eyes.

"Morning," said Alec. "Want some coffee?"

"Oh, yes," Annie answered, as she sat up somewhat shakily.

Daniel reached for the cup and drew it towards his mouth, then drank deeply.

"Ugh! Alec, you better get married quick! Before your coffee kills you!"

"It's your mother's recipe—beet juice and all!"

"Some friend you are," retorted the woodsman. "Now give me a cup of the real stuff!" Alec complied. "This isn't much better," Daniel complained.

"You can make it tomorrow."

"How long are we gonna be here?"

"It'll be five days before you're home. Jake left before sunrise, might get there by dark. But it will take them two days to get back with wagons, then two days to cart you home."

"Why do we need wagons?" Annie asked.

"To take home your apology." At her look of confusion, he explained, "The tribe apologized for Yellow Knife, even though he wasn't one of them. They left you and Daniel gifts. I couldn't refuse, though I didn't take everything they offered. But you're a pretty valuable girl, Annie. You're worth a whole wagonload of baskets, blankets and jewelry. Not to mention a half-dozen ponies."

"Alec, we can't take all that."

"He had to take it, sweetheart," Daniel told her, "or he would have insulted them. The debt had to be paid or their pride would have suffered. Yellow Knife wasn't of the tribe but when they accepted him, they accepted responsibility for what he did. If Alec didn't take the gifts, they'd consider us their enemies. And I don't know what that might lead to."

"But how will they live now, if we have everything they own?"

"We don't," replied Alec. "I mostly took the things they could replace themselves. Baskets, blankets, some pottery—they can make it all again. Ponies they can catch. Some jewelry, not much, but they insisted. Shirts and moccasins, some clothes they made to sell in your father's shop. And enough food to get us home again. That's the only thing that will really cost them anything, but I didn't see how we'd get along without it."

"But, Daniel, what are we going to do with it all?" she asked.

"I don't know, *aroon*. We should keep some of it, at least. It wouldn't be right not to. But the rest..." He shrugged, then grimaced.

"Maybe we could ask Carolyn to set up another auction," Annie said. Daniel's only reply was a smile.

Later in the day, Alec built a wide bed out of pine boughs and helped Daniel onto it. Annie lay down next to him and they slept until suppertime. The next morning, Daniel was up on his feet for a short while, though shakily. His wounds were healing cleanly and when he flexed his arm and found some mobility, he joked, "Back where I was a week ago!"

The following afternoon, Alec declared, "I'm sick of pemmican and jerky. I want a nice roasted bird or some rabbit stew. Do you two think you can entertain yourselves for a while?"

THE WOODSMAN'S ROSE

From his place on the bed of boughs, Daniel waved a hand at him. As his friend stole away into the forest, he reached for his wife. "*Aroon.*" His chest was tight with longing. "I need you."

She slipped in under the blanket. He loosened her hair, let it fall down softly over his arms and chest. With both hands he framed her face, then gazed into her beautiful eyes.

"Annie." He didn't have the words to tell her what he felt. But she smiled at him, coming close to rest her cheek against his heart. "Oh, Annie..."

Her lips brushed softly against his chest. He buried his fingers in her hair, closed his eyes, and lost himself in the love she gave him.

———

THE WAGONS ARRIVED at sunset. Tommy shared a seat with Owen, John Patrick with Irene, and Brian followed behind on Old Son. Owen almost broke his leg climbing down from his perch, so eager was he to see his daughter, to touch her and hold her. As she ran to him, Irene ran to her brother. He was sitting cross-legged by the campfire and stretched his good arm out to her. She fell on her knees at his side, wrapped her arms around his neck and hid her face on his bare shoulder. Her tears fell hot against his skin.

"Hush, *mavourneen*. It's all over."

"Daniel, I was so scared."

"Me, too. Were you brave?"

Her tear-stained face showed him the slightest of smiles. "Yes. But it was so hard!"

He kissed her forehead. "I know. But it wouldn't mean anything if it weren't, would it?"

She leaned back then, and touched the bandage that was wrapped around his chest. "Are you really all right?"

"A little sore, but not badly hurt. I'm glad you came."

She brightened up at that. Annie came back to them and Irene leaped up to hug her, her tears starting anew. Annie whispered something that he didn't hear, and it made his sister laugh.

"Oh, wait!" Irene cried. "I have something for you—where did I put it?" She wore a pair of Jake's discarded denims, a corduroy jacket, cotton shirt and blue bandanna; she had to search through all the pockets to find what she was looking for. "Here!" She thrust a note at Annie.

"*I lov yu, Annie,*" she read aloud. "*I prayd for yu. Yor frend, Norah.* Oh, Daniel, look at this! Isn't it beautiful?"

He took the letter, drew her down next to him, and smiled up at his sister. "Thanks."

"I better go see what I can do to help," she said and left them there together.

The men came one at a time, to inquire after his wounds and Annie's health. His father held his hand tightly for a long moment. Jake had given them an abbreviated story but Alec had filled in the details. Daniel didn't want to discuss it, and they respected his wishes. They ate around the campfire and Brian helped himself to the last of the rabbit stew after everyone else was finished.

"This is real good, Miss Annie," he said.

"Thanks," she drawled, her eyes twinkling at him, "but Alec made it."

"Naw. Did 'e really? Sure don't taste like a man's cookin'."

Laughter rang through the glade as they began to swap cooking stories. Brian insisted that Adam was the worst cook on the range while Irene argued with him. It was Frank, she stated, and by no small margin.

When Annie began to yawn, they all went to bed. Alec had widened the bed of boughs so it would accommodate four. Owen took one side. Annie slept between him and Daniel, her hand in her father's, her husband's arm around her waist. Curled up against the woodsman was Irene, her back to his, the warmth of his body melting the last of the fear from her heart.

Before they settled in, though, Owen hesitantly framed a question.

"Say, lad, you think you'll be up and around by Saturday?"

"What's today?"

"Wednesday."

"Sure. How come?"

"Well, Carolyn really did want to get married in June..."

His daughter's arms were strangling him. "You waited? You waited for me?"

"Silly child, of course we did!"

Chapter 72

JOHN PATRICK AND BRIAN stood watch while Alec slept for the first time in three days. Tommy woke and took Brian's place but when he would have roused his son, John Patrick stopped him.

"Let the lad sleep. He's done more than his share."

At sunrise they were all up, and as Annie disappeared into the forest with Irene and the clean clothes she'd brought, Alec and Tommy spread the gifts out on the grass so they could see what was there. Daniel picked a pair of intricately-designed blankets and a ritual basket, as well as a rugged white pony.

When Annie returned, he could only stare at her—she was dressed as Irene was, in denims, shirt and corduroy jacket. She wore heavy socks but no shoes. She flashed a smile at him and ran to his side. "How come you never told me how comfortable your clothes are?"

He didn't answer but continued to stare at her, until his father made a sound in his throat. Daniel pulled himself together with an effort. "It's your turn, *aroon*. Pick out anything you like."

She reached for a pair of calf-high moccasins and pulled them on. Then she chose three small baskets in shades of blue and ochre, and a delicate necklace of several silver strands. For Jake, the woodsman selected a velveteen shirt and a pinto pony. He offered Alec a fine bay mare.

"And anything else you want," he added. The silversmith chose a wide bracelet studded with turquoise nuggets. Daniel saw Brian eyeing a pair of buckskin boots and handed them to him with a

THE WOODSMAN'S ROSE

knowing laugh. "The kid convinced you, hey?" His brother grunted in response.

"Anything you like, Dad? Owen? Tommy?" His father selected a pair of moccasins for himself and a bracelet for Molly as Tommy helped himself to an oak and hickory bow. But Owen refused the offer, stating that he wanted nothing whatsoever to remind him of their "adventure."

Lastly the woodsman picked out a delicate silver ring and slipped it onto the middle finger of Irene's right hand, murmuring thanks and pinching her cheek. "See anything else?"

"Well..."

"Go ahead, *mavourneen*. Whatever it is, it's yours."

She stepped to the blanket and touched a soft buckskin dress, beaded at the bodice, which Daniel knew had been made to sell to tourists. "Could I have this?" At his nod, she picked it up and rubbed the soft leather against her face.

"You'll need these to go with it," Alec said, and offered her a pair of moccasins that matched the dress.

She accepted them with a smile. "Thank you, Alec. Thank you for everything."

Her hand was on his sleeve. He was bewitched by her smile, by her boy's clothing. Her eyes, usually so deeply blue, were almost green. He held their gaze for a moment then he turned to watch her brother and his wife.

"*De nada*," he replied. It was nothing. There was no debt, for between them, they'd saved his life. But he could see that Irene didn't understand. He closed his hand over hers. "I had a debt to pay," he told her, his voice deep and smooth and rich.

"You would have done it anyway. He's your friend."

"Yes. As is she. As are you."

She beamed at him. "Let's go help."

Alec fashioned hackamores for the ponies, tied them to two long ropes so he and his father could lead them. One wagon was packed with the gifts; Brian helped Daniel up into the other and cushioned his back with blankets. Annie climbed in beside him, while Owen took the driver's seat. Irene rode beside her father in the other wagon. They'd gone a mile when John Patrick pulled his team up and shouted at the passengers in Owen's wagon. "Which way?"

"*Sidhean Annie!*" Daniel cried. He turned to his wife and wrapped his good arm around her, nuzzled into her hair. "Home," he whispered. "I want to go home."

She gave a long sigh. Home. A hot bath and her own bed. Her man beside her every night. Herself, her husband, and their little boy. And the small old voice that had returned to assure her, *He will be with you for as long as you live.*

She sighed again and whispered, as if in prayer or benediction, "Home."

The End

Afterword

DEAR READER,

I hope you enjoyed **THE WOODSMAN'S ROSE**. If so, I'd appreciate it if you'd share it on your favorite social media site, or recommend it to your local library or book club.

The best way for new readers to find an author is by reading reviews. Whether you loved or hated it, or fell somewhere in between, please consider writing a review on your favorite digital retailer or book review site. Just a sentence or two of what you think is all it takes.

Did you like the characters? the plot? Did you find the story believable? inspirational? boring? Are you looking forward to reading new books in the series, or picking up the previous ones? Did something in the story impress? dismay? surprise? Your honest opinion would mean the world to me.

Thanks again for your interest in my work.

Giff

What happens next?

CONTINUING THE SAGA of the Donovans in America, here's an excerpt from Book 3, **RAINBOW MAN:**

§

John Patrick Donovan wore a frown to match his eldest son's. He was a man beginning to feel the effects of seventy years of hard work. His hair had long been gray, his shoulders had begun to slope, his hands to pain him in the cold and damp. Yet none dared to call him old to his face.

"What's going on?" His deep voice was rich with the music of Ireland. "The Army wants to see you." He'd been to their camp trying to negotiate a withdrawal of the troops. In vain, as always.

"They'll have to wait," Adam replied.

"Tell me why."

"They dragged Alec Twelve Trees home at the end of a rope." Adam's words were ripe with disgust. "I don't know where they found him, but he said he'd been walking for two days. That goddamned ugly sergeant was riding his horse. I took it back."

A deep frown creased the old man's brow. "Where is the lad now?"

"I took him home." Adam lit a cigarette, blew a puff of smoke in the direction of the silversmith's cottage. "I came to get Mother to see to him, but..."

"She's already gone."

"So Jake said. He's sending Irene out instead."

THE WOODSMAN'S ROSE

"I'll make sure the Army waits patiently." John Patrick wagged a finger. "But not forever, you hear?"

"Thanks, Dad."

The old man turned on his heel, walked toward the Army encampment on the north end of town, their tents just visible past the stables run by Tommy Twelve Trees. They'd arrived six weeks after the only serious Indian trouble in ten years had occurred. Six weeks after Annie Donovan had come home again, unhurt and unharmed. Six weeks after her husband had fought the renegade who abducted her to the death. And they'd stayed, their commanders convinced the town was in danger from the small band of Navajo who'd lived peacefully in the mountains for that whole ten years.

Adam grimaced at the thought. His sister-in-law was fine now. Or at least as well as she'd ever been. Daniel's wound had healed. There was a nasty scar on his brother's back, but no permanent damage had been done and no blame had ever been attributed to the tribe. The Cavalry wasn't needed, but couldn't be convinced of it. Inwardly, he wished his father luck.

"Adam?"

Irene stood at his elbow. She was tall for a girl of eighteen, slender and graceful. Like his, her hair was black as coal, her face broad at the brow, tapering to a pointed chin. Her skin was perfectly white and flawless, her eyes a deep blue flecked with green. He marveled that this sister who looked so much like him could be so feminine, so beautiful.

"Jake said you wanted me," she continued when he didn't respond.

"Have you got anything with you to use on bruises?"

"Are you hurt?" Her eyebrows drew together, but the graceful arches on her face bore no semblance to the straight black lines on his.

"No, *mavourneen*, but Alec's had a rough time. I think he had a bad fall."

"He got back?"

"A few minutes ago. Do you have anything with you?"

"No. Maybe we could get something at Wang Shen's. They have some herbs for sale."

"Let's go." Adam led her down a narrow side street. Wang Shen's wife had inherited the knowledge of herbal medicines, just as Irene had done. They found her in the shop, but encountered some difficulty in explaining what they needed. Irene's temper was fraying when her brother interrupted.

"Is Jenny here?" Adam knew the Wang's youngest daughter had been tutored in English by Alec. Mrs. Wang nodded and hurried out. When she came back with Jenny, Adam explained what he needed.

"Bruises? Black and blues?"

"Do you have something good for black and blues?" Irene asked eagerly. "Adam, how much do we need?"

"Quite a lot."

His sister stared hard at him. "Is he bleeding?"

"Some."

"Adam, how bad is he?"

"Get as much of everything as you can."

Irene turned back to Jenny, who was offering a bunch of dried leaves.

"Ev-er-las-ting," the girl said. "Good for black and blues."

"Thank you. Do you have any more?" Two more bunches of the same size were produced. It didn't seem like enough to Adam, who said so.

"Jenny," said Irene, "please ask your mother if she has any snakeweed, too. Or arnica."

The answer was negative. After obtaining some long linen bandages and thanking Mrs. Wang, Adam hurried his sister away.

THE WOODSMAN'S ROSE

"Adam, what really happened?"

"I'm not sure. He didn't have the energy to tell me. It doesn't really matter, does it?"

"I guess not. He'll be OK, won't he?"

"He'll be all right," he assured her. *It's funny the way she changes. Some days you'd swear there wasn't a thought in her head but herself, but as soon as something happens she's right there to help. Daniel says we've spoiled her rotten. I guess having seven brothers is enough to spoil any girl. Not to mention that she's got Dad wrapped around her little finger so tight he can't breathe. But she's got a good heart.*

As he opened the door to the silversmith's cottage, he saw that Alec had managed to turn himself over. The marks on his back showed plainly through the dust. Irene gasped and dropped her bundles on the floor. Her hands came up to cover her mouth and she swayed on her feet, just as Alec had done.

"Don't you go fainting on me." Her brother's voice was both stern and compassionate. "I need your help. He needs your help."

She approached the couch with dragging steps and knelt beside it, put a hand gently on Alec's head. Her fingers came away with blood on them.

"Adam..." He was picking up the herbs as she turned to him, reaching up with tears in her eyes. "Adam, what's happened to him?"

He came to kneel beside her, put his arm around her and let her cry for a moment. "Time to pull yourself together, *mavourneen*. He needs your help." She leaned back from him and sniffled. He took the bandanna from his neck and offered it to her.

"What can I do?" he asked, knowing a chore would help her settle down.

"Cool water... I'll need cool water and towels to get this dirt off." She shook her head helplessly. "And cut up some bandages for his head and arms. Adam, someone's tied him up! Who could do this?"

"We'll have to ask him when he wakes up."

She was stroking the silversmith's dark hair when her brother came back with a basin of water and some towels. She began to wash him, but no matter how gently she touched him, he moaned.

"I need some willow bark. Something to ease the pain."

"There might be some whiskey here."

"He won't drink it—you know that," she said. "Go see if Carolyn's got anything."

"I can't leave you here alone."

"Adam, he's unconscious! What could possibly happen?"

"You go, and see if Carolyn can come back with you. And, Irene, don't say anything to Jesse." His wife's pregnancy was advancing without incident, but they were careful with her. Too careful, she would protest, yet she'd lost one baby already.

He turned to the task his sister had abandoned, his hands as gentle as hers. But the obvious pain their patient endured made him stop. A few minutes would make no difference at all.

They were back quickly, Carolyn Griffiths bringing a small glassine envelope containing laudanum, which the doctor had given her husband for toothache.

"Jesse's asking after you," she told Adam. "I told her I'd see if I could find you and send you along."

"Thanks." He gave her a quick peck on the cheek, then turned to his sister. "Everything good now?"

"Yes." She was still shaky, but managed a smile. "We'll take care of him."

...to be continued...

Be the first to get the news!

You can sign up for my newsletter &
get a free book, as well as updates,
early notice of new releases, special promotions, & more.
OR
If you want a copy of my newest books
before they're available to the general public,
consider joining my Launch Team!
Find more information here[1]:

---

1. https://giffordmacshane.com/contact/

Acknowledgments

To my mother, Janet, and my husband, Rich, for their unwavering support;
to the ladies of the Prose & Precision group for their thoughtful input and suggestions;
to Noreen Bennett, Sheila Davis, and Mary Higginson for their keen vision and opinions;
to James and Toni for making sure I got my facts straight—
to all of you, I offer my utmost gratitude.

Songs quoted in THE WOODSMAN'S ROSE

(in order of appearance)

§

BELIEVE ME IF ALL THOSE ENDEARING YOUNG CHARMS
Thomas (Anacreon) Moore, (1779-1852)

§

NONE CAN LOVE LIKE AN IRISHMAN
Traditional, Ireland

§

THE MAID OF LLANWELLYN
Joanna Baillie (1862-1851)

§

MOLLY BAWN
Traditional, Ireland

§

POOR WAYFARING STRANGER
Traditional Spiritual

§

OFT IN THE STILLY NIGHT
Thomas (Anacreon) Moore, (1779-1852)

About the Author

GIFFORD MACSHANE IS the author of historical fiction that celebrates the resilience of the human spirit. Her novels feature a family of Irish immigrants who settle in the Arizona Territory. With an accessible literary style, MacShane draws out her characters' hidden flaws and strengths as they grapple with physical and emotional conflicts.

Singing almost before she could talk, MacShane always loved folk music, whether Irish, Appalachian, or the songs of cowboys. Her love of the Old West goes back to childhood, when her father introduced her to Zane Grey. She became interested in Irish history after realizing her father's family had lived through the Great Potato Famine before emigrating to America.

Writing has allowed Giff to combine her three great interests into a series of family stories, each including romance, traditional song lyrics, and a dash of Celtic mysticism. Having grown up in a large & often boisterous Irish-American family, she is intimately acquainted with the workings of such a clan and uses those experiences to good purpose (though no names will be named!)

MacShane is a member of the Historical Novel Society. She loves to sing, though her cats don't always approve. An avid gardener, Giff cultivates pollinator plants and grows tomatoes (not enough) and zucchini (too much). A self-professed grammar nerd, Giff currently lives in Pennsylvania with her husband Richard, the Pied Piper of stray cats.

What Reviewers say

about the
DONOVAN FAMILY SAGA

§

THE WINDS OF MORNING

- Filled with characters you'll never forget, and historical facts you'll wish you could.

- An excellent portrayal of the human spirit for both love and loss. I look forward to future books about this family.

- In some parts this book would just tear into my very soul, and other parts it touched my heart.

§

WHISPERS IN THE CANYON

- If you're looking for a simple Western romance, this isn't it! Instead, it's a complex family saga steeped in American West history, including the impact of Irish immigration.

- A heartwarming, yet gut-wrenching, romance novel. One of the most well-written and well-developed books I have read in a long time.

- Absolutely breathtaking. I felt every range of emotion reading this book: love, joy, hope, grief, anger.

- A beautiful and heartfelt piece of fiction that goes beyond the simple western romance to deliver a tender, emotional and psychological tale of one woman's bravery in a time when few people really cared or appreciated such strength.

GIFFORD MACSHANE

- MacShane perfectly captures the eternal love of siblings and the deep, deep annoyance, and weaves historical details into the narrative seamlessly.

§

THE WOODSMAN'S ROSE

- Absolutely awesome story and you'll fall in love with all of these characters!
- There were times when I found myself reaching for the tissues, and there were times where I feared for one of the character's life. The author certainly knows how to write a compelling plot.
- There is enough swoon-worthy, though tender, romance to melt even the coldest of hearts, and there is plenty of action and adventure for those who enjoy novels that keep them on the edge of their seat.
- Although the story takes place in savage times and there is an element of that savagery in it, at its heart it is a gentle tale about gentle people. Whilst the book deals with the realities of life, there is a mystical element to it which runs as a distinct thread throughout.

§

RAINBOW MAN:

- You will be drawn in, page by page. Brilliant read.
- Absolutely wonderful book! The story and characters that are so well written I caught myself talking, crying, laughing, and yelling at them!
- A wonderfully descriptive and well researched period novel with a gorgeous hero and a frustratingly naive and clueless heroine.

§

WITHOUT THE THUNDER:

- A very captivating book which drew me in from the beginning until the very satisfying ending.

THE WOODSMAN'S ROSE

- A stunning historical romance set in the heart of the Old West. The descriptive narration and setting plunge the reader into the story. But it's the characters which make it an unforgettable read.